HUGGER-MUGGER IN THE LOUVRE

A Homer Evans Murder Mystery

BY ELLIOT PAUL

DOVER PUBLICATIONS, INC.
NEW YORK

Published in Canada by General Publishing Company, Ltd., 30 Lesmill
Road, Don Mills, Toronto, Ontario.
Published in the United Kingdom by Constable and Company, Ltd., 10
Orange Street, London WC2H 7EG.

This Dover edition, first published in 1986, is an unabridged, unaltered
republication of the work first published by Random House, New York,
1940.

Manufactured in the United States of America
Dover Publications, Inc., 31 East 2nd Street, Mineola, N.Y. 11501

Library of Congress Cataloging-in-Publication Data

Paul, Elliot, 1891–1958.
   Hugger-mugger in the Louvre.

   (Dover mystery classics series)
   I. Title. II. Series.
PS3531.A852H8   1986   813'.52   86-6336
ISBN 0-486-25185-3

To my former colleagues on the staff of the Boston Public Library, from whom I learned much about life and a bit about art and letters now and then.

Author's Preface

Dear Reader:

In accordance with his promise contained in the preface of *The Mysterious Mickey Finn,* the author is beginning *Hugger-Mugger in the Louvre* with the understanding that the principal victim is dead before the reader begins Page One.

This story was written for the reader's amusement, and not for his edification or enlightenment. If he tastes the true flavor of Paris in its best American days, or learns anything about art or antiquity, the author asks him to keep it dark, in order not to frighten timid customers.

Elliot Paul

Contents

HUGGER-MUGGER
IN THE LOUVRE

I

One Way of Getting Back at Women

Six o'clock in the evening is a comforting hour at the Café du Dôme, and especially in the early summer, a season when Paris enjoys a brief stretch of stimulating weather and Montparnasse is in mild transition from the dearth of winter inhabitants to the rush of tourist traffic later on. The regulars of the quarter will have set aside the duties of the day and will not have plunged themselves into the whirl of pleasures of the night. They will be seated on cane-woven chairs around small but sturdy tables, sipping appropriate liquids and conversing, if at all, in a restful easy way. A few will have paper-bound books that require no concentration and the minimum expenditure of effort to hold them up, others will be scanning the headlines of the evening papers or glancing at pages three to eight in the hope of finding amusing or sensational news.

The twilight in Montparnasse is an elusive process, not a matter exclusively of light and shade or the sinking of the sun to rest. There is involved a spiritual significance, a subtle blending of moods and change of pace.

The eventual darkness, stymied by the rose-colored and amber street lamps, does not

> *. . . fall from the wings of night*
> *Like a feather is wafted downward*
> *From an eagle in his flight.*

Neither can it be called, in the words of that other chap from Harvard:

> *The violet hour*
> *That brings the sailor home from sea*
> *The typist home at tea-time . . .*

The fact is, that although the famous quartette of Montparnasse cafés have entertained a staggering number of poets in their time, none of the latter has done justice to the evening hour, when easels and typewriters have been forgotten; when dinner and gay companionship are in prospect; when, in short, there is nothing to do that can be classified as work until tomorrow or the day after. The waiters, of course, are working. But they know their customers' needs and supply them with so few lost motions that they do not seem to be exerting themselves at all.

Homer Evans was sitting near the center of the *terrasse* with a group of his friends; Hjalmar Jansen, the hearty Norwegian-American painter; plump Rosa Stier, who was on her third Pernod in celebration of a portrait that had just been paid for; Tom Jackson, the reporter, who was doing his yearly stretch on the New York *Herald* and had not yet been fired; and Harold Simon, who had been commissioned to do both the Old and New Testaments in woodcuts—text and illustrations—and had rounded out the day by carving that profound passage,

Hebrews 13-8, which read, according to his absent-minded punctuation:

"Jesus Christ! The same yesterday, today, and forever."

It was true that few events had taken place in the quarter in the course of the months just passed. The murder of Ambrose Gring * and the resulting exposure, thanks to Evans, of the Royalist plot and the American tax-dodging ring, had been reposing on the shelves of history slightly more than a year and since that time Montparnasse life had drifted placidly along, with nothing more exciting than an occasional tourist brawl, a wedding of one of the favorite cashiers, and an unforgettable evening when M. Chalgrin, the proprietor of the Dôme, had entertained the Gold Star Mothers. On that occasion, a playful group of models, made up by Jansen and wearing old costumes filched from the Comédie Française, had complicated the party to such an extent that three of the genuine mothers went A.W.O.L. for four days and were retrieved in time to catch the boat back to America only by the heroic work of the former Sergeant Frémont, now chief of detectives of the Paris police.

The evening on which this story begins did not, at first, give promise of being an eventful one. Homer Evans was planning to attend a concert of ancient French music, which he always contended was unjustly neglected, and was waiting for the appearance of Miriam Leonard, who was faithfully completing her afternoon hours of practice on the harpsichord, in order to invite her to accompany him. Now up to the time when they had ex-

The Mysterious Mickey Finn, by Elliot Paul, Modern Age Books, Inc., 1939. (Dover reprint 24751-1.)

perienced their amazing adventure in connection with the case of *The Mysterious Mickey Finn,* Homer would never have asked anyone to go with him where music was to be played. Of all the arts, music meant the most to him and in hearing it he fell into a state of receptivity that was disturbed by human contact. A year ago, if anyone had told him he would listen to Monteclaire's enchanting *Plaisirs champêtres* side by side with a beautiful and eager young woman, Homer would have raised his eyebrows and smiled his sardonic but tolerant smile. However, Miriam, he had long ago decided, was an exception to all rules. The question was: would she consent to go? She had such fine scruples against intruding on his privacy, she was so fanatically insistent on leaving him essentially as he had been before the swift rush of events had brought them together, that Evans was uneasy for fear she might leave him with an empty chair beside him and in his veins that insidious virus of loneliness he had felt, but not often, in the preceding year.

Somewhat behind time, a small truck drove up to the newsstand on the corner of the *rue* Delambre, a bundle of *En-Tout-Cas, Paris-Soir* and other evening papers was dumped roughly to the sidewalk, and a moment later Achilles, the sixty-eight-year-old newsboy with the sparse gray beard, came cackling toward Homer like the Ancient Mariner and, with a malicious look of triumph in his eye, placed a copy of each paper on the table at Evans' place.

It must be explained at this point that Achilles had strict orders not to hand newspapers to Evans but to leave them on a little table in the hallway just outside his apartment in the *rue* Campagne Première. Homer by no means lived in an ivory tower, nor even a zinc one. He kept abreast of world affairs. Indeed, his minute awareness of what was happening elsewhere was a source of continual astonishment to his friends. But he liked to read newspapers when he felt like it, and not at the moment when for obscure commercial reasons some publisher was pleased to dish them out.

"What's the idea? Are you stewed already, you old buzzard?" asked Hjalmar Jansen of the grizzly old man.

"I'm not a sponge like you," Achilles retorted with spirit. "And furthermore, if I claimed to be a painter, I'd learn to paint whiskers that didn't look like putty. A fine one you are to be talking about men being drunk. You haven't gone home sober since your old man took you to the Paris Exposition in 1900."

"Give Achilles a Pernod," roared Rosa Stier.

"It's a wonder you can spare one, the way you pour 'em down," the old man said to her. Then he added to the waiter: "You owe me one Pernod. Don't forget. Just now I've got to sell these papers. I'll make a clean-up this afternoon." With that he hurried away.

Evans, when the old man so pointedly disregarded his instructions, had made no remonstrance. With his deep insight into human nature he had known from the first that old Achilles was no fool. If the man sold papers at the same stand year after year, no doubt he liked it that way. Achilles was sharp and intelligent. His wit had flashed across that same *terrasse* several decades—in lean times and prosperous days, in peace and in war-time. If he impudently planked *En-Tout-Cas* under Evans' nose, Homer was quick to grasp the fact that the occasion was an exceptional one. Nevertheless he sighed. *Les Plaisirs*

7

champêtres of Monteclaire! Was it possible that he would not hear that night the deliberate andante, that movement attuned to the days gone by, the era of kings and courts, of a lusty peasantry and the red-cheeked women of Boucher in the threshing fields? Evans was in every sense of the word a modern man, accepting his own preposterous age with all its implications; but the past, as well, was real to him. And whenever a harpsichord began that slow movement of the *Plaisirs champêtres* he could feel the clock go back—no nervous pulse, no fear of the end of time or of afternoon or evening.

"Well, I'll be damned," said Rosa Stier, who had grabbed a paper, too. Hjalmar gave his knee such a thump with his heavy hand that the drinks on the table shimmered.

"That's rich! By Yee! Can you beat it?" he shouted. The headlines and double-column cuts had struck his eye.

All over the *terrasse,* across the boulevard at the Rotonde, a block farther east at the Coupole and the Select, men and women were leaving their tables and crowding around Achilles, who soon had to go back to his stand for another sheaf of papers. Reluctantly, Evans diverted his mind from the seventeenth-century music and spread *En-Tout-Cas* before him.

WATTEAU WORTH THREE MILLIONS STOLEN FROM LOUVRE

"THE PANSY," COMPANION-PIECE OF "THE FLIRT,"
SPIRITED FROM MUSEUM JUST BEFORE
CLOSING HOUR: ATTENDANTS'
ATTENTION DISTRACTED

SMARTLY DRESSED ACCOMPLICES

With a sigh of relief, Evans laid down the paper again and looked up the boulevard. He was rewarded by the sight of a familiar figure. Miriam was on her way, at last.

"You're late," he said, almost peevishly as she took her place beside him.

She flushed with pleasure. Then, seeing the newspaper, she looked up at him gravely. "Why, Homer," she asked, "what's wrong?" All around them and up and down the street, a sea of spread papers was swelling: waiters had ceased serving drinks and were reading over customers' shoulders. "What's happened?" Miriam asked again.

"From the headlines, it appears that someone has stolen a precious Watteau. You remember. The supercilious young man with a ribbon on his crook. *The Pansy.*"

"Is that all?" Miriam asked. "I'm so glad it's nothing personal, you know. I've been uneasy all afternoon. Forgot once or twice that it was not a piano I was banging and nearly broke a string of my lovely harpsichord. Oh, Homer! It's so beautiful. I can't tell you how those strange sounds make me feel."

Hjalmar Jansen began to roar and slap his knee again.

"I hope they get away with it," he said. "If the Louvre loses enough paintings, maybe some arrangements will be made to let some light into the damned place. Why can't they fill it up with furniture and beads and all that junk and put the paintings in a modern building where somebody can see them?"

"More than half of them are better in the dark,"

Harold Simon said. "But, gee! Three million francs. And the blasted thing wasn't a foot square."

"I haven't been to the Louvre since the day before I kicked my husband out of bed," said Rosa Stier. "Come on, Homer. You know everything. Tell us about this masterpiece. And why did they call it *The Pansy?* Was Watteau queer, or what?"

With an effort observed only by Miriam, Evans aroused himself and good-naturedly began to talk. The others composed themselves to listen, for Homer had been unusually silent of late. Hjalmar sat with his hands firmly placed on both knees, as if he were a second in a heavyweight bout. Tom Jackson looked pained and thought of his paper.

"For God's sake, tell me all I ought to know. Since the Hugo Weiss affair all stories about art are wished on me. God, how I hate oil painting! I hope he's thrown the canvas into the Seine, whoever was ass enough to steal it," the reporter said.

The waiter, who had come closer to hear what Homer had to say, responded to an appealing look and brought quickly a vermouth-cassis and it was not until he returned that Evans began speaking.

"The source of any work of art may be found in the life of the artist," he began, thoughtfully. "Now Watteau was by no means effeminate by nature . . ."

"God be praised," said Rosa Stier.

"He spent most of his life," Homer continued, "in pursuit of a frivolous and calculating woman."

"Hell of a combination," said Hjalmar with feeling, and Jackson groaned again.

"As you know," said Evans, with just the slightest

10

change in his tone which restrained them from interrupting again, "Watteau's enamorata was a ballet dancer at the Opera." (More groans from Hjalmar.) "You all understand that the Opera and the Luxembourg Gardens form the background for all Watteau's work. One, to him, represented indoors, the other was his ideal out-of-doors. In every canvas you will find traces of one or both of those places, and a good choice, too. Watteau was not in good health, weak lungs and all that, so he simplified his world and fashioned his poetry of the brush accordingly.

"*L'Indifferent* or *The Pansy* is only half a work, you might say. It is incomplete without *La Coquette (The Flirt)* that always hangs on its right. Should be in a double frame but frames cost money and the Louvre is always broke, so no one has taken the trouble to hang the paintings properly."

Evans paused to spread *En-Tout-Cas* across the table and Jackson, grinding his teeth, reached for pencil and copy paper.

"You will observe," Evans went on, indicating a blurred reproduction of *La Coquette* with his finger, "that the little lady is smiling at her companion across the frame in a most inviting manner. Thoroughly charming and womanlike she is. Dainty, although buxom. Willing, but not too forward."

"Oh, for Jesus' sake. . . ." said Rosa Stier.

"Patience, Rosa," said Evans, amused. Then he pointed to the other reproduction, that of the painting which had been stolen. "The gentleman in the other picture will have none of her, as one can readily see. He is not trying to inflame her jealousy by suggesting he is on his way to another wench, he simply is trying to show the lady, in every way—by his pose, his facial expression, his supercilious gesture—that she does not interest him. Furthermore, he is implying subtly that none of her sex means a thing in his gay young career."

At that Jackson took off his glasses, wiped them, and stared at the two-column cut.

"On the level," he asked, "do you see all that there? I thought the guy was calling in the sheep or the cows or something. Well, I'm all wet, as usual. Christ! Why must guys paint?"

"The reason Watteau painted these two intriguing little canvases is not difficult to surmise," Evans said. "In his early twenties, and before his gifts were recognized, he fell desperately in love with the young dancer I have mentioned. She was empty-headed in some ways. She knew young Watteau was poor, a bit awkward, not at all sure of himself. Besides, she was being kept by a wealthy roué whose protection she did not care to lose. There is something about genius, however, that makes itself felt through the shyest personality and the least promising exterior. Watteau had no money, no fame, not even robust health to match the vigor of a dancer in the prime of her athletic youth. Still, the girl sensed a part, at least, of his value and was reluctant to turn him down. She strung him along, to the detriment of his art and his health. She deceived him, kept his mind in turmoil, teased him, ridiculed him, but she contrived to keep a hold on him, giving nothing whatever.

"Is it not clear that Watteau's disappointment and resentment would take the form shown so plainly in this pair of paintings? She would never understand. Neither would many of his contemporaries. But every brush-stroke in these little masterpieces gave him relief and satisfaction. It was his revenge on the sex. That, I'm sorry to say, is about the only relief or satisfaction he got."

Evans ceased speaking, and turned to his glass, until Miriam said gently: "Tell us what happened, Homer. We all are not encyclopedias."

"Oh," Homer said, absently. "Watteau became famous, the ballet girl got older and was ditched by her rich protector. She had to go home to Valenciennes where the country life bored her. It was then she thought of Watteau and sent for him. He was delirious with joy, forgot everything and hurried to her side. Since he was very ill, and she was abnormally rapacious after her forced sojourn in the country, the result was quickly tragic for Watteau and for French art as a whole. He stood the strain for a few blissful weeks, then died."

"Another double whiskey," Hjalmar Jansen said.

Drinks were served all around, and the company of friends began to discuss Watteau and the sensational theft with increasing animation, always hoping that the thief would make a clean getaway. The fewer Old Masters there are, the better most hard-working modern artists are pleased. And the antics of French officialdom when on the spot are sure to furnish tiptop entertainment. Miriam, sitting by Homer's side, took little part in the conversation. At first she thought she felt a bit chilly, but the absurdity of that, on a warm summer evening, caused her to look at Evans carefully. He was entering one of his phases of concentration, against his will, it seemed to her. Not a word that was being uttered around the table reached his ears. She sat motionless, trying not to disturb his thoughts and was astonished to see him rise, almost as if he were in a dream, touch her arm to guide her and, without saying good-bye to their friends, lead her toward a waiting taxi.

"Sorry," he said at last. "I had to get away."

She smiled. "Don't think about me. I'm very happy," she said. "Continue with your thoughts."

"That's exactly what I don't propose to do. There are no more newspapers. No man exists or existed who was called Watteau. Montparnasse, for the time being, is out of bounds."

"I don't understand, but that doesn't matter," she said. The taxi was passing the *place* St. Michel. Evans tapped quickly on the window.

"Let's get out here," he said, and led the way across the broad sidewalk to the Café du Départ, where once before, on that memorable night when Hugo Weiss had disappeared, they had taken refuge from their many friends in Montparnasse and, step by step, had been involved in the most strenuous adventure to which Evans, man of contemplation and ease, had ever lent his talents and his latent capacities. The same corner table was vacant, although the *terrasse* and the large square were swarming with busy people who, even more keenly than the idlers of Montparnasse, looked forward to an evening of relaxation and simple pleasures. Already the motley members of that crowd, individually obscure, collectively the soul of France, were feeling the twilight mood. Nervous movements slowed down to a calmer tempo. Tired faces lost the look of daily wear and tear. Somewhere, in cheap restaurants or dim rooms, there would be dinner for all—or nearly all. Seated on cane-woven chairs the Parisians rested a few minutes behind small tables, sometimes rickety, and drank *aperitifs* from bottles similar to those served at the Café du Dôme, with the difference that the glasses were smaller and thicker and made to look ample with false bottoms; that occasionally a struggling *bistrot* keeper felt obliged, in order to defend himself and his family against an increasingly complicated world, to dilute the red wine or vermouth; and that the prices marked on the saucers were modest indeed.

The large newsstand in front of the *terrasse* Homer Evans had chosen was surrounded by eager customers, shoving good-naturedly to get to the front, holding sous in their hands, commenting brightly to one another on the news of the evening, the disappearance of the priceless Watteau. And here, as in the quarter where culture was as thick as gasolene fumes in the air, men and women, even boys and girls, seemed rather pleased than otherwise with the developments. The clever thief, or thieves, had done each citizen a personal favor, one would have said.

"He's got his nerve, that guy," a pert-faced shopgirl said, admiringly.

The chestnut-vendor, who sold peanuts in the off-season, wiped his hands on his apron and grinned. "Took the frame and all," he said, with a true French love of thoroughness.

Notwithstanding the banter, there was a note also of reverence when the sum of three million francs was glimpsed in the headlines. On a midinette or a plumber's apprentice, who by hard toil and unremitting attention was able to earn about a dollar a day, the printed figures representing three million francs had an impact which, though different in nature from that of Nebuchadnezzar's animated wall decorations, was not less awe-inspiring. Had *The Pansy* been painted life size, with, let us say, a couple of grayhounds and an acre of park land behind him, the price of the Watteau gem would not have proved as shocking to the populace. But for a painting only thirty centimeters by twenty, the estimated value seemed fabulous indeed. As Miriam and Homer sat silently waiting for their drinks, they both observed a number of clients asking waiters for the loan of a pencil, so that the price per square centimeter might be computed.

A few of the more sensitive drinkers, however, were not thinking in terms of francs and centimes but were staring at the two-column cuts in search of the beauty they felt sure was therein contained. This latter group was the more bewildered. Homer smiled. Safe from intrusion and with Miriam by his side he felt decidedly better. Directly in front of them three tables had been placed together for a group of young friends who met there daily at the *aperitif* hour. And in the face of each one of the workers, Miriam thought she detected disappointment. *En-Tout-Cas* was spread before them and they all were staring at the reproductions.

Suddenly Miriam was seized with an unprecedented impulse.

"Homer," she said, grasping his sleeve and looking at him appealingly. It was not necessary for her to continue. Evans smiled indulgently, rose from his place and in a moment was leaning over the spread newspaper and explaining to the group the significance of *The Pansy* and the fate of Watteau. To say that his hearers listened eagerly would be a misdemeanor of understatement. Their faces lighted with comprehension, were eloquent with dismay. One of the girls from La Samaritaine, in fact, was so moved that she burst into tears and rushed for a telephone booth.

"So you see, my friends," Homer Evans was concluding, "the first painter who might be called truly French, who didn't copy the Italians, had to die in his thirties when, with luck, he might have lived to a ripe old age and painted so many pictures that the prices of Watteaus today would be only half what they are."

A few minutes after Homer had returned to his place, the group of young people dispersed, mostly two and two, and the huge square grew slowly tranquil. Behind, and to the right, stood Notre Dame. Across the bridge and slightly downstream was the Conciergerie. The fountain on the starboard side introduced a playful note. But it was not the historical monuments on which Evans had his eye. The clock said half past seven, the hour for dinner, so his gaze was resting on the awning of the Restaurant Rouzier where, at just that time of year, the chef was able to procure crayfish that were worthy of what he had learned to do to them. With the ease that characterized all his actions, Evans paid the small sum due the waiter, added a tip that was right for the quarter, and guided Miriam across the cartracks to a table *chez* Rouzier where the headwaiter, after two years, remembered him by name and was immediately solicitous. He did not murmur "crayfish" as if Monsieur Evans were a barbarian and needed prompting. He merely tried to express in pantomime a faint suggestion of what the crustaceans might taste like, and Rouzier's headwaiter, had he chosen, might have been a second Debureau.

First, needless to say, there was a cool dry Pouilly, chilled but by no means iced, and once the meal had reached the coffee stage and the unlabeled brandy known to the wine-steward as "The Opal" had been served, Homer settled back in his chair and assumed that air which Miriam knew preceded a moment of confidence.

"I had a strange feeling at the Dôme tonight," he began. "I hope our friends won't be offended. . . . We left them rather abruptly, you know."

"Of course they won't mind," said Miriam.

"It wasn't when I read the headlines. It was the story that followed," he said. "You know, sometimes I feel quite alone in the world . . . No, not that, exactly." He backed up for a fresh start and reached for her hand, for at the suggestion that he was lonely an icy grip had chilled Miriam's heart until it felt like an over-frosted mint julep.

"I meant that I felt as if *we* were alone in the world," he continued.

"That's better," she said and sighed.

"The point is this. We are all sitting quietly. An old man distributes newspapers. You read. I read. Our friends all read, and so do perfect strangers. This happens at the Dôme, in the *place* St. Michel, the Café de la Paix, in every corner of Paris. Not only the intellectuals but the laborers read, the courtesans, good wives, shop girls, street walkers. Everybody sees the preposterous tale spread with ink upon paper and nobody seems to grasp its absurdity, let alone its implications."

"I love it when you talk this way," said Miriam, so pleased with his sudden animation that she almost purred. She had been uneasy about Homer lately, although she would not admit it even to herself. There had been times when she had been ready to believe she was somehow at fault. But now . . . His voice interrupted her reveries.

"Miriam, my dear. Here is *En-Tout-Cas*. The story is only one column in length. The reporters didn't have much time. Read it carefully, not too fast, and tell me, for the sake of my peace of mind, what seems inconsistent to you."

Obediently she took the paper and read the story, line by line. And at the end she looked up in dismay. "I'm stupid. I know I am. I don't see how you can put up with me," she faltered.

"You mean that you swallow that yarn at its apparent face value?" he asked, astonished.

She reached for his hand and pressed it almost prayerfully. "Tell me what's on your mind. I can listen well, at least . . ."

"That's what I meant about feeling alone. The entire population of this city, the center of world culture, successor to the glories of Greece and Rome, fails to see what is as plain as day. Darling. Think! Reflect! This so-called theft was carefully planned, was it not?"

"I suppose so . . ."

"The exact hour. The most valuable small painting among the thousands in the Museum, in fact, the only one worth anything like three million francs that could be slipped under one's coat without making a bulge. The only painting of such value that was hung, in a small room! One of a series of rooms watched by the same attendants! One of the few paintings that had a literary value, that could be written and talked about world without end! The well-dressed confederates who asked just the right questions and put up just the right front to lure away the unfortunate pair of guardians, named respectively Angorre and Dubonnet! I wouldn't want to be in their shoes, because there's no one under them to whom they can pass on the blame. Now, dear. Have I said enough? What is wrong with the picture? What smells unmistakably of the humble cod?"

"Homer. Let me ask you a question. Suppose you were in a concert hall and Fritz Kreisler were playing the violin? Would you feel like whistling aloud?"

Evans flushed, then smiled with his unfailing good nature.

"All right. I'll stop stalling and get down to cases. Let us approach the matter in another way. Suppose that in Cartier's small show cases in the rear of the store were two expensive pearls, quite carelessly guarded. What should you say about a clever thief who made elaborate and successful plans to steal one and who left the other in the case, although he must have had room in his pocket?"

"You mean *The Flirt?*" Miriam asked, all interest now.

"Precisely. The whole thing doesn't make sense."

"Perhaps the thief was interrupted. Maybe he had to duck with half the loot . . ."

"There is nothing in the story that indicates he may

20

have been interrupted. The attendants were otherwise occupied. The press states categorically that no other persons except the well-tailored pair were seen in the vicinity. The thief, naturally, kept out of sight. But any innocent bystanders or tourists who had wandered in would have been eager to present themselves to the authorities. Think of the publicity . . . No. The interruption theory is not sound, although it was bright of you to think of it."

"Then how do you explain it?" Miriam asked.

"Not so fast, my darling. We haven't considered all the inconsistencies yet. You realize, of course, that Watteau's *The Pansy* or any other of his authenticated paintings is as well known to dealers and collectors as the Eiffel Tower is familiar to the public. The authorities estimate the value of the missing canvas at three million francs, but how and where could it be sold for three francs, three sous, even? Remember the poor duffer who stole the Mona Lisa? He nearly went crazy, and after two years had to give himself up. No, Flower of Montana! The object of this sinister performance is not theft. Not by any stretch of the imagination. And still you have seen a city full of people who have gulped down the tale, hook, line and sinker."

He looked across at Miriam and was disturbed by the change in her. Her eyes were glowing, her breathing had accelerated. Her hands were clasped.

"How wonderful," she said, her words pouring one upon the other. "You're going to solve it, aren't you? We're going to have another unforgettable time. . . ."

But Evans' face grew severe. "Stop that, young lady," he said sharply. "I'm going to do no such thing. I'm going to pursue the even tenor of my way. I'm going to revel in idleness." He leaned closer across the table. "You always forget, my dear, that I've thought this thing out again and again and always have arrived at the same conclusion. A life of action and accomplishment is not for me. I have written one book, painted one quite passable painting, and just once I was trapped by circumstances into playing the detective. Never again. For no reason whatsoever. If the French authorities are so careless as to permit unknown persons to strip the Louvre of its entire collection, I shall stay on the sidelines and remember the paintings as best I can.

"What you don't seem to grasp is that a man must choose one course or another. Either he must be a go-getter and bustle about ruthlessly devouring what and whom he may, or he must develop his faculties of observation and contemplation and refrain from pointless activity. I like life and what it has to offer, when I can be tranquil and enjoy it. Now why on earth should I interfere with this interesting Johnny who has entertained us all today? No doubt he'll carry on farther, if no busybodies intervene. And anyway, if he becomes dangerous to the public, Frémont will have a chance to add to his laurels. It's quite a while since the chief was in the public eye."

"You know how poor Frémont feels about a case in which art is concerned. He gets an inferiority complex you could hang your hat on. Most people do, you know. Couldn't you call on him, at least, and give him the right steer? Tell him just what you've told me, so he won't be all at sea . . ."

"And succumb to his pleadings to give him a hand.

No! I know myself. I can't refuse anyone face to face. I'm going to duck. I'm going to get out of sight until this blows over. Tonight we're going to hear the *Plaisirs champêtres* of Monteclaire . . . Never heard of Monteclaire? I thought so. Nobody knows about the French composers. Well. After you have heard that andante, you'll understand what I mean about tranquillity. And after you've heard the presto at the end we'll take a taxi straight to the Gare du Nord and the next train to Langres. Never heard of Langres? Not surprising. It's one of the most fascinating old walled cities of France but no tourists stray as far east as that, or if they do they can't see the country for the battlefields. Come on. We mustn't be late for the concert. And not one word about the Louvre or Watteau or the troubles of our good friend Frémont, Chief of Detectives. Agreed?"

"If you think best," she said, and meekly followed.

Whenever the French Society of Ancient Instruments got together for a performance or a public rehearsal, Homer Evans was to be found in the audience, seated ten rows back and just left of the center, his sensitive and saturnine face reflecting the moods of the music and the epoch in question. Merely to see the viola da gamba, the viola d'amour, the lute, the harpsichord and the horns just evolving from their use in the hunting field gave Homer a most agreeable sensation, a sort of awareness of the continuity of human effort and the inexhaustibility of the source from which it springs. He liked to enter at the exact moment when he could seat himself in comfort, not so soon as to allow time for nerve strain in waiting, not so late as to be hurried. When he and

Miriam took their places, the Salle Gaveau was half filled and the tone of the audience was more sympathetic than is usually established in the popular concerts, where half of the customers are under some sort of compulsion.

Miriam had eyes for nothing but the clavecin, for it had been at Homer's suggestion that she took up the study of that old instrument after having gone stale with the piano, because of over-emphasis of technical exercises. The first number was a Gavotte by Sartrou, a little-known composer who had been first horn player in the royal orchestra of François I. It began with a haunting, simple theme, a rare combination of spontaneity and sophistication that only the pioneers in the musical art could hope to attain. Miriam listened rapturously, but for once her attention wavered. What was wrong?

As part one of the program proceeded, she was able to crystallize her feelings. She was worried about Evans. No use denying it any longer. He had not, just lately, been at his best. She had listened faithfully to all he had said about the futilities of exertion and the virtues of inaction, nevertheless she could not forget the days when he had been engaged so brilliantly in the rescue of Hugo Weiss and the breaking of the smuggling ring and she wondered if, for once, she might be right and her idol might be wrong. Would not a little excursion in quest of the missing Watteau be just the thing to put Evans in tiptop form again?

When intermission came, and the *Plaisirs champêtres* were imminent she softly excused herself and, as if placed there for her temptation, in the ladies' room was a convenient phone. Trembling with apprehension, but impelled by a force she could scarcely understand she dialed a number and was promptly rewarded by a soft response, the voice of Hydrangea, the former Blackbird who had won the heart of Sergeant Frémont and, at Evans' instigation had forsaken her beloved Harlem for the *place de la Contrescarpe*. Hydrangea's apartment was in the Hotel Murphy et du Danube Bleu and there the Chief of Detectives felt safe from the eyes of the world.

"I'm so glad you called," Hydrangea said in her rich mezzo voice. "The Chief's been looking everywhere for Mr. Evans."

"We're at the Salle Gaveau," whispered Miriam and hurried from the phone with a glance at her shapely hands, as if she feared the instrument had left a guilty impress there. The act of duplicity once having been performed a wave of guilt swept over Miriam. How could Homer fail to read her thoughts? But Evans was thinking of the music to come and scarcely was aware of her return. While the first movement was being played, Miriam found it difficult to compose herself, but once the harpsichord began that deliberate descent that opens the andante she was sure that all was for the best. The theme rose and fell, repeated itself with subtle variations. The 'cello questioned, the viola da gamba replied. Subject was resolved into predicate and through it all the miraculous harpsichord worked out its satisfying pattern of sound, so touching and inevitable, so timeless and of the earth. Evans was lending to the music his refined attention, feeling each nuance, and the magnetic attraction of the firm home tone; the inescapable "do," the natural beginning and ending.

There was a moment of utter silence, then the third movement began, the wild country dance whose only restraint was effectiveness. Then the fourth, from which the great Beethoven was not ashamed to lift a theme for one of his piano sonatas many years later. With the stunned crackle of applause, Evans rose and so did Miriam. There was one more number on the list, but whatever it was would be anticlimax. Side by side they walked up the aisle and noiselessly passed through the doorway. They were aroused by the sound of a familiar voice.

"Ah, my friend," said Chief of Detectives Frémont. "How can I express my joy at having found you! I beg of you to listen. In the name of the happiness you yourself have made possible for me, do not refuse to help me. I am nonplussed. I am floundering. I stand on the brink of disgrace, of shame. I drown in a sea of ignorance . . ."

Miriam's heart stood still. She was burning with a sense of disloyalty and yet . . . Was there hope?

Now Homer Evans, safe on an obscure *terrasse* or fortified by the afterglow of that brandy called "The Opal," was a different man from the Evans confronted with a friend in need. Frémont's distress was too profound, and Homer's heart was his vulnerable spot. He could not quite be gracious, but neither could he be brutal and turn down his thumbs.

"Have things come to such a pass that a man cannot attend a musical performance without being accosted and annoyed by the Paris police?" he grumbled.

"I knew you wouldn't refuse," the chief of detectives said, and wrung Homer's hand. "Good evening, Mademoiselle Montana," he said belatedly to Miriam. Like so many of his countrymen, the Chief was no great shakes

26

at remembering names. He had told numerous acquaintances and had lectured his officers about Miriam's exploits in connection with the Charenton plot and the kidnapping gang at Frontville, but to him she would always remain Mademoiselle Montana, just as Hjalmar Jansen, the big painter who had done yeoman service in the cases mentioned above, would eternally be Gonzo. Actually, in Montparnasse, Miriam and Hjalmar had come to be known almost exclusively by the names the French police, in their consternation, had mistakenly applied to them.

"I knew you would give me your invaluable aid," the delighted Frémont was saying, once again, and again was shaking Evans' hand. "There's something so absurd about having a painting taken right out of the Louvre, and nobody the wiser. The journalists will have a rare time baiting me, and of course, the new prefect has simply passed the buck, as you Americans say."

"What about the Marquis de la Rose d'Antan, director of Beaux Arts? He'll have to take a hand. Pass the buck upward for a change. Let the Marquis take charge. The press can have more fun with him than with you," Evans said. "I'm on my way out of town, to help round out Miss Leonard's education."

"You wouldn't leave me in a fix like this," the chief of detectives said anxiously. "You, yourself, are responsible for my being in my present exalted position. Your modesty, in refusing your large share of the credit in the Weiss case, has led the press and the public to believe that I am conversant with matters of art, and especially of that cursed branch of it known as oil painting. Should my ignorance be exposed now, I shall not only be made ridiculous but it will come to light that I stepped into office on another man's shoulders. In short, that I am a fraud. I shall lose my position and my monthly pay. The only profession I know will be closed to me. My dark jewel, Hydrangea, will starve, or worse, will go back to Harlem far across the sea . . ."

"But the Marquis?" Evans asked, somewhat abruptly.

"The Marquis is away. On one of his frequent voyages, the direction of which he confides in no one. And M. des Murs, Director in Chief of the Louvre, if you please, has been confined to a chair with gout since Easter. No. I am the one who must shoulder the blame, and you know what a daub on a canvas means to me. Why, I've seen a dozen already in store windows that I couldn't distinguish from that pernicious *Pansy* on a bet."

They had left the lobby of the Salle Gaveau and were approaching Frémont's official car, at the wheel of which, in smart plum-colored uniform, sat Melchisadek Knockwoode. The latter greeted Evans with awe.

"Glory be! Here's Mr. Evans himself. I told you, boss, not to worry yourself sick. Why, this case is as good as in the bag right this minute," the Negro chauffeur said, in accents reminiscent of the A. E. F.

In spite of himself, Evans smiled and Miriam relaxed a little.

"All right," he said. "You have me cornered. Let's go on to the Louvre and I'll try to shed a ray of light, if possible."

"I shall never forget your kindness." Frémont said.

2

In Which Notes Are Taken on Finance and Physiology

WHILE in the Salle Gaveau the competent performers of the *Société d'Instruments Anciens* had been drawing sweet sounds from reeds and strings, and in distant parts of France the homebound flocks of sheep had made the low hills seem to creep in the deepening twilight; while, in fact, the Paris police had been combing narrow streets and spacious tree-lined boulevards in search of Homer Evans, Montparnasse had been going its usual leisurely way and was beginning its evening crescendo.

The poets, such of them as were in funds, were at the Falstaff, the Dingo, Au Negre de Toulouse, and elsewhere, dealing with *brindades, ragouts, rotis, soufflés* or sopping up sauces with crisp fresh bread, and were in no position to take on the evening panorama of the Montparnasse sidewalks as a theme for versification. The leaves on the plane trees were softly illumined by the street lamps, in such a way that even the veins showed through. Sidewalk vendors clad in fezzes and burnooses and bearing gaily colored rugs or trays of nuts and sweetmeats strode to and fro in a dignified way and all too seldom made a sale. Still, the Arabs seemed to get along. The tourists and habitués who had dined early were coming back to the *terrasses* of the Dôme, the Select, the Coupole and the Rotonde, there to remain with the general idea of waiting to see what life had to offer, an attitude that made them receptive but not acquisitive. And, as if to celebrate the rising of the evening star, which perhaps unluckily in that season was Venus, a fire-eater sprayed gasolene from his mouth into the air and produced a shapely geyser of flame.

It was at that moment when Dr. Balthazar St.-J. Truc, the proprietor of a rural sanitorium known as the "Sens Unique," came into view, portly and somewhat self-important, wearing as usual a black frock-coat in the buttonhole of which was a damask carnation, a vest across which was a watch-chain that had proved tempting to untold scores of his distraught patients, and striped gray trousers, and shoes with elastic in the sides and no laces. His hair and his beard were dyed a lustrous black. As the doctor walked, he chuckled and removed from his pocket from time to time a sheaf of notes he had scrawled with his gold-embossed fountain pen. In the middle of the Dôme *terrasse,* on the way to his seat near the rear, he paused to slap his thigh and let out a resounding guffaw.

"What's eating the big dude with the stained lilacs?" asked Hjalmar Jansen, good-humoredly, of Tom Jackson. The pair were seated at the self-same table where Evans had left them some three hours before. They had intended to eat dinner but had failed to move when their companions had started out in search of food and were endeavoring to make up the loss by munching handfuls of potato chips, peanuts, hard-boiled eggs and other similar objects that they found close at hand. Their conversation, quite naturally, had had to do with the missing Watteau. One would have thought that had *The Pansy* been left in place, the whole city of Paris would have been tongue-tied that balmy June evening.

"There's something in the wind, when old Homer lights out like that," Hjalmar said. "I hope it's another case and he lets us in on it."

Jackson viewed the prospects of action with Evans in a gloomier light. The last time, only a short year ago, the reporter had not only lost his job temporarily but had been wounded with a fragment of a hand grenade, blown flat by an explosion of T. N. T., knocked cold by being dropped by a thug on a binnacle and had spent hours in the cell at the prefecture known as the Goldfish Bowl, sans belt, sans shoestrings, sans necktie, sans practically everything. And that same evening he had telephoned his editor the gist of what he had learned about the missing Watteau and had been told to drop the matter, since something might creep into print that would embarrass the French Government, and to spend the evening hearing a Grand Rapids widow (golden oak furniture) discourse on the Taj Mahal at the American Students' and Artists' Club.

"Jansen, tell me. Why in hell do men paint? You're supposed to be a painter, and you ought to know," was Jackson's contribution.

Jansen, although a serious artist, was inarticulate on the subject. He hemmed, hawed and reached for his double whiskey.

"Quite a few of us can't help it," he said, apologetically.

"I knew you wouldn't tell me," murmured Jackson, sadly. "Nobody will."

More than an hour before they had talked with Sergeant Frémont, who had driven to the Dôme at breakneck speed, siren shrieking, in the hope of finding Evans there. Since then police officers, singly and in pairs, some on foot, others with bicycles, motorcycles, horses, and automobiles had been scouring the quarter with no success whatever. The tension in the air had done things to Hjalmar Jansen. Feverishly he thought of last year's adventure and was wondering if, after all, the good old days were past and he was already on the skids, at the foot of which lay drabness and respectability.

The advent of Dr. Balthazar Truc served to distract the big Norwegian, for he was puzzled as to how a man who took himself as seriously as the doctor evidently did, and gave himself so much trouble in dressing for the street, could find anything to laugh at.

"That's Dr. Truc," Tom Jackson said, and sighed as he fished in his pockets for copy paper. For Dr. Truc, not six months before, had fought a duel in the Bois de Boulogne against Dr. Hyacinthe Toudoux, the medical examiner, and Truc's sword, after describing an arc through the misty morning air, had landed point down on the toe of Jackson, who, because of his acquaintance with Toudoux in connection with the Dôme murder case, had been the only reporter advised of the meeting and permitted to witness the combat. Tom Jackson, much as appearances pointed against it, was working and drawing pay, however small. Reluctantly he got to his feet and made his way to the rear table where Dr. Truc had taken his place.

"Not often we see you here, doctor," Tom began.

"Er . . . No . . . That is. Yes . . . Too much work. Need relaxation, you know," the doctor said, surprised that anyone in Montparnasse should recognize him so promptly. At any other time, he might have been pleased and flattered, for he responded to free publicity as the nenuphars of the Nile drink in the rising sun. But as it was he smiled professionally and merely waited.

"Any news?" Jackson asked. He knew that the doctor, among his other activities, conducted a health column in the *En-Tout-Cas* which was syndicated to provincial papers throughout France.

At that the doctor brightened. He guffawed again, caused Jansen to turn his head uneasily, three tables forward, and handed Tom the sheaf of hand-written notes he had been carrying and scanning from time to time. Now Jackson's French was not half bad, not quite half at any rate, but he was unequal to deciphering script of the sort Dr. Truc had developed in years of practice in order to bewilder first- and second-class pharmacists and patients.

"Can't you explain, in a few words?" the reporter asked.

"Sit down," said Dr. Truc. "I was expecting friends, or rather, a business appointment. Never rest, you know. But this is too good for you to miss. I've got that fat-head Toudoux where the hair is short. He was lucky, in that duel. Won on a fluke. But now he can't escape. I shall make him publicly ridiculous."

Jackson sat down at the doctor's table and when the

latter asked for a *Vichy fraise* Tom absent-mindedly said "The same." To clear his mind he grabbed a coffee *noir* someone had left sitting around on a near-by table, and gulped it down. Truc's notes had to do with a paper Dr. Toudoux had read before the members of the Academie des Sciences six months before, in which he had described the effect of California wine on the human liver. Toudoux had distinctly said, and had not denied it when it was reported in the press, that an autopsy he had performed on a man who for years had been addicted to a beverage falsely labeled Medoc and bottled in Eureka, California, had shown that the victim's liver, much enlarged, had been streaked with mauve and heliotrope.

"The pink of condition. And why not?" asked Jackson. "I've no doubt yours and mine will be just like that, after drinking this diluted strawberry extract. You ought to try whiskey, if you want to know about American drinks. Bourbon, by preference. It's made of corn." The reporter waved his arms to indicate corn fields and was about to order two double whiskies but the prudent doctor headed him off.

"I smelled a rat," Dr. Truc said, cunningly. "Man and boy, I have seen many livers, and each one of them, if it was discolored at all, had a yellow tinge. Heliotrope, indeed."

"But that Eureka wine, doc . . ."

"I tried it, after having gone to great expense and trouble, on fourteen guinea pigs, a pair of Belgian hares, an old donkey and a gibbon ape that was dying of asthma but otherwise was sound. In sixty-two per cent of the cases, the liver got smaller, not larger, and assumed

34

a faint ochre tint between mustard and honeysuckle," said Dr. Truc, triumphantly.

"What's the difference?"

"Between heliotrope and mustard?" The doctor's face expressed amazement.

"I mean. Who cares?" Jackson asked. The story, he thought, was not going to make the *Herald,* since the advertisers who sold wine would not like to have disturbing chromatic ideas put into customers' heads. It was hard enough, as matters stood, to induce American visitors to drink wine with their meals.

The interview might have continued longer had not two simultaneous occurrences conspired to bring it to an abrupt end. The first, and least important to Jackson, was the arrival of two men, one dark and one light, whom Dr. Truc had been impatiently expecting. The second and decisive event was a taxi that came careening down the boulevard Montparnasse, weaving to and fro among terror-stricken pedestrians and cursing drivers. Hjalmar Jansen rose to his feet and began to shout. Tom Jackson blinked and wiped off his glasses. For as the berserk machine drew near, anyone who had been involved in the Weiss kidnapping case could see that it was the Citroën formerly driven by Lvov Kvek, who had shared the famous millionaire's adventure and had gone with him to America to make his fortune. As the notorious Citroën came still nearer, both Hjalmar and Jackson saw in the driver's seat a tall, distinguished-looking man with a silk hat and a black frock coat, who was waving with his free hand a gold-headed cane. Police began to whistle and women to scream, but the runaway cab pulled up to the curb in front of the Dôme without mishap.

"My friends," the Russian shouted, embracing heartily the painter and the reporter who hurried to meet him. "My brothers but for whom I should have been no doubt already one year in hell. . . . But excuse me . . . I forgot my manners. . . ." And with a sweep of his well-gloved hand he indicated the interior of the cab in which was sitting, ostensibly nervous but game, what appeared at first glance to be an American business man. At second glance, there was no doubt about it.

"Meet Mr. K. Parker Seldon," said Kvek, slapping all three on the back and shoulders. "Mr. Seldon is a friend of Hugo Weiss."

"In that case, have a drink," Hjalmar Jansen said. Before taking his place at the table, Kvek instructed the porter to drive the Citroën around the corner to the *rue* Delambre.

"I've bought my old cab, my former companion in misfortune," the Russian said. "I'm going to drive it until the register has gone as high as it can go, then have another and a larger register installed beside the original one. You don't know what it means to drive without accepting tips."

"Did they ever tip you for driving like that?" asked Mr. Seldon, feeling himself all over.

"My pardonable anxiety to reach my friends . . ." The former colonel paused, then cried out as if in pain: "But Evans! Where's Evans? We can't drink without Evans . . ."

"Oh, yes we can," Tom Jackson assured him. "The dragnet's out for Evans and he's flown the coop."

"Ah, Europe. Ah, old times," said Kvek. "No doubt we shall find him."

"What brings you back to Paris?" Hjalmar asked.

"Orders," Kvek said simply. "Mr. Weiss sent me to take care of Mr. Seldon."

"God help Mr. Seldon," Tom Jackson grunted, and the business man smiled.

"Mr. Seldon is chairman of the board of directors of the American Jar and Bottle Corporation," Kvek continued.

"By Yesus," said Jansen.

"He's a fugitive," the Russian said, and ordered another round of drinks. At those words, both Jansen and the reporter looked at the stranger with heightened interest.

"Shake," the Norwegian said, and wrung the business man's hand.

"Perhaps I should explain," Mr. Seldon began. He was a little out of his element, but anxious to be a good fellow just the same. "Our company . . ."

"Jars and bottles," murmured Jackson.

"Our company," Seldon continued, "in which Mr. Weiss has a controlling interest, is under a cloud. A rival, Mr. T. Prosper Stables . . ."

"We've heard of him, the crook," said Jansen.

"Exactly. Mr. Stables is heavily involved in cans, wants to wreck the bottle trade. With that in mind, he has started a rumor on Wall Street that our company is insolvent, has pulled wires and instigated an official investigation . . ."

"So you flew the coop?" asked Jansen.

"Precisely," Seldon said, and smiled again.

"But Weiss is on the level," Jansen said, firmly. Hugo Weiss was his benefactor and friend and, no matter how many double whiskies the Norwegian painter had drunk, he was not disposed to listen to any slurs on Weiss's integrity. "The man who says he isn't gets his neck broke," Hjalmar added.

"Oh, we're all on the level, more or less," said Seldon. "The fact is, we're leading Stables into a trap. Our company's sound, the books are in order. Between you and me, we're about to declare a good fat dividend. I've disappeared in order to give credence to Stables' rumor. Do you see? Ah, it's perfect. Our stock will go down to the cellar when word gets around that I've fled."

"I don't get you. If your stock goes down, you lose money, don't you?" Jackson interposed.

Seldon winked. "When our stock goes down to the lowest figure, Weiss and a few of the rest of us will buy up what's outstanding. Then, when the investigators find everything shipshape and I show up again, the stock will go up, will rocket, in fact. Weiss will clean up another fortune, Stables will lose millions. Do I make myself clear?"

If he had not made himself clear to Hjalmar Jansen, who never thought about money when he had it, or Jackson, who was beginning to feel the double whiskies, the visiting American had surely got the point across to Dr. Balthazar St.-J. Truc, who had become so intrigued with what he was overhearing that his elbow had slipped and he had doused his pin-striped trousers with *Vichy fraises*. When the dark slim man in powder blue beside him started to make a remark, the doctor held his fingers to his lips for silence. The tanned athletic man with the Wedgwood blue eyes, the other member of the doctor's party, was reading the cricket scores in the London *Times*. Across the notes about livers in mustard and honey-colored shades, Dr. Truc was scribbling hastily "American Bottle and Jar will dive, then rocket."

And all innocent of this, at the other table, K. Parker Seldon was saying to Hjalmar Jansen: "I've heard a lot about you boys."

3

A Husband's Dilemma, and Other Unforeseen Events

THE Salle des Pilulles, or Hall of Pills, in the Louvre Museum was one of a series of small but comparatively well-lighted rooms in the long wing of the palace that stretched eastward on the north side of the large inner courtyard. To reach it, the ordinary tourist would turn left at the Winged Victory, pass through a roomful of pagan jewelry, another in which Egyptian cats predominate, a third filled with vases and pots, and then would brace a guide who, if he didn't misunderstand, would point the way northward, through a series of rooms including the Pavillon Sully, after which the tourist, if still in the money, would turn right and proceed perhaps thirty yards along a narrow passage. Within the memory of the living attendants at the famous Museum, no visitor had ever asked to go there directly, although many had lost their way to the *Spring*, the *Mona Lisa, The Music Lesson* or *Madame Recamier* and had stumbled into the Hall of Pills unawares.

Such wayfarers, were they discerning, had not gone

unrewarded, for in that small secluded room hang several excellent paintings, too small to be effective among the large ones in the main galleries.

It was to the Hall of Pills that Chief of Detectives Frémont led Evans and Miriam, after the short uneventful drive from the Salle Gaveau. The vast national museum, former habitat of kings and courtiers, was surrounded that evening with a cordon of police who were glad of the extra pay, but, inside, the faces of the regular attendants were dismal indeed. At least they seemed that way until one caught sight of the woeful countenances of Attendants Angorre and Dubonnet who had been on duty in the fatal room when the theft had occurred.

Homer Evans said little until he and his companions were face to face with *The Flirt* who was smiling across the frame at a blank and empty space that caused Frémont to groan and wring his hands. The little lady, so deftly painted that she seemed alive, was giving the unsightly wall the eye in a most inviting manner, so wistfully that Miriam caught her breath and sighed. Charming and woman-like was the little figure, dainty although solid, willing, but all in vain.

"Frémont, worthy friend," said Evans. And he put to him the hypothetical case about the two matched pearls at Cartier's.

"I'm an imbecile," the Chief said, miserably. "Perhaps I should resign. . . . But wait. Perhaps the thief was interrupted."

With a few well-chosen words, Evans demolished that theory a second time, and with impressive variations.

"The object of this blatant performance was not theft," he said with finality.

"Not theft? Three million francs not theft? Then what, in the name of God?" the chief of detectives said, with indignation.

"Not a dealer or collector on earth would buy the thing. What's clearer than that?" demanded Evans.

"But there must be thousands of rich Americans who wouldn't know the missing painting," Frémont objected hopefully.

"That type would never buy small paintings, and they'd insist on cracked and faded ones. Watteau used colors that are vivid to this day. Just look at *The Flirt*. Does that painting look old?"

"The devil knows," said Frémont disgustedly. "It surely doesn't look like three million francs or even ten old Russian rubles, as far as I'm concerned. I hope, my friend, that you're not already looking for far-reaching complications. This case is open and shut. Some ass has pinched the smallest chunk of public property belonging to the citizens of France. We've got to get it back, that's all. I ask nothing more than that."

"Unfortunately, our problem is not so simple. Reflect, friend Frémont. Some persons unknown have taken from the wall a completely unsalable canvas."

"Perhaps they didn't know."

"They know a great deal. Too much for our comfort, in fact. They know how the public and guards behave at ten minutes before closing time. They know how inaccessible is the Hall of Pills. They understand the ways of publicity, how much can be said and written of *The Pansy*. They know how to catch the imagination and interest of the people of Paris and of France, that the Marquis de la Rose d'Antan is in parts unknown; that the Louvre's director, M. Pierre Joseph des Murs is confined to his home with the gout and has been since Easter day. It would not be going too far to suggest that they know that the Chief of Detectives Frémont will be held responsible, and to whom he would appeal for help. There's a clever master mind at the back of this, directing every move and laughing, at this moment, most heartily up his sleeve."

Frémont's face had grown, if anything, a shade more gloomy than those of Angorre and Dubonnet, whose spirits Evans' tone of calm authority had perked up a bit. "Don't tell me," groaned the chief of detectives, "that we must make another assault on men of high standing. Already I'm looked on askance by that fortunate and powerful category. They whisper among themselves that I do not know when to stop, that I am ready to upset the political and governmental structure of my country to satisfy an over-reaching personal ambition and vanity. I, who ask only to be a humble officer, inconspicuous and only moderately paid. Did I not refuse the office of prefect?"

"Where is the prefect, by the way? Has he done nothing?"

"The prefect was appointed because of his genius for doing nothing," Frémont said. "He called me in, smiling in that bland way of his. Oh, butter wouldn't melt in his mouth. 'Well, Frémont,' he said to me. 'Here's a case right in your line. Art. I give you a free hand, complete and absolute authority and confidence. To show you how I trust you, I'm going to take a fishing

43

trip at the outset of this important investigation. And when the case is solved I shall obtain for you, if not the Legion of Honor, at least my personal thanks, inscribed on official note paper and bearing the seal of our beloved Third Republic.' That's what he said, and that's what he's done. And between the words his oily voice uttered, I could hear an ominous undertone. 'Here's where I get rid,' he was saying to himself, 'of a troublesome upstart who not long ago presumed to fill large sections of our prison with some of the most illustrious names in heraldry.' "

"By all means let the prefect fish, provided he keeps within bounds of the game laws," Evans said. "At least, this time we won't be handicapped by a hostile official-dom. Now let's get down to business. Let us use those mysterious organs called our brains and see what they will do for us. First of all, the so-called theft of *The Pansy* is of no consequence. It was committed to raise a smoke screen. I doubt if the painting has left the building. In fact, I'd be willing to bet that it's hidden not too far from where we stand. Shall we have a look around?"

At the sound of those words, Messrs. Angorre and Dubonnet began to gesticulate and gasp for words. "Then we'll not lose our jobs and our pensions, and have to beg through the streets," the former said.

"Go home and get some sleep," Evans said, and to Frémont: "Send every guard and watchman away from this wing. We mustn't be disturbed."

Frémont, stunned, turned to Miriam. "Please, Mademoiselle Montana! Talk sense to him. He'll listen to you. I haven't even grilled these men who were lured away by the well-dressed strangers. What shall I write

44

in my report? What shall I say to the press? We are in France, where at least a semblance of order must be followed. We've got to have suspects. We've got to hold someone, and the natural thing would be to arrest M. Angorre and M. Dubonnet, although I'm convinced they were not bribed."

"No such luck," said Angorre, disgustedly. "In my sixteen years of service I've never been offered so much as a bus ticket."

"I'm sure," Frémont went on, "that these men won't mind passing a night or two at the prefecture. I'll make them comfortable, and do my best to convince the Director in Chief, M. Pierre Joseph des Murs, to allow them overtime while they're in custody."

M. Dubonnet, the junior attendant who had but twelve years of service, looked troubled and at last spoke up. "The American savant doesn't understand my predicament," he said. "I've a wife."

The sergeant muttered sympathetically.

"But won't she be glad that you're free?" asked Evans.

The junior attendant's embarrassment increased. "You see, gentlemen. It's like this. Mathilde will have read in the papers that a painting worth three million francs was stolen from the gallery in which she knows I am stationed."

"In accordance with my direction," interposed Angorre.

"Mathilde's natural assumption will be that I shall be held in custody until the painting is found, and if I show up at home, in the middle of the evening like this . . ." Dubonnet emphasized his words with an appealing gesture. "I'm a lost man either way," he concluded. "If

45

everything's aboveboard, she'll upbraid me for spying and setting traps for her. On the other hand . . . Well, messieurs, You all understand. What one has not actually seen and cannot be sure of lacks fire to sear the soul. At least, to goad to violence and the wrecking of humble families. Do I make myself clear?"

Evans, touched, placed his hand on Dubonnet's shoulder.

"You may both remain at the prefecture, of course. It was thoughtless of me to suggest your freedom. And I think I may promise you the overtime, since by masking our real intentions you are serving your country. I did a favor once for M. des Murs, a trivial thing, but he's not the one to forget."

"You are a man with a heart, monsieur," said Dubonnet.

"My little son, poor soul, shall have a bicycle," said Attendant Angorre. "The rest of the supplementary pay my old crowbait will insist on bunging into some bank. Like as not the bank will fail."

"We're not making progress," said Frémont nervously. "Sergeant Schlumberger!" he bellowed, and from the semi-darkness of the long corridor the Alsatian officer known as "The Sunday painter" strode into view.

"Why, good evening, Mr. Evans," the sergeant said. "It's good to have you with us again. Only this time the case is not so grave. After all, as much as I like painting, a Watteau only 30 by 20 . . . That's a waste of genius, don't you think, Mr. Evans? Now I like Watteau when he spreads himself. That wonderful clown in white. Gilles. That's painting. Is it true, monsieur, that the master used a priest's face for that clown?"

46

"Sergeant Schlumberger," interrupted Frémont with asperity. "If you must discuss the revolting details of the ruses adopted by these painters in oil, you had better do so when you are off duty, or at least at some time when the fate of the department is not in precarious balance. I must remind you that there is work to be done."

"I am ready," the Alsatian said.

"Then handcuff these suspects," indicating Angorre and Dubonnet, "and take them as conspicuously as possible to the prefecture. Better use the main exit. Quite a crowd gathered outside the police lines there. Get their descriptions of the two well-dressed accomplices, have the stenographer strike out all conflicting items and if there's anything left have a clean copy made to be distributed to the press. Between you and me, these chaps won't stand on ceremony. They'll revise and trim their stories up a bit if you can make suggestions not too clumsily. Tell the reporters that we're hot on the trail of the thief and hint at clemency if the wretched little daub is kept in A-1 condition."

Schlumberger smiled at Miriam, saluted and led the two attendants away.

"Now please clear the wing. Not a guard or attendant or even a pet cat. I shall trouble you to furnish Miss Leonard and me with belts and automatics, and you can imagine what would happen to one of the poorly paid museum employees if our gentle colleague from Montana caught a glimpse of something moving," Evans said.

"You mean the culprit is actually in the Louvre?" gasped Frémont, reaching instinctively for his own Colt .45.

47

"I cannot impress on you too strongly that we must be prepared for anything," said Evans, gravely.

As if to illustrate the truth of his words, there was a muffled roar from the crowd outside, the shrill whistles of policemen, the banging of a heavy metal door which echoed like artillery through the long corridors. This was followed by the sound of running footsteps, sharp cries and a shot.

Schlumberger, half way to the main entrance with his two suspects, let out a yell, and in a voice that carried above the general din shouted: "Don't shoot, you lunkheads. There are priceless paintings on every wall. I forbid you to shoot."

Evans, Miriam and Frémont were running toward the fracas in the order named, for although Miriam was wearing a moderately high heel in order to bring her head just above the level of Evans' broad shoulder, she had outstripped many a wild steer to a corral fence, and the chief of detectives, since the arrival of Hydrangea from Harlem, had softened up a bit.

To explain the racket and confusion just described it is necessary to leave for a moment the usually sedate confines of the national museum and go southward to Montparnasse. There, it will be remembered, two new arrivals from America, the former Colonel Lvov Kvek and Mr. K. Parker Seldon of the American Jar and Bottle Corporation, were being welcomed at the Dôme by Hjalmar Jansen, nicknamed Gonzo, and Tom Jackson, of the New York *Herald* staff. All of them were waiting, for various reasons, for the reappearance on the *terrasse* of Homer Evans. Jansen, the Norwegian-American painter, had hopes of violent action; Kvek was eager once again to thank Evans for having saved his life a year before; Seldon had been told by Hugo Weiss that Homer would surely put him up in his spacious apartment in the *rue* Campagne Première until bottle stock could be had for a song; and Tom Jackson was expecting Evans to tell him what a Grand Rapids furniture widow would be likely to tell the American Students and Artists about the Taj Mahal.

In their choice of drinks for the evening, the party was divided equally, for Kvek had already exhausted the Dôme's supply of vodka and had switched to double rye, which Hjalmar was drinking. Seldon and Jackson were sticking to double Scotch. Now the American business man had done quite a bit of drinking in his day, what with board meetings, lodge conventions and the like, but he was a shade below the class of such outstanding devotees of Bacchus as Jansen, Tom Jackson and Lvov Kvek. So at the end of a couple of hours he rose politely, brushed a bit of ashes from his sleeve, and said, as if he were addressing the members of his board, "I think, gentlemen, that it might be advisable for the chairman to take a short brisk walk around the block."

None of his companions heard him, or noticed that he was on his feet, so he took their silence for consent and ambled toward the *rue* Delambre, gaining confidence as he proceeded. It is unnecessary to say that he was not aware he was being followed cautiously by Dr. Balthazar St.-J. Truc.

In describing himself to Tom Jackson as a man who never rested, Dr. Truc had not stretched the point very far. The doctor was a man of insatiable ambition, not for glory or the satisfaction of helping mankind. He wanted to be rich. As a boy he had been poor and before he was seven years old had been convinced that it was better to have wads of money. The prospect of wealth had stirred him to effort in his studies and had guided his every action since he had got his degree. He ran his sanitorium at a sizeable profit, soaked rich patients and avoided poor ones, wrote articles for newspapers and magazines, and in a small way speculated on the Bourse. Any ordinary man would have been satisfied with what he had acquired, but not Dr. Truc. He would not rest until he could buy and sell everyone he knew, and while he had earned money steadily in a dozen divers ways, the chances for big clean-ups had eluded him, quite cruelly, it seemed to him. "American Jar and Bottle," he kept murmuring to himself, as he followed the zigzag path of K. Parker Seldon. "It will dive, then rocket. Fortunes will be made. At last I have an iron in the fire."

Meanwhile, on the Dôme *terrasse*, Hjalmar, Kvek and Jackson were debating as to whether they should set a sort of informal dragnet of their own for Chief of Detectives Frémont, in order to find out what, if anything, he had learned about the whereabouts of Evans. There was much to be said on both sides. Jackson, in accordance with his principles of *laissez faire*, was all for remaining where and as they were, until such time in the near or distant future when Evans might return. Kvek was for setting out in his personal taxi and crashing the gates of the Louvre. There he proposed, if Frémont was not in the museum, to find out why and have no nonsense about it. Hjalmar, for nearly the first time in his life, found himself on middle ground. That put him further in the dumps.

"I'm slipping," he said dismally to himself. "Old Achilles was right. The whiskers in all my paintings look like putty." And he was on the point of rushing to his studio and destroying the entire year's output when Kvek began to thump, to yodel and to bellow.

"Mr. Seldon," he shouted with such vehemence that two school teachers from Iowa, in Europe for the first time, upset their cane-woven chairs, becoming entangled with them in such a picturesque way as to attract the favorable attention of a couple of Rumanian boxers who had previously decided to pass them up.

Seldon was nowhere in sight and a rather forceful inquiry among the neighboring clients of the Dôme brought forth no useful information. No one had noticed the bottle magnate's departure or, for that matter, his arrival or his former presence. M. Chalgrin, the proprietor, had been brooding about some new governmental method for saving France, which involved a new tax and a complicated system of daily returns, and would not have noticed what was happening if Aimee McPherson had put on a strip tease act in person.

"Did you look downstairs in the men's room?" Jackson asked, his reporter's instinct asserting itself at once.

Kvek and Hjalmar followed this suggestion, to the acute discomfort of several well-meaning customers who had wished to be alone. No small dapper American business men were among them.

The reporter would not give up so easily. He noticed that while the chair formerly occupied by Dr. Balthazar Truc was empty, the two men who had kept an appointment with the doctor were still in their places.

"I'm Jackson of the *Herald*," he said, approaching their table.

The athletic man with Wedgwood eyes and a vacant tanned expression looked up irritably from the cricket news in the *Times*.

"I beg your pardon," he said, coldly.

"That's it. Jackson. Tom Jackson. I wonder if you gentlemen could tell me about an American my friends and I have lost."

The slim dark man, with bright eyes like coals and heavy eyebrows, was not as distant in his manner as his British colleague.

"I should be glad to help you," he said. "You're a friend of Dr. Truc. I saw you talking together as we came in."

"Has Truc dusted?" Jackson asked.

"I say. What is the fellow talking about? Dusted?" the Englishman said.

Tom Jackson did not like Englishmen, and especially tanned ones. "I asked you a simple question," he said, looking the blue-eyed chap severely in the eye. "Have you seen a business man leaving the café, and if so, in what direction was he headed?"

"Shall I paste him one?" asked Hjalmar, who had come up from the men's room and had overheard a little of the conversation. The former colonel began to cry and to beat his breast, and since he was still clutching his gold-headed cane, there were minor casualties among other innocent bystanders. A number of the police officers who were vainly searching for Evans quickly flocked to the spot, to be met by Hjalmar Jansen in one of his firmest moods.

"My friend's lost the guy he was in charge of," Hjalmar

said. "Let him alone. He'll be all right in a couple of minutes."

Things might have gone better had not an officer new to the quarter put a hand on Hjalmar's shoulder. What followed is not clear in the minds even of the participants. Witnesses agreed that several policemen were seen to turn back handsprings; that an American with glasses started throwing siphons in the air, which exploded when and where they lit; that a large potted palm was uprooted and in its place was wedged a battered blue-eyed Englishman who gave his name as Basil Hamborough; that two Rumanian pugilists who were unwise enough to try to horn into the clash were blinded with perfume thrown into their eyes by a couple of patriotic North-American school teachers; and that, finally, when the affray became general a Citroën taxi was seen retreating down the *rue* Delambre in a manner to suggest that the driver had formerly been employed in Keystone comedies.

From his favorite spot beside a plane tree near the *terrasse* of the Coupole, the animated scene was watched somewhat jealously by M. Delbos, proprietor of that excellent but younger café. The interesting clients stuck faithfully to the Dôme, was his sad reflection.

Meanwhile, the taxi, with Kvek at the wheel and Hjalmar and Tom Jackson in the back seat, was streaking toward the Plaza Athènée, where Kvek and the missing Seldon had stopped five minutes to register and wash on the way from the boat train to the Dôme. There the Russian was met by the doorman, a former captain in his regiment, and while the two embraced, Kvek poured out his story. The doorman swore by the memory of the

Little Father, and the most spotless of the White Russian Saints, that no medium-sized North American having no French had passed his portals since Kvek and Seldon had departed. Words to the same effect were extracted by Hjalmar from the clerk and the telephone girl, who promised in addition to brush up her memory and to come to Jansen's studio the next evening at eleven-thirty, on the chance that she might be able, somehow, to help him. Jackson was on the house phone, conversing with the genial press agent of the hotel, who not only was able to set him right about the Taj Mahal, which the reporter had up to that time believed was a person, but agreed to tap out a story and send it, in Jackson's name, to the *Herald.*

From the Plaza Athènée, after a round of quick drinks in the well-appointed new bar, the trio set out for the Louvre and it was their arrival that occasioned the commotion which disturbed the earlier pages of this chapter. Kvek, because of his top hat and frock coat, had got through the police lines without question. Tom Jackson and Hjalmar had not had the same good fortune. The former, at first asserting that he had a newspaper pass, had been unable to find or produce it. And the sergeant in charge outside the museum had been one of the officers who, a year ago, had been in hospital six weeks on account of the row that followed when Hjalmar Jansen doused the prefect with violet ink. The sergeant took no chances this time. He pulled out his automatic, shoved it into Hjalmar's ribs and made no bones of saying that in case of resistance he would pull the trigger. Hjalmar, depressed as he was about the putty-like whiskers and the date he had inadvertently made with the telephone girl, said, "What the hell." He felt sure he would see Chief of Detectives Frémont at the prefecture eventually, so he and Jackson let themselves be led away.

The former Colonel Kvek, however, having passed the outer lines was challenged in the second line trenches, as it were, and had to resort to fisticuffs in order to get through the main door. He was sprinting down the slippery corridor toward the Winged Victory, and taking great satisfaction in Schlumberger's order that the enemy's fire be withheld, when an attendant stepped out from behind a stone sarcophagus and gave him the leg. In falling, Kvek struck his head on a bunch of bronze grapes being held by the statue of a Roman youth who had belonged to a Nudist cult. The grapes, the gold-headed cane and Kvek all crashed to the floor and, more surprised than injured, the colonel found himself, a few moments later, being transported, surrounded by cops in uniform, in what unquestionably was a Black Maria.

"My taxi," he murmured.

"No need to tell your taxi-man to wait," an officer said. "You'll be lucky if he's still driving a taxi when you get out again."

So it was that Hjalmar, Jackson and Kvek found themselves in separate cells in the prefecture, the one known as the Goldfish Bowl having been chosen for Kvek on account of the additional charge against him of breaking and entering.

Evans, Miriam and Frémont might have reached the Winged Victory in time to witness the arrests and intervene except for one unfortunate happening. Overcautious, one of the guardians-in-chief of the Louvre had caused a barrier to be set up between the room contain-

ing the Egyptian cats and the other filled with pagan
jewelry. Therefore, Evans, in the lead, was forced to
swerve to the right, push open a side door for employees
only, and later found himself in the long ebony-paneled
gallery in which, among priceless exhibits of faiences and
porcelains, repose in showcases the former crown jewels
of the kings of France. Swinging doors joined this with
a rotunda in which the prize piece was Correggio's *Last
Supper*. There the racing trio were blocked again, for
the door into the entrance chamber containing Ingres'
The Spring had been barricaded and nailed. Evans and
Frémont finally were obliged to break it down, so that
when they reached the main exit all violent excitement
there was over.

"A bunch of American drunks tried to crash the gate.
We hauled them in," an officer said.

"Excuse me, but one of them was not American, the
one with the stove-pipe hat. I heard Americans swear in
'17 and '18 and the inflection was not at all the same.
Americans curse short and snappily, like a telegraph.
Dot-dash-dot-dot. That way. The well-dressed party let
it roll just like coal on a chute."

Frémont was relieved, but indignant. "Have I trained
this police force so badly that you let me be interrupted
in a crucial investigation by a passel of inebriates, American, Chinese, no matter what?"

"It wasn't our fault. They just drove up and insisted
on entering," the officer said.

"And who was idiot enough to shoot, in the midst of
the world's greatest collection of objects of art and of
antiquity?" the chief demanded.

"It was a new man, sir, who's only accustomed to strike

duty. I fined him two weeks' pay," the senior officer said.

"If he has shot some valuable painting, he'll have to pay to have it patched. Is that clear?"

The officer saluted and Frémont turned to Evans. "Perhaps now we can pursue our inquiry without further interruption. Ah, there's Bonnet, God be praised. Bonnet, how fortunate. When did you arrive?"

Sergeant Bonnet was one member of the force who knew about art and had worked with Evans on the Weiss case. He had been in Rouen when the news of the theft of the Watteau had reached him and had hurried back without waiting for instructions.

"Bonnet. Take charge out here," the chief of detectives said. "Give guns and ammunition to Mr. Evans and Mademoiselle Montana and explain to all concerned how that amazing young lady can shoot. I want the wing in which we are to work cleared of every living and moving thing, and I want that accomplished without disturbing footprints or fingermarks, without puncturing oil paintings or chipping statues. And I should like to have you explain to these blockheads how many days' pay they would lose if one of the smallest pots or vases should chance to be smashed. It would have suited me better if someone had stolen a boiler from a boiler factory, or all the bonds in the Bank of France. But here we are, in a welter of art again, and we must make the best of it. If it were not for Mr. Evans, I'd resign."

"I'll be careful," Bonnet said.

4

The Quick, The Dead and Some Others In Between

AT LAST an appropriate night silence settled over the Louvre, and Evans, Miriam and Frémont, who had been standing in the Gallery of Apollo while Bonnet was conducting his mopping-up operations in the eastern wing of the museum, started off toward the *Salle des Pilulles,* or the Hall of Pills, so called because in the days of François I it had been used as a laboratory by an apothecary, who conducted a long series of experiments with a view to curing dandruff by homeopathic treatment. It is claimed by one chronicler that King François was so deeply interested in the apothecary's work that once, when the latter spilled a box of pills, the monarch got down on all fours to help look for them. While Homer was telling his companions of this legendary incident, the chief of detectives began to show signs of impatience.

"Don't fidget, Chief," said Evans, smiling. "I'm going to start investigating right away." However, when in the room just east of the Gallery of Apollo they came upon a startling showcase filled with statues of Egyptian cats, and illuminated only by the moonlight through the window, Homer stopped again in amazement.

"Egyptian sculpture reached its highest point when animals served as models. What grace! What subtle lines! What patience personified! The cats have been waiting, all these centuries. And see that hawk on the highest pedestal. He belongs to the air as the cats sit firmly on the ground. You should spend some time here, Miriam," Homer said.

"The cats make me shiver," she said.

The Chief of Detectives Frémont was not fond of cats or owls, alive or dead, although Hydrangea had three of the former and was expecting more. The only use the honest officer could think of for vases and jars might as well be omitted from this story. And the cases of antique jewelry round about reminded him rather painfully of his Harlem sweetheart's childlike extravagance. Hydrangea had been poor, even after she had reached high proficiency in dancing, and consequently had learned to spend as promptly as possible whatever came her way. Frémont was not the man to carp about expenses, but at times he was hard put to make ends meet. His wife was another of those women who have an obsession about putting money into banks.

"Shall we ever get down to business?" the Chief asked, rather peevishly, as Evans was explaining to Miriam that what looked like an ordinary earring to Frémont was the conventionalized left ear of a Goddess named Ru or Rau, and sometimes Esphet-Esphet Ru or Rau.

To ease Frémont's mind, Evans sent him out for three pairs of black silk gloves, after which the Chief was to

59

look behind every painting in the Hall of Pills and to report what, if anything, he discovered there. Meanwhile Homer tore himself from the unusual opportunity to view the treasures of antiquity undisturbed, and focused his mind on the plan of the building.

"Let's have a look downstairs," Evans said, and was about to lead the way when Chief of Detectives Frémont came larruping out of the Hall of Pills with such impetuosity that Miriam, for a moment, was ready to believe he had found *The Pansy*.

"I've an idea! I've a valid theory," the Chief said, gleefully. "The theft is the work of a fanatic. Isn't it as plain as day?"

"Develop your theory, my friend," Evans said, good-naturedly.

"I don't know why I didn't think of it before," said Frémont. "It's the art all around that addles men's brains. My head hasn't been clear since this idiotic theft was announced. M. Angorre, our principal suspect, told me that certain men and women lose their heads about certain of the pictures here, talk to them, even bring them food and leave it surreptitiously, fall in love. Why, there's an old maid who's off her rocker on account of that huge *Last Supper* . . ."

"By Correggio," prompted Evans.

"If one can believe the catalogue," said Frémont. "At any rate, this unfortunate female haunts the rotunda through which we recently ran in vain, and coos and murmurs about the feet of Christ and the disciples. The bottom third of that vast waste of canvas is almost entirely feet, you know. There are rows of them in pairs beneath the table and even the wildest devotee of oil painting could not say that any one of them was beautiful. It's a wonder your Correggio, whoever he was, wasn't excommunicated for what he did to the feet of the Master."

"Sandals, you know. The leakage was inevitable," Evans said, in the best of humor.

"Well, this monstrous woman, as I said, fairly dotes on that array of unsightly feet. She pesters the attendants, asking when the painting is to be washed, as if they sent those things to the cleaners. Wants to be present and sponge off the feet herself, poor thing. Her folks won't lock her up because, except for what I have said and her clinging for forty-odd years to her virginity, she is normal." Frémont's voice rose excitedly. "I tell you, Monsieur Evans, oil painting is sinister and unhealthy. If I were the father of Mademoiselle Montana, here, I'd forbid you to interest her in all this stuff around us. I could see, as you were talking, that she was coming under its spell. Spare this wholesome and resourceful young woman who comes to us fresh from the prairies, the short-horns, coyotes and buckaroos. Take her to the Bois de Boulogne and row around the lake, make trips on river boats, play tennis or croquet, frequent the zoo. But keep her mind out of this warehouse of abnormalities which pass for art, I beg of you, monsieur."

"But, your theory . . ." Evans said.

"Some poor soul, without doubt 'queer,' as you Americans express it, has become enamoured of *The Pansy* and has made away with it. Such a type would not sell the painting for the world, neither would he show it to his friends. He'd hide it away in a bureau drawer, all cushioned and perfumed with lavender, and take it out in secret and at night."

"I'm sorry," Evans said. "Your theory won't do. If such a one had gone dippy about *The Pansy* he would have been haunting the Hall of Pills, and both attendants swear that no one has entered there, except by accident, for at least two years."

The Chief's disappointment was eloquent, so keen that it touched Miriam's heart. "You ought to be glad your theory wasn't sound," she said, kindly. "Had some fanatic stolen the painting to gaze at in the privacy of his bedchamber we should never have found it. As it stands . . ." She looked at Evans hopefully.

"As matters stand, I'm confident we will," he said.

Reluctantly, Frémont went back to his task of peeking behind paintings, drawing on his black silk gloves as he re-entered the Hall of Pills. Homer, after a moment of silence in which he dismissed all extraneous matters from his mind, took Miriam's arm. Except for the six small exhibition rooms and the narrow corridor, the entire wing was in darkness and considering that it was half-dark on a bright sunny day it will readily be understood that the darkness it achieved at midnight was impenetrable if not Stygian. Evans had borrowed a strong flashlight from one of the guards and with that had no difficulty in finding his way. After passing the Hall of Pills, he swerved to the left to find a small doorway, stepped carefully between rows of showcases filled with votive and mortuary statues in miniature, and descended a broad stone stairway on which their footsteps echoed ominously.

"We turn left here," he said, taking a firmer hold on Miriam's arm, which was trembling. The rays of his flashlight, when he raised it, showed a long, low-vaulted chamber. Along the right wall was a long file of stone sarcophagi on the heavy lid of each of which had been carved a full-sized statue of a prince laid out in death. On the left were fragments of sculpture, mounted on pedestals, their grotesque shapes exaggerated by the shadows.

"Oh," gasped Miriam.

"From here," Evans said, to reassure her, "we shall pass beneath that heavy stone archway to the left and enter the chamber where gates and portals from the palaces of the Assyrian and Babylonian kings have been set up, at a stupendous cost of research, exploration and engineering. I should like, if we had time and light, to show you a few of them. Instead, we'll turn again to the left, right here, and enter the Egyptian room."

In the Egyptian room he flashed his torch into the alcove at the left where stood six mummy cases, two of them erect and four resting flat upon the floor.

"We must find the light switch," he said. "I have a hankering to look about me carefully."

He found the light switch, after quite a search, for the palace of the Louvre had not been constructed with a thought for electrical contrivances. Having found the switch, Evans swore. It was not an ordinary one that could be turned by hand but required a key, and to get a key they would have to retrace their steps about a quarter of a mile. Instead, he approached a showcase near by in which were small tools and implements which had been fashioned thousands of years before, of crude metal and stone. He opened the showcase, took out a few of the tools and with one of them was able to turn the switch and flood the room with light.

"Oh," said Miriam, grasping Homer's sleeve. For just outside, in the Salle Henri IV, a huge sphinx in rose-colored granite crouched ominously, as if guarding the tombs. The figure of the Goddess Hathor seemed to spring to life on the wall, where in a bas-relief she was protecting the Pharaoh Seti I. The *Seated Scribe* looked up in astonishment and indignation. Hawk-beaked Horus paused in the act of handing out a libation to the empty air. The towering headdress of Ammon, protector of Tutankhamen, leaned forward in the shadows. Miriam stood perfectly still and as minutes passed noticed that Evans was increasingly baffled. Systematically he passed from one corner to another, his keen eyes scrutinizing each object and container. Once he vaulted to a stone windowsill, shook his head, then jumped lightly to the floor.

"I don't know why I came here first," he said. "Just a hunch, but it seems that my hunches are not worth much, after all."

"I'm sure they are," said Miriam, "I feel as if something were holding me here."

Homer had been examining with a magnifying glass the covering of the mummy cases. Experimentally he tried to lift one, and the lid responded.

"Would you mind holding this open for me?" he asked.

Miriam tried to move her legs to walk toward him and at first could not succeed. Finally she felt herself walking as if against a strong undertow. With all her courage she pulled herself together, attained his side and took a firm but trembling hold on the lid. Inside the case was another of painted wood and the lid of this Homer lifted out and placed on the floor beside them. The mummy was wrapped from head to foot in strips like bandages, exuding an odor that made her feel faint at first but to which she slowly grew accustomed.

"Nothing out of the way here, as far as I can see. I'm as ignorant as a child in matters Egyptian," he said. "Let's have a look at the next one."

The second case was opened and examined, and results were nil. When the inner lid was raised from the fourth, however, Evans drew in his breath sharply. He reached for his magnifying glass, dropped to his knees, and after several minutes to Miriam's astonishment he took out his pocket knife and slit a small sample from the mummy cloth, from the underside of the mummy's broad knee.

"What have you found?" asked Miriam.

"I wonder," he said thoughtfully. "We'll have to look to wiser men than I for an answer to that question."

The echo of a voice from above brought them tensely to their feet and again Miriam's hand clutched her automatic.

"Don't shoot. It's only Frémont and he's far away," Evans said, "Come! We've got to work quickly. I'm afraid the chief of detectives would disapprove of our ghoulish activities."

Hastily he re-opened one of the cases they had already inspected and there again he cut a small sample of the wrappings around the knee. "That's all just now," he said. "Is everything in order?"

They glanced at the six mummy cases to make sure no traces had been left of their investigation, then hurried upstairs to join the bellowing Frémont.

"*Nom de Dieu,* I thought I'd lost you! How long must

we remain in this damnable place? There's nothing hidden behind the paintings," Frémont said.

"We may as well wait until tomorrow," said Evans. "Let's go to the prefecture and find out if anything unusual has been reported. After that, a few hours of sleep won't be amiss. We'd better sleep while we can, for I have a distinct feeling that once this case gets fairly started . . ."

"Started?" said Frémont, indignantly. "It's gone far enough to suit me. I shall be the laughing stock of France. For once, my friend, I fear you have gone astray. You are looking for motes when only a beam is involved, but such a beam. Three million francs! Disgrace! Exposure!"

"Calm yourself, Chief. I promise you developments tomorrow," Evans said.

Disconsolately Frémont let himself be led toward the main exit and there he was pleased to observe that Sergeant Bonnet had restored a semblance of order. The curious crowd, once it had seen a few arrests and a pair of suspects being carted away, had dispersed. Bonnet had sent home the extra officers, given instructions to the attendants-in-chief, and had even been thoughtful enough to telephone Mme. Frémont to the effect that her husband had been given full charge of the spectacular case of the year and probably would not be home for several days and nights.

"One item of interest I have to report, and it may be important," Bonnet said. "There's an empty Citroën taxi parked just inside the southern archway, no passenger, no driver, nothing. And it's been there several hours. None of the blockheads who was here before I came can tell me just how long . . ."

"Ah," said Frémont, immediately hopeful.

"You haven't heard all," continued Bonnet excitedly. "The meter, gentlemen and mademoiselle,"—his voice broke with emotion—"the meter reads 273 francs, and is still ticking."

Within an instant all four were trotting toward the taxi and neither Evans, Miriam or Frémont had approached the battered Citroën nearer than one hundred feet before they called out in unison:

"Lvov Kvek! It's the colonel's taxi!" And, indeed, on closer inspection it proved to be the car in which Hugo Weiss and the Russian had been kidnapped the year before.

The chief of detectives began a kind of rigadoon, clasping and unclasping his hands and making assorted noises which gradually became coherent enough to be classified as speech. "And you," he said excitedly to Evans. "You, yourself, were the one who told me that Kvek was in the habit of stealing small pictures from walls."

Here it should be explained to the reader that in his first days of struggle in Paris, before he knew enough French to drive a taxi, the former colonel had eked out a bare existence by exchanging old engravings that chanced to be on the walls of the Hotel Voltaire for new ones he could pick up for a franc or two on the *quais*.

Evans, as certain as he was that Frémont's hasty suspicions were groundless, decided to let them ride. The Chief needed cheer of some kind and Evans needed time.

"Let's go at once to Montparnasse and see what this is all about," he said. "I thought our friend the colonel was in America. Perhaps he is."

A four-minute ride in the official car, with the aid of the siren, brought them all to the curb in front of the Dôme and there they found, in the center of the *terrasse:* Rosa Stier with her ninth Pernod, Harold Simon, a rangy Finnish painter named Snorre Sturlusson, and a Juno-esque Swedish actress called Olga. The last named had reached the point where she was rendering, to the delight of the regulars and tourists assembled, her version of *Barbara Frietchie* in Swedish dialect. To say that the newcomers were greeted warmly is an illustration of the shortcomings of mere words. Rosa Stier yelled *"Sauve qui peut."* The Finn shook Frémont's hand until it felt as if it had passed through a clothes wringer. And Olga stepped down from the table and threw her shapely arms around Evans' neck. It was only the extraordinary force of Homer's personality that within a reasonable time restored enough order for the questioning to begin. M. Chalgrin, the proprietor, was called away from his gloomy computations, the waiters rallied around, and soon it was established that Kvek had appeared out of the blue, as it were, with a middle-sized American business man in tow, the latter having been introduced as a friend of Hugo Weiss.

"Was the colonel in possession of any small package or packages?" asked Frémont severely.

"He acquired a package in a hurry, but not a small one," Rosa said. "From what I hear it was a beaut."

From then on M. Chalgrin took up the narrative. He explained that the Russian and his dapper American had been received by Hjalmar Jansen and Tom Jackson; that after a stupendous number of double whiskies the American had got lost, that the resulting search for him had ended in a riot, after which Kvek, Hjalmar and Jackson had escaped in a taxi and had not been heard from since.

"My God! The drunken Americans," Frémont said, and within five seconds the Chief, with Miriam, Evans and Sergeant Bonnet, were speeding to the prefecture with small regard for life and limb. They burst in on Sergeant Schlumberger, who was still in the act of questioning the suspects, Angorre and Dubonnet, and a moment later found themselves in front of a trio of cells in which the Russian, the reporter and the painter known as Jansen or Gonzo were snoring, which gave proof that life was still extant, but nothing more. The chief of detectives, having had previous experience with those same gentlemen, called feebly for the medical examiner, Dr. Hyacinthe Toudoux.

Fortunately, the doctor was still in his laboratory, engaged in deep research, and was soon on the scene.

"Monsieur Evans," he cried, delightedly. "How good it is to see you again! I am so far in your debt that I am almost ashamed to ask you what I can do for you."

"How long will it be," asked the Chief, somewhat abruptly, "before these incorrigibles can be revived again?"

The medical examiner passed leisurely from one cell to another, sighed, listened through his stethoscope, tested the breaths with a lighted match, and said: "Not before morning, between eleven and two."

"Impossible. I must speak with them immediately. At once. Do you hear?" Frémont said.

The doctor raised his eyebrows. "I have given my best opinion," he said. "And I beg you to remember that my text-book on the resuscitation of drunken men is the standard work on the subject, not only in France but in other lands as well. These men drink with a singleness of purpose that makes necessary a set of special calculations. Instead of swallowing and absorbing tranquilly, as we do in France, they fill themselves to the brim and only begin the absorption process after they have taken in enough to stagger a whole company of soldiers. You may try to wake them, if you wish, but I warn you against it."

"The press is waiting to talk with you," an officer said to Frémont, from the doorway, and in despair the Chief left the corridor, followed by Bonnet.

5

Of the Ravages of Discourtesy

THE laboratory of Dr. Hyacinthe Toudoux was on the western side of the prefecture, separated from the prefect's office and the retention cells by yards and yards of administrative offices in which, during the daylight hours, hordes of harassed clerks wrestled with passports, identity cards and reams of records which, if they served no other purpose, helped reduce substantially the numbers of the unemployed in France. At the entrance, Miriam, at the doctor's suggestion, paused a moment while a sheet was hastily thrown over a couple of corpses that had recently been brought in, and a case of American prairie rattlesnakes that had crossed the ocean in the self-same liner, the *Ile de France,* which also had transported Lvov Kvek and his missing charge, Mr. K. Parker Seldon, of the American Jar and Bottle Corporation. The good doctor, while he had scrupulously kept his word to Evans about divulging the formula for making Mickey Finns, which Evans had given him in connection with the death of Ambrose Gring, had been intrigued by the properties of the excellent oil those serpents provided and had kept a few on hand for his personal use and private experiments.

The main room smelled rather strongly of formaldehyde, so, following the doctor's lead, Evans and Miriam stepped out on a balcony which overlooked the Flower Market. Although it was not yet dawn, the stalls were already being filled with fresh roses, lilies, gladioli and other seasonal plants and flowers.

"How lovely," Miriam sighed, glancing from the verdant scene below to the fading stars above.

The doctor smiled. Already he had forgotten about the drunken men in the prefecture, so intent he was on his investigations and research.

"My calling," he said to Miriam and Homer, "may seem sordid at first glance, but there are compensations. You may recall, Monsieur Evans, that some time ago I read a paper before the Academy of Science in which I stated that I had found an over-strained liver streaked with heliotrope and mauve."

"I read the report in *Le Temps* with great interest," Homer said. "And I was amused to find that you imputed that unusual size and coloring to California Medoc. I wouldn't mind the Californians manufacturing or drinking such stuff, if it pleases them, but when they label it with the time-honored names of French vintages, then I object most strenuously."

"Today I found another pink liver, and the corpse had also spent several years in California," the medical examiner said, triumphantly. "But pardon me, mademoiselle and monsieur. I see by your expressions that something unusual is in the wind, and surely our chief of detectives would not be in such a state from any trivial cause. But that affair of the Louvre, as I see by the papers, is a spectacular theft. So much the better. I shall not be involved."

"I wouldn't be too sure," said Evans. "To be frank, I am out of my depth. In a moment of weakness I agreed to help our friend, the Chief, and I fear I shall prove a broken reed, or such a limp one that no breakage will be necessary. Tell me, Dr. Toudoux, to whom would you turn for enlightenment on Egyptian questions?"

"Has there been trouble there again?" the doctor enquired.

"I do not mean the Egypt of today, which has fallen so far below its former glories. I refer to that Egypt of yore, the land which led the way toward that which we call civilization, the times of the building of the pyramids and the Sphinx."

"Oh, those," said Dr. Toudoux. "Well, if that's what's on your mind, I think I know your man. My old friend Zacharie de la Poussière, who held the chair of Egyptology at the Sorbonne until he retired in order to pursue his studies uninterruptedly. He lives in the *place* Dauphine, not three hundred yards from here. I'm sure he'd be happy to be of service."

"No doubt Professor de la Poussière has long since been in bed. I've read of his deciphering of hieroglyphics. Is he conversant with materials and fabrics as well?" Evans asked.

"First of all, I'm sure he's not asleep, since he works nearly every night. And scholars come to him all the way from Egypt itself to learn about what went on there centuries ago," said the doctor.

"You'll excuse me then," said Evans, noting the exact

address on a card. "If you think he wouldn't mind, I'll try to see him at once."

"Remind him that on Friday he's playing parchesi with me," the doctor said. "It's a silly game, I know, but we both seem to like it."

As Miriam and Evans entered the *place* Dauphine, they noticed a single lighted window, and since it was in the building the doctor had indicated Homer pressed the doorbell. The door was opened so suddenly that both of them recoiled, confronted by a distracted woman in negligée, her hair awry, her face showing marks of recent tears. The woman screamed and the concierge, close behind her, grunted.

"But it's not Zacharie! It's not my husband! Where is he? What's been done with him? He left home this morning, early, and I haven't heard a word," the woman sobbed.

"I'm very sorry to have disturbed you," Evans said. "I had been told by Dr. Hyacinthe Toudoux . . ."

"Has he seen my husband?"

"Not today, I feel sure. I've just come from the prefecture . . ."

"The prefecture," repeated the woman, dazed. "Then there is something wrong! I beg of you to tell me."

"I have nothing to tell. I came on a personal errand, because I'd been given to understand that Professor de la Poussière was in the habit of working at night. But if I can be of assistance?"

"He's never stayed away like this before, without a word. What shall I do?"

"The most sensible course would be to notify the police. They'll telephone the hospitals . . ."

74

At the mention of hospitals, Mme. de la Poussière fainted. Her face, already pale, turned paler. Her eyelids fluttered, then closed, and she collapsed, not without natural grace, into the arms of the concierge.

"Now we're in a fix," the concierge said. "You've made her ill, and there's no place to stretch her out down here, not even room to sit down in that lodge of mine when my wife's in bed and her duds are all over the only chair." With that, he handed the unconscious woman to Evans and shrugged his shoulders.

"I'll take her upstairs," Evans said, "Which floor?"

"The top," said the concierge. "I'll give the key to your girl friend, here." Having handed a key to Miriam, the concierge said good night and slammed the door of his cubbyhole.

The stairs of No. 12 *place* Dauphine were steep, narrow and numerous, but Evans, now thoroughly committed to the new adventure, bore Mme. de la Poussière aloft with ease. Just after they had passed the third floor landing she began to revive but, finding herself secure, remained limp and motionless until the sixth floor, her habitation, was attained. There, after Miriam had opened the door and Evans had stretched her on the couch, the wife of the Egyptologist murmured her apologies. Already, Evans' reassuring presence had had the effect of calming her overwrought nerves. She sat up, smoothed her hair and listened quite bravely while Homer phoned the prefecture. The chief of detectives was no longer there but Sergeant Schlumberger assured Evans that no reports had come in concerning Professor de la Poussière or any other man of his approximate age or description.

"He's probably with a woman," the bluff Alsatian said,

and in spite of Homer's efforts to muffle the remark it carried to the couch on which Mme. de la Poussière was sitting, in faded but becoming negligée.

"I think that is highly improbable, unless the woman has been dead these hundreds of years and is wrapped in kilometers of bandages," Madame said with dignity. "I would pray in church for any girl who could get his mind away from antiquity for a while." She bowed her head. "I tried, when I was younger . . . I don't mean to say," she added, loyally, "that Zacharie has callously neglected me. But one doesn't like to feel, when one is the object of affectionate attentions, that one's husband has his mind on occurrences several thousands of years before Our Saviour . . . But forgive me. I'm burdening you with my confidences. I assure you, monsieur and mademoiselle, that I've not said as much, in the nature of complaint, since our marriage in 1903."

"Perhaps he's carrying on his studies elsewhere," Evans said. "There are mummies in various museums."

"I telephoned the Louvre several times," she said. "That's where he started for, I think. Someone called him from there. But the operator was very short with me, and told me grudgingly that the Professor was not in the building. Ah! Manners these days."

"He works there frequently?" Homer asked.

"There's a mummy there about whom or which he's recently unearthed new information. You'll see the tablets spread out on his desk in his study just to your right. Since those things were shipped to him, he has spent half his time laughing, the Lord knows why. At all hours of the night one could hear him guffaw, to such a point that the neighbors put in a complaint. Since then

76

he's tried to chuckle, but he can't. He's got a hearty laugh, and a sense of humor, so they say. I know nothing of ancient Egypt so I can't share his merriment."

It could be seen that Mme. de la Poussière was by no means devoid of humor herself, and that, in her normal condition, she had put up with her lot with admirable philosophy. She was past middle age but carried her years extremely well, with much of her former beauty and all of her charm. Readily she granted Evans permission to enter the professor's study, and Miriam followed as far as the door. The large low-vaulted room had three dormer windows. The floors and all the furniture were strewn with open books, papyrus scrolls, photographs, engravings and drawings of pharaohs, queens, artisans, toilers and slaves. The walls were papered with pictures and blueprints of monuments, idols, obelisks, cross sections of pyramids, plans of palaces, maps of plains and of rivers, gods and goddesses in profile, generals and armies, players of the harp and psaltery, blowers of horns and trumpets. In spite of the multitude of objects, a sort of order seemed to show through the appearance of confusion.

Evans went straight to the desk on which were spread five broken tablets, pieced together like jigsaw puzzles. He stared at the hieroglyphics chiseled upon them and turned to Miriam with eloquent dismay.

"And to think," he said, "that for a man who knows enough, these tablets are filled with laughter that is fresh and irresistible after five thousand years. And also to think, that with all the nonsense with which I have crammed my idle head, not a single scrap of knowledge helpful to us now can be found. I have never felt so completely a fool."

77

"You couldn't help it," Miriam said, defensively. "How were you to know what to study?"

"How, indeed . . . Well. No use weeping over sins of omission. Let's be on our way." Returning to the salon, where Mme. de la Poussière rose to bid them good night, Miriam put her arm impulsively around the older woman's waist.

"Mr. Evans will find your husband. Will you try to go to sleep?" she said.

"You're both very kind. I'll try," said Mme. de la Poussière.

The *place* Dauphine is a quiet little square on the Ile de la Cité, with a small park in the center and a few obscure hotels and old residences ranged closely on all sides. Not fifty yards away is the busy Pont Neuf, where market trucks and wagons rumble all night long to help in the colossal task of feeding Paris, but the sounds that reach the *place* are softened and subdued. On the eastern side, the jail, the Palais de la Justice, and the Sainte Chapelle introduce an atmosphere of spiritual and temporal authority which does not overshadow the square. There are dim doorways, shuttered windows, time-stained walls and in the center a few chestnut trees beneath which are short cement walks and a half dozen benches. Two street lamps, spaced well apart and cloaked with foliage, furnish just the right amount of light. It was in that *place,* that had been Paris when cows were still grazing in St. Germain des Pres, where Evans and Miriam found themselves standing after their interview with Mme. de la Poussière. Homer was in a brown study, walking as if in his sleep, his mind, now thoroughly aroused, making ineffectual sallies in all directions. Miriam, who was accustomed to his moods, kept step with him, her hand on his arm, and followed his lead as carefully as if they had been in the midst of a crowded dance floor, notwithstanding the emptiness and silence of the *place*. Scarcely without his knowing it, Evans decided abruptly to sit down on a bench and undoubtedly that impulse saved his life. A shot rang out, a flash lighted one of the shade trees. Another shot followed before the echo of the first got started. As, with a horrid crash, a body dropped heavily through the branches of the tree and collided with the concrete walk, Homer saw Miriam standing tensely, smoking automatic in hand.

"Look out! There may be more of them," he said, and drew her to the shelter of the nearest tree trunk. There was no further sound and no motion, except for a single twitch on the part of the man on the walk. They waited a breathless moment, then hurried toward him.

"Oh, Homer!" whispered Miriam, almost in tears. "Have I been hasty again? Was I wrong to fire when I saw that flash?"

For answer Evans showed her his hat, through the top of which a bullet had passed. "It's lucky one of us was on the job," he said. "Let's have a look at this chap. . . . But, of course, with the prefecture so near, we'll have to call Schlumberger and let him start from scratch." He looked at Miriam steadily. "How are the nerves? O.K.?"

"If you're not going to scold me," she said.

"Stand guard half a minute, and I'll call the regulars," he said, and set off at a brisk walk for the prefecture. Within a few seconds he was standing beneath the balcony of Dr. Hyacinthe Toudoux. The doctor was inside, engaged in color photography.

"I say, doctor," Evans called, and the medical examiner appeared on the balcony. "Sorry to interrupt, you know, but Miss Leonard's just shot a man. He's dead, worse luck, so you'll have to rally round."

"You're joking," said the doctor incredulously.

"Honor bright! And I've got to notify the sergeant, or can you do it by phone? The body's in the *place* Dauphine."

"The devil!" said Toudoux, tearing off his white apron and muttering. Hearing the doctor's irate voice on the phone, Evans hastened back to where Miriam was standing. Except for a small pool of blood in the shadow of the corpse, no change had come about. That is, no outward change. Inwardly, Miriam had suffered what practically amounted to a revolution. She remembered Evans' words in the Hall of Pills, how he had hinted so strongly that the thief who had taken *The Pansy* had known whom Frémont would call on for aid. The whole thing was a trap, she believed, and it was she who had deceitfully led Homer into it. Already he had missed death by an accidental three centimeters and Heaven only knew what was to follow. She must confess her duplicity, she had decided, and that, she was sure, would mar their remarkable friendship. The first act of trickery, the first lack of straightforwardness. Would he ever trust her again? And after all her resolutions and talk about non-interference with his life and habits. She almost dreaded his return but when finally he reached her side she had no time to unburden herself, for Sergeant Schlumberger, sprinting well for a man of his age and even disposition,

80

was only two seconds behind. Later, they heard the measured tread of Dr. Hyacinthe Toudoux who was rounding the corner from the Quai de l'Horloge and growling audibly as he carried his well-worn satchel.

"Little thanks for a scientist in the public service," he said aloud, to all whom it might concern. "Not an atom of consideration. Young women are given guns. They go off. Pouf! And not only some bum or other bites the concrete but the best photograph of the effects of California wine, mixed fruit salads and improperly prepared abalone is over-exposed and spoiled. *Zut, alors!* Show me what's left of this intruding nitwit. Hmmmm. Death was instantaneous, occurred about five minutes ago—between five and six—from a bullet wound, Colt .45 caliber, fired by . . . What the devil is your name, Mademoiselle? . . . Thank you. Good evening or morning. I trust I shan't be troubled again."

And the irate doctor scribbled a certificate, using the back of the bench as a desk, signed it with a flourish and handed it gruffly to Sergeant Schlumberger, who had already ascertained that the corpse had not even as much as a used Metro stub for papers.

Having received the sergeant's permission, Evans knelt beside the body. He pried open the mouth and switched on his flashlight.

"Hmmmm. Doesn't speak English," he said, and rose to his feet again.

The Alsatian officer, already unnerved, almost exploded.

"Would you mind telling me," he asked, "how the devil you are so sure this man was not conversant with your illogical and bothersome lingo? And perhaps, since

I've got to make a stab at handling this case, you'd go further and tell me what difference it makes, even if he had spoken Portuguese or Sanskrit? He took a shot at you, was blown from a tree with a most lucky shot . . ."

"Lucky, indeed," said Miriam, indignantly. Then a window was opened far above and faint screams were heard. Dr. Toudoux, who had not reached the corner, wheeled impatiently.

"One moment, doctor, if you please," Evans said. He sensed at once that Madame de la Poussière had heard the shots and had dragged herself at last, in terror, to the window. Miriam already was pushing the concierge's bell but the latter was not responding. It took several sharp raps of Sergeant Schlumberger's club on the windowsill to bring the concierge to his senses.

"Can a man never sleep?" he shouted.

"Wake up, in the name of the law," said Schlumberger gruffly.

Evans, meanwhile, had explained the situation as best he could. They all accompanied Dr. Toudoux to the sixth floor of No. 12 where the professor's wife was struggling heroically against incipient hysterics.

"My husband," she gasped, beginning to shake, then go rigid.

Dr. Toudoux, meanwhile, had taken a small phial from his case and, in his agitation, failed to conceal it from Evans. On the label was written:

Oleum crotali confluenti *
Tinc, argalli Texarkanae * *

* Prairie rattlesnake oil.
** Arkansas lettuce, a variety of loco weed found only in eastern Texas and Arkansas.

Seeing that Evans had read the label, the doctor's ruffled face relaxed and he smiled somewhat sheepishly. "The American Mickey Finn," he murmured, and within a few minutes Mme. de la Poussière was sleeping soundly, if not peacefully.

"I have found your formula invaluable in certain emergencies," the doctor said, when all was quiet again.

They took seats in the salon and refreshed themselves with a glass of excellent wine. Its soothing effect was soon apparent, and Evans spoke first.

"You asked me, a while ago, how I knew that the corpse spoke no English," he said to the perspiring sergeant. "As you know, the 'th' sound occurs often in that language, and to pronounce a 'th' one must press with considerable force with the top of the tongue against the upper front teeth. The chap who passed away just now had not pressed against those teeth with his tongue or even a toothbrush for a considerable length of time. Do I make myself clear?"

"To a certain point," said the sergeant, "but why that mildly disgusting fact is important to us I still cannot fathom."

"A French gang is involved, the members of which spend much of their time dancing. That I deduced from the soles of the shoes, which are worn smooth to the tips of the toes. Now which French gang, unilingual and having headquarters in a Bal Musette, would go to extreme lengths to shorten my inoffensive existence?"

"The St. Julien Rollers, I suppose," the sergeant admitted grudgingly. "But nearly all of them are on Devil's Island."

"The few who are left must have gathered other undesirables around them. I propose that you see what you can learn about the recent activities between the *rue* des Deux Ponts and the boulevard St. Germain," Homer said.

"I'll have to inform M. Frémont," the sergeant said. "And the way he was feeling tonight, I don't relish the experience."

"Why not let him sleep until morning? It's well after dawn as it is," Evans asked. "He solicited my help on this case, and I'll take the responsibility. But," he continued, turning to Dr. Toudoux, who was pouring another round of drinks, "since Professor de la Poussière is nowhere to be found, could you perhaps recommend another learned man who might serve my purpose?"

"With pleasure," said Dr. Toudoux, whom the smooth white Bordeaux had thawed more than a little. "I happen to know that when the absent professor was wrestling with a problem particularly difficult he was in the habit of consulting a man who, although unknown among the savants and explorers, had a knowledge of ancient Egypt that commanded the respect of friend Zacharie. I refer to Lazare, of the *place* St. André des Arts, Hot-seat Lazare as he was brutally called in his school days. And that, my friends, reminds me of an old and nearly forgotten story. I see that the sergeant's able assistants are removing the body to the morgue and since we all have time and the tale is not without relevance, if you are going to interview the man, I'll begin."

He settled himself in an easy chair, lighted a fresh cigar, and, with a glance at the sleeping patient, continued.

"When Professor de la Poussière was at the height of

his fame as a teacher at the Sorbonne, he had in his class one pupil for whom he had the highest hopes. The young man was poor, so poor that he was conspicuous among his classmates, who, for the most part, were rich and aristocratic. I am speaking of Lazare Dufour, who today is the humble proprietor of that taxidermy shop named *Au Sens de Mesur* in the *place* St. André des Arts.

"Lazare was brilliant, but incurably shy, lacking social graces and living completely alone. As long as he could remain inconspicuous, he was able to absorb knowledge with fantastic aptitude. The moment he thought he was attracting attention, he grew tongue-tied and miserable. For that reason, Professor de la Poussière seldom called on him in class, but he had won the young man's confidence and friendship so that they had long talks in private, talks which quickly became, to all intents and purposes, consultations.

"Having a free ticket one night to the Comèdie Française and being unable to use it, the professor offered it to Lazare, who accepted eagerly. He had never been inside a theater and the performance entranced him. The piece, I believe, was Molière's *Les Femmes Savants* and the unhappy young student, lonely beyond belief, felt himself a part of a living, speaking company in which he could remain invisible. That, for him, was Paradise. The performance that night was poorly attended, so after the intermission, Lazare stole up to a seat nearer the stage. Before the act had proceeded far, there was a tug at his shoulder, and an angry old woman began upbraiding him in hoarse whispers, other spectators began to hiss for silence, and a crotchety old man in evening clothes began making a terrible scene. The old man was the late Marquis de la Rose d'Antan, father of the present minister of Beaux Arts, I believe.

"Well, the upshot was that the curtain was rung down and an altercation followed in which young Lazare was so crushed and embarrassed that he nearly swooned. The Marquis, it seemed, did not care for the opening acts of the play and Lazare had taken the seat he had reserved for the finale. For the young man to retreat to the seat he should have occupied was not enough. The irate nobleman, inflamed by the jibes of the hostile crowd, asserted that he would not accept a hot seat, nor change it for another. He called in the police and the next day entered suit against Lazare and the Comèdie Française. The case was the talk of Paris, Lazare, more dead than alive, was lampooned in the press, laughed at in the streets and, after becoming a comic celebrity, was reprimanded and fined and for weeks was unable to force himself to return to school. When he did appear in class, his classmates, for the most part, refrained even from smiling, but in his consternation Lazare took the wrong seat again, this time the one belonging to the Marquis' son and the latter, an arrogant fellow, complained that the chair was too hot when he tardily entered the classroom.

"The Sorbonne, mademoiselle and gentlemen, lost a brilliant student that day and Lazare, instead of becoming our foremost Egyptologist, became proprietor of a taxidermy shop that came to him from a distant relative he had never seen. Bear in mind poor Lazare, my friends, when you are on the verge of discourtesy. Remember that one drop of ridicule may burn like an acid and destroy a priceless fabric fate is weaving."

There were tears in Miriam's eyes as the doctor finished speaking and she was about to confess, again, when Evans rose and beckoned her to follow.

"I shall have words with this sensitive man," he said, "and shall take the utmost care not to bruise his tender feelings."

6

A Sock Filled with Sand, and Joyce's Ulysses

THE Chief of Detectives Frémont, after a harrowing session with the star reporters of the morning papers, had rushed out of the prefecture without making his usual tour of inspection. The journalists, outwardly, had been respectful but in each of their questions the worried Chief had felt an undercurrent of mockery and of glee. The theft of the famous *Pansy*, coming as it did after a long dearth of piquant news, was proving to be jam for the Paris papers. The suspects, Angorre and Dubonnet, had failed to impress the gentlemen of the fourth estate, although the pair had been photographed in various poses and their statement, carefully edited by the prefectorial stenographer, had been accepted under protest. A round of the art dealers in the *rue* la Boëtie and the boulevard Haussmann had netted an even half dozen copies of the missing painting, but only two of them had been done with sufficient skill to warrant their submission to a board of experts. In short, not only the veteran reporters but also the cubs had seen clearly that Frémont was stalling and sparring for time, and they all made much of the fact that both the prefect, Philippe de la Chemise Farcie, and the minister of Beaux Arts, the Marquis de la Rose d'Antan, had found it convenient to remain away from the center of activities.

Having at last shaken off the watchdogs of the press, Frémont had dismissed for the night his faithful chauffeur, Melchisadek Knockwoode, and had walked all the way to the *place* de la Contrescarpe. He tried to snatch a comforting beer in several of the cafés en route, only to be driven away by the constant chatter about the stolen Watteau and the laxness of officialdom generally and of the police in particular. Now and then the Chief derived comfort from his recollection of Evans' promise of developments tomorrow, but in his heart of hearts he feared that the said developments, if they occurred, would prove more embarrassing, if possible, than those of the day just passed. Alone on the narrow streets he skirted the Pantheon and L'Eglise de la Montagne St. Genevieve and a few moments later inserted his key in the door of the Hotel Murphy et du Danube Bleu.

Hydrangea, her dusky countenance eloquent with solicitude, received him with open arms.

"Man. Your poor head is burning hot," she murmured tenderly, and busied herself with cool towels, aspirin and simple household remedies to which the Chief found it difficult to respond. "Has Mr. Evans found that little picture yet?" she asked. "I declare, I don't see why everybody should make such a fuss about a thing like that."

The chief of detectives was too tired to attempt an explanation. He had found in the past that his sweetheart's sense of values differed radically from that of

89

the Paris public, in more ways than one, and he loved her for her simplicity. As weary as he was, the Chief was in no mood for sleep, so he sat at the back window for a breath of air and Hydrangea, after mild attempts to induce him to rest, gave up and soon was in slumber. How long he sat there, Frémont did not know. The stars grew dim and disappeared, the first rays of dawn sought out familiar towers. His window looked out over the *rue* Cardinal Lemoine and directly beneath it was a two-story structure on the ground floor of which was a popular dance hall, the Bal des Vêtements Brulés. The second floor contained six rooms, five of which were rented to transients for periods ranging from twenty minutes to forty-eight or even sixty hours.

The neighborhood clocks had been striking five, at intervals, for nearly half an hour when Frémont saw a slim young man, with checkered cap drawn over one eye and a suit of loud but faded pattern fitting snugly in the back, leave the front doorway of the long-dark Bal des Vêtements Brulés and, staying close to the wall as if by long habit, start walking toward the boulevard St. Germain. Had the Chief not been sure he had seen that cap and suit before, and always in suspicious circumstances, he would have stifled his impulse to follow. As it was, he felt impelled to do so.

Tiptoeing from the room in which Hydrangea slept, he descended the stairs, made his way hastily to the boulevard and was rewarded by seeing his quarry cut across toward the *place* St. Michel. There Frémont picked him up again, and, with the skill he had acquired when he had occupied a much less important position in the force, he shadowed the cap and pinch-back coat across the Pont

St. Michel, along the *quai* and into the *place* Dauphine. There, the young man become noticeably cautious, and Frémont ducked into a doorway to watch. The other looked in every direction and finally darting with address from lamppost to tree, stood still beneath a quiet chestnut in the center of the *place*. The young man gazed upward into the thick foliage of the tree. He spoke a few words which Frémont couldn't catch, looked more closely, then seemed to be startled by something he saw on the concrete walk. So suddenly and quickly that Frémont himself had difficulty in following his movements, the youth hurried out of the *place*, alarm written all over his wasp-like back.

The chief of detectives was torn between two impulses: first, to have a look at the tree and the sidewalk; and second, to continue the chase. It was the first to which he succumbed. The tree looked very much like other chestnut trees, but on the sidewalk was a stain, rather carelessly swabbed up, of what Frémont thought was blood. In an instant his brain, hitherto lethargic, got into action and with it his legs. He caught a taxi on the fly as it was passing the statue of Henri IV.

"The *place* de la Contrescarpe," he said, showing his badge, "and don't stop for anything."

Luckily the traffic was light at that hour, so in record time the Chief was again at the window of Hydrangea's apartment in the Hotel Murphy et du Danube Bleu, not without, however, having passed beneath the eagle eye of Bridgette Murphy, the proprietress. The taxi waited, according to instructions.

Frémont reached his vantage point none too soon. The young man in cap and tight suit, now practically on the run, rushed into the Bal des Vêtements Brulés and closed the door behind him. That was enough for Frémont. He decided to investigate. Leaving Hydrangea still sound asleep he descended softly the rear flight of stairs to the kitchen, this time without being observed by the proprietress, and in less time than it takes to tell was out of doors and in the *rue* Cardinal Lemoine. He tried the door of the dance hall, found it was not locked, and entered. The light was dim inside and the Chief could hardly make out the empty tables and chairs around the rim of the dance floor. With uncertain step he continued, trying to make no sound, but it had been many years since he had trod a dance floor and that of the Bal des Vêtements Brulés had been waxed to a point where only experts could safely venture on it. His foot slipped, there was a crash and the back of Frémont's head came in brusque contact with the polished boards. He was not quite unconscious but definitely *hors de combat*. When he felt himself pinned by several sets of arms and heard himself cursed in the spiciest slang to be heard on the entire Left Bank, he tried to resist. Promptly he felt a thud on his already battered head and after that, oblivion. Had the Chief known it, it was a silk sock stuffed with sand that had accomplished his final downfall.

In front of the Hotel Murphy et du Danube Bleu, in the neighboring street, the taxi driver waited patiently until after breakfast time. Then he began to grumble and to fidget. Eventually he got out and paced the sidewalk so nervously that Bridgette Murphy, who had inherited a certain aggressiveness from her Irish father and more than her share of curiosity from her French mother, pushed open her front-room windows and said:

"What's eating you?"

"Don't speak of eating, I beg of you, madam. I was cruising along peaceably when a man who claimed to be a police officer hopped my running board . . ."

"Claimed to be," repeated Bridgette. "That's a good one! His claim was a pippin! You were driving the Chief of Detectives Frémont, the best of luck to him."

"That doesn't take the place of breakfast," the chauffeur said. "And what would the chief of detectives be doing so long in a dump like this?"

"That's none of your business," said Bridgette, thoroughly nettled. "So you're calling it a dump, my respectable hotel. I was on the point of feeding you, you big palooka, never having turned away a man who was hungry. But I draw the line at a bum like you. A dump, indeed! I'll have you know that if I hadn't heard the Chief himself tell you to wait, I'd crown you with a mug I've got handy."

"I spoke hastily, madam," the taxi driver said, for he saw that he had made a tactical error. "Had I reflected, I should have remarked that your establishment would do honor to a classier quarter than this."

"And what's wrong with this quarter? Respectable workingmen we have here, all up and down the street, as far as the Gobelins, I'll have you know. Who are you, with a rattle-trap a decent moth would pass up, there's such a stink in the cushions, and the parts clanking underneath like tin cans in an ash wagon, to be casting aspersions on the men who have to work for pay, and not have tips thrown at 'em like dogs at the feast of Nebuchadnezzar?"

"I'm a union man myself," the driver said.

"In that case, shut your trap and come in," said Bridgette. "Did you think that I'd let you starve right in front of my window?"

So it happened that the driver, after coffee spiked with rum and a couple of crisp rolls, lost much of his impatience, and with a glance to make sure the meter was running properly, curled up in the back seat of his taxi, to which Bridgette in her description had not done full justice, and was soon fast asleep.

Now Frémont had mentioned to Hydrangea that he was due at the prefecture at eleven o'clock, to interview some countrymen of hers who had been brought in drunk the night before, so at half-past ten her alarm clock sounded and she sat up, rubbed her large dark eyes, and saw she was alone in the room. Bewildered, she dressed hastily and hurried down stairs.

"At what time did the Chief go out?" she asked anxiously of Bridgette.

"He didn't go out, he came in," the proprietress said, "and furthermore he left a taxi waiting at the door that will cost the state aplenty."

"But he's not upstairs," Hydrangea said, now thoroughly alarmed.

"The hell you say," retorted Bridgette and together they made a quick search of the building. The cook, who had been unavoidably absent at the moment the Chief had hurried through the kitchen, swore no one had left by the back door, and the situation was further complicated by the arrival of Sergeant Schlumberger who informed them that Frémont had not put in an appearance at the prefecture. Hydrangea began to shudder and to wail. The taxi man was aroused and questioned but he stuck to his original story, namely, that a man who had represented himself as a police officer had leaped on his running board about five-thirty in the morning in front of the statue of Henri IV; had been driven full speed to the hotel; and had not been heard from since. At that point Hydrangea began to moan and to call for Mr. Evans.

"He should be at the prefecture by now," Sergeant Schlumberger said. With that he bundled the terrified ex-Blackbird into the taxi and told the driver to take them to the prefecture. There they found Miriam, Evans and Dr. Hyacinthe Toudoux, the latter having snatched a very few hours of the deep and dreamy on the couch in the salon of Professor de la Poussière.

What Evans would have said, had he not given thought to the fears of Hydrangea, was that he did not like the look of things at all. As it was he said: "Don't worry about the Chief. No doubt he's hot on the trail of a suspect," and knowing that action of some sort would relieve her troubled mind he asked her to go to the kitchen of the Salle Ste. Anne near by and prepare three orders of American ham and eggs, as only she could prepare them. This having been done, he placed a steaming plate in each of the cells occupied by the slumbering Jansen, Tom Jackson and Lvov Kvek, and waited.

The fragrance of grilled ham and fried eggs soon permeated the entire corridor and when to this was added the aroma of black coffee, Jansen sat up and rubbed his eyes.

"Good morning, folks," Hjalmar said, seeing his friends out in front and only a rickety set of bars in between. He was accustomed to awakening in all sorts of circumstances. Tom Jackson, on his right, was blinking, by that time, and reached for his breakfast without vouchsafing a word, after having ascertained that he had not lost his glasses.

Kvek, however, was less passive in his reactions. He rose to his feet, clutched at his falling trousers, and began to roar. "Where is K. Parker Seldon?" he demanded. "I insist that he be produced at once. He was sent abroad in my charge, and I must find him. Where is Frémont? Where am I, for that matter? . . . Ah, Evans, my friend!"

The sight of Homer Evans inspired the colonel with such hope and vigor that he broke open his cell door with a lusty shove. The lock, in several pieces, went clanking to the floor. In a second the Russian was holding Homer in an affectionate embrace and pouring out his story. Before he had finished, Sergeant Schlumberger lost his usual calm.

"In the name of all that's holy," he said, "I plead for moderation. Is it not enough that Professor Zacharie de la Poussière, professor emeritus of the Sorbonne, is lost without trace; that our Chief of Detectives Frémont is unaccountably missing: that a priceless Watteau has been spirited away? Now you tell us that an American, who makes bottles, has added himself to this already imposing array. May the devil take all business men, American or otherwise. He'll have to wait his turn."

An officer who had just returned from Montparnasse stepped up, saluted the sergeant, and said: "I have information about this so-called business man, sir."

"Out with it," said the sergeant, and Kvek caught the officer in a suffocating embrace.

The latter, having with difficulty extricated himself, reported that early in the evening preceding, a dapper middle-sized American had entered a book shop in the *rue* Delambre and had purchased a copy of a book called *Ulysses* which he said his daughter, then in high school, had asked him to give her as a graduation present. It was a large blue book with paper covers, the officer said, and although he knew very little English he was convinced that it was not the book for a high-school girl to read.

"Never mind the book. What happened then?" asked the sergeant impatiently.

The officer replied that the middle-sized purchaser had then started walking down the *rue* Delambre, in the direction of the river, and had narrowly been missed by a mail truck in attempting to cross the street while reading aloud.

"You say Mr. Seldon was registered at the Plaza Athènée?" asked Evans.

"Check up there at once," the sergeant told the officer. "If the book is as large as you say it is, he won't have got half way through it yet. Ah, these Americans."

The officer saluted and was instantly on his way.

7

The Equivalent of a Third-Class Funeral

BEFORE continuing with the account of what was happening at the prefecture, it will be well to relate the adventures of Evans and Miriam between the time they left the *place* Dauphine and the hour when they kept their official rendezvous at eleven o'clock. As they walked along the *quai* and crossed the Pont St. Michel, Aurora, rosy-fingered goddess of the morning, had got in some of her snappiest work. The windows of the grim Conciergerie were aglow with faintly colored light, reflecting the earliest beams of the rising sun. Cafés were opening, sleepy *patrons* were greeting their matutinal customers and serving them with brandy and coffee, bakers' boys were bringing in the fresh hot rolls and sticks of golden-crusted bread.

It was but a step from the *place* St. Michel to the adjacent *place* St. André des Arts and, as if the patron saint were aware of the desecration of his favorite national museum, the shadows in his narrow street seemed reluctant to respond to Aurora's ministrations. Facing the entrance, near which some early buses were waiting, Evans found at once the shop named *Au Sens de Mesur,* in the windows of which were stuffed cats, glaring hostilely at the intruders; pug dogs with beady eyes; great horned owls with snowy plumage; peacocks with tails stiffly spread. There were mounted heads of deer and mountain goats, brought by hunters to untimely ends; on a branch was neatly coiled an Asiatic python; there were hat racks fashioned of antlers, for customers who were not superstitious, and in the center a brown cub bear.

The iron grille was loosely padlocked but the officer on the beat, in response to Evans' question, said that Lazare, the proprietor, lived near by in the *rue* de la Huchette and, although an early riser, rarely opened his shop before nine or ten in the morning, he having found by long experience that purchasers of stuffed birds or animals seldom had the urge to buy in the early morning hours.

"I can't say that I blame them," the officer said. "For my part, when a beast is dead, I'm willing to let it go at that. I'm fond of plants and flowers, within reason, but deliver me from stuffed kittens or Pekingese."

Having thanked the officer, and agreed with him, Homer set out for the Hotel du Caveau. M. Julliard, the proprietor, knew everyone on the street and after having greeted Evans and Miriam and cheered them with a quick but substantial breakfast, he told them that the man they sought lived in his own hotel.

"I served him his coffee half an hour ago," M. Julliard said. "His room is on the top, right under the roof. I've offered him a better one but he says he likes the view. Well, who can blame him?"

In single file, Evans and Miriam mounted the narrow flights of stairs and, from the fourth floor upward, were aware of hearty laughter. At the sixth floor, the stairs petered out and they were obliged to climb a ladder. Aloft they paused for breath and tapped gently on the only door. Inside, the laughter continued, and Homer had to knock quite forcibly before it stopped and the door was opened by a man with thick steel-rimmed spectacles and sparse gray hair. Seeing Miriam, and because he was wearing slippers and a night shirt, the gray-haired man stepped back and hastily closed the door.

"I was sent by Dr. Hyacinthe Toudoux," said Evans, gently.

"Toudoux. Ah, yes. Toudoux. I'll slip some clothes on," said a voice from within, and the sounds the man made as he dressed in haste were punctuated by chuckles and subdued guffaws.

Evans, who had expected a more melancholy reception, adjusted his agile mind as best he could. When Lazare finally admitted them, with an apologetic glance at the rumpled bed and the disarray of books, plans and scattered papers, he had what seemed to be a letter in his hand. Without preliminary words he handed the missive to Evans and sat down on the bed, holding his sides and trying to control his merriment.

The dismay Evans felt cannot be reduced to prose, for he saw scribbled over five sheets of unlined notepaper rows of hieroglyphs which to him meant volumes less than nothing.

"I'm sorry," he said at last. "I'm ignorant of ancient

writings, an ignorance I'm determined to remedy at the earliest possible moment."

"At your leisure, my lad," the old man said, still chuckling. "What's a year or two, in the infinity of time?"

"What, indeed?" agreed Evans, and Miriam stifled the objections that arose in her mind. Having been brought up on a Montana ranch, in a country that was admitted to have practically no past, and a fairly uncertain future, she found the long view of things disconcerting. Homer, noticing her slight agitation, murmured a favorite quotation: "Eternal enemy of the absolute." Then he glanced again at the letter in his hand and saw the signature, a loosely scrawled "Z" that in his former haste he had mistaken for an Egyptian character which might have meant anything at all.

"This document, I take it," he said to Lazare, "was sent you by Professor de la Poussière."

"Who else would have been so thoughtful?" Lazare replied. Under ordinary circumstances, with strangers, Lazare was shy and awkward, but in Homer Evans, notwithstanding that the latter had no ancient Egyptian, the old man had instantly recognized a kindred soul, a man of understanding, tolerance and boundless good will. And such men, wherever they may be found, are members of a closely knit fraternity.

"When did you see the professor last, may I ask?" Evans inquired.

"I think it was Easter morning," Lazare replied. "It happened that this year the Christian Easter coincided with the opening of the old Egyptian spring festival, in celebration of the rebirth of the nature god. So Zacharie and I slipped over to Pharamond's for a breakfast of tripe and a bottle of wine, and after the second bottle we were able, quite successfully, to imagine we were back in the good old days. We chose, I believe, the reign of Otlas, whose Hawk name was Sekhemib Uothnes (3019-3003 B.C.), although, had we known then what the professor has discovered since, we should undoubtedly have spent the morning in the court of another pharaoh, who, although little known to scholars today, is soon, thanks to de la Poussière, to take his proper place in the hall of fame."

And again the old man excused himself, sat down on the bed, and tried to control his laughter.

"If you chance to see the professor today," Evans suggested, "please remind him that his wife is uneasy about him. It seems that yesterday he started out in the morning, probably bound for the Louvre. He didn't get to the Louvre and he didn't come home last night. Do you think that is cause for alarm?"

Lazare stopped laughing and was much perturbed. "Dear me," he said. "Now that's strange. Had he been engaged in some new investigation he would probably have let me know. The letter I showed you was mailed day before yesterday. He was in excellent spirits then."

"No doubt it will all be explained," said Homer, not wishing to frighten the old man. "What I came to you about is quite a different matter. Are you familiar . . . ? But of course you are. I want your opinion about some samples of mummy wrappings I have with me. As outrageous as it may seem to you, I was obliged to snip them from two mummies in the Louvre, in the interest of justice, you know."

"Dear me," said Lazare, "snipping mummies."

"I know little of Egyptian textiles, or the practices of Egyptian embalmers," Homer went on. "But I happen to have read that the best linen woven by the ancients had as many as 450 warp threads to the inch. And I assume that for the grave clothes of a pharaoh, the best was none too good. Am I correct in that assumption?"

"Unquestionably," said Lazare, and began pawing the bed and the table top for his other glasses. "I'm sorry," he said. "We'll have to go to my shop before we can examine your samples properly." And the old man, thoroughly intrigued, snatched his rumpled felt hat, had a tug at his string tie, and led the way briskly down the ladder and the six steep flights of stairs. The trio trudged wordlessly through the *rue* de la Huchette, across the boulevard St. Michel and entered the shop *Au Sens de Mesur* where Lazare was promptly confronted by an angry woman who had been glaring through the window at a stuffed three-toed sloth which hung indolently from a sawed-off limb of a tree.

"I shall keep this revolting creature hanging at the foot of my husband's bed," the woman said, with considerable vehemence.

"That should have a salutary effect," said Lazare.

It seems that the woman's husband had lost his job, which had involved the wearing of a pale green uniform and standing at the foot of a stairway in a haberdasher's shop. And, according to the woman, the husband had accepted his new condition, that of a man with no pay coming in, too calmly, and merely because his wife had contrived to bank a part of his wages over a period of twenty-eight years. The man, if the woman could be believed, spent half of his time in bed, and ate as much, or more, as he had eaten before. The three-toed sloth had been a gentleman friend's idea, a man who had a business of his own and understood a woman's troubles.

"You'd better let me send it to you," Lazare suggested, for the animal, with its tree trunk, branch and pedestal made a package as large as the customer herself. The woman turned down his suggestion, with muttered comments about delivery charges, and left the shop lugging her ungainly purchase, hard put to keep the pedestal from dragging on the ground.

The old man smiled. "One meets all kinds of people in this business," he said, "but mostly folks who are slightly original in their ways."

He led the way to his commodious warehouse in the back, opening the door and waiting politely for Miriam to pass through. To his and Evans' surprise, after they had caught their breath again, the girl recoiled with an exclamation of fright and in a split second a shot rang out and sawdust and bits of snake's skin filled the air. For just inside the door was a prairie rattler, viciously coiled, and Miriam's light step on a loose floor-board had caused the tail to vibrate.

Miriam's contrition surpassed that of poor Lazare, who was apologizing profusely and trying to explain. "I'm terribly sorry," she said. "I could have sworn the snake was alive, and he wasn't a foot from my ankle."

The policeman on the beat had heard the explosion, but he was accustomed to hearing the backfire of buses in the *place* St. André des Arts and decided quickly that if anything worse had occurred, someone would promptly inform him.

"When I stuff an animal for my own amusement,

which is seldom," Lazare explained, "I make it really life-like. The customers, most of them, don't like that. They want a dead cat to appear different from a live one, in order to stir more deeply their emotions. They want to be constantly reminded that poor Minou or Frou-Frou is no more, and what a little darling she used to be. That snake . . . My dear girl, it's no matter . . . was given me by our mutual friend, Dr. Hyacinthe Toudoux, who seemed to have several others. I had forgotten that it was coiled near the door. A thousand pardons. What a shock it must have given your nerves."

The back part of the warehouse was filled with stuffed monkeys, zebras, cassowaries, gnus, jaguars and other wild and domestic beasts, and rows of shelves contained gulls, macaws, loons, iguanas and other birds and reptiles. At least half the space, however, was devoted to relics of Egypt and volumes, notes and drawings relating thereto.

Evans eagerly produced his two bits of cloth, and Lazare as eagerly reached for them. "This first sample," Evans said, "is an exceptionally fine piece of cloth, is it not?"

Lazare took the small sample, felt it, sniffed its odor, held it to the light and then put it under a small microscope that was set up on his table.

"I have seldom seen a better example of weaving, of the period just before 2900 B.C.," he said, without hesitation.

"And what have you to say about this one?" asked Evans, handing over the second sample, which was the one he had taken first, from the mummy case which stood fourth from the left.

Lazare stroked, sniffed, held the cloth to the light and, without resorting to the microscope said: "I regret to inform you that this one is not Egyptian at all. Offhand, I should say it was French, and of comparatively recent date."

"Ah! Modern?" asked Evans, eagerly.

"To all intents and purposes," replied Lazare. "It was woven not earlier than Napoleon's time. I haven't counted the warp, but it's not far from one hundred threads to the inch. You surely must be mistaken in saying that it was taken from an Egyptian mummy of high rank. My dear young man, that would be equivalent to giving a marshal of France a third-class funeral."

Miriam glanced hastily at Evans, ready, as always, to share his disappointments. To her surprise, Homer was elated.

"Thank you, M. Lazare," he said, shaking the old man's hand. "You have told me exactly what I wanted to know. I wonder if I might presume still further on your good nature, since Professor de la Poussière is nowhere to be found. Could you come with us, without delay, to the Louvre?"

"If you wish," said Lazare, excitedly reaching for his hat. "I should like to have a look at the mummy in modern wrappings."

"We'll stop at the prefecture for Chief of Detectives Frémont," Homer said.

8

When a Body Meets a Body

THE officer who was sent to the Plaza Athènée in quest of K. Parker Seldon returned to the prefecture just in time to meet Evans, Miriam and old Lazare in the corridor. Sergeant Schlumberger was not long in joining them.

"Where's Frémont?" asked Homer. "We've got to go back to the Louvre, and in a hurry. I've come across a clue at last."

"Where's Frémont, indeed? I wish you could answer the question for me," the Alsatian said, gloomily, and told what had happened at the Hotel Murphy et du Danube Bleu.

"The devil," Evans said. "We'll have to carry on without him. Too bad."

"Let's hear what this man has to say about the American, and them I'm ready," said Schlumberger, sighing.

The officer made his report. Following the arrival in Paris the day before of the boat train from the *Ile de France,* forty-two American business men had registered at that comfortable hotel, the Plaza Athénée, but only twelve of them could be classed as middle-sized and eleven of them were satisfactorily accounted for. Furthermore none of them was in possession of a book called *Ulysses* or had even heard of it. The resourceful policeman, however, had examined the room in which Kvek and Seldon had paused to wash, on the way to the Dôme, and had gathered up all the baggage and brought it back with him for examination by his superiors.

Lvov Kvek sorted out his own valises, which narrowed the examination down to four suitcases and a flat, oblong package wrapped carefully in cotton wool and waterproof black paper. The suitcases having yielded nothing except clothes and noncommittal personal effects, Evans carefully unwrapped the package.

Both he and Lazare gasped, for the package contained only a tablet of sandstone on which had been recently carved some hieroglyphics. No attempt had been made to make the tablet appear ancient, but Kvek came forward with the information that a messenger from the Manhattan Museum had brought the package to the boat, handed it to Mr. Seldon in the name of Hugo Weiss, and had transmitted with it a note saying that it was to be delivered to Professor Zacharie de la Poussière, 12 *place* Dauphine.

"Now you see what you've done," said Sergeant Schlumberger in despair. "You've linked two of these abominable cases. What shall I do? Is a mere sergeant expected to read Egyptian or Chinese, to replace in such complicated emergencies his chief, his prefect and the Minister of Beaux Arts and Monuments Publiques?"

"Peace, sergeant," said Evans, introducing Lazare. "We

have here a man to whom this tablet will be as clear as the letters which blaze out at night from the Tour Eiffel. And you should be glad your cases are inter-related. That means, solve one, solve all. And think of the credit and promotion."

"I shall lose my stripes, that's all," said the Alsatian, "but I thank you for your well-meant words. Am I to understand that you'll not desert me in this pickle of the century?"

"I'll carry on," Evans said. "But I'll need the services of your prisoners here. Just unlock the two remaining cells, like a good fellow, and we'll hold a council of war."

The face of the honest Alsatian was a picture of woe.

"Mr. Evans," he said, miserably. "In your country, still in the pioneer stage, there are no such things as formalities. Precedents do not exist. It is expressly stated in our general orders that no prisoner may be released except on written order of the prefect or the chief of detectives. That rule is iron-clad, and has never been broken. These men have attacked and assaulted more than a dozen officers in performance of their duty, and one of them has forced his way into a public building. The moment we find Frémont, all will be well, but in the meantime . . ."

"Call the Minister of Justice," Evans said. Then he turned to Lazare. "Do you think the professor, under the circumstances, would object to having us tamper with his mail?" he asked.

"Not at all. By all means, let's have a look," replied Lazare. "Oh, it's modern," he said, when the sandstone slab was handed to him. Overcoming his disappointment, he placed the tablet on a desk, got out another pair of glasses, and peered at the characters spread before him. His eagerness changed to bewilderment, and then to dismay. "Dear me," he said. "I can read what it says but I can't understand it. There is something about a stable . . . er . . . shipments to a stable which is joined to a museum. And that is followed by a text still more cryptic. A Nubian, it seems, has concealed himself or is about to conceal himself in a helter-skelter stack of sawed and split wood. Ah. The end is clear. It's in the nature of a request or warning. 'Examine secretly and report to H-U-' then comes G or J or perhaps Y . . ."

"Hugo Weiss," suggested Evans, eagerly.

"Why, yes. Hugo Weiss. Is he someone you know? . . . Too bad the message doesn't make sense. Doubtless it's in code, and the professor has the key," the old man said.

But Evans, to the astonishment of his companions, was pleased.

"You have given me invaluable aid," he said to the bewildered old man. "For the first time since I was dragged into this puzzling case, I see a gleam of light. Not blinding, by any means, but a streak which may precede the dawn. Monsieur Lazare. Had you been aware that in the United States is a multi-millionaire named T. Prosper Stables, who has put even philanthropy on a paying basis; that the Croesus just mentioned is the patron and at the same time the beneficiary of several museums; and that he is an enemy of Hugo Weiss, you would not have been bewildered by that inscription. Shipments, certainly of articles Egyptian, are about to be made to Stables' museums. Is that clear?"

"Oh, Homer," gasped Miriam, and clutched his sleeve.

"As for the Nubian and the sawed and split wood . . . Miss Leonard, what would you say about that?" Homer asked, with a smile.

"A nigger in the woodpile," she said, her breath coming quickly.

"Exactly," Evans said. Then he saw that Lazare was still in the fog. "That is an American idiom," he explained, "meaning that something shady is afoot, that sawed and split wood, metaphorically speaking, is about to be appropriated by unauthorized persons, represented in the figure of speech by a dark-colored stranger. In other words, *Il-y-a quelque chose de louche.* Do you follow me?"

"Ingenious, indeed! I take it that the precious articles in question are not necessarily of wood, but might be of other materials, and that the color of the intruder's skin does not imply a slur on any particular race but rather represents the forces of darkness and evil, personified in Christian mythology by the Devil and in Egypt by the God of Necessity, Mutt-Thaa."

"You get the idea," Evans said. "Now let's hurry to the Louvre."

An attendant entered with the early editions of the afternoon papers. Schlumberger, in the absence of his chief, had been obliged to face the representatives of the press and had stuttered and contradicted himself so badly in trying to explain the absence of the chief of detectives that the reporters had left in high dudgeon and each edition outdid the preceding in lambasting the department.

III

PARIS LEFT WITHOUT PROTECTION
HIGH OFFICIALS IN HIDING
UNDERLINGS EVASIVE

The above was one of the milder headlines which was eagerly read when the clients of cafés from one end of Paris to the other gathered to enjoy aperitifs and scandal. The *En-Tout-Cas*, however, went further than its competitors. Its editor proclaimed that an American fugitive who was wanted by the police in the United States for having played fast and loose with a large bottle corporation was being sheltered and abetted in his crime against widows and orphans by high officials of the Paris police. In substantiation of its charges, this vehement newspaper stated that the culprit, a Mr. K-S. Porcière, had arrived on the *Ile de France,* had been whisked to the Plaza Athènée, and within five minutes had disappeared. No word of this had been given the press, which was the only guardian of public interest, the *En-Tout-Cas* asserted, and cited this as proof of official complicity.

"The public demands that the prefect divulge these important and shady occurrences, with a full explanation of his silence to date," an editorial began. It got hotter as the writer warmed to his task.

"Will the Prefect, Monsieur de la Chemise Farcie, respond to this reasonable demand? That, Parisians and Frenchmen, is unlikely. Monsieur is busy, fishing. Where? Ask the chief of detectives, if you please.

"The chief of detectives, it seems, is not in his office. Neither is he in the Musée du Louvre, from which priceless paintings disappear like carp from a tank. Where is he? Ask one of the sergeants. Which one? The senior. Only he is in authority.

"The senior sergeant, one Schlumberger, nearly bites off his tongue. The Chief is out, he says. Out where? He's working on the case. Which case? The sergeant stammers. He does not know."

The demoralization of Sergeant Schlumberger was complete. It was the only time in the course of his long faithful service that his name had been mentioned in the papers. "One Schlumberger. Bites tongue. Police complicity," he was muttering, as he started for the national museum. But since no word had been received from the Minister of Justice, he agreed to take along Kvek, Hjalmar and Tom Jackson in his personal custody.

At the main entrance of the Louvre, Sergeant Bonnet was waiting. With him, in a state of hysteria because of the disappearance of Frémont, was Melchisadek Knockwoode. The east wing had been cleared and the guards and watchmen who had been removed from their posts of duty were playing cards and chatting in the entrance lobby. Evans and Lazare took the lead, with Miriam, Jansen and Schlumberger close behind them. Kvek and Bonnet brought up the rear. They proceeded through a long subterranean passage between files of Roman sculptures, passed through arches and up and down short stairways until none of them except Homer or Lazare could have found his way out in an hour. When finally they entered the long narrow chamber in which were the heavy stone sarcophagi, Evans halted, sat down on the edge of one of the ponderous lids, and gathered his forces for instructions. First he warned them to touch nothing and to keep well behind him when he went into the Egyptian room, but as he was talking he suddenly rose to his feet and started examining the lid of the sarcophagus.

"This has been chipped," he said, in astonishment. "And recently." He took out his magnifying glass, then searched the floor for the missing fragment of stone. It was not to be found.

"Sergeant Bonnet," he asked. "Has anyone been in this chamber today?"

"Not a soul, I assure you," the sergeant said.

"You're sure it hasn't been swept?"

"I swear it," replied the earnest detective.

"I'd like to have a look at the under side," Homer said. For he had determined not to let the minutest detail escape him.

Hjalmar and Kvek stepped forward, and with grateful grins which bespoke how glad they were to have something tangible to do, took hold of the enormous stone lid. Stretched between them was the granite statue of an Assyrian prince of whom little else was known. They tightened their grips and lifted. Centimeter by centimeter the great lid rose. It was without hinges, its weight having been considered sufficient to keep it in place.

"What shall we do with it?" Hjalmar asked.

"Turn it crosswise and rest it near the foot, so we can look in," Evans said.

They all peered in, and Melchisadek started running, dodging wildly between statues, for in the ungainly stone chest was reposing, face down, a wrapped Egyptian mummy. Instantly Lazare took charge, and motioned the others back. He beckoned Homer to stand by and help him.

114

"Lift it carefully," he said. "I'll take the head and you the feet. Ah! Thank God it's uninjured! There now. Upsy daisy, slowly. Capital! Now we'll turn him over, left over right. That's the way. Let him down gently to the floor."

That having been accomplished, the old man knelt quickly, stared at the cobra-shaped hood, swathed in bandages, and then, to the astonishment of everyone present began to laugh uproariously.

The two sergeants frowned. There was a time and place for everything according to their notion, and the fact that an Egyptian mummy had been lying face downward in an Assyrian sarcophagus meant nothing whatever to them.

"It's Tout-or-Nada, the young wag, himself! In death as in life, forever the clown," said Lazare, holding his sides. His laughter was so contagious that Lvov Kvek and Jansen could not help joining in, until the solemn walls of the chamber set up a rumble of echoes.

Then, as suddenly as he had grown merry, Lazare became grave. Admonishing the others by no means to approach or touch the mummy, the old man, followed by Homer, set out at a brisk trot for the Egyptian room. There, before their companions had had time to catch up with them, they began lifting the cover of the mummy case fourth from the left, removed the inner lid, and both dropped down to their knees.

"A table! We must unwrap him," said Lazare. So Hjalmar and Kvek removed a glass case of ancient tools and relics from the bench on which it had rested. Hastily Evans and the old man brought forth and stretched on his back what seemed to be another well-wrapped mummy.

"Begin at the knee," said Evans tensely. "That's where I got the sample." And to Sergeant Bonnet he whispered a terse request for the official photographer. Before the latter had arrived, Lazare had removed the wrappings from the knee and the upper calf of the leg, disclosing, not the dry preserved flesh of an Egyptian monarch but the slightly discolored skin of a corpse.

Sergeant Schlumberger began to clutch at his hair and to burble, and Evans, to calm him, said soothingly:

"Now here's your story for the papers! And it ought to satisfy the most exacting of them, for, unless I am mistaken, this unfortunate man is the Marquis de la Rose d'Antan."

"Not the Minister of Beaux Arts?" the officers exclaimed with horror.

"The same," said Evans. In their excitement, none of them noticed the change that had come over Lazare. He had ceased unwrapping abruptly. His formerly benevolent face was distorted with emotion the nature of which was impossible to fathom. Miriam, remembering what a tragic part the dead marquis had played in the old man's career, hastened to Lazare's side. He seemed to be afraid of her, in an agony of embarrassment and self-consciousness.

Sergeant Schlumberger, still hoping the wrapped corpse might not prove to be a high official, was not as considerate as he might have been in less trying circumstances.

"Unwrap the face, if you please," he said. "There's no time to be lost."

Because of the harshness of his tone, Lazare lost all control of his nerves and backed away into a corner. "No! Not that one," he muttered. "Excuse me, gentlemen. I'm not well. I shall have to leave you." In trying to get out he stumbled against a small showcase which crashed to the floor, scattering signet rings on which were carved the hawk and the vulture, first dynasty bracelets of gold, turquoise, amethyst and lapis lazuli, and a small ivory tablet which set forth, had anyone except the distracted Lazare known it, the prescription for hair restorer used by Khenti Athuthi's queen (3345-3289 B.C.), a mixture of dog's claws, donkey's hooves and boiled dates. Weeping and mumbling the old man sat on the floor, trying to gather the ancient treasures in his hands.

Evans whispered quickly to Miriam and gently she led Lazare away. Of those present, they were the only ones who understood in part what had happened. "Don't leave him until he's himself again," said Homer and Miriam nodded, tremulously.

A moment later, the official photographers came panting in, followed by Dr. Hyacinthe Toudoux. Evans, meanwhile, continued unwrapping the remains.

"What now?" demanded the doctor, gruffly. His study of human livers and California wine had been interrupted again and he was so much disturbed by that fact that he had not looked closely at the swathed object stretched out on the bench. In his haste, in fact, he mistook it for a mummy and almost exploded.

"I am willing and it is my duty," he said, "to deal with bodies, but there's a limit. If you think I shall try to fix the time of death of prehistoric relics you have overestimated my amiability." The doctor turned on his heel

117

and was about to leave the room when Evans suavely tried to set him right.

"What you see here," he said, "unless I am very much mistaken, has been until very recently the Marquis de la Rose d'Antan."

"An insufferable fathead," grunted the doctor, still unconvinced.

"I'm not disputing that, but he's entitled to the service the Republic gives freely to all citizens," Evans said. "His body, wrapped as you see it here, was placed in the mummy case which properly belonged to a chap named Tout-or-Nada just before five o'clock yesterday afternoon, and if death occurred before this bandaging began, the late Marquis must have been dead before half past three."

"What makes you so sure this is the Marquis?" asked Dr. Toudoux. "As far as I'm concerned, it could be Mata Hari."

"Not with hair on her leg," Sergeant Schlumberger said. "But I should like an answer to the question, just the same."

Evans smiled. "Of all the missing men connected with this case, M. de la Rose d'Antan is the only one who fits this particular mummy case. Professor de la Poussière is far too tall, and even our middle-sized American, who furthermore was alive long after five yesterday afternoon . . ."

Kvek began to weep and to bellow. "Do you mean K. Parker Seldon has been murdered, too? I'm disgraced. I shall never live it down. What shall I say to Mr. Weiss, my benefactor, who entrusted him to my care?"

"Be patient, all of you," Evans said. "Here, Kvek. Start

in on the left leg. Hjalmar, continue with the right, where Lazare left off. I'll have a go at the head, and we'll make better progress. And please do not think that an unrelated series of murders and kidnappings have taken place on the same day, by chance. The incidents are all of a piece, and were carefully planned, excepting the disappearance of Frémont. His removal, you may be sure, was decided upon on the spur of the moment. It does not fit into the picture."

The Russian and the husky painter were making the bandages fly, and it was not five minutes before even the most skeptical among those present was sure that the corpse was not that of Mata Hari. At the head, Evans was making rapid progress, too.

"Don't be afraid of tearing the cloth," he said. "It's not Egyptian but modern. Ah! It's the Marquis, all right."

The medical examiner brought out his bandage scissors and after snipping the remaining linen away he made a brief examination, much handicapped by the fact that the inner organs had been removed and the Marquis had been hastily embalmed in the style of bygone days.

"How the devil can I say how he died, when he's as full of foreign gums and asphalt as a third class pharmacy in Belgium?" spluttered Dr. Toudoux. "We'll have to remove him to my laboratory, where probably I can do no better."

9

A Little Algebra Proves a Dangerous Thing

THE modest success of Sergeant Schlumberger in his police career had been due to his sterling Alsatian character, generous but stubborn, and his simple common sense. His mind, never brilliant, worked on principles he had learned in the early grades of school. In the words of the immortal Rabelais, "He had both feet firmly on the ground." Astounded and dismayed as he was by the discovery of the body of the Marquis de la Rose d'Antan, he did not lose his head or indulge in flights of fancy.

"If one Egyptian mummy contains one corpse, x Egyptian mummies contain x corpses," was the way he worked it out.

Consequently, after the remains of the minister of Beaux Arts had been carted away, Evans had to restrain the sergeant, almost forcibly, from ripping open with a pair of garden shears from the Louvre's broad green lawn, the mummy of Tout-or-Nada which was still lying on its back near the Assyrian sarcophagus.

"How do we know that it does not have the President

of the Republic inside?" demanded Schlumberger, sweat beading his broad wrinkled forehead. "And look at this one." He made a pass with the shears at the remains of Kephere, Neferkere or Keneferre Huui (2837 to 2814 B.C.). It's about the size of the prefect, Monsieur de la Chemise Farcie. It might even be your middle-sized business man."

"God forbid! Don't say that," groaned Kvek.

"I assure you, sergeant," Evans said. "There are no more modern corpses in the building. Each one of the mummies is wrapped in the best Egyptian linen of their epoch. I beg of you, put down those garden tools and do not destroy the work of glorious past ages."

The sergeant muttered, and still held on to the shears.

Evans, to comfort him, elaborated his explanation. He took from his pocket the two pieces of linen and handed them to the sergeant, along with his magnifying glass. "See how fine the Egyptian cloth is woven?" he said. "Imagine. Four hundred and fifty threads to the inch. Who has the patience to weave like that today? Now look at the other. It's French, and modern. Not more than a hundred years old. That's what gave the show away."

The Alsatian grunted and looked at the second sample through the reading glass. "Hmph!" he said. "My mother used to make sheets just like that. I'll bet this came from Alsace. See how the little warts on the threads make it rough and strong? I can see my mother, now, working hour after hour in the long winter evenings. Candlelight, we had then. A fire on the hearth, and apples roasting. I used to sit in the corner, monsieur, and try to draw her picture. She would smile and nod and never make fun of me, monsieur. This little piece of cloth brings back memories to me, and makes me wonder if, after all, I should have come to Paris and joined the police."

The simple words of Sergeant Schlumberger were touching to Evans, whose human sympathies were always easily aroused, but in the midst of the recital his mind began to clutch at threads of thought and try to untangle them. "Are you sure the cloth was made in Alsace?" Homer asked. "If so, it might be traced."

At those words, the sergeant forgot his misgivings about the remaining mummies and beamed. "I know just the man, an old auctioneer from Strasbourg, who sells antique furniture and fabrics all over the province."

Quickly Homer gathered up a few yards of the wrappings that had covered de la Rose d'Antan and handed them to Schlumberger. "Do what you can," he said. "And go the limit with the newspaper men. Explain about the differences in the linen, the genuine pharaoh and the false, without mentioning my name. After this, the press will eat out of your hand."

Evans' next task, after the sergeant had departed, was to put Tout-or-Nada back in his mummy case and close the lid. The photographers, having taken not only the pictures necessary for the criminal records, but an assortment for the newspapers and agencies, packed up their apparatus and left the building, after promising not to snap Homer Evans unawares and receiving his promise, in turn, that when anything turned up for them he would let them know. Like all men who came in contact with Evans, even casually, the cynical cameramen trusted and respected him on sight and were willing to help him remain anonymous.

The odor of musty linen, natron, dried pharaohs and asphalt had irritated the parched throats of Hjalmar, Tom Jackson and Lvov Kvek to such a point that Evans led them all to the Café de l'Univers just across from the Hotel du Louvre, where after having ordered drinks for them, and before settling down to a bout of hard thinking, Homer telephoned the Minister of Justice to find out about their technical release. The minister, who liked Evans and was anxious to do what he could for him, was apologetic. His legal advisers, it seemed, were deadlocked 91 to 91 on the question and a final decision could not be reached before September.

Seated on the *terrasse* at the table with his three convivial friends, with near-by traffic swirling in all directions, and pedestrians scurrying to and fro, Evans was able to detach himself and to consider the problems he was called upon to solve. There were many of them, and all were urgent, but he decided that first of all he must devote himself to finding Frémont. Without the Chief the department was at sixes and sevens, and there was a staggering amount of purely routine work to be done.

Frémont had left the prefecture about two o'clock in the morning, and according to Hydrangea, had reached the Hotel Murphy et du Danube Bleu soon after half past two. According to Bridgette Murphy the chief of detectives had arrived again in a taxi, about half past five, much agitated, and had hurried upstairs, telling the taxi to wait. Nothing had been heard from him since.

Immediately Homer decided that the St. Julien Rollers were involved, although a year ago their leaders and most of their members had been sent to Devil's Island on evidence unearthed by Evans and presented in court by Frémont. There, amid the Corsicans, fevers, tarantulas, whips, dungeon cells and tropical vapors they had, according to the continual complaints received by the Minister of Justice from the guards and other convicts in French Guinea, made the world's toughest place immeasurably tougher. Had the remnants of the gang been reorganized and a new leader found? Most likely, Evans thought. The man who had shot at him from the tree in the *place* Dauphine had been stationed there, probably, to watch the doorway of Professor de la Poussière and report when the alarm was given about the professor's disappearance. It was significant, however, that the sentry, on seeing Evans crossing the *place* at a lonely hour of the night, had, on the spur of the moment, fired with intent to kill. No other gang had a grudge against Homer, or even knew of his existence. Therefore, a St. Julien Roller had been in the tree, and the gang had kidnapped Professor de la Poussière.

By logical steps of reasoning, Homer built up his theory. Professor de la Poussière, from all Evans had been able to learn of him, was in himself dangerous to no one. He was an inoffensive learned man wrapt up in Egyptology. Whoever wanted the professor removed was not afraid of the man, but of his knowledge, and certainly not of the knowledge he had possessed many years, but some important item recently acquired. That would have to do with the Pharaoh Tout-or-Nada, whose mummy had been mishandled in the Louvre and whose ornate casket had been used as a hiding place for the body of the Marquis de la Rose d'Antan. The St. Julien gang had the professor, of that Evans was convinced, but he knew they would not dare to kill Frémont, and much less would they risk kidnapping him.

Excusing himself, he left his friends at the table, cut across the street to the Hotel du Louvre and there put in a call for Hugo Weiss in New York. Within an hour he heard the voice of the genial millionaire and asked Weiss what Stables was buying. He had to hold the line a few minutes while Weiss made inquiries at the museum and then was disappointed to learn that Weiss's enemy had been offered the mummy, in perfect condition, of a pharaoh called Neferkesokar.

"You're sure it's not Tout-or-Nada?" Evans asked.

Another long wait ensued, and Weiss returned to the phone. "Sorry," he said. "It's Neferkesokar. N for Nathaniel, E for Ethel, F for François . . . Neferkesokar. That was his hawk name, my young expert tells me. His given name was Sesochr. He reigned from 2933 to 2926 B.C., and nothing else is known of the chap."

Evans made rapid notes, again cursing his ignorance of Egyptology.

"How's my friend, Parker Seldon?" Weiss asked. "Enjoying his exile, no doubt."

"He's bought a copy of *Ulysses*, that's all I can tell you just now," Evans said. "He did that last night, then disappeared."

"Clever chap," said Weiss. "Well, so long."

The distant receiver clicked and severed the connection.

"I'd better concentrate on Frémont," said Homer, ruefully. "And save ancient Egypt for poor Lazare." He had been thinking of Lazare from time to time, but assumed he was safe with Miriam.

Rapidly, Homer made his plans. First, to find out what he could about the St. Julien Rollers, as reorganized, and then to learn what had happened to Frémont. He recrossed the street from the Hotel du Louvre and found his friends contentedly chatting and singing on the *terrasse* of the Café de l'Univers.

"Come with me," Homer said, and as they sprang to their feet eagerly he added: "And from now on, keep reasonably sober." Hjalmar, somewhat piqued at the suggestion that he could not hold his liquor, walked the entire length of the *terrasse* on his hands, his legs in the air, without as much as knocking off a glass of beer from one of the tables. Kvek and Tom Jackson swore they would be careful, in the manner of their respective races and countries. To their surprise Evans led them across the *place*, through a tangle of traffic rushing helter-skelter to and from five directions, to the stage entrance of the Comédie Française. The wardrobe mistress was an old friend of Homer Evans. As a matter of fact, Homer had got her daughter a job at the American Embassy, where, although the girl had learned little English, she had been the cause of several other persons learning French. Old Madeleine received Evans cordially and shook hands with his companions, secretly envying them their glow, since the old woman liked a nip herself, on occasion.

With a minimum of words consistent with Gallic politeness, Evans explained what he wanted, namely, French gangsters' costumes for all four of them, and the services of a makeup artist. Hjalmar Jansen's broad face beamed.

If they were going out dressed as Apaches, there would be rough stuff, and that was what he craved to round out a satisfactory day. Kvek seemed to have the same idea, for his aristocratic face also was eloquent with satisfaction. The *Herald* reporter, however, made a mild objection.

"You may as well save yourself the trouble of dressing me up," he said. "Within two minutes I'll be spotted as an American. It's always the same, no matter what I do or where I go. No one listens to my French, and the whole neighborhood starts trying to speak English. I'll do whatever you say, but I'm warning you."

The makeup man, who had just been led in by old Madeleine, after looking Jackson over, was inclined to agree.

"Father and son, the Merles have been making up all kinds of faces for four generations," the man said. "But to make this man look like a Frenchman . . ." He spread his hands, narrowly missing Hjalmar's solar plexus with the handle of a paint brush.

It was finally decided that Jackson should be left as he was, except for a snappy new American hat and a pressed coat and trousers. And, on second thought, Homer obtained for Kvek a Volga boatman's outfit, so he could pose as a doorman from Montmartre who had picked up a promising tourist from the U.S.A. Hjalmar got into a *chantier* or coalman's outfit, with cap turned backward, a worn sweater and a soiled dark blue sash a foot wide around his middle. Old Madeleine, with her liking for Homer, saved the best for him, a gangster's costume that had just come in from a second-hand dealer who supplied old clothes to the theater from time to time. And for a proper understanding of what happened later, the recent history of the costume is indispensable.

The night watchman at the morgue was very poorly paid and had a wife who objected to getting out of bed and lighting up the charcoal stove in the middle of the night. Consequently, the family was all out of proportion to the watchman's regular income. Now according to the orthodox procedure, when a body was brought into the morgue and the police had got through with the clothes, they were wrapped in a bundle bearing the name, if any, of the deceased, and were held a reasonable time in a corner closet, to be placed at the disposition of the dead man's relatives, if any of them showed up. The gangster whom Miriam had shot from the tree in the *place* Dauphine had no identifying marks or papers and did not look, to the practiced eye of the watchman, like a chap who would be likely to have relatives who would advertise the fact. So the watchman, hard pressed for cash because his wife was about to give birth to their ninth offspring, stretched a point of procedure and rushed the corpse's clothes to the Flea Market before they were fairly cool. The dealer in the Flea Market had just been fined for obstructing a sidewalk with his pushcart, so he hurried the bundle, in turn, to the Comédie Française and sold it for eight francs, although protesting to heaven that it was worth at least ten. So it happened that Homer Evans, in starting out to stalk the St. Julien Rollers, chanced to be wearing the cap, wasplike coat and high-buttoned trousers of the man who had shot at him less than twelve hours previously. The cap was shaded by a particularly villainous visor and, had Evans ever seen it on its former owner, he undoubtedly might have recog-

nized it. Had he failed to do that, he would have remembered the peculiar color of the scarf that took the place
of collar and necktie, for it was of a plaid that combined
the ideas of Drs. Toudoux and Truc as to what the color
of an overstrained liver should be.

It was quickly agreed that while Evans should do a
little scouting in the *rue* St. Severin, former hangout
of the St. Julien gang, the others should test their dis-
guises by entering a small café near the Hotel Murphy
et du Danube Bleu in the *place* de la Contrescarpe, where
Evans would call for them when they were needed. The
appearance of an American tourist and a Volga boatman
would not be incongruous in that neighborhood, since
the Russian cabaret, the Coque d'Or, was near by in the
rue Mouffetard.

10

In Which the Dragnet Tangles with Ben Hur

SERGEANT SCHLUMBERGER, in the gloomy prefecture, was sitting alone and signing, counter-signing and stamping basketfuls of documents in triplicate and quadruplicate, almost at random. For relief from his troubled thoughts, the honest Alsatian dropped in from time to time on Dr. Hyacinthe Toudoux, whose temper was rising by leaps and bounds.

"How in God's name can I be expected to find causes of death in a corpse from which practically everything of importance has been extracted and which, in the bargain, is stuffed to overflowing with asphalt?" the harassed doctor demanded. Then, seeing that the sergeant was in worse shape than he was, the doctor pulled himself together and, to distract the sergeant's mind, told him the story of the unfortunate school-day episode in the life of old Lazare.

To say that the anecdote had a bracing effect on the Alsatian would be beggarly, indeed. "Why, that's a perfect motive for the crime," he shouted, fishing around for buttons to press and, in his excitement, getting his right hand glued up in a pan of a sticky substance the nature of which Toudoux would not have even dared to hazard a guess about. "And this Lazare, who acted so suspiciously in the presence of the corpse, spends his time embalming all kinds of gruesome animals. Of course he's our man, the ideal suspect. Why did no one inform me before about his grievance against the Marquis and all the family? No doubt he's been brooding and scheming all these years."

The doctor was aghast, and did what he could to defend the taxidermist, but nothing he could say was effective. Within five minutes the dragnet was spread and officers were galloping up the steep stairs of the Hotel du Caveau, where, finding their quarry had fled, they completed the disarray of notebooks, plans, specimens, relics and papers. Coincidentally the flimsy grille had been crashed and the door forced open of the shop *Au Sens de Mesur* in the *place* St. André des Arts and another squad of policemen was peering behind stuffed zebras, cassowaries, tigers, loons and adjutant cranes, in the hope that the proprietor had hidden himself in his place of business, which they found not at all banal.

After those initial failures had been reported, the chase became general and spread to all quarters of Paris. Old men with sparse gray hair were spotted and inconvenienced, until the numbers of them ran into the hundreds, and all young American girls wearing blue tailored clothes were questioned and asked for passports and identity cards. All but thirty-six of them were able to convince the officers that they were not Mademoiselle Montana, and none of them was carrying a gun, but the unlucky three dozen were taken to the prefecture where Schlumberger, dreading the press interview that was imminent, could not tell one from the other and in desperation ordered all of them to be held.

Miriam, filled with compassion for the demoralized Lazare, had taken him to Evans' apartment where, after almost exhausting the resources of her gentle nature, she had calmed the old man to the point where he was able to sit quietly in a chair. There, she had told him that she knew about the tragedy of his youth, the mention of which set him off again. Lazare tried to control himself, but the wound was too deep and too raw. When for a second time Miriam had quieted him, she sat down at the piano and began to play. She tried Mozart, Bach and Haydn, with negligible effect. The taxidermist responded slowly to musical therapy. At her wits' end, Miriam suddenly remembered a piece she had learned from the Seek and Ye Shall Find Correspondence School, which, before she had come abroad to study, had mailed her lessons all the way from Omaha to the Montana ranch. The title of the piece was the *Ben Hur Chariot Race.*

At the sound of the stirring introduction, Lazare began to blink and twiddle his fingers, much as Miriam's father had done under similar circumstances. Before the chariots were neck and neck, it seemed to the girl that her charge was working himself slowly away from the deep end. She redoubled her efforts. First Ben was ahead, then the other chap. They were rounding the bend on one wheel . . .

The door burst open and four officers in uniform bustled into the hallway, followed by Evans' indignant concierge. The close finish of the chariot race had drowned out their knocking. That both Miriam's hands and her mind were fully occupied undoubtedly saved the lives of all five of the intruders. Her gun was ready in its holster but she saw the color of the uniforms and controlled her reflexes in time.

"What does this mean?" she asked, her eyes blazing.

Two officers had already laid hands on Lazare and when they told him he was wanted in connection with a murder, the old man suffered a relapse. Cringing and muttering, and acting in every way as a trapped culprit is supposed to act just before his confession, Lazare was bundled into a police car, handcuffed and whisked away to the prefecture. Miriam followed in another vehicle and the ride was so short that, on the way, she was able to tell the officers only a part of what she thought of them.

Schlumberger, with an air of reproachful dignity, was closeted with the gentlemen of the press. He told them about finding the mutilated remains of the Marquis de la Rose d'Antan, wrapped in yards of linen and hidden in a mummy case. Then he regaled them with a recital of the behavior of Lazare, taxidermist of the *place* St. André des Arts, of his deep grudge against the family of the late Marquis, and the evidences in his room and his shop, of how he had studied feverishly the mysteries and questionable practices of the ancient Egyptians. The official photographer passed out prints of the body, before and after unwrapping, with painted mummy cases and relics in the background. The reporters apologized profusely for their shabby treatment of Schlumberger the day before and promised him full credit on the morrow. As they were filing out, they met the officers bringing in Lazare, more dead than alive. The policemen who had found the wanted taxidermist cowering in a Montparnasse apartment were questioned, and flashlights illumined the dim corridor as the old man was hustled into the Goldfish Bowl. Miriam, who was determined to carry out Evans' instructions and stick close to the old man, insisted on being allowed to occupy the adjacent cell.

Meanwhile, Homer Evans, not suspecting what had happened to Lazare, or that he, himself, was wearing the clothes of the defunct gangster, made his way to the *rue* de la Huchette. The Hotel du Caveau, the host of which was the gay Savoyard, M. Henri Julliard, stood back to back to the buildings in which was the Bal St. Severin. Up to the time of the gang's exposure, the Bal St. Severin had been the headquarters of the St. Julien Rollers. M. Julliard listened with great interest to Evans' story of the shooting in the *place* Dauphine, once he had got over his astonishment at the perfection of Homer's disguise. And the Savoyard, after consulting his Serbian *garçon*, who knew everything that took place in the quarter, had two items to contribute. The St. Julien Rollers had reorganized, and were being led by a mysterious man called Le Singe (The Monkey) who kept himself completely out of sight. And the new headquarters were not far away, because a girl named Nicole, who consorted with the gangsters, still lived in Julliard's hotel.

"Here's a letter for her now," the Savoyard said, indicating a plain manila envelope, carefully lined with purple tissue paper. "It came in this morning," the hotel keeper added.

"I'm going out to find Nicole. Could I deliver the letter

to her?" Evans asked. "If I don't find her, I'll bring it right back."

"Why not? But don't lose it," M. Julliard said.

With the letter in his pocket, Homer gave just the right twist to his incredible cap and started for the *place* de la Contrescarpe, where, on entering the Hotel Murphy et du Danube Bleu, he startled Bridgette Murphy so badly that she attacked him with a broomstick. Once having been admitted, his appearance proved no more reassuring to Hydrangea, who was lying face downward on the bed and moaning when, in response to her invitation, he opened the door and went in.

After a few comforting words which soothed the sorrowing ex-Blackbird to the point where she hurried to the washstand to bathe her eyes and arrange her hair, Evans sat down at the back window and tried to put himself in Frémont's frame of mind. Harassed by enforced proximity to objects of art, and especially oil paintings, and unnerved by Evans' own suggestion that back of the theft of *The Pansy* was a malicious master mind, the chief of detectives had been too distraught for sleep. He had gone to the window for a breath of air, looked out, and . . . at that moment Evans caught sight of the Bal des Vêtements Brulés. There were other buildings in view: a parochial school with a high-walled yard and half-grown trees, a residence or two that once had been respectable but had fallen into disrepair, a store in which were sold articles of piety, and a fruit and vegetable stand. Among all those, the dance hall held Homer's keen attention.

"What did the Chief say, when he came in last night?" Evans asked.

"The poor man was too exhausted to say a word,"

Hydrangea said. "I rubbed his head with this tonic . . . Smell it. . . ." She held out the bottle, unstoppered, and Evans sniffed. It was not for him, or any Anglo-Saxon, but if the Chief liked it, why spoil his fun? Homer thought.

"What time does the dance hall close?" he asked.

"Two o'clock," Hydrangea said. "That's when the music stops. Sometimes they keep on talking and drinking for hours after that. I don't mind. Let 'em make all the noise they like. It reminds me of Harlem, on a warm summer night. Don't tell the Chief that, though. He's scared sick that I'll go back some time."

There was no shaking either Hydrangea's or Bridgette Murphy's stories. The former repeated that Frémont had come in at three o'clock, and had walked all the way from the prefecture, the Franco-Irish proprietress insisted she had seen him enter hurriedly at five-thirty, leaving a taxi ticking at the door. Both tales were true, Evans felt sure, and based his conjectures accordingly. Frémont had seen something that drew him from his sweetheart's bedroom and brought him back there later. What could it have been? At that moment the orchestra of the Bal des Vêtements Brulés hit up the first tune of their afternoon grind, a popular Java with words containing much sound sense, to the effect that one cannot tell from where one is sitting, how one's picture is going to turn out. The moment had come, decided Evans, to investigate the dance hall and its clientele.

Tom Jackson, Hjalmar and Lvov Kvek were showing admirable restraint, and when Homer found them, in the small café near Bridgette's hotel, they were as sober as they ever needed to be. The reporter had called the day city editor and by giving him the story about the Marquis de la Rose d'Antan had got another feeble clutch on his job. The editor, however, had refused to let him follow up the case, saying that the *Herald* would clip the murder news from the French papers, and had given him an assignment he had accepted with relief. He had been instructed to find K. Parker Seldon, chairman of the board of directors of the American Jar and Bottle Corporation and ask his opinion about the five-point drop in Jar and Bottle stock that had occurred the day before.

"Don't come back until you find him," the editor had said. "The boss has bottle stock, and he's tearing his hair."

"I'll hold you to that," Jackson had said, and smiled for the first time that day.

Evans' plan for entering the Bal des Vêtements Brulés was as follows: Hjalmar, who was most convincing in his underworld disguise, and who had a slight edge on the lusty Kvek in throwing the hammer, the discus, cops, siphons or whatever needed throwing, was to enter first, alone, and take a seat as near the door as possible, with his back to the wall. He was to appear drowsy and show no signs of paying attention to what was going on, until he got a signal from Evans.

The big Norwegian started down the slight incline of the *rue* Cardinal Lemoine toward the entrance of the Bal des Vêtements Brulés, whistling somewhat gaily for a drowsy man, but otherwise in character. The fight at the Dôme the evening before had raised his spirits, he had passed a comfortable night at the prefecture, the discovery that the mummy in the Louvre was a dead Marquis had given promise of further adventure. In short, Hjalmar was himself again and vowed, as he walked and whistled, that when the present case was over he would paint whiskers as whiskers had never been painted before. He pushed the swinging doors, swept the assembled dancers and drinkers with a noncommittal glance, and selected a small table near the entrance and not too far from the bar, behind which the proprietor, M. Trouvaille, was pouring drinks in the best French style, so that they overran the brim of the glass, messed up the tray, the table and the drinker's clothes and fingers. Noticing Trouvaille's technique, the big painter ordered cognac, which evaporates quickly and is not very sticky.

The sharp-edged voice of the accordion, tracing variations on a popular air, was abetted by a brace of shrill violins. A drummer was doing what he could with the snare, the bass drum, cymbals and a modest array of kitchen utensils. A shuffling sound arose from the floor, where several pairs of dancers were locked in picturesque postures.

"They keep good time," Hjalmar said, for he liked to dance as well as he liked to paint, and for such a big man was light on his feet.

According to the plan, Tom Jackson, as a prosperous and reckless American, and Kvek as a Russian doorman who was acting as his protector were to come in several minutes later, after the customers had got accustomed to seeing Hjalmar around. So the latter, catching the eye of a dark-eyed curly-haired girl, decided he'd have time for one dance before his act went on. He walked over to the girl, rolling a bit from side to side because of his years at sea, and looked down, half-amused, at her escort, a slim pale young man with a face too old for his years and long nervous hands that twitched with disapproval.

"How about it?" Hjalmar asked.

The pale young man shot him a venemous look, tried to refuse, and lacking the nerve, gave the girl a slight shove in Hjalmar's direction.

"What's your name, kid?" Jansen asked, as they glided easily among the dancers.

"Nicole," she said, raising the fringe of her long lashes as she looked up at his face. The other men dancing, having seen Nicole's former escort make a sign with his thumb, one by one left their girls in the middle of a measure and formed a hostile group near the door of the back room. After whispering there a moment, they found their girls again and finished the dance.

"That mug you were with is sore," Hjalmar said, happily.

Nicole was not as cheerful about the situation. She might have communicated her misgivings to Hjalmar had not the music stopped at that moment, just as the swinging doors opened and Tom Jackson came in, followed closely by Lvov Kvek in Volga boatman's costume. In the general silence that followed, Tom Jackson yelled, "Whoopee."

The proprietor, who was tact personified, smiled at the orchestra and the musicians plunged into "Tipperary," which in many parts of France is believed to be the English and American anthem. Kvek winked broadly across the bar and said, "Champagne." That was enough, and when the Russian added, "For the house," the effect was electrical. The regular customers, even the reluctant young man who had been deprived of Nicole, rallied around to swell the proprietor's profits. Kvek led the way to a table across the dance floor from where

Hjalmar was chatting with Nicole, who, because she was afraid to go back to her former partner, stayed as close as she could to Jansen's broad shoulder. Champagne was served all around, with a bottle for the band, and when the music started up again, Hjalmar found himself on the horns of a dilemma. Evans had told him to drowse, but if he drowsed, Nicole's boy friend, whose name he had learned was Godasse, or Godo the Whack, would beat up the girl. With the aid of a fresh cognac to spike the sweet champagne, the painter reasoned it out this way. The drowsiness he had been instructed to feign was to indicate that he was paying no attention to the others. If he danced with Nicole, in a nonchalant way, the same result would be attained.

"Come on, kid," he said, and she snuggled up to him in a fatalistic way he could not help admiring. He had got in deeper than at first he had intended, still there was no deserting a frail young girl in such an emergency.

The entrance of Homer Evans just then shifted the focus of attention and had an effect way beyond anything Homer had planned or expected. The men who were dancing, except for Hjalmar, and Kvek, who had annexed a supple blonde called Nadia, stopped dead in their tracks. Trouvaille, the proprietor, ducked behind the bar. And Tom Jackson, to relieve the situation, let out another "Whoopee" that fell entirely flat.

"What's wrong?" asked Hjalmar, keeping step with the music and bending down until the girl's lips were close to his ear.

Nicole was trembling violently, looking first at Evans' low-slung cap and mustard-colored scarf streaked with heliotrope, then at the doorway of the back room, in which was standing Godo the Whack, his malevolent eyes protruding from their sockets.

"He's got on Sancho's clothes," the girl whispered.

"Sancho? Who's he?" asked Hjalmar.

"The guy who got killed last night," Nicole said.

"Dance with him, and put him wise. He's a friend of mine," Hjalmar said.

Nicole, right then and there, had to make a decision. Either she had to go back to Godo the Whack and take her medicine or she had to string along with Hjalmar. The latter course she chose. In dancing, Hjalmar maneuvered the girl near the table Homer had chosen and said, in English, under his breath, "Dance the next one with this baby. She's got news for you." And with that, the big Norwegian began to choke and splutter. Hastily he glided away, taking such long steps that Nicole was dragged along with only the tips of her toes on the floor. In front of the bar, Hjalmar burst into such hearty laughter that the disgruntled Apaches came scurrying to the doorway and glared in from the back room and Lvov Kvek burst into a Russian song about crows and the beautiful month of May. Jackson got up and did a tap dance, the beat of which the orchestra caught promptly.

Surprised as he was by his reception, Evans did not think for a moment that Hjalmar would have disregarded his instructions without purpose, so when Jackson had subsided and called for more champagne, Homer crossed the floor and asked the Norwegian curtly, in gashouse French, if he might dance with his girl.

Hjalmar nodded, but in order to keep up pretenses,

also scowled so savagely that Nicole, for a moment, was in doubt as to what she should do.

"Get some others on the floor," Homer muttered, for he knew that if he and Nicole were performing alone they would have little chance to talk. Hjalmar lumbered over to Jackson's table and grabbed Nadia. The reporter objected, and was pushed back into his chair. Kvek began to bellow and received a kick on the shins underneath the table. Four or five girls, all having been deserted by their men, were huddled around the bar. Tom and the Russian approached them, took the first two handy, and began dancing around. As the reporter passed the half-open doorway of the back room he noticed that it was empty. All the Apaches had disappeared.

Coincidently Homer was receiving and digesting information, and to say that he was dismayed would be putting it mildly. He was sure, however, that the regulars who had quit the Bal des Vêtements Brulés were members of the reorganized St. Julien Rollers. Instead of handing Nicole back to Hjalmar, when the dance was over, he sat at the table with them. The Norwegian had stopped laughing, but his face was decidedly gay.

"Will those birds be back?" he asked.

"If not, they'll be shadowed," Homer said. He had taken the precaution to get four plainclothes men from the prefecture and station them in near-by doorways.

"I hope they come back," the painter said, and his wish was fulfilled on the instant. The swinging doors parted and Godo the Whack came in like an eel through the entrance of a trap. He was followed by his six pals who had left him by way of the back door, and two more gangsters they had picked up outside. Homer stared calmly at their faces, to see if he could recognize any of them and to be sure he would know them when he met them again. Hjalmar, prompted by his experience on the waterfronts of the world, began his inspection at the other end and noticed at once that each of the gangsters was wearing only one sock, and had a bulge in his right coat pocket. There flashed into his mind simultaneously the memory of a large sandpile just up the hill from the entrance of the hall. At the same time, Kvek chanced to look behind him, since he had seated himself carelessly in front of a window, and on the sill he saw a sock stuffed with sand.

"I shall remember this date. It's one of my lucky days, my friend," the Russian said to Jackson. Tom was thinking quite the opposite. Eight thugs were standing purposefully between him and the swinging doors; still he had the presence of mind to order more champagne, reflecting that a full bottle was better than an empty one if it had to be used as a weapon. That was the only use that came readily to mind for the champagne Trouvaille served to stray Americans.

The atmosphere was so tense that Nicole's large dark eyes glowed with apprehension and something violent would surely have happened had not the swinging doors opened slowly, once more, causing the gangsters who had their backs to them to jump like cats and land on the balls of their feet. A sleek little man with a bronze complexion, black hair and shapely black eyebrows came in, smiling experimentally. He was dressed all in brown, hat, tie, socks, gloves and everything to match. Behind him, in correct tweed, was an athletic blue-eyed Englishman who looked around him with unconcealed distaste.

His discomfiture increased when he saw Tom Jackson, in rather loud clothes, his arm around the blonde called Nadia and with four champagne bottles in front of him, three being empty and the fourth in a bucket of ice. The Englishman pretended so pointedly that he hadn't recognized the reporter that the latter took the matter to heart.

"If there's any place in town you don't patronize," Jackson said, "I'd like the address, so I can go there myself."

"It's the press johnny," said the Englishman to his dark companion. "Can you make out what the fellow says?"

That was enough for Tom Jackson. Unmindful that Evans was trying to attract his attention and signal "As you were," the reporter untangled himself from the blonde, took off his glasses, and socked the Englishman in the jaw.

"Well struck," roared Hjalmar, clapping the tips of his fingers gently together. The gangsters, however, who had been set to go over the top, were precipitated into action. In a body, they started toward Homer. Kvek, with a Cossack yell, picked up his table and, using it as a shield, charged into the Rollers from the left. Hjalmar, following suit, drove into them with his table from the right until the gangsters were squeezed together like steers in a loading corral. Jackson and the Englishman were having a strictly private fight in the corner by the bar. Trouvaille, the proprietor, was yelling for order and expecting the police, the loss of his license, and other calamities. Along the right hand wall, Nicole was sitting wide-eyed and pale in her chair, the table having been jerked from in front of her. It was thus that she attracted the attention of Godo the Whack, who squirmed out of the solid mass of his pals and started in her direction.

Evans, who had been about to finish off the Rollers with a frontal attack, paused a moment to take a swing at Godo, who was within a foot of the terrified Nicole. The Whack was knocked flat on his face and passed out, and Homer tossed his limp body on top of the seven thugs wedged in between Kvek and Hjalmar, who were increasing the pressure gleefully.

"Don't let 'em get out the back way," Homer said, and his lieutenants nodded. "Chase 'em out through the swinging doors."

"Hold my table a minute," Hjalmar said, and Evans took it from his hands. The big Norwegian grabbed the hindmost gangster and heaved him like a sack of meal in the direction of the main exit. The Roller hit the swinging doors head first and passed through them as they flapped outward. As the doors were swinging inward, the second thug was stunned by them but managed to pull himself together and start down the hill. The remaining five who were conscious, and as anxious to get out before the cops arrived as Evans seemed to be to get rid of them, charged out of the Bal, propelled by the boots of Hjalmar and Kvek. Godo the Whack still was unconscious but he began to twitch and mutter, so Hjalmar tossed him over behind the bar with such accuracy that practically no glassware was broken.

Doggedly in the corner Tom Jackson and the Englishmen with blue eyes were pummeling and trundling one another, with strict adherence to the Marquis of Queensberry rules. The contest seemed to be horse and horse. The reporter could hit his opponent but could not knock him out. The Englishman, who boxed formally and stiffly, like an old engraving of prizefighters of yore, had a punch but couldn't land it. Had not the dark partner of the Englishman seen fit to interfere, the fight would have been allowed to progress uninterruptedly until one or both contestants got tired. As it was, the black-haired stranger tried to trip Tom from behind and Kvek felt justified in evening up the odds. He paid no attention to the slim dark man, who was obviously inexperienced in free-for-alls. Instead, the Russian caught hold of the Englishman's suspenders and, after jerking the buttons out by the roots, he ripped open the fly and the trousers were soon down around the Englishman's well-tanned knees.

That gave Homer the opportunity he had been waiting for. The mysterious pair, of whose appearance at the Dôme he had already been told, intrigued his interest. Swiftly he went to the exit, opened the doors and beckoned a patrolman he had previously instructed to stay out of the fray. Trouvaille groaned and began to protest innocence. Nicole and the other girls huddled together in a corner. Jackson and the Englishman stopped fighting.

"What's this?" the policeman inquired.

"Take their names and addresses," Evans whispered.

The dark-haired partner, who was more presentable than his confrere whose pants were down, produced a card which read:

LEWSON-PHIPPS & XERXES

IMPORTERS AND EXPORTERS

69 RUE REAUMUR, PARIS

"Your papers," the *agent* demanded.

The dark man, of Armenian origin, had an Egyptian passport with a name the officer did not attempt to read but which Evans quickly memorized for future reference: Hagup Bogigian. The Englishman, holding up his buttonless trousers with one hand, fished in his coat pockets with the other and produced a British passport which gave his name as Basil Hamborough. They were the members of the importing and exporting firm. The dark one explained to the bewildered policeman that he had taken the names of Xerxes because foreigners could remember it, even if they couldn't say it. Basil Hamborough, it developed, had an uncle named Lewson-Phipps who had given him his share in the business with the understanding that Hamborough should not come to England more than twice a year, and never stay more than forty-eight hours.

"What were you doing here? Why did you come, and in business hours? Surely not to dance," the officer said.

The Englishman gave a contemptuous look at the frightened girls in the corner. "Most certainly not," he said.

Tom Jackson, annoyed by the man's assumption of social superiority, made another pass at him, and was restrained by Homer.

"I like to dance," the dark one said. "My friend and partner came with me, simply to watch."

"Oh, I say," the Englishman said.

Evans winked at the officer to let it pass, and the latter, after warning the proprietor against further outbreaks of violence, went back to his post near the summit of the hill. The members of the firm of Lewson-Phipps & Xerxes left hastily in the other direction, the Anglo-Saxon partner spluttering indignantly as he trekked downhill with both hands gripping his neatly-tailored trousers. Nicole, with true French thrift, was on her hands and knees retrieving the buttons which had been scattered from one end of the dance hall to the other. When she saw that Evans, Hjalmar and Jackson were about to go, however, she abandoned her minor economy and stood up, chilled with fright.

"We'll have to take the kid along," Hjalmar said. "If we don't, those scissorbills will murder her."

Evans, who wanted to talk with Nicole on his own account, nodded his agreement and Nicole, snatching her hat from a peg in the back room, picked up her worn handbag and stood obediently at Jansen's side. The big Norwegian had misgivings, but he also had a heart. It was one thing to acquire women, and quite another to get loose from them, he knew from bitter experience. Nevertheless, the girl was with them when they entered the Hotel Murphy et du Danube Bleu. Bridgette Murphy eyed her somewhat coldly until Evans asked her to take care of the girl and not to let any pimps come near her.

"I'll skin 'em alive," Bridgette said, and the pale scared girl wanly smiled.

"I'm not so much afraid of Godo," she began.

"He takes orders from someone?" Evans asked, kindly.

Nicole began to tremble and to cry. Homer placed his hand on her shoulder. "You don't have to tell me. I'll find out for myself," he said. Leaving the others for a moment, he descended to the kitchen and examined the envelope addressed to Nicole. It was postmarked "Luneville-sur-Seine." Hastily he steamed it open and gasped with satisfaction as he read:

FIND AMERICAN K.S. PORKER DELIVER HIM
ALIVE   (Signed)   THE SINGE

Immediately many things began to be clear to him. None of the gangsters dared call at the postoffice for his mail, so the leader sent his correspondence through Nicole, who probably gave the messages to Godo unopened. Carefully re-sealing the envelope he put it back in his pocket. Obviously, the St. Julien Rollers, who had kidnapped the professor, did not have K. Parker Seldon, who had become known as K.-S. Porker in the French press and to French officialdom generally. The Singe, who must be the new leader, was as much in the dark about the bottle magnate as Evans was himself, and wanted the middle-sized millionaire as badly. Bridgette produced, at Homer's request, an atlas and he found Luneville marked by a small dot, on the west bank of the river about fifty kilometers upstream from Rouen. A quick call to the prefecture brought to Homer's ears the troubled voice of Sergeant Schlumberger who promised to send the prefectorial launch, the *Deuxieme Pays de Tout le Monde,* to the landing near the Pont Royal and to dispatch Melchisadek Knockwoode post haste to the *place* de la Contrescarpe.

At the prospect of a river voyage, Hjalmar Jansen began bellowing a chanty, the words of which drew forth an admonition from Bridgette to respect himself. Kvek, reaching in his pocket to see if he had enough cigarettes for the cruise, came upon the sock filled with sand, which he had utterly forgotten.

"It's sticky," he said to Evans, as he explained how he had come by it.

Evans, when he examined the sock, let out an exclamation of satisfaction. Three at a time he leaped up the stairs and knocked on Hydrangea's door. Without waiting for her to get up from the bed, where she was still weeping, face downward, he rushed into the alcove and took from the shelf above the washstand a bottle of hair tonic labeled "Psalm XXIII Anointment" and sniffed first the stuffed sock, then the unstoppered bottle. Hydrangea, who was standing close behind him, slid senseless to the floor, as if her wild-rose negligée had been empty and had slipped from a hook. With a stiff shot of gin, Evans revived the fainting Blackbird and verified the fact that she had rubbed Frémont's head with liquid from the bottle in question, a process in which, she tearfully said, the Chief took a deep delight.

"Someone's gone and slugged him right on his po' head," she wailed, and promptly passed out again.

Conjectures were swarming through Evans' brain, to use the words of the Chinese poet "like bees through black hair" but his line of action was well defined. The St. Julien Rollers, originally a smuggling gang, had always used the river, and since their upstream hangout, at Frontville, had been found and raided the year before, it was natural that they should seek a hideout in the opposite direction. Hjalmar, with Kvek and Jackson as crew, was to take the *Deuxieme Pays* downstream as far as Rouen and inquire of all his acquaintances among the river men if any suspicious-looking craft had been seen on the Seine in the days just past. Evans decided to have

Melchisadek drive him at once to Luneville, where he would have a look for The Singe.

"You'll write to me, won't you?" murmured Nicole, as Hjalmar went whistling away.

II

Certain Pitfalls That Travelers Should Keep in Mind

SINCE it has developed that the leaders of the St. Julien Rollers are as deep, or deeper in the fog, and are more anxious concerning the whereabouts of K. Parker Seldon than are Homer Evans, Lvov Kvek and the Paris police, it may increase the reader's confidence in himself, and dispel any unfortunate feeling of inferiority that may have been instilled in him in his childhood, if he is able to review the adventures of the missing business man since the latter took leave of his friends on the *terrasse* of the Café du Dôme with the expressed intention of taking a walk around the block.

It was true that his daughter Isabel had asked Mr. Seldon to buy her a copy of *Ulysses* and that, drunk as he was, he had remembered the girl's request and had purchased the book in the *rue* Delambre. The bottle magnate, like so many modern parents, had tried to keep abreast of his offspring's interests and with that in mind had opened up the book and had seen some words which, while they seemed to make the story less suitable for a sweet girl graduate, stirred an interest in Seldon that surpassed anything he had ever felt for *Paradise Lost* or *Lorna Doone,* the only other works of fiction whose names he could call to mind.

As he had walked along the *rue* Delambre, reading, he was followed eagerly by Dr. Balthazar St.-Jean Truc, to whom he represented untold wealth and prosperity. He had made a turn to the right and, later, another, dimly thinking he was getting back to his friends at the Dôme. Before long he was lost and, in order to clear his head, he decided to drop in at a convenient saloon for a glass of beer. Now the French word for beer is *biere* (pronounced bee-air) but those ingenious people have invented an *aperitif* named Byrrh (pronounced beer) and it was this latter that the well-intentioned barkeep set out for K. Parker Seldon.

The American, thinking the barman had made an innocent mistake, tossed down the Byrrh and for a moment thought he had swallowed some old-fashioned spring medicine. He smiled politely, offered a ten-dollar bill in payment, having nothing smaller in his wallet, and listened to assorted noises to which he could not reply. The bartender was an accommodating fellow and, tumbling to the fact that his client did not understand either French or the customs of the country, he got out a copy of *En-Tout-Cas,* looked up the exchange, and, deducting a few francs to be on the safe side, handed back three hundred and ninety-six francs. K. Parker Seldon thought he had all the best of the encounter. He still wanted beer, however, and stopped in a neighboring bar where he asked for it again. A second time he was served with the dark liquid tasting like sarsaparilla in which a few young owls had been bathing.

It should be explained that two elements had contributed largely to the success in business of the bottle and jar king, not counting the bottles and jars themselves. The first was the friendship of Hugo Weiss, the second, Seldon's own persistence. It was the latter quality that was brought into play, after the second Byrrh had come his way. He sat down at a near-by table, and with *Ulysses* before him, waited until someone else came in and received what looked like a glass of beer. Then he rose, and with a creditable bit of pantomime, indicated to the barman that he wanted the same. Promptly he got it, but after trying three or four of them, the bottle king concluded that beer in gay Paris was not what it was in the old country. With that he tried another saloon and asked for whiskey.

That time they got him the first crack out of the box. He found himself facing a tall glass with Black and White in it, and splashed in a moderate amount of siphon.

As he started off again he had dimly in his mind that he must find the café where he had left Kvek, and for the life of him he could not remember its name. Neither did he know the name of his hotel. That discouraged him to the point where he wanted another Scotch and soda.

At eleven o'clock that evening, Seldon's pilgrimage had brought him, by a devious route through the *place* du Chatelet, the Porte St. Denis and other historical points of interest, to a bench near the *place* Pigalle, in the heart of Montmartre, and there the chairman of the Board of Directors of the American Jar and Bottle Corporation fell asleep. Dr. Balthazar Truc, who was not accustomed to long walks in city streets, was footsore and hungry, and seeing that his incipient benefactor was dead to the world the doctor felt safe in slipping into a near-by *bistrot* for a ham sandwich and a cup of coffee. Like so many who, in Shakespeare's word, "are fit for stratagems and plots," Dr. Truc did not touch alcohol.

The sandwich bread was tough and the ham sliced very thin, and it cost the doctor plenty, for while he was eating it some anonymous dip relieved K. Parker Seldon of his wallet, which contained several hundred dollars and about eighteen francs left from the ten-dollar bill. The thief, although having been reduced by hard circumstances to picking pockets, had not lost the last spark of human kindness, so he left his victim his passport and a sheaf of American Express checks which were not convertible without another signature.

Having eaten the unsatisfactory and expensive sandwich, Dr. Balthazar Truc came out of the café and took a seat on the bench beside the drunken man. A policeman approached but the doctor looked so respectable that the officer was satisfied all was well. Under the pretext of examining Seldon, in his professional capacity, Dr. Truc came into possession of the passport and the traveler's checks the pickpocket had passed up, and as an additional precaution, removed Seldon's unusually fine and expensive sets of upper and lower false teeth. Then he hustled into a telephone booth to call the garage where he had left his limousine. In his absence, someone got Seldon's hat, coat and shoes.

As the clock was striking midnight, the bottle magnate began to be aware of headlights passing and a taste in his mouth like leaf mold trampled by hyenas who were shedding their hair. His head was aching and around inside it rattled some phrases from the prayerbook, to the effect that he had done some things he ought not to have done and had left undone other things he ought to have done. Beside him, on the bench, was the copy of *Ulysses*. Just then there were plenty of passers-by and their interest in Seldon was instrumental in his finding out that he was lacking hat, coat and shoes. He staggered to his feet and, in trying to yell, discovered that his teeth were gone.

A crowd gathered, including several Americans, but none of them suspected from the bottle man's appearance or the sounds he made that he was a countryman in distress. Another policeman came on the scene and, being younger and less experienced than the first officer, led Seldon to the commissariat.

The commissariat just off the *place* Pigalle is one of the liveliest in Paris, or anywhere else in the world, and because so many foreigners from every land and belonging to every race seek diversion in Montmartre, the commissaire had secured the services of a squad of interpreters and linguists who would do credit to any university. When Seldon began emitting sounds and syllables, in an endeavor to explain himself and report that he had been robbed, the commissaire decided that he was probably Maltese, and rang for the Maltese interpreter. The only result was more animation and less articulateness, if possible, on the part of K. Parker Seldon. In turn, the commissaire tried Flemish, Turkish, Swedish, Indo-Chinese and Turkestan. When these failed, as did German, Dutch, Norwegian, Hebrew, Italian, Finnish, Spanish, Malay and Portuguese, the commissaire began to get fed up with the case.

It cannot be said, in all justice, that the commissaire was not a thorough man. He handed the frenzied American a well-crusted pen and a container in which was a mixture of dust and violet ink of about the consistency of cream of wheat. The marks Seldon made did nothing to shed light on his nationality, for although they resembled Chinese they ran from left to right and horizontally, not up and down.

Noticing that Seldon was clutching under one elbow a large blue-covered book, the chief interpreter took it gently away from him, opened to page 401 and was confronted by the following words:

"Deshill Holles Eamus. Send us, bright one, light one. Horhorn, quickening and wombfruit. Hoopsa, boyaboy, hoopsa."

"*Zut, alors,*" the interpreter said, and turned back to page 264. There he lamped "Imperthnthn thnthnthn. Chips, picking chips off rocky thumbnail, chips. Horrid. And gold flushed more. A husky fifenote blew. . . . Rrrpr. Kraa. Kraandl. . . . My eppripfftaph be pfrwritt."

"Throw him out," the interpreter said. "He doesn't belong on this planet at all."

The commissaire was just about to take his subordinate's advice when Dr. Balthazar St.-J. Truc came in, exuding his best bedside manner. He removed with a flourish from a vest pocket a neatly engraved card and handed it to the presiding official, and let it be known that he was the proprietor of a sanitorium between Paris and Rouen. He said suavely that he had taken an interest in the pitiable alcoholic without language, script or country and asked permission to take him to his hospital for observation. Relieved because the sanitorium was in Luneville, many miles from his arrondissement, the commissaire made out and signed the necessary papers and wiped his brow with relief.

Of course, Seldon, having a violent headache and no French, understood nothing of what had occurred, except that he had been hustled into a police station and was being hustled out again.

He awoke early in the morning in a narrow room of which the walls and the floors were of a rather soft composition like rubber and smelled like carbolic acid and musk. The cot was peculiarly constructed, the windows were heavily screened and barred, and the door, when he tried it, was locked. Dimly he remembered his portly rescuer and a long automobile ride, still more dimly the evening that had preceded it. In his mouth and throat persisted still the vile after-taste he identified with Byrrh, *biere,* bee-air and what, if it had been about six times stronger, would have resembled just plain beer. Nothing happened, so, lying miserably on the bed, he gazed at the ceiling and tried to enumerate and classify his problems. Thus far, his first trip abroad had proved a disappointment. He had heard Weiss speak highly of France, he knew Kvek had been so eager for a glimpse of French shores that he had with difficulty been restrained from climbing one of the smokestacks of the *Ile de France.* The jar king tried to keep an open mind, and found the going very hard.

He decided (a) that he must get the door unlocked, (b) that he must arouse Dr. Truc, (c) that he must go to a dentist and be fitted out with teeth. Then he could get money, if he could get to a phone, telegraph or cable office. After that he could buy some clothes, apply for a new passport, report the loss of his travelers' checks, get a drink of water, some champagne and a good square meal. There would still remain the task of locating Kvek and his hotel, in which his baggage was reposing. At that point he remembered the headstone, or whatever it was, that he must deliver to a professor so-and-so at a certain address. All in all, it was a longer list of problems than had ever been presented to the directors of his corporation in a calendar year.

His pillow was thin and hard and, turning it over, he found *Ulysses*, somewhat battered but still legible. The volume had flown open at a point where a Corporal in the British Army was announcing, in Dublin, what he would do to any b———, f———, b——— who said a word against the b———, f——— king. From there on the narrative was so compelling that Seldon's aching eyes were riveted to the page, and he decided that if ever he got back to America he would plunk his precocious daughter into a Baptist finishing school and have a heart to heart talk with the mistress about reading lists. It was one thing to let the younger generation in on a few of the facts of life, but quite another to allow drunken soldiers to talk naturally in print. The thick blue book, however, served to take the bottle tycoon's mind away from his immediate plight and gradually worked him into better shape to be overjoyed when he heard a key inserted in the lock and his door swung open about ten inches. Through the opening sidled a huge square-headed blond man with expressionless blue eyes and sandy hair and freckles all over his bare arms and his chest. The giant pointed toward himself and said: "Gus." That was all he attempted in the way of self-introduction.

Seldon began to gibber and gesticulate, to which Gus paid small attention. From a bucket he poured a brown warm liquid into a paper cup, broke off a chunk from a loaf of coarse gray bread, turned around, left the room and locked the door behind him.

The first locking of the door K. Parker Seldon had been willing to assume was accidental. The second was intentional beyond a doubt. During about three-quarters of an hour the bottle magnate danced with rage, tried to shout for help, and pounded on the heavy panels. After that he tried the coffee, howled and yammered indignantly and spewed it all over the floor.

The flap of the peephole winked, the latch turned, and Gus stepped in again. With a jerk of his head he indicated that Seldon was to precede him into the hallway, which sent a wave of joy over the harassed business man. His elation did not last more than a minute. He was led into a courtyard, with walls six meters high and unscalable. The door clanked behind him. In the yard were a dozen men in all sorts of nondescript attire. The nearest one was on his hands and knees, with an ear flat to the ground. It turned out that he was listening for worms.

Another chap, more than six feet tall and wearing faded pink pajamas several sizes too small, made a furtive sign to Seldon and led him to a corner of the yard, away from the others. The American felt a faint temblor of hope until the man started speaking.

"They think I'm crazy but I'm not," he said.

The truth dawned on K. Parker Seldon like thunder

across any number of bays. He was in a lunatic asylum. The eruption of what he intended to be speech, resulting from his discovery, caused his fellow-inmates to conclude that Seldon was no man to offer confidences. The man with the high-water pajamas backed hastily away, with pity written all over his cadaverous face. Seldon, nettled, pursued him, baying, burbling and waving his arms. He was determined to get his points across, namely: that he had been robbed and victimized; that he was an American citizen and, by God, someone would have something to answer for; and furthermore that when he found Dr. Balthazar Truc he was going to reach down his throat and turn him inside out. To escape what he thought would be physical violence, the man in pink pajamas climbed the only tree. Other inmates, alarmed, began to yawp and to howl, bumping each other as they ran pointlessly to and fro.

A large black-haired woman in white, one of the nurses, saw the commotion from an upper window and reached for the house telephone.

"Tell Gus there's trouble in Courtyard Seven," she cooed and went on with her work.

By that time K. Parker Seldon was so determined to make someone understand, that he tried, by jumping a foot or so off the ground, to catch hold of the pajamas of the man in the tree. He had just succeeded when Gus, very bored, came on the scene. His coming had a quieting effect on everyone except Seldon who, waving the torn fragment of pink cloth he had in his hand, walked straight up to the big gorilla and socked him in the nose.

A howl of approval rose from every quarter, including the window where the black-haired nurse was standing, arms akimbo. Gus, who had a hopeless yen for the big handsome woman, was chagrined at showing up so badly.

"Naughty," he said, in some kind of Scandinavian French.

The irate jar magnate took a healthy swing and hit Gus again.

The smooth voice of Dr. Truc was heard, just behind the freckled attendant. The doctor had a way of appearing and disappearing unexpectedly.

"I should have warned you, Gus. The new patient is dangerous," the doctor said.

Seldon thought no more about Gus, except to dive between his legs to get at Dr. Truc. Gus, at best a slow thinker, had not been prepared for that maneuver. The doctor abandoned his bedside manner and his professional dignity and started to run, only to be tackled from behind. Before Gus could interfere, his boss was flat on his face in the dust with the new patient sitting on him and pounding the back of his head with both fists. The other patients, whose life contained so little cheer, were being repaid for months of hardship but none of them enjoyed the incident as did the black-haired nurse. Above the din her hearty laugh rang out, and she shouted encouragement to the game little business man in German, French, Hungarian and her native Russian, which seemed to have an edge on the other languages for booming mirth above the noise of crowds.

Of course, Courtyard Seven was between Courtyards Six and Eight and the racket spread all over the large institution until old ladies were clawing at bric-a-brac, young girls tearing off their clothes, old men prancing like stallions and nurses, guards and attendants running every which way.

Gus's arrival at the doctor's side would, in ordinary circumstances, have put an end to the conflict, but in falling, Dr. Truc had spilled Seldon's express checks from his pocket. Those Seldon had recognized in time to slip from Gus's grasp and start giving Dr. Truc the boots. Of course, the American's efforts were accompanied by lisps, gurgles and squeaks that would have caused the occupants of the Tower of Babel to jump from high windows and perish.

Having reduced the proprietor of the Sens Unique to a pulp, Seldon eluded Gus's ham-like hands again and grabbed up the checks, which in the scuffle had been loosened from their binding. Waving them in his hand, and pointing to himself and then upward toward God, he raced wildly around the yard and a general alarm was sounded. Gongs clanged, attendants in duck and bruisers in white jerseys poured in from doorways and windows. The hilarious nurse upstairs started rooting in English.

"Throw them over the wall," she yelled.

Seldon, harassed as he was, heard the encouraging words and glanced upward at their source.

"Throw them, little dove! Little wild duck of the north!"

The bottle king caught on. He drew back his arm and without a windup sent the wad of checks and his card case flying over the high barrier, and the breeze from the near-by river scattered calling cards, telephone numbers, contraceptive devices, Life Savers, a Chinese laundry check, and a letter of introduction to Professor Zacharie de la Poussière, in all directions.

"I adore you," shouted the nurse. "I throw you a hundred kisses."

Dr. Balthazar Truc was still on the ground, too woozy to attempt to rise. Gus was no match for the American patient, as a sprinter, and several of the other patients were joining in the game and forming a sort of interference for Seldon as he charged back and forth. Finally, the Russian nurse decided it was time to take a hand. She hurried down into Courtyard Seven.

"You've done enough for today," she said, smiling, to Seldon. "It's time for your shower."

He ran to her side, she took his arm and led him away. "This afternoon," she whispered, as he was being locked in his room.

12

Which Causes a Lawyer to Burst into Song

WHEN it is taken into consideration that at the time
Miriam was born there was scarcely a fence in all Montana, and that her father, from whom she had inherited
her sometimes hasty temper, had considered moving his
ranch to a secluded spot because in a single week in 1903
two covered wagons had passed westward along the trail,
it can be better understood how the Western girl reacted
when she found herself between four stained and moldy
walls, a dank low ceiling and a rough concrete floor not
more than ten feet by twelve. Moreover, her recollections
of the tang of the sage brush with which the great open
spaces are generously carpeted did not make it easier to
endure the fumes which arose from a certain corner of
her cell.

To be sure, she was in quod voluntarily and the door
was not locked, but the struggle between her inherited
claustrophobia and her determination to stick with the
suspect, Lazare, was closely contested and did not tend
to make her more amenable to Sergeant Schlumberger's

well-meant suggestions. In fact, she went so far as to infer, in a talk with him, that there is something in kraut, which if indulged in to excess, dulls the wits and renders the eater unfit for human society, and particularly for holding public office or employment. That was a sore point with the Alsatian, whose mother had always stored away a barrel or two of sauerkraut in case of sickness, and who had been ridiculed before on the same score by members of the force who hailed from the Midi or the Western provinces of France.

By the time the sergeant sent for Lazare to be brought to the office for preliminary grilling, such friction had developed that Miriam dashed through two hundred yards of offices in order to protest to Dr. Hyacinthe Toudoux, and on her way upset approximately four cubic yards of wire baskets filled with documents, six swivel chairs and two villainous-looking old women who tried to stab her with rusty ink-crushed pens as she passed.

Dr. Toudoux responded with alacrity, as soon as he had scrubbed some of the asphalt from beneath his worn finger-nails. The corpse or mummy of the late Marquis de la Rose d'Antan was still stretched on his laboratory table and the doctor was, if possible, further than ever from arriving at the cause or hour of death. In the prefect's office, where Schlumberger had confronted the demoralized taxidermist, Toudoux really let himself go.

"This man, your prisoner, is on the verge of a nervous collapse," the doctor said, glaring at the Alsatian. "If you persist in questioning him now I shall prefer charges against you, personally, and your negligent superiors who, in this case, are showing the ineptitude for police work that they habitually display in the field of science."

"But it's not my fault that I find myself in charge of this hornet's nest of related cases," protested Schlumberger.

"Why not resign?" the doctor asked.

"I must eat," said the Alsatian with dignity.

"Not necessarily," the medical examiner said. "In any event, this unfortunate man, who is as innocent of wrongdoing as I am, should be sent to a comfortable hospital for rest and observation, and must not be disturbed again until he has recovered from the shock of his false arrest."

The doctor slammed the door and left the room, and restrained himself just in time from kicking the two old women who claimed they had been injured when Miriam upset them and demanded certificates for accident compensation and leave. "Was ever a man of science subjected to such outrageous interruptions?" he said, when once he had reached his laboratory again. But his previous outburst was nothing compared with what followed when he picked up the *En-Tout-Cas* from the chest of the defunct marquis, where the messenger had laid it, and read the health column signed by Dr. Balthazar St.-J. Truc. Tearing off his white apron and white linen coat, he got into his street clothes, nearly ripping them to pieces in the process, snatched two sharp pointed foils from the wall and caromed down the stairs to the sidewalk where he hailed a taxicab.

"So I'm an impostor! I'm color blind, eh? Livers do not show streaks of heliotrope, as any experienced dissector knows! And wine of California does not swell them, but shrinks them! We shall settle these points in the Bois," were some of the exclamations overheard by the chauffeur as the taxi careened toward the Café du Dôme. The wild

167

look on the face of the doctor, the way he laid about him with the foils, and the cryptic nature of his soliloquies, made the driver so nervous that he sideswiped an empty hearse which was speeding back from a second-class funeral and was so delayed by the resultant formalities that Toudoux, handing him distractedly a hundred-franc note, continued his journey on foot and, because of his manner and his weapons, was given a wide berth by the sidewalk crowd.

Miriam, as soon as the doctor had left the prefect's office, led Lazare back to his cell and tried to comfort him, but she was alarmed to notice that, while the unfortunate taxidermist had lost his attitude of fear, he was beginning to take less and less interest in what was going on around him. He had been deprived of his belt, his string tie, his spectacles and his shoestrings but the searchers had overlooked a small piece of carpenter's chalk in one of his pockets, so, after Miriam had assured him that she would see him through and that once Evans found out about his arrest, he would promptly be released, the old man sat cross-legged on the concrete floor and started scribbling hieroglyphics on the wall. A guard whose attention had been attracted by the strange scrawls and the behavior of the prisoner, generally, tossed into the cell through the bars a copy of one of the newspapers.

"There. Read the news. You'll feel better having something to read," the guard said. "Here's one for you, too, mademoiselle," he added to Miriam, and smiled.

A glance at the headlines brought about a change for the worse in old Lazare. The long-buried incident of the hot-seat in the Comédie Française had been revived, and even enlarged upon. Beside flashlight pictures of the taxidermist, wild-eyed and with bars in the foreground, were tintypes of the old Marquis, and Lazare as a student, in court. The Marquis, whose murder and mutilation covered half the page, was shown at the Jockey Club, in Louis XIV costume, and half-wrapped in bandages, quite obviously dead.

Columns followed about Lazare's arrest: how he was taken in the apartment of a Montparnasse demimondaine called Mireille Montana. And there was a touching paragraph about the way in which the handsome young adventuress was sticking by her sexagenarian Lothario, who was in a state of collapse. The newspaper men, having been starved for news since *The Pansy* had been stolen, had let themselves go.

But it was not the plight of Lazare, nor the unflattering snapshots of herself that chilled Miriam's heart and drove all else from her mind. It was the realization that Homer Evans had not read the papers. Otherwise he would have rescued the taxidermist long ago. Something must have happened to him to put him out of touch with events. Her heart stood still as she paced the floor in agony. It took her a full hour to get a grip on herself.

"I must have confidence, and carry out his instructions," she said. Then she had an inspiration. The suspects she had heard about had always refused to talk, if they knew what was good for them, until a lawyer had been found to represent them. With that she began to rattle the bars.

"Don't get excited," said the amiable guard, who had been staying fairly close to her cell in the hope of catching her eye.

"Call the sergeant at once," she said. "I've a right to have a lawyer. So has Monsieur Lazare."

The taxidermist only shuddered.

Reluctantly the guard complied, and the sergeant, gray from worry, walked down the corridor and said, "Well?"

"I want a lawyer. I insist . . . ." Miriam began.

"You won't find any lawyer in his office until after lunch," Schlumberger said. "They take things very easy, the lawyers do."

"Then I shall phone one at home."

"In a case like this, the telephone is unsatisfactory," the sergeant said. "It's much better to see a lawyer face to face."

"You want to get rid of me, but I'll be back," she said, and with a few comforting words which Lazare scarcely heard, she left the prefecture, hurried to her hotel for a bath and change of clothes, then drew all her money from the bank and took a taxi to the boulevard St. Germain. She thought she remembered having seen lawyers' shingles there, and she was right. In the first block eastward from the Deux Magots she saw a sign: Me. François Ronron, Avocat. She dismissed her taxi, found the entrance with some difficulty, since it was wedged in between a window full of dusty trusses and a shop where clerical vestments and articles of piety were on display. She mounted a narrow stairway and, after lighting a match, tried to read the doorplates, in the few instances in which the doors were not blank.

The concierge, who had been eyeing her from the ground-floor entry, upbraided her in a shrill cracked voice. "No smoking on the stairways, mademoiselle."

"I'm not smoking. I'm looking for a lawyer," Miriam replied.

"Which one? I have three. How should I know which lawyer you want? What's your business with a lawyer, anyway? If it's divorce or any kind of blackmail, you'll have to go down to No. 217," the concierge said.

"I want Maitre Ronron," said Miriam.

"Third floor left, and no more matches," snapped the concierge. There was something in the atmosphere that made Miriam fear that a lawyer wouldn't help her much, after all. Gritting her teeth and setting her shoulders, she climbed to the third, which in France is the fourth and sometimes the fifth, and there, by the light that filtered through a fly-specked skylight she read: Me. François Ronron, Avocat.

Vigorously she pushed the bell button and thought for a moment she had set off a burglar alarm. However, nothing happened, so she touched the button again, that time with a staccato attack from the wrist with fingers relaxed, as she had learned from the Seek and Ye Shall Find Correspondence School and the Paris Conservatoire. It was one of the few points on which their teachings had coincided. She paused and listened and was rewarded by the shuffling of a pair of slippered feet. The door opened slowly and she was faced with a crotchety old man with heavy eyebrows and a bulging forehead.

"What do you want?" asked the old man, peering into the darkness. "Oh, a woman," he added, crossly. Women almost invariably called on Maitre Ronron much later in the afternoon. So did men, if they wanted to get the best run for their money.

"I want to see Maitre Ronron right away," Miriam said

and nearly upset the clerk as she stepped brusquely into what proved to be a narrow waiting room.

"He's not in the office, and won't be for an hour," the clerk said. He was holding in his hand a wet stub pen with a feather for a handle. At his desk a huge volume that looked like a scrapbook was open, and on a near-by wall were shelves of similar books.

"Where is the Maitre?" Miriam asked.

"In his apartment. Did you have an appointment?"

"No."

"Who sent you to Maitre Ronron?"

"I saw the sign on the door below."

"You mean to say that you came here without references? You have made an error, Madame. Maitre Ronron's practice is an old established one. He hasn't taken on a new client in several years. Would it not be as well . . ."

"Where is the Maitre's apartment?"

The old man began to stammer. He didn't like the glint in Miriam's eye. He tried to stall but she caught him firmly by the shoulder and gave an admonitory shake. Reluctantly the clerk told her that the lawyer lived in the rooms directly behind his office, and before he could stop her, Miriam had brushed him aside, strode through the office and banged on the door that chanced to open into Maitre Ronron's bedroom. The building in question had been built just after the Franco-Prussian War, which had used up the best workmen. It was none too solid. The latch of the door gave way and so did the lock.

Maitre François Ronron sat up in bed, blinking, and saw before him an angry young woman, unquestionably chic and attractive, who was waving his faithful clerk,

Hector Camphre, as if he were a flag. But the Maitre, although conservative to the hilt in the matter of decor and clientele, was rather open-minded and had seen enough of life, as reflected in courts and law books, to be able to retain a certain poise in all kinds of situations. He smiled, reached for his toupée, adjusted his pillows and asked Camphre if he would mind opening the window shades.

Miriam, relieved to find someone at last who didn't treat her as if she were about to steal the law books, was the first to speak.

"Forgive me, Maitre, for bursting in on you like this, but the case I want you to take is one of great emergency. An innocent Frenchman's reason and his life are at stake. Your Government is on the verge of committing a terrible mistake . . ."

"That's where governments are teetering continually, mademoiselle," he said. "But if you'll wait in the office until I am dressed, I'll hear what you have to say. Monsieur Camphre, if you please. Give our client something to read, and dust off a comfortable chair."

The clerk, muttering, handed Miriam a copy of *L'Illustration* dated March, 1909, after dusting off the chair with it. He was so much like a ruffled bantam rooster that Miriam, with difficulty, refrained from tickling him under the chin. In about three-quarters of an hour Maitre Ronron came in, pommaded, groomed and corseted, and started rubbing his hands. As he rubbed, Miriam told him what had happened.

"We must establish an alibi," the Maitre said.

"I thought of that, and questioned M. Lazare," said Miriam. "It's not going to be easy, because on the day of the crime he was in his shop all day, alone. Not a single customer came in."

"It's those radicals in the Chamber. They're to blame for our slump in trade. Only last week they authorized the use of typewriters in the Department of Justice. Typewriters, mind you, those soulless instruments responsible for half the sloppy writing and thinking of today. The wise Chinese use chopsticks, Mademoiselle Montana, not because such a resourceful people could not invent a small shovel for cramming food into their mouths. Indeed, not! Chopsticks require slow eating and that means good digestion, health, economy, and above all a mind clear as crystal. A typewriter, mademoiselle, slays the identity, confuses the ears with clattering noises, frustrates the flow of reason by mechanical defects. Do you see in this office a single one of those bothersome machines? Why, I would discharge after thirty years of service my good clerk, M. Camphre, if I even caught him using a fountain pen. Our forefathers wrote immortal prose and reached profound decisions without mechanical claptrap to addle their brains. A quill, mademoiselle. That's the ideal writing instrument. A balm to the intellect."

"You are eloquent, Maitre," murmured Miriam. "I agree that whenever possible, one should go about things slowly. But in this case, sir, there is need for haste." Before the lawyer could interrupt her, she continued with the story, and only when she repeated Dr. Toudoux's words about sending Lazare to a quiet place for observation did the Maitre perk up a bit.

"Ah! Excellent! Of course . . . And not a public institution where the flunkies of our reckless government will maul him and shove him from pillar to post. Were it not for the expense . . ." the Maitre paused tactfully.

"Don't give a thought to that. I'll cable Hugo Weiss."

"Ah! Weiss! That will be splendid," said the lawyer, fumbling in dusty pigeonholes until he found a cable blank which he handed to Miriam suavely. Maitre Ronron had heard of Weiss and his millions. "In that case, some reputable private institution where my client will have the best of care. That will be good for him, and, I'm frank to tell you, mademoiselle, it will give us a breathing space to see what can be done about the alibi. Often one can be proven, if tact is used with reluctant witnesses, persons who perhaps have denied any knowledge of the case or have neglected to come forward because of the fear of notoriety. You'll readily admit, mademoiselle, that it would be hard to remember the exact day on which one had bought a stuffed weasel or a pigeon-hawk."

Miriam nodded.

The Maitre summoned the clerk, who was buried deep in his enormous scrapbook, and soon M. Camphre had deposited on his employer's already over-loaded desk another huge volume in which the Maitre began exploring, with "Ah's" and refined exclamations from time to time.

"I had another case in which my client went daffy . . ."

"Lazare's not daffy."

"Let us say, then, in need of a tranquil regime. Let me see. It was the year just after the War. And we sent the fellow . . . Camphre, can't you remember?"

"February, 1920," snapped the clerk, still ruffled, "People vs. Passepartout."

"Exactly. Joseph Passepartout. And where did the inventor go?"

"To the Sanitorium Sens Unique, Dr. Balthazar Truc, Luneville-sur-Seine," was the prompt answer.

"That's just the place for Monsieur Lazare. For observation and rest. Just send your cable, my dear, and leave the rest to me. I've seldom, in the course of more decades of practice than I care to admit, had a more charming or intelligent client. Good day."

So it was, that after much deft maneuvering on the part of Maitre Ronron, with the aid of the minister of justice, who, while politically of another camp, was at one with the maitre on the subject of dominoes, a well-cushioned limousine drove up to the prefecture. Lazare, comparatively calm because Miriam was at his side, was led from his cell and started out, at a rate of speed appropriate for strained nerves, for Luneville-sur-Seine. Maitre Ronron, who had seen the answer to Miriam's cable to Hugo Weiss, the philanthropist, which cordial message had ended with the words "Spare no expense," rode with them as far as the gates of Paris, humming gaily an old French tune:

> *Oh! Le bon siècle, mes frères,*
> *Que le siècle ou nous vivons!*
> *On ne craint plus les carrières*
> *Pour quelques opinions.**

As the limousine rolled out of sight, beyond the Porte de Neuilly, Maitre Ronron repeated "Spare no expense,"

* Oh, what a good century, my brothers,
Is the one in which we live.
No longer we dread the rock pile
On account of a few opinions.

and added: "A beautiful and expressive phrase for such a harsh language as English. I have never had similar instructions from a client in fifty years at the bar. But then . . . Americans."

13

A Miraculous Draft of Calling Cards

THE crew of the *Deuxieme Pays,* when the launch pulled up near the Pont Royal, was more than mildly astonished to see waiting for them a tall husky man with huge hands, in coalheaver's garb, a gaily colored Volga boatman humming Russian songs, and a prosperous-looking American with rimless glasses who surveyed the boat, the river and the whole scene doubtfully. Hjalmar, the coalheaver, had thought it best not to change to their ordinary clothes, considering that violent action was afoot, but had suggested to his companions that they roll their duds into a bundle which could be stowed away in the cabin for future use if necessary.

The big painter, having convinced the boat crew of his authority, notwithstanding his disguise, dismissed the regular boatmen and at once took charge. He was convinced that the St. Julien Rollers had not hidden their victim or victims within the city limits, so Parisians who were strolling along the *quais* in anticipation of the *aperitif* hour were astonished by the spectacle of a speed boat rushing down stream at thirty-five miles an hour, weaving recklessly in and out between tugs, scows, barges and pleasure craft and leaving a tempestuous wake that sent its waves splashing noisily against the ancient walls and bridge abutments. The *Deuxieme Pays* ducked around the Ile du Cygne (Swan Island), passed the stark rows of factory chimneys at Suresnes and was approaching St. Germain, to the delight of bathers and pleasure seekers in canoes and rowboats who liked being jounced by the waves.

As soon as he had left behind the river resorts on the outskirts of Paris, Hjalmar throttled down the engine and swept both shores with practiced eye.

"He said to inquire along the way," said Kvek, hopefully, as a riverside café swept into view when they rounded a bend.

The big Norwegian, who also was thirsty, steered the craft to the bank, where its splutter caused a team of plow horses to forget their day of toil and stand on their hind legs. The landscape, with trees clustered and drooping by the riverside, long straight roads with double files of poplars stretching toward the hills in the distance, dark patches of alfalfa, fields of ripening grain, caused Lvov Kvek to gasp with admiration and relief. He had liked New York and had been hospitably received there, but the hunger he had developed for trees and green fields was appeased by his nearness to the French countryside. Tom Jackson, on the other hand, was hankering for solid city pavements, and when it was suggested by his companions that he get up from his bunk and have a drink, he turned the color of spread Roquefort cheese and threatened his shipmates with bodily harm.

The proprietor of the café recognized Hjalmar, who was known all up and down the river because of his frequent trips on barges, but could tell him nothing strange or interesting. At the next five stops the success of the investigators was equally barren. Just upstream from Mantes, however, was moored an ungainly barge in need of paint which was labeled "The Poor but Honest" *(Le Pauvre, Neammoins Honnête)* on which Hjalmar had made the trip from Paris to Havre more than once, because of his fondness for old Matthieu, the owner, his wife, and particularly his daughter Marie who was at the tiller. The barge was loaded with asphalt, in sacks, and Matthieu told them that on Sunday, two days before *The Pansy* was stolen, a car with a Paris number had driven alongside and a dark man dressed in brown, with heavy eyebrows, had climbed awkwardly up the ladder to the deck and had purchased two sacks of asphalt, at a price old Matthieu had mentioned only as a ceiling for bargaining. In order that the well-dressed customer might avoid soiling his clothes, Matthieu had carried the two sacks to the automobile and placed them in the back, where a rumble seat had evidently been removed to make room for a baggage compartment. Furthermore, a bottle-green launch about fifteen feet long, with a coffin-shaped cabin, black oil-cloth cushions and a crooked rudder, had hove to at seven in the morning, only the day before, and a city chap, wearing a cap and a scarf around his neck, but no sash to indicate that he was a workman, had asked Matthieu where, if anywhere in the vicinity, one could buy a can of gasolene. The bargeman had directed them to a wayside filling station not five hundred yards away, after trying to convince the launchful of suspicious-looking characters that in Mantes, just downstream, they could buy all the gasolene they wanted at the *quai*.

"That's the gang we're looking for," Hjalmar said. His problem had been simplified. Instead of a blanket order to gather information, he now had a definite aim, to find the bottle-green launch.

"They can't eat the damn thing," he reflected, but he knew that from Mantes to the sea the Seine was fed by innumerable creeks and rivulets concealed by saplings, willows and high marsh grasses and that several canals afforded detours which complicated his task. There was a clear stretch of river before them, however, so Hjalmar started off at full speed. The *Deuxieme Pays* cut through the water, bow rising, stern almost submerged and above the groans of Tom Jackson, Hjalmar thought he detected a knocking, so he lashed the helm and hopped forward to investigate. He was still tinkering with the engine when the launch passed Luneville.

Lvov Kvek, who was acting as lookout in the bow, saw at that moment rippling on the river's surface a small school of what appeared to be calling cards, and scooping up one he read the words: "K. Parker Seldon." Without hesitation he dove into the current, and, expecting that his shipmates would see him and stop the launch, he struck out for the shore with his powerful Caucasian crawl. Unfortunately, Tom Jackson just then was suffering a spasm of what he insisted was indigestion and Hjalmar had his ear close to the roaring engine, which was performing in a way that would have satisfied many a less critical master. It was only when, after leaping back to the tiller to negotiate a sharp bend, he noticed Kvek was not in the bow. He assumed that the wine aboard the "Poor but Honest" had made the Russian drowsy and that Lvov had gone below for a snooze.

Homer Evans, at the moment when Kvek quit the *Deuxieme Pays,* was sitting on the running board of the chief of detectives' limousine while Melchisadek was struggling with the second flat tire that had delayed them. Reluctantly, Homer had to give up the idea of reaching Luneville ahead of Hjalmar and the launch. In trying to keep watch of the river traffic, he had got into dead end roads several times and one of them, the one on which the limousine was resting with a list to starboard, had been sprinkled with horseshoe nails. Nevertheless, Evans was not depressed. He had been thinking hard since he had set out from the Hotel Murphy et du Danube Bleu and had reached some definite conclusions.

The Singe and his gang had got Frémont, entirely un-according to plan, and didn't know what to do with him. That to Evans was as clear as day. The chief of detectives, who had been slugged by mistake, probably in the dark, was not an asset to the Rollers, but a liability.

"If I can make a trade . . . if by agreeing to take back Frémont, no questions asked, I can also get Professor de la Poussière, or at least ensure his safety, I shall have made a fair start on this case," Homer said to himself. "After that, with Frémont directing the police, we can start looking for the murderer of the Marquis de la Rose d'Antan."

A black cat more than two feet long glared at Homer and Melchisadek from a clump of rushes, then stepped malevolently across the road in front of them. Mel-

182

chisadek, who had not liked the omens before, tried in vain to keep his knees from knocking together.

"Are you sure, Mr. Evans, that you ought to go to Luneville? You won't find no million-dollar pictures down there. They used calendars to put up on the walls," Melchisadek said.

"Come on. There's no time to lose," said Evans.

The chauffeur sighed, and they started off again. Fifteen minutes of hard going, through dust and ruts, brought them to a paved road on which was a sign: Luneville, 1 kl.

"Drive in, and stop at the paint store," Evans said.

"You won't find no paintings . . ." the nervous chauffeur began, but he checked himself and tried to mind his own business. Mr. Evans got men into tight places, but contrived to get them out again, was the assurance he tried to dish out to himself. In the central square of Luneville stood a shop with a brightly striped awning and pillars painted green and yellow. It was the local paint shop, all right, and Melchisadek pulled up in front of it, expecting at the very least a shower of machine-gun bullets. Instead of that, a pleasant old man wearing a smock and artist's flowing tie came toward them from a near-by saloon.

"Good afternoon," Evans said, in his most winning manner. He had forgotten again that he was dressed as an Apache and, until he recalled that unfortunate fact, was at a loss to understand the misgivings reflected in the paint dealer's face.

"Have you any quick-drying paint?" Evans asked.

The paint man looked relieved but Melchisadek's face

fell. He liked the limousine as it was, a shiny dignified black.

"For autos?" the paint dealer asked.

"No. Boats," Evans said. "Which color dries quickest?"

"You know, monsieur, you're the second man from Paris who's asked me that. Just yesterday a fellow came in, dressed as you are, and he wanted some boat paint too. 'What color gets dry quickest?' the fellow asked me."

"And what did you tell him?" Evans inquired.

" 'Terre verte. Earth green,' I said. But he didn't want green. He took Indian red. That dries almost as quick, but if you slap in a lot of drier it doesn't look as well."

Homer bought two cans, one green, one red. The paint man, still puzzled, and not without reason, watched his customer drive away and scratched his head. Evans directed Melchisadek to leave the car in the shade of a tree just off the lane that led to the river.

"Can you swim?" Evans asked.

"I never had to," Melchisadek answered. "See here, Mr. Evans, do you think sho'nuff we'll find the Chief in a town like this? He's never been in swimmin' since I've known him."

"You'll see the Chief before dinner time," Evans said.

He walked along the bank until he saw a sign "Boats for Rent" and hired a small flat skiff and some fishing tackle. Melchisadek brightened still more. Above all things he loved to fish at twilight and had not had a chance to do so since the days of the A. E. F. Smiling, Homer took the oars and handed the tackle and bait to the chauffeur. They idled along, downstream, passing boathouse after boathouse and any number of motorboats, sailboats and rowboats moored to posts along the banks. Evans' face showed disappointment. Not one of the shelters or crafts he saw had any discernible marks upon them of the St. Julien Rollers. At last, to Melchisadek's surprise, Homer opened the can of red paint and emptied the contents into the river.

"That won't do no good to the fish, Mr. Evans," the chauffeur said. He had already caught four *goujons* and his fisherman's instincts were thoroughly aroused. At that, Evans tossed in the empty can and watched it carefully. It floated a few feet, then filled, capsized and sank to the bottom, where it caught, now and then, a stray beam of the setting sun and flashed back a wavering reflection.

"No good," said Evans. "The Singe is too bright to leave cans in plain sight. He would have buried them."

Around a bend, and in a sheltered cove, Evans nosed the skiff to the bank, got out, and told Melchisadek to find a good spot for fishing near by and to wait for him. The Negro scarcely heard him, so intent he was in fondling the four small fish he had.

"Ah, the simple candid mind," said Homer to himself, wistfully. "The spirit akin to nature, in tune with its logic, unaware of complications. Enjoy yourself, my friend. I, less fortunate, must root and grub for hidden cans."

Behind the boathouses along the shore was a growth of scrub alders and, among them, cat-o'-nine-tails and rushes. Near by, on a light rise of ground stood a deserted blacksmith's shop. Evans crawled on his hands and knees, for once thankful he was wearing someone else's trousers, and gasped with pleasure when he saw, on some leaves

185

of a bush, two small spots of Indian red. It was not long before he had also found some loose earth, which he explored with his jack-knife and was rewarded by uncovering three empty cans, with labels identical with that he had thrown into the river.

"But where is the boat?" he asked himself. From a point as near as he could approach without exposing himself, it did not appear that the craft could have been dragged into the shop. There were no signs of Rollers, no trodden grasses, except in the rear. Aware that darkness would soon be upon him, he worked his way in the upstream direction into the thicket and soon found some swampy land with a small creek connecting with the Seine and concealed by such a rank growth of plants that from the river it was practically invisible. There, on its side in only three or four inches of water, lay a motorboat freshly painted Indian red and covered with branches.

That was enough for Evans. Straightening himself and brushing off his damp knees as best he could, he walked back to the rear of the blacksmith's shop and pounded on the door. There was no answer, but faint slits of light indicated that someone was inside.

"I want to see The Singe," he said, loudly. "Open up. I've got news from Godo."

There was no answer, but Homer thought he heard a muffled consultation.

"Who are you?" someone asked gruffly, from inside, after a tense pause.

"I'll tell that to The Singe," Homer said. "Do you want everyone in town to hear us talking?"

The door creaked, then opened a crack, and a pair of

wary eyes looked out from the dimness. Abruptly the door closed again, there was more muttering, then someone said, "Come in."

As he entered, Evans was tackled from three directions. One gangster dived at his legs, another tried to pin his arms, a third raised a sock stuffed with sand. Homer made no resistance.

"What the hell?" he asked calmly. "You're three against one. Why don't you hear what I've got to say? Then do what you like, you damn fools. I've got news, I tell you."

"What news?" asked the man who had hold of Homer's arms, and who smelled of Eau de Quinine.

"I'm telling it to The Singe. Not you mugs," said Evans, relieved that the sock had been slipped back in its owner's pocket.

"You'll tell us, all right, if we get to work on you," said the man at his legs, loosening his grip. That was his mistake. With his knee, Evans flopped him over while he caught the heads of the other pair and banged them, face foremost, together. When the trio began to recover, Homer had them covered with his automatic and their hands went reluctantly upward.

"Now, you fatheads. Do I see The Singe, or don't I? I'm going to let one of you go, and if he doesn't come back with the man I want in five minutes, the other two get plugged. Understand? You can settle it between yourselves who goes and who stays, but quick. For that you get one minute," Evans said, narrowing his eyes.

For three men who had their hands up, the gangsters put up a wonderful argument. No two of them, it appeared, were willing to take a chance on the third.

"All right, you, in the middle there. Get going." Homer said. "Five minutes . . ."

"Have a heart. We can't make it in less than ten," the middle gangster said. The others nodded confirmation.

"I'll make it eight, just to give these guys a break," said Homer, indicating with his gun the pair he had selected to remain. "And time is called right now." With that he kicked a sheet of steel that roared like a gong.

The messenger dived through the doorway and the others tried to plead with Evans to be lenient in the matter of time, and they did succeed in convincing him that The Singe was a good ten minutes' distance from the blacksmith's shop, allowing for a round trip. The relief of the captive pair, when footsteps were heard outside, was so eloquent that Evans could not keep from smiling.

A tall well-built Norman, sturdy and tanned and in early middle age stepped in brusquely. No doubt of it. He was the boss.

"Well?" he asked, his blue eyes cold in the lantern light, his voice steady.

"Thank God, here's a man one can talk sense to," said Evans quite as cool and much more suave.

"Start talking," The Singe said, ignoring completely the gun in Homer's hand.

Evans, not to be outdone, tossed the weapon to the floor between them. "Send these bloody fools away. I'll talk to nobody but you."

"Get going," The Singe said to the three bewildered Rollers and they had not received an order that season that had been as musical to their ears. They simply vanished. No other word is adequate.

"Well?" The Singe said again.

"Listen," Evans said. "You've got the chief of detectives and you don't know what to do with him."

"You talk, and make it fast," The Singe said, noncommittally.

"After all, what can you do with him? You can't bump him off. You can't let him go. Either way, you lose."

"So what?"

"I am offering to take him off your hands, no questions asked."

Even as cool a customer as The Singe could not hide a flicker of interest. "And who are you?"

"A friend of his."

"The dick who sent my pals to Devil's Island," said The Singe, but with little emotion.

"Do they like it down there?" Evans asked. "There must be lots of room."

"You haven't got a thing on me," said The Singe.

"You've only kidnapped the chief of detectives. That's all. What a droll idea. I thought better of you than that," Evans said. "That's one of the few things even you know well that you can't get away with."

The slur on The Singe's judgment was a little more than he could stand. Like other professionals, he took pride in his technique.

"What could I do? The damn fool stumbled in on my boys in the dark. One of them slugged him before he knew who it was. Anyone would have done the same."

"I appreciate that you're not entirely to blame. Your boys are careless. One of them took a shot at me from a treetop. I hope you have cautioned the survivors about trying that again . . . But let's not quarrel. I'm making you a *bona fide* offer to take Frémont off your hands, and give you my word and his that the incident will be closed. I'm not after you, this time. I want at least two other fellows. Now think my proposition over. You've nothing to lose, and much to gain."

The Singe was thinking hard, and there was much intelligence behind his steady eyes. It was apparent that it was not concerned with the brotherhood of man, but neither was it likely to muff a golden opportunity. The Singe was not simple enough to imagine that Evans had suddenly decided to do him a favor. And if Evans wanted Frémont badly enough to risk his life and good looks, he might be willing to raise the ante. Swiftly The Singe whipped into shape a counter proposition and one that would have done credit to a Richelieu.

"I'll tell you what I'll do," he said. "I've got another duffer who's a drug on the market. Never mind who he is, but he's not a crook or anything. And he hasn't been missing so long that it can't be explained by a guy as bright as you seem to be."

Evans nodded, and tried to restrain his laughter. He felt sure The Singe was referring to none other than Professor de la Poussière. But instead of appearing over-anxious Homer resorted to poker tactics, although he despised the game.

"If I'm going to take two, you ought to do something for me," said Homer.

"Go on," said The Singe.

"There's a girl I've taken a fancy to, a kid named

Nicole in the Bal des Vêtements Brulés. Do I get her too?"

The Singe searched his mind a moment, then nodded, and even brightened. "Why, sure," he said. "To tell you the truth, I'm glad she's struck a bit of luck. She never was tough enough for my business."

"You'll send word to the gang? I don't want her to be afraid to go out of doors."

"Say, when I give a girl away, it don't mean maybe. And if she makes you any trouble, just let me know."

"Thanks. I will," said Evans. "Then it's a deal. I'll take Frémont and the other bozo, and for that I get Nicole."

The Singe stepped forward and shook hands. "I don't know what your game is, but I'm not curious. How soon can you take this pair of guys?"

"Right away."

"I'll fetch 'em," The Singe said, and left the shop.

14

As It Was in the Beginning, More or Less

Lvov Kvek stood on the bank of the Seine, a limp card clutched in his hand, and eyed with dismay his dripping Volga boatman's costume. In the waning light of a quiet evening, in a strange locality, he was ruefully aware that it would not do. He must think, and for that purpose, he would have to get out of sight. Near by was an ivy-covered wall, six meters high, which seemed to enclose some sort of an imposing institution. Not far from the wall was a clump of trees. The Russian jumped for a sturdy limb, hauled himself upward and climbed into the thickest of the foliage, from which he could see over the wall and into a number of empty courtyards.

The period of exercise and recreation was short in the Sanitorium Sens Unique, and for the afternoon in question it was over. Dr. Balthazar Truc had found through long experience that if he kept his patients in good physical condition they gave more trouble to the guards, the nurses and himself. And furthermore, a *corpore sano* was more than likely to restore a *mens sana,* which put an end to fees.

Thus it was that Kvek, in a near-by tree and drying slowly, beset with questions as to how he should proceed, saw only the empty courtyards and a dim face or two behind heavily screened windows. He had swallowed a quantity of river water but that had not slaked his thirst. Neither did the words "K. Parker Seldon" on the card he had retrieved serve to make his forced inaction more bearable. His surprise and joy cannot be over-estimated when he saw, leaning from one of the unscreened windows, a familiar head and set of shapely shoulders. It was only by clutching his own throat tightly with his free hand that he choked off a wild cry of "Sofia Alexandrovna. Sonia, my pigeon. My lost cousin Sonshka."

These were one and the same person, namely Sofia (or Sonia or Sonshka) Alexandrovna Dargomyzshkov, one of his first cousins, whose fate he had not known since she had escaped from Odessa, through Constantinople in 1917.

The sight of her, so radiant and clothed in white, prompted him to cross himself fervently and was nearly instrumental in causing him to fall from his perch in the tree. At once, he saw an objective. To get into communication with Sonia and, after embracing her and weeping, to ask her what she could do for him in the way of procuring suitable clothes.

Now Dr. Truc had taken elaborate precautions against any of his patients getting out of the Sanitorium Sens Unique, but had never found it necessary to guard against outsiders coming in. Working himself perilously from tree to tree, Lvov reached another limb which was only a meter from the wall around the courtyards. Unwrapping his long Volga boatman's sash, he tied one end firmly to the tree and threw the other inside the wall. It was the work of a moment for him to swing over to the wall and descend to within ten feet of the ground. From there he jumped down.

Sofia Alexandrovna was about to let out a shriek when she recognized her cousin Lvov, and nearly swooned with joy. She ran down the stairs, upsetting an attendant with a tray, and opening the door, beckoned Kvek to enter. Inside, they hastily wept and embraced and she led him through an unfrequented corridor and into her room. There they repeated with less haste and more fervor their embrace of reunion and mingled their tears with a torrent of whispered words. Eventually they got to the point where Lvov thought it best to explain his attire and his presence in the neighboring tree. At his mention of K. Parker Seldon and the sight of the damp calling card, Sofia's tear-stained face lighted up with fresh joy. By her woman's intuition, rather than any resemblance between the American business man described by Lvov and the game little party who had pummeled the doctor, the nurse arrived at a swift conclusion. She was sure that the new patient was the man her cousin sought.

Sofia Alexandrovna was impulsive, but she had a good head on her shoulders and immediately emphasized the need for caution. The man who tackled doctors and made nondescript noises had, she had learned from the records, been committed to Dr. Truc's care by a Paris official. The doctor, she knew, had never been known to slip up on the legal phases of his practice. To Lvov's appeal for clothes she was at loss for a reply. There were no men except the attendants who were of her cousin's stature. Then she thought of Gus. Gus would be on duty in a ward quite distant from his sleeping quarters, she knew. Hastily she left Kvek alone and in a few minutes returned with an outfit that, while it was not much of an improvement on the togs Lvov already had, was less conspicuous. Sofia knew that the doctor was short of male huskies. The spring and early summer are the seasons most often chosen by unfortunates to lose their minds and cut loose from drab reality. So the sanitorium had several new patients. Rapidly the cousin decided that Lvov should make his way outside, then present himself for employment and give Sofia as a reference. That would bring them together in a plausible way and obtain for Kvek the run of the institution.

A half hour later, Kvek, with certain pardonable misgivings, wearing Gus's clothes, pressed the bell at the outside gate and was ushered into the presence of Dr. Balthazar Truc, for whom the Russian felt an instantaneous aversion that almost amounted to a mania. The doctor, bruised and battered, had been thinking that he must put Gus in a ward where the patients were not so spry. He mistook Kvek's black looks for wholesome ferocity and hired him on the spot.

"I can give you as a reference my cousin, Sofia Dargomyzshkov," Lvov said.

"Never mind references. Are you solid and strong?"

For answer, Lvov picked up a thick sheaf of index cards and tore the pack as if it were tissue paper.

"Those cards cost six francs fifty," said the doctor, angrily. "That will be deducted from your first week's pay." He was impressed, nonetheless, and promised himself that the obstreperous American, who was booked as S-K. Chaudron, nationality unknown, would promptly be discouraged from further demonstrations of dissatisfaction such as the one that had spoiled the doctor's morning and had lost for him at least three of the American Express checks.

It was just then that Hjalmar, roaring a ballad called "Samuel Hall," and chagrined that he had so little to show for his voyage downstream, caught sight of the tower of Rouen and decided that it was time to awaken his companions.

"Where's Kvek?" he asked Tom Jackson, when the reporter sat up, reaching for his glasses.

"Oh, he must be around somewhere," the reporter said.

"That's what I thought, but he isn't," said Hjalmar, making a dash for the tiller to avoid a snag.

The big painter was alarmed at once, and so was Jackson as soon as he had roused himself enough to feel any emotion at all. In a panic, Hjalmar shoved over the tiller and the *Deuxieme Pays* nearly snapped off her rudder in making a sharp U turn.

In the blacksmith's shop, on the outskirts of Luneville, Homer Evans was waiting in the gathering darkness for the delivery of The Singe's two prisoners, and he didn't have long to wait. A nondescript car drove down the lane, without lights and turned in between two clumps of alders. The Singe got out and was followed by a stocky irate man who was protesting and resisting as best he could, considering that he was blindfolded, bound and gagged.

"Frémont, by God. And in the vilest of tempers," Evans chuckled.

The struggling Chief was followed by a man of more

196

phlegmatic temperament, a tall stoop-shouldered fellow who was hoodwinked and gagged in a perfunctory way and whose hands were bound behind him with his own flowing tie. The Singe, with skill and an instinctive gentleness, propelled the pair to the doorway of the blacksmith's shop and eased them in, and with a finger on his lips requested Evans to keep silent.

Before The Singe turned to go, he handed Homer a scrawled sheet of notepaper, then returned to the car with his firm athletic stride, waved his hand, and the chauffeur, who had kept the engine running, released the clutch and drove away. Evans, without saying a word, removed the gag from the professor's mouth, whisked off his blindfold and untied his hands.

"Good evening, sir," the professor said, politely, looking around him in a bewildered way. He knew all about gold and copper, those metals having been used freely in ancient Egypt, but iron work was a closed book to him, so he squinted uneasily at the bellows and the forge.

"Professor de la Poussière, I believe," said Evans, shaking hands. At the sound of Evans' voice, the trussed-up chief of detectives began a sort of rigadoon and had Homer not caught him and steadied him, would have stumbled headlong into the cinders. Rapidly Evans snatched off the blindfold, took the gag from Frémont's mouth and cut the cords from his ankles and wrists.

The chief of detectives was anything but proud of himself. His thanks to Evans he mumbled as graciously as he could, then he stared at the tall professor who was peering up the chimney of the forge and reaching for another pair of spectacles.

"Have you two met?" Evans asked, for it was evident that The Singe had kept his prisoners separate and that Frémont did not know who his companion in the back seat of the delivery car had been. In fact, the Chief had never heard of de la Poussière, and knew nothing of the developments in the case beyond the mere theft of *The Pansy* and the dressing down he had received at the hands of the newspaper men. Frémont's mind, in fact, was torn between two impulses. One had to do with phoning Hydrangea to inform her that he was safe, the second was to take up the trail and get even with the gang who had sandbagged and kidnapped him in the midst of an important investigation.

"Not so fast," Evans said, as the Chief hit for the door. "There's much for you to hear and assimilate before you barge into any more dens. By the way, perhaps first you'll tell me how you contrived to get yourself removed from our midst?"

"Have you found that insufferable painting?" counter-questioned the Chief, who was not cooling off to any noticeable degree.

"Oh, the painting," Homer said. "I'd almost let the painting slip my mind. Time has not been standing still while you were the guest of the Rollers, you know."

"Must we stand here and talk? Those crooks will all get away," said the Chief.

"A heart to heart talk is often helpful," Evans replied. "Besides I took the liberty of promising, in your name, that the little incident of your forcible removal would be overlooked. Wiped from the slate of our memory, in fact. And, if it makes you feel better, I don't mind saying that your impromptu adventure has helped, no end, in unraveling this tangle of iniquities. Now please calm yourself, my friend, and tell me about your late indiscretions, which have turned out so luckily for all concerned."

Frémont's face had turned a deep shade of old rose and was showing some purple streaks and patches. He reached for a horseshoe, but the winning smile on Homer's face recalled him to his senses and he was forced to struggle with a rueful grin himself. He recounted what he had seen from Hydrangea's window and the hunch that had caused him to follow the young man with the tight coat and cap. When he got as far as the blood stains in the *place* Dauphine, he was surprised to see Evans nod with satisfaction. Succinctly the Chief wound up with the tale of the taxi ride, his entrance into the Bal des Vêtements Brulés, and his subsequent awakening in a motorboat.

Homer, in turn, told the Chief about his scrutiny of the mummies in the Egyptian room of the Louvre, and that brought the professor to his side in an instant.

"The fourth from the left. Ha, ha! The fourth from the left, you say. Ho, ho! Excuse me, gentlemen," and holding his sides the savant sank down on an anvil and laughed so heartily that the Chief began spluttering and turning purple again.

"What is there to laugh about?" he demanded.

"The fourth from the left was Tout-or-Nada," said the professor, between gasps. "Oh, dear me. Bless my soul." And he clutched his tired ribs again.

"I noticed that your amusing friend, Tout-or-Nada, was wrapped in a kind of linen that was much inferior to that of his social equals all around him," Evans went on.

"Oh, no. The best was none too good for him," said de la Poussière.

"Hear me out, I beg of you, gentlemen," said Evans, earnestly.

At that, his hearers struck an average between the professor's merriment and the Chief's indignation. The latter, however, could not refrain from asking what Egyptian mummies had to do with a Watteau painting less than a foot square.

"That's the point," Homer said. "I'm glad you are showing an intelligent interest, at last. According to the emergency plans worked out in advance by the guards in the Louvre, an alarm coming from the Hall of Pills would remove both guards from the Egyptian room and the rooms adjoining." He sketched rapidly a plan of the rooms and stairways. "You see," he continued. "That would give any evil-minded visitors in the Egyptian room a perfect avenue of escape toward the west. And since the painting was and is completely unsalable, little else could be accomplished by stealing it and by the resultant hue and cry. Do I make myself clear?"

"Go on," urged the Chief, now thoroughly alert.

"I simply examined the room in question in the hope of finding some suspicious circumstance. And all I found, that did not seem to be in order, was a cheap modern wrapping on what was supposed to be an ancient pharaoh. I snipped off a sample of the bandages from Tout-or-Nada and another chap, the second from the left . . ."

"Ah, yes. Suph, or Chefre, if you prefer," murmured the professor.

The look on the Chief's honest face seemed to indicate that Suph or Chefre were all the same to him.

"With my samples," Evans continued, "I went to Dr. Hyacinthe Toudoux and asked him who was tops on Egyptian questions." Homer bowed to Professor de la Poussière. "The doctor was kind enough to refer me to you," he said.

"Too generous," the professor said, and bowed. The Chief nearly twisted off his neck in turning from one to the other.

"I won't bore you with details," Evans said. "I walked across the *place* Dauphine to find the professor and was informed by his charming wife that he had not been home since early morning."

"I trust Hélene was not unduly anxious," de la Poussière said.

"We reassured her. Miriam . . . Miss Leonard was with me. We returned to the *place* Dauphine, disappointed at not finding you in, and some unlucky man in one of the trees took a shot at me, missing by only the narrowest margin." He turned to the Chief. "You know how Miss Leonard is. She shot the fellow dead and he crashed to the pavement. That accounts for your bloodstains, and the interest of your young chap with the cap."

"The devil," said the Chief.

"Why, that's strange," remarked the professor. "I've walked through the *place* at all hours of the night for forty years, and never have been molested."

"I must get on with my story," said Evans. "Dr. Toudoux, although annoyed because his studies had been interrupted by the corpse from the tree, gave me a second-string Egyptian expert, a charming man named Lazare, who stuffs animals by day and roots in Egyptology at night. Miss Leonard and I found Lazare, just after breakfast time . . ."

"You couldn't have done better," murmured de la Poussière.

"Lazare was in a capital mood, just having received your letter about Tout-or-Nada, I presume," Homer said to the professor, who nodded. "He told me promptly that skulduggery was afoot. Tout-or-Nada's wrapping was not Egyptian but Alsatian and had been manufactured thousands of years after Tout had died. You see, Frémont, that is like finding the body of Vercingetorix in Sascha Guitry's clothes."

"That ham would do anything for publicity," Frémont said.

"Publicity was Tout-or-Nada's longest suit," interposed the professor.

Evans took the floor again. "Of course, an examination of the mummy who reposed fourth from the left was in order, and Lazare was the man to conduct it. Unfortunately, our case at that point was complicated further. A middle-sized business man, K. Parker Seldon, of the American Jar and Bottle Corporation . . ."

"I shall lose my mind," said Frémont, clutching his forehead. "Egyptians are bad enough. Couldn't you spare me the American?"

"Mr. Seldon," Evans continued severely, "arrived in Paris on the evening of the theft, accompanied by our old friend, Lvov Kvek."

"Oh, vodka! Whiskey! Stuffed cold fish! Rioting in Montparnasse," the chief of detectives groaned.

"Mr. Seldon," Evans began again, "was the bearer of a message from Hugo Weiss to Professor de la Poussière." The professor bowed again. "And the message was carved on sandstone in ancient Egyptian characters, first dynasty, I believe."

"Not only I, but everyone has gone crazy," sighed the Chief.

"Seldon disappeared, but we found the message. About that time our chief of detectives left us to carry on alone. I can't tell you how we missed him, and how the journalists seemed to resent his absence."

The Chief buried his face in his hands and suffered.

"I did the best I could without official support," Evans went on. "I took the sandstone tablet to Lazare and learned that it was a warning and a request addressed to the professor here. Weiss had got wind of a proposed sale of Egyptian relics to a rival collector and urged the professor to investigate secretly and report.

"Well, with Sergeant Schlumberger as our only salaried prop, I took Lazare, Miss Leonard and our Montparnasse friends who did us such good service last year, Messrs. Kvek, Hjalmar Jansen and Tom Jackson the reporter, to the Louvre. In the long corridor filled with statues and empty sarcophagi, just outside the Babylonian and Egyptian rooms, I paused to give last-minute instructions, sort of a pep talk, you know. There I noticed that a sarcophagus had been tampered with. Jansen and Kvek lifted off the lid and inside was the mummy of Tout-or-Nada wrapped in the finest Egyptian linen of his day.

"Lazare and I started on the hot foot for the Egyptian room and in the mummy case belonging to Tout-or-Nada we found the dead body of the Marquis de la Rose

203

d'Antan, swathed and camouflaged by the tell-tale Alsatian grave clothes."

"Impossible! Not the Minister of Beaux Arts," said Frémont, in horror.

"If there had to be a sacrifice, the choice was not bad," the professor said. "The Marquis, an old pupil of mine, was not the man to direct the Ministry of Beaux Arts. I trust that his successor . . ."

"I've got to get back to Paris. I'm disgraced. Ruined. Done for," Frémont cried.

"Patience, Chief. You have covered yourself with glory. You will have Paris at your feet again, if only you'll develop a bit of poise. I have had your interests at heart and have not been idle an instant. Instead of probing the demise of the late Marquis, or chasing stray Watteaus, I bent my efforts toward finding you, with success, you must admit. No one except us and The Singe's cohorts knows you have been kidnapped. Posterity will marvel at how you have tracked down Professor de la Poussière and rescued him in a deserted blacksmith shop. Tell the press that presently you will also produce K. Parker Seldon, the missing American; the slayers of the Marquis; and the precious little picture. By the way, we should all have a look at the newspapers. Let's amble up to Luneville center, telephone the anxious women, snatch a bite to eat, lay plans for the future and read what the journalists, in the absence of facts, have turned out in the way of fiction and comment."

Frémont sighed, and shamefacedly extended his hand. "I shall have you to thank, my inscrutable friend, if I escape humiliation and my dependents are not reduced to begging in the streets. There are times when I think my old father was right, and that I should have carried on his humble tobacco shop, as he counseled. There I should not have been continually in the public eye, not called upon to be at once a clairvoyant and a shelf of encyclopedias. The Marquis de la Rose d'Antan! Egyptians! Pansies! American bottle chairmen! Ah, well. Lead me by the hand, as if I were a wayward little child. But cover me with false glories no more. I cannot live up to them. This time, dear friend, the credit shall go to you . . . No. Don't protest. Your genius will be proclaimed."

"In that case, you will have to excuse me. I shall abandon the inquiry," said Evans, firmly, and the Chief was obliged, reluctantly, to yield.

"One thing I haven't made clear," Homer continued. "The Singe, who leads the reorganized St. Julien Rollers, is a fine upstanding man. I like him, and in this case he's not to be badgered. You see, I only agreed to take you back, friend Frémont, on certain conditions, and you are the last man to suggest that an honorable bargain should not be fulfilled."

"As you say," said Frémont, meekly, and followed Evans to the river bank.

"I brought along your chauffeur and the car, for your convenience," said Evans, indicating Melchisadek, who had anchored the skiff to a snag and with the aid of his powerful flashlight had just succeeded in catching an eighteen-inch *lotte*. The scene that ensued was touching indeed, and gave such proof of mutual affection and esteem between master and man that the professor wiped a tear from his eye.

"It was often thus in ancient Egypt," he said. "The

205

paintings that remain contain many whips, mostly for decorative purposes. The writings, if only they could be generally read, would do much to correct the impression of Egyptian brutality created by the purely visual arts. The slaves, for the most part, were quite as well off, or better, in the reign of Tout-or-Nada, than workers are today. They worked leisurely, and man-power was not stinted when heavy tasks had to be performed. Had a king like Mykeri or Shepseskef tried to institute a modern speed-up, or turned his subjects loose by tens of thousands to starve in the rainy season, his kingdom would have crashed about his ears."

"Which is precisely what is occurring today in the industrial world," said Evans.

"Indeed," said the professor, in astonishment. "Is that so? How logical. I cannot thank you enough for calling that to my attention. I shall read up on the matter without delay."

15

The Crossing of Trails in a Madhouse

In the neat and tidy bedroom of his cousin, Sofia Alexandrovna, Lvov Kvek sat in a rocking chair. He was still wearing Gus's clothes and he was very hungry, but he had a job and prospects of interviewing K. Parker Seldon later in the evening. Since he was not to begin active duty until after dinner time, Sofia advised him to walk the short distance to the town and stow away as much good food as he could. It seems that Dr. Truc fed his employees badly and his patients much worse.

They heard a light tap on the door.

"May I come in?" inquired a voice, softly modulated and of pleasing mezzo quality.

"Of course," answered Sofia, rising.

The door opened timidly and Kvek saw a tall gray-haired woman in a dress that, although worn and old-fashioned, carried with it an air of dignity.

"Excuse me, Mademoiselle Sonia. I didn't know you had a caller," the woman said, and was about to withdraw.

"My dear Marchioness," said the nurse, putting an arm around the other's waist. "Come in and share my joy. I have found today my long-lost cousin, Lvov, who used to pull my sled for miles in the streets of old Moscow. My childhood playmate . . ."

"But I'm sure I shall be *de trop*. Another time, my dear. Perhaps this afternoon. My nerves have been troubling me . . . Oh, nothing. Just the uneasiness that comes with the fragrance of the fields and the warm summer sunshine. I am French, you know, and not like you full-blooded Russians. The very mention of miles in the snow has made me shiver."

Lvov Kvek was a picture of sympathetic courtesy. "There was sunshine in Russia, too, madame, in the days of the Little Father," he said, with feeling. "Ah, Sonia, the meadows, the wasps, the hayfields."

His impetuous cousin threw her arms around his neck and when she released Lvov, their caller had stolen away in a manner that would make an Arab sound like a tank by comparison.

"She's been locked up here five years," said Sonia, indignantly.

"Don't tell me she's a patient," said Kvek. "Why, she's saner than I am."

"Much saner, little dove," Sonia agreed. "But only just lately the doctor has allowed her a little liberty."

"Who is she? You addressed her as the Marchioness?"

"The Marchioness de la Rose d'Antan," Sofia said.

"My God. Then she's the widow of that mummy we found in the Louvre."

"I think the news of her husband's death improved her condition. He was responsible for her having been sent here. I'm sure, now he's out of the way, that she hopes to regain her freedom."

"The devil," said Kvek. "Why, this place is filled with victims. Just outside the doctor's doorway I was braced by a chap named Passepartout, an inventor, who said, 'They think I'm crazy, but I'm not.' "

"That's one of the few who really is off his rocker," Sonia said. "I advise you to keep an eye on him."

While the two impetuous cousins were enjoying their fortunate reunion, Homer Evans, with the chastened Frémont on his left and Professor de la Poussière on his right, was finishing off a very decent meal in the Restaurant Sérieux, just across the square from the Luneville town hall.

"You won't forget about *The Pansy?*" asked Frémont anxiously, for the conversation had dealt largely with matters dating far back of the time when all Gaul was divided into three parts.

Evans, appreciating his uneasiness, smiled. "I promise again, to find your little painting, once the murder of the Marquis has been solved. That shall be my last act before I retire forever from detective work. From that time onward I shall devote myself to contemplation."

"And study," added Professor de la Poussière, who had been enchanted to find a man who listened so attentively when ancient Egypt was discussed.

It was then that Evans took the opportunity of telling the professor about K. Parker Seldon and the message carved on sandstone he had brought from Hugo Weiss. When, however, Homer scrawled from memory on a sheet of notepaper the hieroglyphics in question and explained their meaning, the chief of detectives groaned.

"I telephoned Weiss today," Homer said to the professor, "and learned that a sale is afoot, involving the mummy of a king called Neferkesokar."

"The twin brother of Tout-or-Nada," the professor murmured. "But no one can sell his mummy, which consists only of a shin bone and a fragment of skull. For the existence and the whereabouts of those relics are known only to me and a trusted family of natives on the vastness of the upper Nile. There must be some mistake."

"An American museum has been offered the mummy of Neferkesokar in perfect condition," insisted Evans.

"I have seen with my own eyes, on my last expedition, his plundered pyramid and the only two of his bones remaining," said Professor de la Poussière.

The chief of detectives began to roll his eyes, clasp his forehead, extend his palms to heaven and give other symptoms of extreme agitation. "But the painting? The Marquis? The American business man? Who cares if some American has bought the carcass of Julius Caesar, or has made a bid for the whole French Pantheon? For the sake of my sanity, if for no better reason, let's get down to work. The theft, the murder, the abduction. Take your choice!"

"The cases are all related," Evans said, "and are bound up closely with the Pharaohs Tout-or-Nada and his twin brother, Neferkesokar. I'll demonstrate that without delay."

"I should remind you, perhaps," the professor began, "that for many years the mummy of Tout-or-Nada remained unidentified in the Louvre. The king's name was not known, and no record had been found of his reign. Egyptologists had assumed that Neferkesokar held the throne from 2933 to 2926 B.C. And those seven years were completely blank in Egyptian history.

"Last year, when I was exploring near Sokencor, I found a pyramid from which a pharaoh's mummy and his jewels had been removed soon after his burial. Imagine my delight when I noticed that the designs painted on the mortuary chamber corresponded exactly with the decorations on the casket of the unknown mummy in the Louvre. I will not bore you with needless details, but my investigations revealed that the unknown's name was Tout-or-Nada, that he was Neferkesokar's twin brother and that he had reigned for two months and a half, from December 2933, until sometime in February, 2932.

"The fact that Tout-or-Nada was born a minute in advance of Neferkesokar made the former the heir to the throne their father, the bastard king Seudi, had usurped. This fact caused Neferkesokar to hate his brother, and not only did he have him murdered but he had the remains removed from the pyramid and hidden in a libation priest's burial chamber in the lower kingdom.

"The records of Tout-or-Nada's reign his brother caused to be destroyed, so successfully that Egyptologists for untold centuries did not even know of Tout-or-Nada's existence."

The professor began to laugh. "Neferkesokar's treachery came back to him, with interest. His oldest son, Huthefi Kere, was as vain as his father and when he came to the throne in 2925, he wiped out all records of

Neferkesokar excepting his name. That, for religious reasons, he did not dare to do. It was permissible between brothers, apparently, but not between father and son."

"I can't tell you how much you've helped me," Evans said, rising in his enthusiasm and pacing the room, which was empty of diners except for the three who were in conference.

"Disgrace and exposure," Frémont moaned. "Hydrangea dark beauty, how shall I nourish and pamper you when bereft of my monthly pay?"

Evans was thoroughly aroused, as always when confronted by intellectual problems. "Professor," he asked, "how long ago did you publish your findings, the results of your exploration at Sokencor?"

"I haven't published them, as yet. I've been getting my report in shape," the professor answered.

"You haven't confided them to anyone?"

"Lazare, of course. He's worked on my notes as hard as I have."

"You didn't, by any chance, tell the Marquis de la Rose d'Antan?" asked Evans.

"As a matter of fact, I told him last week, perhaps Wednesday or Thursday, that I had identified the mysterious pharaoh of the Louvre. Now that you mention the incident, I seem to remember that the Minister of Beaux Arts was not as pleased as I had expected. But then, he was thoroughly incompetent. At the Sorbonne, he was always at the foot of my class," said Professor de la Poussière.

Homer turned to Frémont, who was continuing his lamentations.

"Are you satisfied now that our cases are linked with Egypt?" he asked. "Hence, loathed melancholy! Reflect! A few days after our friend, the professor, tells the late Marquis about his discoveries, the professor is kidnapped . . ."

"And the Marquis is killed," said Frémont, whose lethargy left him in an instant. "If the Rollers did one job, of course they did the other."

"Not so fast," objected Homer. "If the estimable Singe had been so foolish as to kill the Marquis, why would he have taken the trouble to embalm him and hide him in the Louvre? No, my friend! We've already forgiven The Singe for having borrowed you and the professor. We can't pin the murder on him, not by any stretch of the imagination."

"Then who killed the fathead and stuffed him to the gills with asphalt? There's no likelihood that he committed suicide, you'll have to admit," the Chief said, testily.

"Just now, I'm absorbed by another question," said Evans. "I've got to figure out why, on Tuesday morning, The Singe wanted Professor de la Poussière badly enough to snatch him from the very doorsteps of the national museum, and today, on Thursday, was so keen about giving him away. What happened between those dates to make so careful and efficient an executive change his mind?"

"I'm worse than useless," Frémont said.

A cry of joy was heard at the door, and Lvov Kvek came rushing in and embraced Frémont affectionately. It will be remembered that, although the Chief had seen the Russian, the latter had not seen the Chief since their thrilling adventure upriver more than twelve months before. The greetings having been disposed of, Kvek told Evans excitedly that he had found K. Parker Seldon in the Sanitorium Sens Unique without passport, money, false teeth or suitable clothes. Also that Dr. Truc had been custodian of the Marchioness de la Rose d'Antan for five years, and that the lady was saner than seven-eighths of the clients of the Dôme.

In the midst of his recital, Hjalmar, Tom Jackson and Melchisadek appeared on the scene. The big Norwegian was relieved to find Kvek in safety and was chagrined because there was so little to report. The bottle-green launch, now red, Homer had already found. Hjalmar told him about the odd purchase of two sacks of asphalt from the "Poor but Honest." Instead of appearing disappointed when Hjalmar had finished his story, Evans was enormously interested. Of course, there were many men with heavy eyebrows who wore brown, but the description fitted Hagup Bogigian, or Xerxes, of the firm of Lewson-Phipps & Xerxes, so perfectly that an inquiry was in order.

Quickly Evans decided on the disposition of his forces. The Chief was to return to the prefecture to get the department back into running order and check up on all routine. Hjalmar was instructed to return with Kvek to the Sanitorium Sens Unique and present himself for employment. Dr. Truc was short of husky help, according to Sofia's statement, relayed by Kvek. Inside the institution both men were to use their ears and eyes to best advantage and refrain from arousing the doctor's suspicion until further notice. Particularly they were to watch the doctor and the Marchioness de la Rose d'Antan.

They were also asked to persuade K. Parker Seldon to bear his incarceration a little longer, in the interest of justice and an adequate revenge.

It was not often that Tom Jackson showed pleasurable emotion, but when Homer suggested that the reporter accompany him to the premises of Lewson-Phipps & Xerxes, Tom actually beamed. The prospect of another crack at the Englishman drove off the last vestige of *mal de fleuve,* or river sickness, and started him briskly chewing on a long loaf of bread. Professor de la Poussière, anxious for once to take part in an enterprise of his own era, was assigned to the task of finding Lazare and Miriam, whom Evans supposed to be still in Paris.

As a matter of fact, Miriam and her charge had not yet entered the Sanitorium Sens Unique. It developed that Lazare had never ridden in an automobile and was fearful at every turn that the vehicle would be demolished with all hands. Likewise, he had never been in the country before, having grown accustomed as a lad to the fifth and sixth arrondissements of Paris and his natural timidity having restrained him for venturing on strange ground. Therefore, in order not to frighten the old man, Miriam had asked the chauffeur to drive not faster than twenty miles an hour and once, when the latter had shown some reluctance to carry out her suggestion, she had taken a playful shot at a cigarette butt he had tossed out with a gesture of defiance and had shattered it in mid-air. From that time on, the driver was even more solicitous than Miriam herself.

They approached the high walls of the Sanitorium in the starlight of mid-evening and the nearer they came the less Miriam liked the look of the place. She had never consulted a lawyer before she tried Maitre François Ronron and in spite of the latter's cheery and reassuring manner odd bits of gossip she had heard about members of that relentless profession began to drift into her mind. There they mingled with ominous tales she had heard about madhouses, both public and private, until she was almost ready to defy the court order and rush her protégé to the nearest foothills, a toss-up between the Vosges and the Pyrenees, there to lie in wait and shoot it out with whom it might concern till Homer Evans came. She reflected, though, that such a course might prove more disturbing to Lazare than a day or two in a country booby-hatch.

Miriam was young and had by no means lost her capacity for surprise and astonishment. This was fully utilized when, on entering the corridor leading to the office of Doctor Balthazar Truc, she passed between Hjalmar Jansen and Lvov Kvek, both attired in starched white uniforms. The painter had his finger to his lips and the Russian winked his off eye meaningfully, so the girl's remarkable presence of mind, which had stood her in good stead many times on the prairie, did not let her down in the Sanitorium. Her pardonable agitation was not soothed, exactly, when, after the formalities of Lazare's registration had been accomplished and a stack of documents four inches thick had been signed and witnessed, a large handsome woman, also in white duck, entered precipitously and greeted her effusively.

"My darling Miriam," the stranger said. "Whatever brings you here? You must come to my room for a chat before you go away."

Dr. Truc, who was nervous whenever two of his acquaintances met, seemed displeased but made no oral objection when the woman in white led Miriam away. But a moment later, Miriam was weeping with relief in Sonia's rocking chair, having been informed that Homer Evans was safe and had dined in Luneville that very evening.

16

In Which Some of the Findings Are Pickled, While Others Are Not

THE firm of Lewson-Phipps & Xerxes had a swanky store in the avenue de l'Opéra just far enough from the American Express and the Café de la Paix so that tourists, in reaching it, would be stimulated but not exhausted by the short walk involved. The windows on either side of the entrance were filled with gaily colored objects of art from Cathay and the Indies, Tibet, Mongolia, Cochin-China and Persia. There were rugs and carpets, some of which were Oriental and others which looked so much like the real thing that only experts could tell the difference. Phoenicia was represented by a collection of votive statuary and coins, many of which had been made by Phoenicians; Egypt by a remarkable exhibition of paintings and sculpture and, on the back shelves, where they would not frighten the ordinary customers, reposed primitive charms, ornaments and statues from the Congo.

By a system of mirrors, carefully concealed, the Armenian Xerxes and his British partner were able to see clearly each customer as he or she entered the store.

Hamborough, with his cold *savoir faire* and public-school English, stepped forward if the purchaser's eyes were blue or gray. Members of other races were met by Xerxes, whose ancestors had been traders when those of his partner were in that wing of the primitive inhabitants of the British Isles who held out longest for the caves, suspicious of innovations.

The showiest of their stock the importers kept in their windows and shelves. The rest was carefully stored away in their large loft in the *rue* Réaumur. It was to the warehouse that Homer Evans and Tom Jackson made their way, after a careful inspection of the windows in the avenue de l'Opéra. Chief of Detectives Frémont met them in the gloomy doorway and followed them up four long flights of stairs. The watchman did not prove difficult to deal with. When the Chief showed his badge, the man turned pale and made a dive for the window, only to be restrained and reassured by Evans, who promised him that if he kept his mouth shut about the visit, the police would overlook the past and would not even ask to see his papers. With relief and alacrity, the watchman agreed and opened the huge loft protected by fireproof metal doors, automatic sprinklers and a set of burglar alarms which would have done credit to the Bank of England.

To have searched the place thoroughly would have required many days. Thin moonlight filtered through the large skylights and Frémont's torch revealed rows of bundles and cases of odd shapes and with prices and contents lists scrawled or stenciled in a code known only to Hagup Bogigian. The nimble-witted Xerxes had tried, once or twice, to explain it to his partner and had relinquished the project. On the other hand, it is only fair to state that Bogigian had proved to be a hopeless washout at tennis and golf, and could not have ridden to the hounds unless a camel had been furnished him, and the capture of the fox had involved a pecuniary prize.

Evans, followed by Jackson and Frémont, peered into corners, glanced at labels and finally, from behind a barricade of packing cases in one of the least accessible corners, Homer came forth triumphantly with a mounted chimpanzee. To say that Frémont greeted his discovery with enthusiasm would not be candid.

"You do not seem to be impressed," Evans said, smiling.

"I'm not bowled over," the chief of detectives said. "We have a Marquis on our hands, stuffed with paving materials. Now you drag out a monkey, filled, as likely as not, with excelsior. The connection is too remote."

"Tom," said Evans, addressing the reporter. "In your profession you see the affairs of the world go ticking and revolving like the works of a watch. The spectacle, according to tradition, is supposed to sharpen the wits and heighten the faculties. Does the presence here of this excellent specimen of the genus *anthropopithecus troglodytes* mean anything to you?"

"I can't say that it does," Jackson said.

"Look around you, gentlemen," continued Evans. "Every object in this large warehouse, if we can believe the labels and the samples we saw in the display windows, has been shaped by an artist of some distant land. It has an aesthetic value, a decorative quality, an exotic appeal. They represent art, not nature. Does it not seem strange that, in the midst of masterpieces in faience, porcelain, bronze and precious metal, there should be hidden carefully a single chimpanzee? And not a stuffed chimpanzee, but one which has been skillfully mounted. In fact, so skillfully that only one man in Paris could have done it. I refer to Monsieur Lazare."

"I'm sorry," Frémont began. "I had intended to tell you but it slipped my mind. That lunkhead Schlumberger arrested Lazare while we were away. Said he acted suspiciously when the body of the Marquis was found, had a grudge against the family, God knows what."

"You mean he's accused Lazare of the murder?" asked Evans, incredulously. "Preposterous. Let the old man go at once."

Frémont was even more uncomfortable. "I'd gladly let him go, but he's out of our hands," the Chief said.

"In whose hands is he then? I insist that he be released," said Homer.

"The court has sent him for observation to the Sanitorium Sens Unique. Mademoiselle Montana went with him, so they say," the Chief said.

"But the poor chap's in danger of a nervous breakdown. We must get him away from Dr. Truc, or he will go crazy. He's pathologically shy," insisted Evans.

"You'll have to apply to the court. In fact, the commitment was made on motion of Lazare's own lawyer."

"His lawyer?" exclaimed Evans.

"The Maitre François Ronron," Frémont said. "He was dragged into the case by Miss Montana, according to Schlumberger."

"We shall have to wait until morning," Homer said, disgustedly. "Just now we've got business."

He pointed to the chimpanzee. "When I am in the course of an investigation and find a fact or an object as incongruous as this, I examine it closely. If you will do the same, you will see, concealed in the fur at the back of the neck a thin strong linen cord. And if you examine the cord you will find, suspended where the hair is thickest, two keys, both for old-fashioned padlocks. Now you'll admit that if those keys are well hidden, the man who hung them around the monkey's neck would not risk putting them in one of his pockets, or a drawer of his desk. He obviously did not have occasion to use them frequently."

"No one would lock up valuables with a padlock having such a key, or a padlock of any description," objected Frémont. "Look at the locks in this place. The best on the market."

"Another reason for suspicion when two old-fashioned keys of a flimsy lock are guarded and hidden so elaborately," Homer said. "Do you mind, Frémont, if I take away these keys and later tonight substitute another pair that look like them?"

"By all means, take the monkey too if you like," said Frémont, disappointed.

"That would be crude," said Evans. "I don't want to warn the chap who hid those keys. In fact, I want you to plant one of your best men in here. He can keep out of sight behind the packing cases. Have him report at once if anyone goes near the chimpanzee."

After the mounted chimpanzee had been replaced exactly where Evans had found it, the Chief warned the watchman once more not to disclose the fact that the warehouse had been searched and made arrangements for the entrance of an officer to carry out Homer's instructions. Then they made their way to the prefecture, got two padlocked keys that would pass muster, and handed them to the officer assigned to the vigil in the *rue* Réaumur. They were giving the detective his final instructions when the door of Frémont's office flew open and Miriam came in.

"I'm sorry," she began . . .

"Is it a comfortable madhouse where you left Lazare?" Evans asked, with a smile.

"I don't like it at all," said Miriam, almost on the verge of tears.

"Don't worry. We'll soon get him out. And I think," he said, turning to the Chief, "that we'd better send Schlumberger to Alsace to help his friend, the auctioneer, trace samples of linen. Otherwise, he may take it into his head to make another absurd arrest."

"Absurd!" repeated Schlumberger vehemently. He had entered unnoticed as Homer was speaking. "Absurd, indeed! You were fortunate in solving the Weiss case last year, Monsieur Evans, but the one before us now requires a lowlier brand of thinking than yours. It is not my fault that the court has seen fit to give the murderer a loophole for pleading insanity. But it may interest you to know that I have proven Lazare's guilt beyond the shadow of a doubt. Would you mind," the sergeant said, facing Frémont, "calling Dr. Hyacinthe Toudoux?"

Frémont, impressed by Schlumberger's unusual confidence and self-assertion, phoned the medical examiner and in a moment the doctor's footsteps were heard in the corridor. Toudoux was anything but tranquil. He had cooled off a little since his trip to the Dôme with the foils.

His expression as he entered the office showed more dismay than anger.

"Good evening," he said sadly.

"Will you please tell the Chief and Monsieur Evans what I have found?" Sergeant Schlumberger said, his air of injured dignity deepening.

"A jar, containing the missing parts of the Marquis de la Rose d'Antan preserved in alcohol," the doctor said, miserably.

Schlumberger looked defiantly at Evans, and was surprised to see the latter smile. "Shall I tell you where you found them?" Homer asked.

"Impossible! I have told no one except the doctor," said the sergeant. "I was on my way to make my report."

"Exactly. You found the tell-tale jar concealed on a shelf in the taxidermist's shop called *Au Sens de Mesur,* proprietor, the suspect Lazare. Am I right or wrong?" demanded Homer.

Not only Schlumberger, but everyone in the room except Toudoux gasped with astonishment. Frémont's face fell. "I guess that settles it," he sighed. "It wasn't the St. Julien gang, after all."

"I don't believe Lazare did it," said Miriam, stamping her foot so hard that Jackson's glasses almost fell off his nose.

"Can I phone that to the paper?" the reporter asked. "The deadline's not far off."

"By all means. Plaster the discovery all over the press. Lazare won't read the papers, so the news won't disturb him. The public surely is entitled to such an important fact," Homer said. "But if any officer of the Paris police wants to avoid making himself ridiculous, I should suggest that he avoid being quoted as saying that the evidence is conclusive against Lazare."

"I don't know what more you want," said Schlumberger, and Frémont was inclined to agree.

"I was only making friendly suggestions," Evans said. "Come, Miriam. We'd better find the murderer, if for no other reason, to protect our colleagues against their own ill-considered impulses." To Jackson he said that he might as well get a good night's sleep, and to Frémont he made the same recommendation. The night telephone operator at the prefecture was instructed to tell Professor de la Poussière that there was no need of searching farther for Lazare. Then Homer and Miriam, arm in arm, walked slowly down the corridor and out into the square. The famous clock on the corner of the Palais de la Justice was striking one as they turned toward the *place* St. André des Arts.

The space in front of the grille at the taxidermist's shop was devoid of pedestrians at that hour, although the sidewalks on the boulevard St. Michel not thirty yards away were still fairly active. Homer reached for one of the padlock keys and tried it.

"A good omen," he said, for the first key opened the grille. The second loosened the padlock on its hasp on the door of the shop. Miriam clung close to his arm as Evans traversed the front room and made his way to the back, where Lazare's littered desk stood among stuffed specimens of beasts and animals. Shielding his flashlight with one hand, he mounted a short stepladder and started examining the dusty jars on the shelves.

"Hm, I thought so," was his only comment.

"What have you found?" asked Miriam.

225

"Two more sets of human inner organs, neatly pickled," said Evans.

Miriam could not repress an exclamation of horror. "But what shall we do?" she asked.

"Nothing for the present. This will be a lesson to our Alsatian comrade. He should learn to be thorough," Evans said.

They walked along the boulevard St. Michel toward Montparnasse and Miriam knew that Homer was entering one of his phases of intense concentration. She was dismayed that more of what she thought was incriminating evidence had been found on the premises of the harassed Lazare. There were dozens of questions she was eager to ask, but there was nothing to do except wait. As they passed the *terrasse* of the Coupole, the proprietor, M. Delbos, nodded hopefully, then noticed with satisfaction that the preoccupied couple did not turn in at the Dôme, either. In Homer's salon, a few minutes later, he motioned to Miriam to make herself comfortable in an easy chair while he selected a straight-backed wooden-seated chair for himself. Miriam was scarcely breathing, she was so anxious not to disturb him, but he looked at her presently, almost petulantly, and said:

"Forget Lazare for the moment. He's in no danger. My immediate problem has to do with The Singe."

This was followed by another long silence, then he began to speak as if he were thinking aloud.

"Of all the people concerned in this case, The Singe is the most logical and able. His motives are clear. He wants to make large sums of money without work, as the term is generally understood, and at a minimum risk of being imprisoned or guillotined. His gang, you must remember,

226

has been deprived of all its best talent. That makes it necessary for him to be all the more watchful and careful. Such a man kidnaps a well-known professor with intent to kill, then does his best to get rid of him."

Miriam, trying to lend her best attention without intruding, barely nodded.

"What happened between the day de la Poussière was seized and the day I rescued him?"

Involuntarily Miriam let a few words escape. "The Marquis was murdered," she said.

The effect on Evans was astonishing. It was almost as if he had had a paralytic shock. His body grew rigid, veins swelled on his forehead. Pale with fright, Miriam held her breath until he showed signs of relaxation.

"You've solved the problem," he said, simply.

"The thought must have come from you," she said. "I wasn't really thinking. The words slipped out."

"By Jove," said Evans, thoughtfully. Then he rose and placed his hand on Miriam's shoulder. "Darling," he continued. "Try to place yourself in the same receptive attitude again. I'll sketch the outline of events, as I understand them, and perhaps you can fill in the blanks. Our minds must be in tune."

Overcome with happiness, the girl tried to compose herself. For a while she could hear the beating of her heart, then a feeling of delicious languor stole over her as Homer began speaking.

"The murder of the Marquis caused The Singe to change his mind. Why?" He motioned her not to answer. "Because," he continued, "the Marquis had hired him to kidnap Professor de la Poussière."

"Ah," she murmured.

227

"And why did the Marquis want the professor put out of the way? Because de la Poussière had discovered the identity of Tout-or-Nada. The Singe nabs the professor, but does not kill him outright. Why not? Much easier to hide a body than a living well-known scholar."

Miriam's face showed almost childish disappointment. "I don't seem to have an answer for that," she said.

He smiled reassuringly and stroked her hair lightly. "You're not at ease. Relax. I don't need any help to answer that simple question. Ah, it's lucky we have a rational man involved in this crime. The Singe does not work for pleasure, or to satisfy his vanity. He works for money, and not any kind of money. He wants cash. . . . By Jove," Evans exclaimed, and made a dash for the telephone. He dialed a number and in a moment was talking with the night clerk of the archives at the prefecture.

"The *dossier* of the Marquis de la Rose d'Antan . . . You have it? Good . . . Glance over it and tell me what you can about his financial condition."

After a moment, the receiver began to spout sounds and Evans showed signs, first of satisfaction, then of delight. "Thanks," he said. "Good night. That's enough."

"The Marquis was broke," Homer said, turning to Miriam. "He had long ago run through his inherited fortune, and the large holdings of his wife are intact, the principal, that is. He can only spend the interest. He's borrowed from everybody, and especially . . ."

"Xerxes," gasped Miriam.

"Xerxes?" repeated Homer, bewildered. Then he slapped his knee, and grabbed for the phone. The clerk, when asked if among the Marquis's creditors was Hagup Bogigian, the answer was "Yes."

228

"Heavily in debt to Bogigian?"

"At least two hundred thousand francs," the clerk said.

Miriam was game but frightened. That she had become an instrument accessory to Homer Evans' brilliant mind thrilled her and terrified her at the same time. Suppose she should blurt out the wrong answer, some day. There would be another day, of course. He thought he was going to retire, but other emergencies would arise.

"We must go back to The Singe," Evans said. "Steady now. Unclasp your fingers and let them rest lightly on your knees. Wait for the heart to get back to its tempo. Now. The Singe works for cash, the Marquis had none. He couldn't borrow any more from Xerxes or anyone else he knew. Pampered and spoiled from his youth, the threat to his extravagance made him arrogant and desperate. The world not only owed him a living, but a sumptuous one, anything and everything he wanted.

"The Marquis learned that millionaires in America wanted Egyptian relics for their museums, and would pay fabulous prices. Perhaps Xerxes told him. But no one could sell an antique statue or a mummy without official authentication. That was where the Marquis came in, let us assume. A couple of mummies were made to order, and sold for fair prices, thanks to the Marquis's O.K. Then the No. 1 American client, Prosper Stables, wanted to enrich his Egyptian collection in the Manhattan Museum. There, where a staff of experts was employed, no makeshift would do. A real mummy which could pass muster meant a fortune. Therefore, the Marquis decided to peddle the unknown in the Louvre, and pass him off as Neferkesokar, about whom nothing whatever was known except his name."

"Then the professor spilled the beans," said Miriam, eagerly.

"That's right. Professor de la Poussière found the real Neferkesokar, consisting of a shin bone and a bit of skull, and identified the twin brother Tout-or-Nada, who was about to be sold into American captivity," said Evans. "But let's not forget The Singe. He's our yardstick, our control. Why did he undertake such a dangerous job on credit? Evidently because the stakes were large and he had some hold on the Marquis. The Marquis could give him no security. He had no convertible assets. What could he have offered?"

"*The Pansy*," gasped Miriam, turning white as chalk.

Evans was visibly shocked. He stood as if stunned, then gradually considered the suggestion.

"But, Homer," the girl protested. "I didn't realize what I was saying. I'm afraid . . . Forgive me, darling." And she hurried into the next room and threw herself on the bed, clenching her fists in an effort to hold back her sobs.

Evans scarcely paid attention to what she was doing. "*The Pansy*," he murmured. "How perfectly it fits! Of course! The three-million-dollar Watteau, that couldn't be sold. Why should it be sold? The Singe could dangle it like the sword of Damocles until he got his ducats. He kidnapped the professor, and probably let the Marquis believe he had killed him. Not only the painting, but the ghost of the professor was held in reserve. Sound fellow, The Singe. He must have been hard hit when he learned that his client, the Marquis, had been murdered."

With an air of satisfaction, Evans strolled out to the kitchen and mixed two brandies and soda. "All right, dear. Call off the hysterics and have a drink," he called.

"I'm not having hysterics," said Miriam's faint voice. "You'd feel funny yourself if your voice started answering questions right off the bat, as if it didn't belong to you at all." Nevertheless, she got up from the rumpled bed cover, washed her face with cool water, rearranged her hair, smoothed her skirt, looked at her automatic to make sure the safety was on, straightened her girdle and her stockings, recovered one shoe that had slipped off, and returned to the salon timidly.

"Try this cognac I just received from the Charente," said Evans. "It's as good as is permissible to mix with water. In fact, in a pinch one could drink it straight."

That meant that the case was to be forgotten until morning.

17

Aurora, Pluvius and Cupid All Play the Field

It is common knowledge that the rain falls on the just and the unjust. Even more impartial is the Goddess Aurora, whose rosy fingers, after touching softly the towers of Paris—Notre Dame, the Sainte Chapelle, the grotesque Tour St. Jacques, the domes of St. Paul, the Pantheon, Sacré Coeur, and the Institute—crept fragrantly down river, over dewy willows, cafés, cat-o'-nine-tails, red-tiled rooftops, haystacks, boats at anchor, wayside filling sta-tions, and fields of grain and grasses, until she was in a position to gild the barred windows of the Sanitorium Sens Unique. And since Hjalmar Jansen, though on the payroll as a bouncer, had the blood of Norse sea kings in his veins, he stirred from force of long habit when the rays of the morning sun aroused a couple of house flies to action. Having subdued the flies with a folded copy of *L'Action Francaise* left behind by his predecessor, the husky painter might have gone to sleep again had not Kvek tapped on his door. The Russian, it seems, had been restless, not having had time to get accustomed to the moaning and wailing in the violent ward, and had scoured the institution in search of a bracer. Thus it was that when he entered Hjalmar's bedroom, which barely would contain two such sizeable men, the former Colonel was holding in his hand a beaker of medicinal alcohol he had filched from the laboratory of Dr. Balthazar St.-J. Truc. In the kitchen he had found a case of Coca Cola, six bottles of which were in his pockets.

"I'm nervous. Let's have a snifter and look around," said Kvek. "Then we must have a talk with K. Parker Seldon."

Because they had suspected they were being watched closely by the doctor and his bodyguard, Gus, they had postponed the visit scheduled for the previous evening.

"I never tried Coca Cola," said Hjalmar doubtfully.

"They say straight alcohol will kill you, unless you dilute it," counseled Kvek, pouring the alcohol and the Coca Cola into the large crockery water pitcher on Hjalmar's washstand.

It was a matter of a few brisk minutes for Hjalmar to dress and for the two men to dispose of the contents of the pitcher. The drink made them both hungry, so they started out to find the kitchen and ask the cook to fix them some eggs. The latter, a surly chap, had strict orders to give the help nothing but the regulation breakfast, thin coffee flavored with chicory and gray soggy bread. The alternative presented him, however, was that if he didn't produce an omelet and some ham, the two new guards would lug out the cookstove and heave it into the river.

Refreshed by the alcohol and the breakfast and cheered by the morning chorus of the birds, Kvek and Jansen were on the point of looking for Seldon among the patients when they saw, pacing anxiously on one of the gravel walks below the windows, Dr. Truc, their employer.

"Now, what the devil is he up to, at this hour of the morning?" Hjalmar said.

The doctor was not long in demonstrating. He stooped, not too easily, picked up a small pebble and shied it at one of the second-story windows. Hjalmar and Kvek immediately got themselves out of sight and watched. The long French windows opened inward and through a painted set of bars half obscured with ivy, the Marchioness de la Rose d'Antan looked out and waved her hand. A moment later she descended and, clad in her old-fashioned dress, with high collar and wide puff sleeves, her hat that looked like one of François I's tilted coyly on her head, she walked slowly by the doctor's side to the spacious grounds outside the gate leading from the patients' courtyards.

"I'll be damned," said the painter.

Kvek was indignant that a blighter like Dr. Balthazar Truc should presume to be on familiar terms with a member of the nobility, whether she were crazy or not.

In his narrow cell off Courtyard Seven, K. Parker Seldon was lying tightly bound in a straitjacket, his legs in a sack, the prey of the keenest disappointment. He remembered with pleasure the trundling he had handed out to Dr. Truc, but that was blotted out because the black-haired nurse had failed to keep her promise to see him the previous afternoon. The day had been endless, the night even longer. When Aurora could spare a few rays for his small window, he squirmed himself into a

234

reading position, opened *Ulysses* with the aid of the stubble on his determined chin, and tried to lose himself in the chapter in which some citizens and students stage an intellectual debauch in a lying-in hospital. It is a tribute to the author of that masterpiece to relate that the harassed business man was so deep in prose when his door softly opened that he asked, somewhat impatiently, without looking around:

"Say, what's this 'agenbite of inwit' the guy talks so much about?"

That is what Seldon thought he had said. The sounds that reached the shapely ears of Sofia Alexandrovna were similar to those made by French plumbing about four o'clock of a winter morning.

"Why, you've lost your teeth, poor man," said Sonia, after locking the door behind her. "That's why you can't talk."

"Gubbubshunbishes pinchtum," was the only comment he could make, but his face expressed his joy.

"You understand my faulty English?" asked Sonia, her cool hand on his forehead.

Seldon tried to make gestures with his head that would convey that he understood, and that her English was the most lyrical and musical he had heard since Sothern and Marlowe had played Des Moines in 1906.

"Then listen carefully," she said. "Your friends, my darling childhood playmate and cousin, Lvov Kvek, and Hjalmar Jansen, are in the sanitorium."

Seldon began to weep, assuming that his companions had been overtaken with the D.T's and were as helpless as he was.

"There! Quiet, little dove! You didn't understand,"

said Sonia. "They're not patients. They're attendants. They're going to get you out of here."

At that, Seldon began to laugh and wiggle like an eel. Deftly the nurse unstrapped his arms and handed him a pencil and her memorandum pad.

"Are you married?" he wrote, feverishly.

She smiled and shook her head.

"Engaged?" he scribbled.

She shook her head again. It is always difficult to record how such things happen, but K. Parker Seldon found himself enclosed in eager arms and practically over-powered. He had played around a bit in the Middle West, at Shriner's conventions, Chamber of Commerce get-to-gethers, etc., but nothing in his experience had prepared him for Slavic outbursts of affection. Nevertheless, he did the best he could, and was first to hear a tap on the door.

"Let us in," whispered Kvek and Hjalmar, and an in-stant afterward were wringing the bottle magnate's hand. They urged Seldon to be patient for a day or two, if need be, promised to get his teeth for him at the earliest pos-sible moment, and hastily departed. Hjalmar started out to stalk the Marchioness and her frock-coated medico, while Kvek decided to have a look around the doctor's office before the other guards got up. The patients, most of whom slept fitfully, began howling for breakfast but no one paid the slightest attention to them.

Finding himself in the spacious grounds in front of the Sens Unique, Jansen began to regret that he was wearing white duck and that the terrain afforded so little cover. By flitting from shrub to shrub, however, he managed to work his way unobserved into a damp patch of raspberry bushes from which he could see Dr. Truc and the Marchioness and overhear every word they said. The pair were seated on a bench beneath an apple tree that spread its limbs over a secluded mossy pathway and, because it interfered with conversation and the long hat pins had narrowly missed putting out the doctor's left eye, the Marchioness had removed her broad-brimmed hat and placed it on the seat beside them.

"Christ, what are patterns for!" muttered Hjalmar as in shifting his position he practically impaled himself on raspberry thorns.

"To think that I shall know happiness at last," the Marchioness murmured.

"That you shall, my dear," responded Dr. Truc. "I shall devote myself to you alone. I'll give up my profession, my practice, the institution I have built up so painstakingly. We'll go to a foreign land, where no word of the recent unfortunate happenings can reach you."

"But, when, Balthazar? How long must we wait?"

"As soon as I can set you free, we'll fly. There are technicalities, my dear. Technicalities," the doctor said.

"How relieved I shall be, when I can give everything I have to you," the Marchioness said. "I hope the details won't prove a burden to you. I've much more money, I'm afraid, than I had when I first came here. The Marquis could only use the income. And now his property, which he couldn't squander, the apartment and its contents, the chateau in the Ain . . . Perhaps I should ask my old lawyer, Maitre François Ronron, to administer . . ."

"Ah, no. Not necessary, my dear."

"Of course, I'd feel safer if you'd take charge. And

237

wouldn't it simplify matters to place all my property in your name? Then I wouldn't be obliged continually to be signing things."

"All that will be arranged," the doctor said, so pleased with the prospect that he reached for her hand and started humming an aria of Massenet to which he fitted mentally a lyric substantially as follows:

(Tenor)
> Les titres vont dégringoler
> (Hélas pour les bouteilles)
> Mais le business man va s'employer
> A les faire regrimper.

(Chorus)
> Ah, vive les jolis titres
> Qui vont bien s'amplifier.

If the doctor had been singing in English, the words would have gone something like this:

(Tenor)
> The stocks will take a nose-dive
> Now the business man's away
> But when it's known that he's alive
> They'll go up till there's hell to pay.

(Chorus)
> Three cheers for jar and bottle stock
> That'll hit the sky that day.

Hjalmar was eager to be off and away, and to report to Evans the strange turn of events that had come to his attention. But the lovers lingered until, one by one, and then in droves, the day-shift mosquitoes got into action. Their first choice was undoubtedly Hjalmar, although they by no means neglected Dr. Balthazar St.-Jean Truc. The Marchioness, wrapped in thought, seemed not to mind them but when the doctor arose and suggested they go inside, she acquiesced with the gentle grace that characterized all her movements.

While this touching scene was being enacted, Lvov Kvek was making progress also. The heavy door of the doctor's office was locked, the windows were fastened from inside, but by standing on the doorknob Kvek was able to force open the transom, through which he wormed his way in. The office contained a flat-topped desk the top of which was covered with a writing pad, wire baskets marked "Incoming" and "For Future Reference" and a pair of telephones. The side drawers of the desk were locked by patent fasteners connected with the central drawer which had been locked with a key. Hastily Lvov cleared everything from the desk, picked it up with its contents and turned it upside down. Then he shook it until the fasteners worked loose and the drawers came open. That accomplished, he righted the desk again and placed the articles that belonged on top where he had found them, as nearly as he could remember. A hasty search yielded K. Parker Seldon's passport and, wrapped in tissue paper, the set of false teeth.

Elated, the Russian closed the desk drawers again, and let himself out of the office, the door of which had a spring lock. In less than a minute he was at the door of Seldon's cell, which he entered joyfully but, in his haste, forgot to lock behind him. Seldon, the moment he was unstrapped, shook hands, began to babble and, when

Lvov took the teeth from his pocket the American fitted them into place and told his story, as much of it as was known to him. He had taken a walk, got lost, had a drink or two and instead of finding the Dôme, he had dim recollections of a bench on some boulevard, a police station, a ride in the doctor's car and his awakening in the booby-hatch.

Kvek expressed surprise that his charge was so little shaken by the experience, and was further astonished to see, rising on the cheeks of the business man, a pair of blushes that would have done credit to a schoolboy in his first game of postoffice.

"Your cousin!" murmured K. Parker Seldon. "The beautiful Sofia! Now that I have my teeth, I shall ask her hand in marriage."

"She always wanted to go to the States," said Kvek. "Let us go and drink, let us feast; I will give her away, and such a wedding. *Da*, dum dum *dum*. *Da* da de *dum*. Can you not hear the peal of the organ? Can you not smell the bridesmaids, the vodka, the heaps of caviar?"

His rhapsody, in which Seldon had joined by marching up and down the cell to measures of Lohengrin, was interrupted by a grunt of rage as Gus tackled Kvek from behind. The powerful and disgruntled guard, whose passion for Sofia had kept him near the boiling point for weeks on end, had overheard the last part of the conversation and could contain himself no longer. He had the advantage of weight and surprise and for a moment it looked as if Kvek would be battered to a pulp before he could strike a blow. But the floor was soft, as floors go, and once he had recovered his presence of mind, the Russian managed to get a half-Nelson and even up the contest. K. Parker Seldon, finding that what strength he had made little difference, one way or another, started using his head. There was nothing in the room that would serve for a weapon except the straitjacket. One sleeve of this Seldon wound around Gus's thick neck, then began twisting from behind. Gus began to soften up, and soon he was limp. Kvek slipped the straitjacket over his legs, strapped his arms, and unmindful of Seldon's protest, made an impromptu gag from the soliloquy of Marion Bloom, hastily wrenched from *Ulysses*.

In the corridor was a telephone booth for use of the employees, operated, of course, by coins. Kvek, with what little help Seldon could give him, dragged the unconscious guard to the booth and dumped him in. Tearing off the fly leaf of *Ulysses* the Russian printed "OUT OF ORDER" in large block letters, and, taking the thumbtacks from a notice signed by the doctor, to the effect that employees were forbidden to use the other phones, he replaced it with the placard he had improvised. He had barely got Seldon safely back in his room when Hjalmar came in from the raspberry patch, his skin scratched and swollen with mosquito bites and his white duck uniform stained with raspberry juice.

"We'll chuck him into the launch tonight after dark," said Jansen, when told what had happened to Gus.

18

Dealing in Part with the Psychology of Attire

IN THE laboratory of Dr. Hyacinthe Toudoux, bright lights shone pitilessly through the night and their brittle rays bounced on and off the eyeballs of the medical examiner from all directions. The cabinets were filled with nickel-plated instruments. Most of the furnishings were nickel plated, including the coffee machine Toudoux had accepted years before from a café keeper in lieu of an obstetrician's fee. Table surfaces were of white enamel, walls and ceiling painted white. The setting was by no means restful or conducive to calm.

On the slab, in the near-by fish tank, were the remains of the Marquis de la Rose d'Antan. Muttering imprecations, the doctor walked circles around them, trying to extract the clue to the cause of death that had eluded all his tests. Had the doctor been able to keep his mind entirely on the autopsy before him, he might have got better results, but each time he allowed his eyes or thoughts to wander from the gruesome task, he saw, dancing in the air before him, like fumes from alphabet soup, the mocking words of Dr. Balthazar Truc as printed in the *En-Tout-Cas*.

"Livers do not swell but shrink! The scoundrel! Saffron and mustard. Bah! I shall run him through the heart. I shall run . . ."

At that point, the doctor got his wires crossed and switched back to the corpse. "Run through the heart" was the *leitmotif* that was carried over from one theme to the other, so absent-mindedly the doctor picked up a powerful magnifying glass, a 500 candle-power flashlight, and turned both on the heart of the former Minister of Beaux Arts and Public Monuments. Dr. Toudoux's hair stood on end and seemed to give out electric sparks. He began babbling, walking in circles, then returned with glass and flashlight. No doubt about it! The heart had been pierced with a slender instrument, not larger than a sail needle, which had left a scar the size of a thumbtack hole but which, under the doctor's powerful glass, looked like a bird's-eye view of Mount Vesuvius.

"I've got it! The Marquis was stabbed," he said, executing a sprightly "forward and back" as he used to do as a lad when dancing the quadrille. He paused in front of a life-size chart on the wall, which showed exactly what Adonis would have looked like if Venus had sliced him in halves. Squinting and peering, and skillfully estimating angles, Dr. Toudoux loosened a safety-pin he had used to hold up his shorts and touched with the point the spot on Adonis's heart corresponding to the puncture in that of the late Marquis de la Rose d'Antan.

"Stabbed from directly in front," the doctor said, "by someone with a steady hand who was approximately five feet seven inches tall. Death must have been instantaneous. Practically no bleeding. Afterward, cleaned like a haddock and stuffed with natron and asphalt. Ah, now I am free to seek out that unspeakable Truc. This time he shall not escape me. I shall run him through . . . Damnation!" In his excitement he had ruined the forty-dollar chart of Adonis by slashing it in a vital spot with the safety pin.

Raising the heavy shades of the laboratory, Dr. Toudoux was astonished to find that it was broad daylight, in fact, about eight o'clock. The Chief of Detectives Frémont had not yet put in an appearance at the prefecture and Toudoux had no intention of giving important news to Schlumberger, who had arrested his friend, Lazare. The worst of it was that Lazare, as the doctor remembered him, had a marvelously steady hand, acquired by stuffing the tiniest insects, and was exactly five feet seven inches tall.

"I must telephone Monsieur Evans, and at the same time I can ask him to act as my second when I perforate Truc. Had the former been a member of my fencing team in 1910 . . . but then, I suppose he was scarcely in his 'teens. Ah, time. Ah, exactions of science. California Medoc! Heliotrope! Vindication!"

In the course of the year that had passed since Dr. Toudoux had first been associated with Evans, and at his suggestion had traced the mysterious Mickey Finn, their acquaintance had ripened and the doctor had learned that his new friend did not like to be disturbed at eight o'clock in the morning. So the doctor crossed the Pont St. Michel and ordered breakfast, if that is not too dignified a term for what the French eat in the morning, at the Café du Départ. Nine o'clock was the deadline he set for Evans' slumber.

At nine the phone rang and Evans, sighing, walked toward it in his pyjamas. He listened carefully to the medical examiner's report, and told Dr. Toudoux, in confidence, about the two extra jars of hearts, livers and lights on the shelf in *Au Sens de Mesur.*

"Good God! Do you mean to say I've two more autopsies to perform? I shall resign. I shall go back to the Congo . . ." the doctor said.

"No need to concern yourself with the new exhibits. I'll find out all about those deaths myself, without dissecting anything. In fact, already I've quite a definite idea," said Homer. "And furthermore, put off plans for dueling, at least for a while. I want you to come with me to Luneville, where I am sure we shall discover that Dr. Balthazar St.-Jean Truc has placed himself so far below the level of a gentleman that meeting him on the field of honor would be unthinkable."

"All right, if you say so," said Dr. Toudoux, reluctantly. "I'd much rather run him through, no matter about his social standing."

"No telling what might happen," said Homer. "Goodbye. I'll call you later. And please don't tell anyone else, at least until tomorrow, about the skewered heart. I'll notify Frémont in private, just to cover the law."

The receiver had scarcely been balanced on the hook when the phone rang again. That time a female voice, with a Russian accent, introduced its owner as Sofia Alexandrovna Dargomyzshkov, speaking from the Restaurant Sérieux, at Luneville-sur-Seine, in behalf of her cousin Lvov and a big man named Hjalmar. Sofia repeated, word for word, the conversation the painter had overheard between Dr. Truc and Madame de la Rose d'Antan, and could not withhold her indignant comment. She could not believe it of the Marchioness. It was horrible that a gentle high-born lady should attach herself to an oily crook and thief and throw her fortune at him, even to get out of a madhouse. Perhaps the poor woman, after five years of torture, had actually lost her mind, the nurse suggested.

Another voice broke in on the line. "Monsieur Evans," said the voice of The Singe. "Oh, the line's busy. Excuse me."

"Don't hang up," Evans said, anxiously. "I was talking with Luneville and have nothing more to say."

Sofia hung up the receiver, and The Singe carried on.

"Could I see you for a few minutes? It's important," he said.

"Are you in Paris?" Homer asked.

"Yes."

"I'll meet you in an hour, at the Hotel Murphy et du Danube Bleu," Evans said.

"Much obliged," said The Singe.

Evans went back to his bedside and pulled an ornamental cord that set a small American flag fluttering outside his window. That was the signal for his barber, Henri Duplessis, to come over and shave him. It had seldom flown before mid-day, but the barber happened to see it and arrived with his implements soon afterward. While Homer was in the needle-bath, he had Duplessis telephone to Miriam, asking her to meet him at the Dôme for breakfast in half an hour. Sleep and the short walk from the *rue* Vavin had restored the color in her cheeks, for during roundups and wars with the sheep men she had grown accustomed to snatching a few hours of rest, often with only the sage brush for a mattress and the stars for a canopy overhead. Nevertheless, she approached Homer somewhat warily, for she had reflected that if he had the power to manipulate her thoughts he probably could read them, and would have figured out how she had dragged him into the complicated case that was beginning to look so black for old Lazare. His warm greeting dispelled her uneasiness instantly.

"I have news from all quarters," he said. "My modest establishment, formerly obscure and tranquil, has become practically a telephone exchange. I shall have the instrument removed just as soon as this case is over." Then he told her about the scene on the rustic bench beneath the apple tree beside a mossy path that had uncovered the asylum romance of the ages, the hole in the Marquis' heart that had been made with a steady hand by a party five feet seven inches tall, and lastly, about the S.O.S. from The Singe. That seemed to please Homer Evans more than all the information he had received.

"I want you to meet The Singe," Evans said. "I've taken quite a fancy to the fellow. One meets so few people, you know, whose brains work well, in an orderly way, and whose nerves are functioning properly. He's a good-looking chap, blue eyes, six feet tall . . ."

"He might have stooped five inches," said Miriam, more interested in finding a defense for Lazare than in the gang leader Homer liked so much. She wasn't jealous of his men friends, but her experience thus far had taught her to distrust the St. Julien Rollers.

Evans enjoyed a leisurely breakfast, then led Miriam

to a taxi and they set out for the *place* de la Contrescarpe. The Singe was chatting easily with Bridgette Murphy, who had a weakness for strong men with cold blue eyes. He acknowledged the introduction to Miriam with a flicker of surprise on his face, pardonable when it is remembered that she had ended the careers, here below, of a round half dozen of his gangsters. He had expected something sterner than the rosy-cheeked clear-eyed young girl who, except for her rather sturdy handclasp and the style of her shoes, was as feminine as any maiden in his native Normandie.

Miriam was left to talk with Bridgette while the two men retired to an adjacent room. Once alone with Homer, the broad freckled face of The Singe showed some embarrassment.

"It was cheeky to call you," he began.

"Not at all. I'm glad to hear from you," Evans said.

"As a matter of fact, perhaps I can do you a favor," The Singe continued. "You've been looking for a little painting . . ."

"Ah, *The Pansy*," Evans said surprised. Then the Marquis must have delivered it, after all, he thought. How could he have delivered it, three days or so after his death? The painting was in the Louvre until Tuesday afternoon.

"It's the one the papers made such a row about not long ago. I can lay my hands on it, if that will do you any good," The Singe continued.

Homer smiled in his most winning way. "Monsieur," he said, facing the stalwart Norman squarely. "Let us be frank. Why not say that you have the painting, and want to be rid of it."

248

The Singe grinned appreciatively. "I have to get used to talking with a sensible guy like you," he said. "Most people can't stand the truth. It rattles 'em. You have to beat around the bush . . ."

"Exactly," Evans agreed. "Now I'll tell you what I'll do. I'll take the painting, and never disclose where I got it, if you'll tell me how you came by it."

"I didn't steal it," The Singe said. "I wouldn't be stupid enough for that. Might as well steal Notre Dame."

"I'm sure of that. And I'm not interested in any deals you might have made, in which the painting was involved. I want to know simply how it came into your hands just now."

The Singe struggled with a look of annoyance, not directed at Evans, but some unknown person or persons not then in the room. "My gang isn't organized yet," he said.

"I've noticed," Evans said, but not unkindly.

"I may as well come out with it. One of my boys, a sap called Godo the Whack, took it on himself to get the Watteau from somewhere where a certain party had cached it . . ."

Homer laughed good-naturedly. "Which French philosopher was it who said, 'Surtout, pas de zêle?' (Above all, no zeal)."

"Talleyrand, God blast it all," muttered The Singe.

"Well," said Evans. "Send me the painting, carefully wrapped. Have your messenger leave it on the table in my outer hallway, any time at all. No one will bother him. If the concierge asks questions, tell her the package is for me . . . And, by the way, if by any chance you should be tempted to kidnap a fellow named K. Parker

Seldon, alias K. S. Porker, or Porcière, lay off, like a good fellow. The man's particularly hot. To make up any loss of money such forebearance would entail, why not buy a block of American Jar and Bottle stock while it's down in the cellar."

"No, thanks," replied The Singe. "I've had temptations before to play the market. It's just as risky as my game, and if you win you never know where the money comes from. I appreciate the tip, though. Well. So long."

As The Singe, after bidding *au revoir* to Bridgette Murphy, was passing out the doorway, the Chief of Detectives Frémont came down the stairs, followed by Hydrangea, in a natty street costume of Nile green with a fluffy summer fur almost white in color, to set off her ebony skin.

"Who was that chap?" the Chief inquired, who had got used to having Evans turn up at all times and places.

"Oh, someone you've never seen," answered Homer, nonchalantly. Again he excused himself from the others and led Frémont into the room where his erstwhile captor had been standing just a minute before. There Homer told the Chief about the Marquis' diminutive stab wound, and hesitantly added the items about the height of the murderer and the steady hand.

"Don't be obstinate," Frémont said, while Evans was still debating with himself as to whether to mention the pickled innards of two other victims in Lazare's little shop. "Lazare's our man, without a doubt," the Chief continued. "I'm as sorry as you are, but what can we do?"

"My friends," Evans said. "I warned you last night that if you put your money on Lazare your choice would not be in at the finish."

"But the motive, the pickled parts, the collapse in the Louvre, his lifelong experience in stuffing things . . ."

"That will all be explained when the murderer is found," Homer said.

The Chief looked more than doubtful. Hydrangea, however, had made up her mind. "Bertram," she said, severely. "Don't you do nothin' Mistah Evans says not to do. You'll go get yourself in trouble."

Frémont sighed. "I may as well join the prefect on his fishing trip," he said.

At that Hydrangea brightened. "Now you're talkin'," she said, with a gleaming smile. "You better jus' let Mistah Evans handle his case his own way, an' show me a river where I can catch some croakers."

As the Chief and his sweetheart strolled down the hill toward the Pantheon, it looked from behind as if he were having a hard time explaining just why such an excursion was not feasible.

Evans and Miriam were not long in descending the hill, where in the *rue* des Ecoles they found a taxi.

"No. 12 *place* Dauphine," Evans said to the driver, and to Miriam: "We've got several calls to make this morning."

When the door of Professor de la Poussière's apartment was opened softly by his charming wife, Evans apologized for calling at such an hour. The professor was asleep, having worked on his book about Tout-or-Nada all night, but Homer, having learned from Dr. Toudoux that Hélène de la Poussière and the Marchioness de la Rose d'Antan had been schoolmates in the same convent, did not seek enlightenment concerning

Egypt, but Madame's recollections of her unfortunate friend.

"I have never thanked you properly for rescuing my husband," Madame de la Poussière began.

"It was a pleasure," said Evans. "And I shall ask but one reward, namely, that when this case is over your husband shall forget Egyptology for a while and take you on a trip to New York. It's time you both saw the modern world, for purposes of comparison."

Her gratitude was so touching that Miriam placed an arm around the older woman's shoulders. On the subject of the Marchioness, it was not difficult to get Hélène to talk.

"Was she normal, like other girls, I mean, in the convent?" Evans asked.

"She was more sensitive than most of us," Madame said, sadly. "At times more given to day dreams, and always more intelligent. The sisters were troubled by her thirst for information and her gift for logic. I am sure the restricted nature of our life there irked Eugénie more than she let it be known. To me and a few other intimates she said she would marry the moment she was released from school, that she would see the world for herself and learn of its freedom and the joys of privacy and solitude. Her nature was contradictory; in a way, she was finer than her classmates, more responsive, and at the same time more determined and capable of higher initiative."

"She was rich?"

"Very rich."

"And her dot? Do you know anything about the arrangements?"

"She never mentioned them, even to me. You see, she had never known about money matters and her parents, ultra-conservative and pious, liked to think of her as feminine and innocent. But the marriage contract . . . It must be on record . . ."

"Many thanks," Evans said.

Madame de la Poussière leaned forward and for once her eagerness showed through her remarkable restraint. "Monsieur Evans, I trust you. You have done for us what never can be forgotten. If you could help that unfortunate woman, if you could be instrumental in saving for her the last years of a cruelly thwarted life . . ."

Miriam could contain herself no longer. "You will, Homer?" she asked breathlessly. "You won't let her stay in that terrible place?"

"I will do what I can," Homer said. "But tell me, madame. Was her mind unsettled? And what led up to her incarceration?"

"The Marquis," Madame de la Poussière said bitterly. "He hated women . . . I don't mean that there has been any scandal, in the obvious way. But he has always been surrounded by men, who, like himself, thought of our sex as distasteful, as property, one might say. He married Eugénie believing she was submissive and inconsequential, and was enraged when he found she had a will of her own and a faculty of seeing through his subterfuge. I tried to keep up our friendship, but he made it impossible. After she was sent to that institution, I made repeated attempts to visit her and always was dissuaded, on the ground that my presence would aggravate her condition. I wrote letters, and received no replies. No doubt she never saw them. The doctors who testified that she was ill and irresponsible were both cronies of the Marquis, the judge was a bachelor and in his dotage. Her parents were dead!"

"Then you've never seen her in the Sanitorium Sens Unique?" Evans asked.

"Once I gained admission there," said Madame de la Poussière. "For several days and nights I had been thinking about her, and seeing her in my dreams . . . Two years ago, I think it was. To impress the doctor in charge, I got a letter from my lawyer, Maitre François Ronron . . ."

"Oh, he's my lawyer, too," said Miriam, relieved that she belonged to such a respectable clientele.

"Eugénie was especially troubled about her clothes," the professor's wife continued. "The beastly Marquis had sent her only heirlooms his own mother had worn, outmoded dresses, hats, shoes and even underclothes he had kept in mothballs in the attic since the old Marchioness had died. To be dressed so ridiculously preyed on Eugénie's mind and the other patients looked at her askance. I promised to send what she needed, and did so . . ."

"Excuse me. What did you send?" interrupted Evans.

"Two complete outfits, each, for winter and summer. I took her measurements myself, while the doctor was out of the room, and had the clothes made by my dressmaker."

"Maggy Rouff," Homer added, smiling.

"Don't mind him. He knows everything," Miriam said, when Madame showed polite surprise.

"You have helped me, and also I hope, your friend the Marchioness," said Evans cordially, when the interview was finished. "Perhaps you'll be able to take her to America with you."

Miriam smiled, shook her head affirmatively and nodded, behind Evans' back, as if to say that the Marchioness was as good as aboard ship that very minute.

19

Another Calculation Involving X, *the Unknown Quantity*

DR. BALTHAZAR ST.-JEAN TRUC, after his stroll with the Marchioness de la Rose d'Antan, sat down to breakfast in his spacious living quarters. He had built a small wing on the old asylum for his own use, and because he had always dreamed of being fabulously rich he had fitted it out for living in the style to which he was determined to get accustomed. His bedroom contained a huge four-posted bed with a canopy, dating from the time of Louis XIV, ornately framed mirrors, rich upholstered chairs, and an Aubusson carpet he had accepted from Lewson-Phipps & Xerxes as payment for having pulled the British partner through a rather tough siege of delirium tremens following the Christmas holidays in the Armistice year. When he had been informed by a patient who had been in the rug business that the Aubusson had been made in Japan, the doctor had been deeply hurt, until he reflected that his patient, Basil Hamborough, had not really had the D.T.'s. He had merely been afflicted with a case of the shakes, which by a tapering treatment involving California wine Dr. Truc had prolonged six weeks.

Adjacent to the bedroom was an alcove in which the doctor breakfasted. He did not, like the patients, restrict himself to a diet that would have driven the Spartans to a hunger strike. He ate rather well, in fact, and particularly in the morning, after a stroll in the grounds. His usual snack consisted of herring and potatoes, four or five slices of assorted cheeses, coffee with cream, and several Alsatian *brioches,* a pastry shaped something like a snail, and containing raisins and citron soaked in brandy. On the morning in question, his regular bill of fare did not seem adequate to him and he decided to augment it with a lark omelet. Luxurious plans were forming and reforming in his head. At last, after a lifetime of scheming and slaving, big money loomed on his horizon. The Marchioness, just lately, he had permitted to breakfast in her own room and not gather with the other inmates at the long dreary table covered with white oil cloth and patrolled by the nurses and huskies. His thoughts of her were so tender, when he remembered her words, "Everything I have will be yours," that he pulled a bell cord, intending to send her one of his six Alsatian *brioches* to brighten her uneventful day.

A second time the doctor pulled, then he yelled "Gus!"

There was no reply.

The third yank brought the bell cord right out by the roots and the metal contraption to which it was attached, in crashing, tore the doctor's striped gray trousers.

Another attendant answered and informed the doctor

that Gus was nowhere to be found. He had disappeared in uniform, and his street clothes were gone from his room.

At any other time Dr. Truc would have raised a hue and cry, but he had to make grave decisions, so he let the other attendant serve him while he pondered the questions which swarmed in his mind. American Jar and Bottle stock, according to the *Herald* of the day before, had hit a new low. In a week it had tumbled from 104 to 32. What should he do? There were several alternatives. He could put it up to K. Parker Seldon, convince the jar satrap that legally he could never get out of the Sens Unique unless he played ball with the proprietor, then convert his assets into cash and buy the stock at thirty-two. On the other hand, he could communicate with the rival millionaire, whose name was Stables, and offer to double-cross the jar and bottle concern by keeping the chairman in the loony-bin until the company failed. According to Bradstreet, which the doctor thumbed tenderly as he turned over the various possibilities in his mind, Stables had twice as much money as Hugo Weiss.

Then, as so often happens, the doctor saw that his two projects—that of marrying the Marchioness' fortune and of cleaning up the bottle market—could be combined. He made up his mind to keep Seldon in captivity, without his teeth or contact with the outside world, until after Eugénie's cash was in his name. Then he could plunge in bottle stock in a major league fashion. His joy at the prospect was so intense that, in spite of the fact that his awkward attendant had let the lark omelet get cold in transit from the kitchen, the doctor burst into song, to the tune of Massenet's *Frolic in D* slightly modified to fit the words:

> *"Mais, vive l'amour, le business man*
> *Et le médicin culotté,*
> *Ainsi les veuves et orphelins*
> *Qui paieront tous les frais."*

> (So here's to love and the business man
>   And the doctor blithe and gay,
>   Also the widows and the orphans
>   Who'll have the bill to pay.)

In an expansive humor Dr. Balthazar Truc polished off the last of the Alsatian *brioches* and, before settling down to his morning routine at his desk, walked slowly through his laboratory where, under blue lights such as those used by painters at night, two rows of guinea-hen livers rested side by side. Row "A" was from fowls whose food had been doused with certified French wine, Row "B" was from those who had unwittingly swallowed the California imitation.

Dr. Truc stuck his hand between the buttons of his coat and cleared his throat, as if addressing the Academy of Science, with Dr. Hyacinthe Toudoux cowering in the front row. "Gentlemen," he began. "As you see by comparing exhibits 'A' and 'B', the latter are slightly shrunken, and are streaked with honeysuckle, perhaps a bit on the mustard side."

If it came to a duel after that, he reflected, Toudoux would be too humiliated for effective fencing.

At his desk in his office the doctor's mood veered abruptly. He fumbled for the basket marked "Incoming" and began to holler and growl. On form 356-D, supposed to be a cook's requisition for supplies, there was scrawled a complaint that two new huskies, Kvaque and Gonzo by name, had obtained by threats of bodily harm and sabotage a ham omelet from the doctor's private stores. Truc pressed buttons so viciously that he broke two fingernails. "Send those two bandits to me this instant," he roared when four attendants came in on the hot foot, expecting to find that Passepartout, the inventor, had got a toe-hold on the doc.

A moment later Kvek and Hjalmar entered, both with their sleeves rolled up and scowls on their foreheads. They both had forgotten the ham and eggs and thought they were up on much graver charges. They looked at the furious doctor, grinned and Hjalmar asked, in English: "Shall I poke him one in the snoot, just for luck?"

"Forbearance, my boy," counseled the former Colonel. "We don't want to get canned until the time comes."

Dr. Truc seemed to be fascinated by the sight of their brawny arms. He had seen huskies before, but this pair looked like destruction personified. Besides, Gus had flown the coop in an inexplicable fashion and the doctor was short of help. He contented himself with rebuking the new men and telling them that the value of the ham, the eggs and the cook's extra time would be deducted from their pay.

"Oh, that's all right, old man," said Kvek, to smooth things over. Hjalmar was still toying with his first idea, that is to say, a poke in the snoot, but reluctantly let it pass and followed Kvek from the room. The inventor, Joseph Passepartout, having clandestinely secured a stick of stovewood, was lying in wait behind the telephone booth but he too, notwithstanding his cloudy mind, was impressed by the bare arms and resolute stride of the new pair of guards and decided to withhold his attack until Gus, his Nemesis, passed that way.

In a narrow white-walled room, Lazare was testing his bit of carpenter's chalk, the only possession he had retained after Dr. Truc and frisked him. Upstairs, in the midst of her antique furniture, the Marchioness was playing the spinet softly as she watched the play of shadows from the foliage outside her windowpane. The man in Courtyard Seven who habitually listened for worms, thought he had heard one and started scratching the hard-packed earth. Sonia Alexandrovna was gazing with rapture at an old copy of a New York Sunday supplement and wondering if there were skyscrapers in Des Moines, and if the Atlantic Ocean was bluer than the Adriatic Sea. Of one thing she was certain, she would not be married in white. Once out of the Sens Unique, she would never wear white again, she promised herself.

At the Paris prefecture, the proceedings were on a more rational plane than those in the Sens Unique. Schlumberger, after a session with a handwriting expert, had learned that a page of notes concerning an Egyptian King named Tout-or-Nada had been penned by Lazare on the very day of the murder, which Dr. Toudoux had finally reported must have been the Saturday preceding the Tuesday on which *The Pansy* had been stolen. Together with Frémont, who tried to defend Evans' theory of Lazare's innocence, the Alsatian sergeant led the way to the *place* Dauphine and consulted with Professor de la Poussière.

When handed the page of notes, the professor began to roar with laughter. "Dear me, I shall split my sides," he said, waving the paper and his spectacles in one hand and wiping his eyes with the other.

"Then it makes sense?" asked Schlumberger, with a significant glance at the Chief.

"Gentlemen, it's a wonderful story. It was in Tout-or-Nada's reign, you know, that the properties of hasheesh were discovered, accidentally . . . In the year 2933, a gardener attached to the pharaoh's court burned off a field which had become overgrown with weeds, in order to plant blueberries. Some camels in a near-by lot, while the smoke from the fire was drifting in their direction, began dancing and snorting in a most unusual fashion. In fact, they lost their dignity entirely and behaved like colts, afterward settling down for a peaceful nap lasting forty-eight hours.

"Tout-or-Nada, who was then the crown prince, being one minute older than Neferkesokar, his brother, had a scientific turn of mind, and having noticed the behavior of the camels, after sniffing the smoke, had his wise men investigate the nature of the vegetation in the burned field. They found one hundred and seventeen kinds of weeds and grasses and each one in turn was tried on camels.

"The ninety-fourth was *cannabis indica* and caused the laboratory camel to pursue a female ostrich until hopelessly outdistanced, then mount a minor pyramid and slide down on his haunches, smiling and chuckling the while.

"The next week, old Setheri, the bastard pharaoh, died and Tout-or-Nada ascended to the throne. On the occasion of his father's funeral, Tout ordered incense pots of burning hasheesh to be set out at intervals of ten yards all along the route, with the result that the animals in the procession stampeded and the populace, overcome with merriment, staged an orgy to which the scribes in the kingdom were never able to do justice. The body of the king, it seems, got lost in the shuffle and was found, some weeks later, about two hundred miles down the Nile. From that time on, until Tout-or-Nada was pushed into the Nile and drowned by his treacherous twin brother while looking at the reflection of a double moon, afterward advanced as proof of Tout's divinity, every feast day or religious celebration meant free hasheesh for the populace and slaves. Such as were overcome by the smoke were dragged into the royal laboratories and carefully studied as they came out of their stupor. It was the conclusion of the wise men that *cannabis indica* was non-habit forming and comparatively uninjurious in its effects, that it could be produced cheaply on a large scale and would add much to the joy of the nation. But because it was associated with Tout-or-Nada in the public mind, Neferkesokar spitefully stamped it out and became so unpopular that when it got to be common knowledge in the streets that his son was putting bamboo needles in the pharaoh's soup, there was not an Egyptian or a foreign subject to be found who would warn Neferkesokar."

"In your opinion, professor, could a man who was crazy translate all that from the Egyptian?"

"Of course not! Nonsense! There are not a half dozen men alive who could read the old characters so accurately, and not many who could put the story in such lucid French. I have always told my pupils that the contents of their minds will avail the world nothing unless they learn to express themselves . . . But, you know. Youth . . . Distractions . . . Scholarship is not what it was, gentlemen. Ah, no, I fear not," the professor said, and went back to his closely written notebook which still was gritty with Sahara sand.

Downcast and bewildered, Frémont went back to the prefecture. Lazare's plea of insanity had been badly dented by Schlumberger even before it had been offered. And as the Chief sat at his desk, waiting for a word from Homer Evans, he began to envy the ancient Egyptians, who could drown, knife or poison anyone, up to and including the President of the Republic, without putting the local police to infinite trouble. He had heard much talk about Egypt of late, so much that his head was ringing. But no one had mentioned Egyptian detectives. They must have been an easy-going lot.

In the loft of Lewson-Phipps & Xerxes, Sergeant Bonnet was seated precariously on a case of warming pans with intricately carved handles, from northern Sweden, with his feet on a porcelain dragon of the Sui dynasty, early seventh century. He was concealed from the doorway by a huge packing case containing a state carriage, embossed in gold, of Philip II of Spain. Through a rift between boxes, he could see the somewhat bored expression on the face of the mounted chimpanzee and the sergeant was beginning to share the monkey's ennui. Nothing whatever had happened since Bonnet had been stationed in the warehouse. As the streaming of employees from near-by mercantile establishments indicated the hour of noon, however, the sergeant was startled by the opening of the metal doors. Crouching in his hiding place, he saw Monsieur "X," which was as far as the police force could get with Xerxes or Hagup Bogigian, enter the warehouse, after looking carefully around him. The Armenian paused a moment, then tiptoed to the other end of the spacious room, making his way skillfully between the multitude of hazards in the shape of packing cases, rolls of carpets, etc. Approaching the chimpanzee, Xerxes paused again, to look and listen. Then he reached for the keys, and hastily tucked them into his pocket.

When the Armenian left the warehouse, Bonnet was not half a block behind him. But long experience in the devious paths of Egypt and Morocco, and a rather candid tendency toward self-analysis, had taught the importer that if he was not being followed, he deserved to be. Consequently, Bonnet was so hard put to keep his man in sight that he had not a moment to give the high sign to a fellow officer, although he passed within hailing distance of any number of them. The quarry headed down the *rue* Montmartre, a sartorial symphony in brown which blended with the sides of beef and stained aprons in front of the meat and poultry shops. He cut closely around the huge market shed, hugged the circular wall of the Bourse, darted across the *rue* du Louvre, through the *rue* Jean-Jacques Rousseau, mingled with the crowd under the archway near the Café du Rohan and leaned over the subway entrance stairway.

Had not Bonnet been watching Xerxes so closely he would not have seen him drop the keys into the crowd that was descending the stairs. As it was, the sergeant let out a yell, involuntarily, that caused Xerxes to make a quick about-face, like a cat. Seeing Bonnet approaching at high speed, the Armenian ran down the subway station stairs and delivered brief but fervent thanks to God when he heard the rumble of an approaching train. He squeezed through just as the automatic doors were closing, leaving Bonnet panting and swearing outside, and in less than thirty seconds was being transported at high speed toward the Tuileries.

The disgruntled Bonnet reached the prefecture just in time to hear Schlumberger, his rival for the next promotion, recount with satisfaction how he had trapped Professor de la Poussière into betraying his colleague, Lazare.

"Insane, my eye," said Schlumberger. "He performed a mental feat, on the day he stuffed the poor Marquis, that only six men in France could accomplish."

"Enough," said Frémont, who was not only on the horns of a dilemma but felt himself being punctured in a tender spot by both of them. Hydrangea, piqued because he would not take her croaker fishing, had laid down the law in no uncertain terms. When Mr. Evans said a man was innocent, he was blameless and white as snow, was the Blackbird's dictum. Yet Schlumberger was piling up the most imposing evidence to the contrary. As so many men before him, the Chief was trying to choose between domestic peace and professional integrity. To divert his mind, he turned to Bonnet, who had been watching the stuffed monkey.

"Well?" the Chief began. "Don't tell me your man showed up and got away."

"That's about the size of it," said Bonnet, disconsolately.

Tom Jackson, whose reporter's instinct was ever uppermost, asked: "Who was he?"

"The dark one, Monsieur 'X' etc. . . ." said Bonnet. "He came in, nervous as a woodchuck, tiptoed up to the monkey and took the keys and cord from around his neck. Then he beat it. I trailed him to the Metro Palais Royal where he chucked the keys into the crowd. Then he spotted me. I must have yelled or something . . ."

"You should carry a bugle, to make it easier . . ." the Chief began.

"Well, I didn't know what to do. Whether to follow Monsieur 'X' or look for the keys."

"Of course, you couldn't be expected to remember that the keys were phony, and the gent was real. That would have required quick thinking, putting two and two together," was Frémont's peevish rejoinder.

Schlumberger tried not to look superior, but the going was very hard. He had been bawled out unmercifully for pinching Lazare, and he needed a raise in pay. Bonnet had given him the laugh when, just recently, he had shadowed the wrong clergyman in a Rosary set-up and dragged into the prefecture a young nephew of the Archbishop of York. The resulting protest by the British Embassy had brought an even sixteen tall hats into the prefect's office. Bonnet, however, knew the Alsatian was secretly enjoying the performance.

"I'll find the man, don't worry," he said.

"Pray do," said the Chief. "Preferably, before you come back into the prefecture again, even on payday."

Tom Jackson, who always had a twinge of feeling for the underdog and who was still hoping to catch up with the Englishman again, overtook Bonnet in the avenue and suggested that they call at Lewson-Phipps & Xerxes, as representatives of the New York *Herald,* and offer to give the firm some free advertising on condition that photographs of both partners be furnished. After lunch time the English partner went in for some form of stiff exercise, so he would be feeling fit when tea came along. Xerxes, as the reader knows, was just then in the subway. The clerk, a hold-over from the days of Lewson-Phipps himself, looked at the reporter and his plain-clothes escort disdainfully. Old Lewson-Phipps had never held with publicity.

"I have just left Mr. Xerxes," Jackson said, feeling sure that the Armenian would not break in on them. "He said for you to give me a picture."

Exuding disapproval, the clerk complied, and Jackson agreed to take the photograph back to the prefecture to have it rephotographed so that several prints could be made. Bonnet, on his mettle, refused to enter, and waited at the Café au Marché des Fleurs, so indignant that he piled one Pernod right on top of another and was muttering when the reporter returned.

Had the sergeant noticed the satisfaction written on Jackson's face, he would have known in advance that his luck had changed. As it was, he had to wait for Jackson's drink to come and go before the latter told him what had happened.

Since the day of their arrest, the suspects Angorre and Dubonnet had been receiving their pay on the basis of an eight-hour day, with time and a half for overtime. When no outsiders were around, the Chief had given them the run of the prefecture, so they chanced to be in the office playing parchesi when Jackson came in with the picture. Homer Evans had been there, also the Chief and Sergeant Schlumberger. Of those present, only Evans had noticed that when the photograph of Xerxes was produced, Dubonnet, the junior guard from the Hall of Pills, turned greenish white, like the inside of a fallen pear-blossom, and, slamming down the dice box, left the room and re-entered his cell, where he sat morosely with his back to the door. Evans, after waiting a moment tactfully, joined him and little by little drew forth the admission that on an occasion all too recent Dubonnet, having found a letter addressed to his wife, Mathilde, and signed "X," had in a rage ransacked their lodgings and come upon a photograph, affectionately inscribed, from "X" and corresponding to the one brought in by reporter Jackson.

"I do not wish to know who the man is, monsieur. Spare me that, I beg of you. But if he has been given the designation 'X' by Mathilde, does that not presuppose a series of lovers A, B, C, D, etc., all through the alphabet? A man as poor as I am, who marries a girl with Mathilde's face and figure, cannot expect to go through life unscathed. But 'X,' after all. There are such things as restraint and moderation."

20

The Sudden Death of a Couple of Grasshoppers

IN MONTPARNASSE, and elsewhere in the same chrono-
metrical zone, the *aperitif* hour was approaching. Five
more liners loaded with Americans had landed at Cher-
bourg and Le Havre and the boat trains had brought
the visitors to the Gare St. Lazare, from which they had
scattered to various hotels. Of those who chose the Right
Bank of the Seine, it is better not to speak, but the thou-
sand-odd who preferred the Left were seated in the four
principal cafés, the Dôme, the Coupole, the Rotonde and
the Select, enjoying the play of sunlight among the leaves
of the plane trees, the easy tread of Algerian and Moroc-
can rug peddlers and the drinks with which they were
working up a thirst for the appetizer proper. The afternoon was several degrees balmier than that on which the
terrasses had been animated by the news that *The Pansy*
had been stolen.

Miriam, as she turned from the *rue* Vavin into the
boulevard Montparnasse, was agreeably surprised as she
noticed that the colorful crowd had been augmented by

another influx of her compatriots. She liked Americans, especially in large numbers. The fact is that in the Montparnasse quarter spiritual solitude is more easily obtained when the district is filled with people. In the dreary winter months, those quarterites who do not have the price of a trip southward stand out like brick outhouses in a fog and are easily spotted by the possessors of glittering eyes.

Having tired of herself in dark blue, Miriam had changed to a becoming beige ensemble, embroidered in the same color and showing off to excellent advantage her clear complexion and expressive eyes. Throughout several changes of mode, since the Hugo Weiss case had brought her into association with Homer Evans, she had stuck to the normal waistline, in spite of the pleas of *couturiers* with other styles to sell. She couldn't explain to the dress designers, quite naturally, that it would be awkward to have a holstered automatic dragging down around her knees, like the clapper of a churchbell, and again there were aesthetic reasons why she did not want to wear her gun too high. The dressmakers concluded she was merely obstinate, but could not withhold their admiration when they saw her in street attire. In choosing the beige, notwithstanding its high visibility, she had remembered that Homer had liked it especially, and although she had involved him in the Louvre murder case in order to provide distraction for his mind she did not want him to lapse into the habit of intellectual pursuits, to the exclusion of other piquant phases of life. Her stockings were of flesh-colored silk, her shoes of beige canvas, garnished lightly with brown leather. The handbag provided a note of color, echoed by the topaz brooch Evans himself had selected.

It was understood between them that at five o'clock or thereabout they should meet, when it was convenient, for a drink at the Dôme, but, knowing how much routine Evans had had before him when they parted at lunch time, she hardly dared hope to find him in his place just left of the center and well toward the rear. When finally she saw that he was there waiting for her, in one of his best moods, which combined physical relaxation with humorous mental activity, she hurried her pace until she was almost on a trot.

"I was afraid you'd be late," she said, settling comfortably beside him.

"I had plenty of time to spare," he said, his sensitive fingers touching lightly the cool frosted glass. "In fact, I walked over from the prefecture and spent half an hour in the Delacroix museum. Strange chap, Delacroix. Couldn't draw very well, was as full of absurd and romantic ideas as our chimpanzee is full of Lazare's home-made stuffing, but what gusto when he got a paint brush in his hand! Ah, paint. How pale and lifeless on a pallette, how deeply imbued with verve and spirit when applied to a canvas by a master, be he a wise man or a magnificent fool . . . Ah, yes. I had another few moments that were by no means dull. I found a laundry, over near the old morgue, for men with only one shirt. They sit there, naked to the waist, and chat while their shirt is washed and ironed, fee 1 franc. You wouldn't believe how varied the conversation was . . ."

"Homer, you didn't . . ." She was looking hard at his shirt, which was freshly laundered.

"But why not?" he asked.

"Excuse me, dear," she said. "I should know, by this time, that no door is closed to you. But, Homer . . . I know I shouldn't talk shop at this hour . . . Still . . ." She looked at him anxiously.

"You're troubled about Lazare," he said kindly. Then his eyes lighted and he smiled his most tolerant smile. "All of my associates seem to have some pet obsession. Frémont can't sleep nights because of *The Pansy;* Schlumberger loses weight before one's eyes, trying to figure out what Maitre François Ronron will use as a defense; Madame de la Poussière's peace of mind is tied up with the freedom of her friend, the Marchioness; Bonnet's future happiness depends on finding the wily Armenian, Xerxes; the Prefect of Police, M. de la Chemise Farcie, dotes on mountain trout; Seldon wants to nobble the arch-crook Stables, and add lists of figures to those already in his bankbooks; Hjalmar and Kvek crave violent exercise and entertainment in the Roman style; lastly, you, my darling, are inviting wrinkles and gray hairs on behalf of a captive taxidermist. Of all my acquaintances, I seem to be the only one who needs nothing at all."

The gasp that came from Miriam and the agonized look that crossed her face caused him hastily to add "That is to say, nothing more than I have." As he reached for her hand, the color returned to her cheeks, and her lips. "Forgive me, I'm long-winded," Homer continued. "You shall have your heart's desire this very night. So, within certain limits, shall the rest of our merry throng. We shall have dinner . . . let me see . . . One has to select one's menu with care when the meal is to be followed by an active adventure. Certain foods induce contemplation, but the contemplation's all over in this case. I must find something that stimulates energy, tunes up the nerves and the circulation. As a matter of fact, shellfish and a tinge of saffron seem to be indicated. An *arroz marinero* in the Basque restaurant near the gare de l'Est. Achuri is the name. A cousin of the proprietor was very decent to me when I was in Madrid. Taught me the secret of *chipirones*."

Miriam was trembling with excitement. In actual emergencies she was as cool and steady as Homer himself, and had even quicker reactions. But to be told in advance that after a meal of rice and shellfish a murderer was to be run to earth and old wrongs righted caused a momentary flutter. "Oh," she said, paused a while and repeated, "Oh." That was all she could seem to contribute, since questions were forbidden in the progress of a case.

Acquaintances nodded or paused at their table to pass the time of day, tourists stared at them admiringly, being sure at first glance that they belonged in Montparnasse and were acquainted with all its mysteries. The hour passed pleasantly but Miriam's excitement did not subside. On the contrary it rose, and when, in the ladies' room she held out her hands, palms up, experimentally, she saw with dismay that they were shimmering. "Steady, my girl," she said to herself, unconsciously imitating her father, who had pronounced the same words so many times in the cattle and sheep men's clashes. She wondered if Homer had noticed her agitation, and if he would blame her or be disappointed. Could she shoot straight, with her hand wobbling to and fro, she wondered. There was no possibility of taking a practice shot in the ladies'

274

room of the Dôme, where a bullet would ricochet viciously between marble slabs and metal fixtures.

A moment later, when she rejoined Evans he had lost all inclination to tease her. They walked slowly to his apartment, where he took a package from the table in his outer corridor. This, the contents of which were unknown to Miriam, he tucked under his arm.

"And now," he said, "we've just time for a ride in the Bois. A turn or two around the lake, at thirty miles an hour, no more, no less, should put me in a frame of mind to solve the one remaining problem, the riddle confronting our friend, Dr. Hyacinthe Toudoux. About the livers, you know. Do they swell or shrink, and are they streaked with heliotrope or honeysuckle? Truc wouldn't dare to fake his experiments, not that I would put it beyond him, but he couldn't get away with it. Ah, well. Forget it. I'll work it out somehow. Toudoux's been very decent about Lazare."

As they rode side by side in the taxi, Miriam felt the strange chill that always came over her when Evans brought his powerful mind to a focus, and the focus was distant from her. She sat erect, hands motionless in her lap, and breathed as lightly as she could. Should she have continued to wear blue? A marksman could see beige two hundred yards away. What, exactly, was before them? When suddenly Homer turned to her, obviously elated, she was startled so that she felt a tingling around the roots of her hair.

"You've got the answer," she said.

"I don't see how I could have failed to get it instantly," he said. "It's so simple it's fairly ludicrous. Dr. Truc will be laughed out of the Academy, if he ever sees the

Academy again. You see, he tried the Eureka wine on guinea hens, gibbon apes, donkeys, Belgian hares and calves. Toudoux got his data from human beings, or what was left of them."

"But," objected Miriam. "Dr. Truc's first post mortem was on a man, according to his column."

"Exactly," said Evans, "and, unless I lose my guess, one will find on investigation that the benighted chap was a vegetarian, as are the gibbon apes, guinea hens, the donkeys, etc. Toudoux got hold of a good lusty meat eater. That's the answer. I'll tip him off this very evening. In fact, I'll insist that he trail along."

Miriam bit her lips with mortification. At the mention of the evening, her nerves began to vibrate again. As if Homer understood what was taking place within her, he asked the driver to seek a secluded roadway, stopped the taxi, and led Miriam into a thick grove of tall moss-stained trees. At a distance of thirty yards, a couple of grasshoppers had lit on the lower part of a venerable tree trunk and were clinging there, side by side. Without warning, Evans whipped out his automatic and shot the grasshopper on his, the right-hand, side. The report of his gun was followed so closely by another that the two shots could hardly be distinguished. Miriam, aghast, found herself holding her smoking automatic and saw that the second, or left-hand grasshopper, was no more.

"Now, for the rice, in the mariner's style, with shrimp and lobster meat, *almejas,* and the sausage of Perdrazo," Evans said and, although there were tears in her eyes, Miriam knew that her self-confidence had returned to stay.

276

The rice, when it was brought on, decorated with strips of roasted scarlet peppers that enhanced the glow of the saffron and the pinkness of the shrimps, was all that Evans had promised it would be, and they left the restaurant gaily, almost like a pair of irresponsible children. The package, however, was still tucked safely under Homer's arm.

"Now for the gathering of our forces," he said. "We shall take with us Chief Frémont, of course, and Schlumberger. They both will be surprised, and the latter, I fear, will return sadder but wiser. Bonnet and Tom Jackson I have asked to collect Xerxes, *chez* Madame Dubonnet, and bring them both along. Professor de la Poussière must be on hand, to help us when we get out of our depth in forgotten centuries, and his good wife, Hélène, has had so little recreation that the excursion would cheer her no end.

"The Alsatian auctioneer who has been so clever as to trace the linen in which the Marquis was wrapped will be absent, also the wholesome family who dwell on the 'Poor but Honest.' Melchisadek, naturally, will pilot his chief and Hydrangea, who refuses point blank to let Frémont enter the borders of Luneville again unless she is present. You see, to the simple mind nourished on Harlem tradition, a story to the effect that a notorious bandit kidnaps a man, holds him a day or two, then sends him on his way and is not prosecuted, sounds a bit fishy. I fear the former Blackbird suspects there is a woman in Luneville, most likely a blonde. The fact that Frémont was slugged so deftly that there is absolutely no bump or scar does much to make his explanation of his absence unconvincing. Ah, well. There is so much virtue in a childlike nature that its few inconveniences may be forgiven."

"We shall have a small army," Miriam said.

"In Luneville we shall find K. Parker Seldon, Hjalmar, Kvek, his cousin Sofia Alexandrovna, to say nothing of Lazare and Dr. Balthazar Truc, the Marchioness, and a husky named Gus."

"But my lawyer," said Miriam. "He's drawing Weiss's money. Can't we get some work out of him?"

"Ah, Maitre François Ronron. By all means. A fine old gentleman of a school almost extinct. I have never complimented you on your choice of attorneys, but you couldn't have done better."

Astonished, Miriam glanced at Homer's face and saw that he was entirely in earnest. "But," she objected, "he hasn't done a thing except to get poor Lazare locked up in the trickiest bughouse this side of Vienna, with slim prospects of ever getting out again. That poor inventor, Passepartout, was all right when he went into the Sens Unique in 1919. Now look at him."

"Perhaps the virtues of your counselor-at-law will disclose themselves more fully as the evening wears on," Evans said.

"He'd better show some stuff, since his fees will pass through my hands," Miriam said. "I was smart enough for that, at least."

The prefecture, when Homer and Miriam arrived there shortly after eight o'clock, was steeped in gloom. Chief Frémont, having just concluded a telephonic bout with Hydrangea, sat morosely at his desk wondering why it was that women who had cause for jealousy were blind, deaf and dumb, while those fortunate enough to possess an honest man's entire affection never tumbled to that simple fact. If ever he got slugged again, he swore silently, he would see to it that he came back with a scar, even if he had to inflict it himself.

Near him, his face buried in his hands, was Schlumberger. He was cocky, but disappointed. He had counted heavily on the Alsatian linen, as evidence against Lazare, but his auctioneer had found that it had been woven by a harmless old woman who, in order to get funds to have her spectacles repaired, had sold several meters of the cloth to a passing Englishman who wanted to make a shroud for his doodlesack collection, to protect it from dust and sunshine when he was away for the shooting in the fall.

Both of the good officers were worried about Bonnet, who had not reported his success in finding Xerxes because of Homer's instructions.

Evans was not crude enough to be breezy, but did his best to inject a bit of cheer into the atmosphere. "Meet me at the Hotel Serieux at Luneville promptly at eleven o'clock," he said.

"What for? *The Pansy?*" asked Frémont, without hope.

"The murderer," Evans said. "But no telling what else we may find."

"You can't take the murderer out of the asylum," Schlumberger said. "He's sent there by the court, although God knows why. You're just wasting your time."

"Better come along, anyway," said Evans, and led Miriam toward the laboratory of Dr. Hyacinthe Toudoux. On the way, they paused to glance through the bars at Angorre, who was reading the *En-Tout-Cas* to find out how long his overtime was likely to continue, and Dubon-

279

net who was counting in a mechanical way on his fingers, from A to X.

"What's the noise about?" asked Miriam, as they traversed the bleak area of deserted officers. A clatter such as travelers attribute to angry flocks of birds in the jungles or Arctic wastes was rising and swelling. Opening the door of the laboratory gently, they saw the medical examiner in his shirtsleeves, hair awry, chucking guinea hens out of the open window and into the night. It turned out that the doctor had ordered a crate of the hens, in order to show up Dr. Truc, and had found that, actually, California wine did tend to shrink their livers and that the livers, when extracted, showed a detestable mustard-colored stain which Toudoux, in his rage, and not seeing Miriam in the doorway, described quite otherwise. His joy, when Homer offered the simple explanation, was equaled only by his impatience to get at Dr. Truc. Again grasping the sharp pointed foils and tearing them from the wall, he hustled himself into his coat and started down the stairs.

"Where are you going?" Homer asked.

"Luneville," the medical examiner said. "I shall offer that scoundrel two alternatives. Either he shall eat without butter or sauce of any kind an entire copy of *En-Tout-Cas,* in which shall be printed his apology to me and an unequivocal admission that he made an ass of himself with herbivores, or I shall churn his tripes . . . On second thought, I shall churn them anyway." And he made off again.

"I'm going that way. Let me drive you down," Evans said, and the doctor, who had made no plans for transportation, calmed himself and proffered his thanks.

21

Nocturne

WHEN Luna, pale goddess of the moon, surveyed the land from the dusky horizon, her first glance was directed toward the Sanitorium Sens Unique. For between those grim walls, with bars to streak the silver light sent by their symbol and protector, were her favorites among men. The goddess, in contrast with her rival, the pink-fingered Aurora, took little interest in humans whose lives had the traditional beginning, middle and ending. She would shine disdainfully, if at all, upon bores who insisted that two and two were four. In Dr. Truc's asylum dwelled a company exactly to her taste, whose actions were unpredictable, whose conversation was by no means confined to "Yea yea" and "Nay nay" but had a satisfactory range and variety, and who showed more verve when the moon was shining than Aurora could ever evoke from them.

As the goddess attained the altitude necessary for an effective entrance into the sky's great amphitheater and her most beloved among rivers, the Seine, sent back to her a beauteous reflection as tribute, Luna was startled to observe that the narrow road leading into Luneville was carrying unusually heavy traffic that evening. Silently she raised the back curtain of a roadster that had a large baggage compartment where the rumble seat used to be and peeped inside, annoyed by the impudent tail-light that winked in her face. Hastily she lowered the curtain and turned away, for sitting three abreast, left to right, were Hagup Bogigian, or Xerxes, at the wheel; Mathilde Dubonnet, a natural blonde whose face was extraordinarily familiar to the goddess, in fact, so familiar that Luna scarcely recognized her wayward devotee in a sitting position; and Sergeant Bonnet of the Paris police, an organization in excellent standing with the celestial guardian of eccentrics. Mathilde had been upbraiding Xerxes for having got himself and her in the toils of the law. At the time Luna ceased eavesdropping, the young woman was asserting that if Dubonnet got wind of the affair and threw her out of the house, Xerxes would have to marry her, even if it made her an Armenian. The negative was being argued by Xerxes, as hotly as was consistent with safe night driving. Bonnet, who had slipped up once that day, was taking no chances. His gun was in his hand and ready.

At random, Luna selected a long limousine that was proceeding deliberately, perhaps two miles behind the roadster just touched upon. In its cushioned interior the gaze of Luna lingered with pleasure, the sole occupant, not counting an anonymous chauffeur, being Maitre François Ronron of the boulevard St. Germain. When lawyers started night riding into the country, Luna knew she was in for some kind of a treat. Legal phraseology was her particular delight, such sonorous words and phrases as "with malice aforethought," "felonious intent," etc., and of all the ladies on Olympus she held most rigidly to the doctrine of *caveat emptor*.* But Maitre Ronron was not talking to himself just then, so she passed along a few more kilometers and spied Melchisadek at the wheel of the chief of detectives' car. Beside him, and much easier to spot by moonlight, was Sergeant Schlumberger, formerly of Alsace. The back seat offered a spectacle so intimate that even Luna smiled and turned away. Hydrangea had concluded, since Frémont had shown a willingness to take her along to Luneville, that he must have been slugged, after all, and the Blackbird was trying with all the resources of her affectionate nature to make the Chief forget her unwarranted suspicions. She had not only succeeded in that objective, but was well on the way toward making him forget *The Pansy*, the Marquis de la Rose d'Antan, and the fact that Mrs. Frémont was on the rampage and that a talk with her, face to face, could not be postponed much longer. In a way, the Chief was dreading the moment when the papers would announce that the case was over. He did not expect Evans to exonerate Lazare but figured that if Homer failed to do so, he would offer no further objections to having the taxidermist tried.

The auto driven by Homer Evans contained Hélène de la Poussière, whose delight because she was to take part in a modern adventure had revived the faded roses on her cheeks so noticeably that she had been forced to wear a brighter scarf than usual, to match. She sat on the left-hand side of the rear seat, almost dazed by the

* Let the buyer beware.

loveliness of the fields and villages, the winding roads on the hillsides and tangents across the plains, the summer fragrance and the river mists. In the center was the professor, who was trying to figure out when the moon would rise that night on the stretches of the upper Nile and wondering if the shin bone and skull of Neferkesokar were just as he had left them. Dr. Hyacinthe Toudoux was by far the most promising passenger, from Luna's point of view, since he was muttering about livers and tripes and toying with a couple of foils in a meaningful way. Notwithstanding all the dark deeds she had witnessed, the goddess had never seen one man run through another with two swords at once, so she resolved to stick close to the dynamic medico and his companions. Miriam, of course, was in the front seat beside Evans, just close enough so he would be constantly aware of her presence, not pressed against him so tightly that his thoughts would be sidetracked or addled.

"In five minutes, we'll be at the hotel," he said. And when she said "Oh" there was no tremor in her voice. She held her right-hand palm up, and as far as she could discover by moonlight, it was as steady as American Jar and Bottle stock, which had not budged from 32 all day long.

Against the bar of the Hotel Sérieux at Luneville-sur-Seine, Tom Jackson was leaning, in the act of wiping off his glasses. He glanced at the clock, which indicated the hour as being ten forty, then asked the proprietor if it was correct. The proprietor's watch said ten twenty-five.

"In that case, I'll have another," Jackson said. He wanted to be in good shape for the raid on the asylum, but even more he wanted to forget that he had lost his

284

job. The afternoon spent with Bonnet, in pursuit of Xerxes, had done the trick. The *Herald* would stagger along without him, and that was that. When he was about half way outside the whiskey and soda, he heard an outburst of Russian song the words of which, had he but known it, dealt with folks dying young or living to be too old, in inverse ratio to their merits and good fortune. Coincidently another voice, not as well trained but quite as powerful, was singing "Samuel Hall." The proprietor's face lighted, and a second later the door opened and the ex-reporter was greeted by Hjalmar and Kvek. They had scaled the asylum wall by means of the Volga boatman's sash, fed beer and sandwiches to the taciturn Gus, who had been installed aboard the *Deuxieme Pays,* firmly lashed to a stanchion. Neither one had tasted alcohol, figuratively speaking, since the day before. The first couple of whiskies they took straight, swallowing boiled eggs and *brioches* practically whole the while. Then they settled down to wait for Homer Evans.

The first arrivals were Bonnet with Xerxes and Mathilde, the former of which was warning the woman not to damage the Armenian, who had become public property by virtue of the sergeant's authority. He made it clear, however, that were it not his official duty to protect his prisoner, he would offer no personal objections to anything she might care to do. Mathilde catching sight of Kvek and Hjalmar, forgot her anger and paused in the doorway, her head slightly tilted to show her winning profile, which was as good as that of Isis, and maybe better. Without ado, the Russian and the big painter flipped a coin and Hjalmar won.

"Hello, kid," he said. "Where you from?"

The Maitre François Ronron and the officials from the prefecture pulled up at the hotel entrance almost simultaneously, and the lawyer noticed that Sergeant Schlumberger was glowering at him ferociously. That was a good sign that the sergeant was worried about his evidence, Maitre François Ronron concluded, and the resulting smile caused the Alsatian to splutter with rage.

Dr. Hyacinthe Toudoux, who was first out of the other limousine, started hell bent into the darkness, foils in hand, in the direction of the Sens Unique, until overtaken by Evans and persuaded to bide his time, since it would be short. Miriam joined Kvek and Jackson at the bar for a bracer, and smiled tolerantly as she saw Hjalmar and Mathilde at a table in the corner, the latter in the act of asserting that she had not found such a droll and amusing companion, and big and strong to boot, since she had been silly enough to marry a watchman, and such an ineffectual watchman that paintings were stolen right from under his nose. Hjalmar was pointing out that, on the other hand, if one has to have a husband, it is better to have one with fixed hours of work which can fairly well be counted upon not to vary.

In the billiard room, Homer assembled the members of the party and gave them their instructions. Frémont and Schlumberger, with Professor de la Poussière, were to go to the main entrance of the Sens Unique and present the document the Chief had secured from the court, authorizing him to visit the suspect, Lazare, and question him. Maitre François Ronron, as Lazare's attorney, was to accompany them and assure Dr. Truc that the defense had consented to the examination.

Bonnet was told to take Mme. de la Poussière, Mathilde and Xerxes, the latter to be handcuffed and hobbled, to the asylum boathouse, there to wait the signal for their entrance through the front gate. Then, after escorting them inside, the sergeant was to fetch Gus, securely tied, from the *Deuxieme Pays*.

Homer, Miriam and Dr. Hyacinthe Toudoux saw the first two detachments on their way before they joined Jackson, Hjalmar and Kvek in the bar.

"Let's go," Evans said simply. "Hjalmar, show us the way."

In single file they passed along the moonlit pathway, Jansen in the lead and Dr. Toudoux, foils still in hand, bringing up the rear. A rope ladder had been rigged and one by one they scrambled over the wall and let themselves down into Courtyard Seven, at the entrance of which they were met by Sofia Alexandrovna.

"Where's the doctor?" asked Evans, in a whisper.

"In his private wing," the nurse replied.

"And Seldon?"

"In his room, reading the same ungainly blue book. I don't know what he finds so fascinating in it. My English is not bad, but I couldn't make head or tail of it," said Sofia, whose tone indicated that she considered *Ulysses* a waste of time.

"Let him out," said Evans.

"But he hasn't any clothes. He wouldn't want to appear in company in his night shirt. He's very shy. I like that in a man," Sofia said.

Hjalmar put in a helpful suggestion. "He's just about the size of that Armenian," he said.

Since it was not practicable to retrieve Xerxes and

strip him just then, they had to fall back on the Volga boatman's costume, more or less adjustable in size, that Kvek had hidden in his cousin's room.

Cautioning the others to make no unnecessary noise, Evans concealed them in the corridor by the telephone booth while he and Miriam tiptoed upstairs, skirted the violent ward in which howls rose to Heaven, ranging from those of ecstasy to despair, and including several shades and kinds of feeling Miriam, young as she was, had not yet experienced. The volume of sound increased as the moon rose higher and faded from henna to platinum. Homer felt her hand on his arm and patted it reassuringly.

"We're going to see Lazare," he said.

The taxidermist-savant was not in a general ward, where mad-folk of moderate resources were herded together. Lazare had a private room, since his bill would be paid by the Third Republic, if the latter survived the annual financial crisis which was due in the fall. Dr. Truc had selected No. 14-A, which had no view to distract a nervous patient and was sound-proofed against incoming or outgoing howls, prayers, imprecations or soliloquies. For once, and entirely by accident, Dr. Truc had hit upon just the treatment the patient needed, namely, solitude. With his piece of chalk and a wall on which to write hieroglyphics, Lazare could have lived on a diet of roots and herbs. In fact, he had wished absent-mindedly for a wholesome root to gnaw when he had tasted the asylum bread and coffee. The old man had improved rapidly, being left to his own devices. He didn't worry about his shop, because in the new dispensation of things there seemed to be no need for ready money. His rent had been paid up two months in advance, just after the sale of a large chimpanzee. The sympathetic young lady who had gone to jail with him had even promised to bring him some books. Lazare was simply letting things ride. He allowed his thoughts to stray, not too often, to the stuffed Marquis and regretted faintly that he had not done the job himself, for at a glance he had noticed that in mixing the stuffing, some amateur had forgotten the sesquicarbonate of sodium, which always contains sulphate and chlorides of sodium. The mummy de la Rose d'Antan would look pretty crummy before five hundred years had elapsed, was Lazare's opinion. He was just as well pleased.

He heard a tap on his door, which was not according to Hoyle. Regular attendants peeked in, then opened the door without knocking. When in response to the taxidermist's "Come in," Miriam appeared on the scene, followed by Homer Evans, the old man rose to greet them and apologized for the trouble his temporary lapse had given them.

"I'm quite all right now," he said, "but please, if you can, avoid a public trial. This place has done me a world of good, but you know how I feel about crowds. I've never grown accustomed to them. I should not appear at my best. Most likely I'd cause embarrassment to Maitre Ronron, make him lose face, perhaps."

"You'll be back in your shop in the morning," Evans said, "unless you care to take a holiday."

"Oh, no, thanks," said Lazare. "I'm rested and fit. I'd been in a rut for years, and I'll admit, now that I've seen what a short stay in a sanitorium will do for a man, that I'd overdone it a bit preparing notes on Tout-or-

289

Nada. Ha! ha! ha! Ho! ho! Well worth a collapse, that chap."

Evans chuckled and agreed. "I'm going to hold a little meeting in the doctor's salon tonight," he said. "I hope you'll be present. Professor de la Poussière will be there, and there will be several interesting points brought up concerning Egypt."

"By all means," Lazare said. "What an amazing institution! I confess that I had not realized that our madhouses had reached such a cultural level. By all means."

"Miss Leonard will call for you when the time comes," Homer said.

"I hope she'll play that piece I like, if there's a piano," said Lazare. "Let me see. How does it go? *T*atatata *la* mi *tum* tum (Boom!). *T*atatata *la* mi *tee* tee. (Wham!) *T*otototo *to* la *tee* tee, (rest) la tum tum, (rest), la tee tee, (Zowie)."

"That's *Ben Hur*. You remember the tune," said Miriam. "It was my father's favorite."

In the hallway, their voices safely covered by the wails and whoops from Ward 9, Homer and Miriam completed their final plans. White-coated attendants and soft-footed nurses passed them by, assuming that they had brought with them, or were about to bring, a new patient for whom the resplendent full moon had proved to be the last straw.

"Oh, Homer. You are so satisfactory," Miriam said. "Why couldn't I have known that, if you were not worrying about Lazare, I could be sure he was all right?"

"Dr. Truc slipped up badly, for once," Homer said. "I've seldom seen such an improvement in so short a time."

In the old mossy boathouse by the river bank, the chorus of frogs would have delighted Aristophanes. On Mathilde, who had spent her life in the city, it produced the opposite effect and necessitated the raising of her voice to a pitch unbecomingly shrill as she upbraided the handcuffed Xerxes. It was already apparent that whatever else might be accomplished by the Luneville pilgrimage, the suspect Dubonnet would have nothing more to worry about between his wife and M. "X." Madame de la Poussière, who was of the patient and fore-bearing school of womanhood, listened in amazement, and even at moments secretly envied her outspoken, if wayward, sister. Two hundred yards upstream, Gus, trussed up in the official motorboat, was cursing his luck. For the first time since he had been employed in the Sens Unique he had money in his pocket, and a couple of roughnecks had tied him so securely that he couldn't use it. The knowledge that Sofia was betrothed to a medium-sized and violent patient had stirred in him an old lust for rum and riot. Gus was a frustrated man, with no relief in sight. He could feel the roll of bills by stooping and bending one elbow, and his mind, that worked slowly at best, had come to a full stop in trying to figure out why a couple of bruisers would take the trouble to fan him into insensibility, bung him into a telephone booth and then shanghai him without rolling him.

When the signal was given from the window of Sofia Alexandrovna (two dots and a dash, repeated, with the light), Frémont, waiting resolutely near the outside gates, was suffering a fit of despondency. True, he had pacified Hydrangea, who was being well guarded by Melchisadek in the limousine, parked near the boathouse. But the Chief did not see what was to be gained by crashing an asylum. Madhouses made him nervous.

Schlumberger, grunting and muttering to himself, was eager to break in, confident that his arrest of Lazare would be more than justified and that Evans would go down in history with his compatriot, the athlete Snodgrass. The professor was puzzled by the unconventional approach of the party to the institution, attributing it to a change of local customs he had not previously noticed in his brief contacts with the workaday world. Hélène had looked well and charming, he reflected, and he attributed her excellent state of nerves and preservation to the tranquillity of her life with him. Just lately, for some reason he could not fathom, she had mentioned more than once a voyage to New York. In fact, the chap known as Evans had said something about it, too.

"Dear me," the professor said, and wrapped his scarf around his lean throat as he noticed that the river mist was rising. "One learns to be careful of one's health on the Nile," he said to the Alsatian. "The Euphrates, too, for that matter."

22

An American Falls Under the Spell of the Old World Charm

AT THE hour when the Louis XIV clock in Dr. Balthazar Truc's luxurious salon should have been striking eleven, the proprietor of the Sens Unique, who was lounging in his satin dressing-gown and moleskin slippers, was startled by a vigorous peal of the bell at the outer gate.

"Ah! Another patient," he said, clasping his plump hands behind his back and peering out through a slit between the draperies of the window that commanded the entrance. Instead, he saw his night watchman arguing with a party of three men, one stocky and determined who seemed to be in charge, another heavy-set and ponderous, and the third who had a lean but not exactly hungry look about him. As the doctor watched, he saw a fourth man join the party. "What the devil," exclaimed Dr. Truc, impatiently.

Taking down a large book from one of the convenient shelves, the doctor advanced to the office doorway to confront the intruders. The volume was a Codification of the Laws relating to the Insane or Feeble-minded, with an appendix dealing with the rights and duties of physicians with reference to the mentally incompetent. He turned the leaves rapidly, placed a thumb between two pages, and waited. He did not have long to wait.

"I am Frémont, Chief of Paris Detectives," the stocky visitor said, brandishing a document which he handed to the doctor. "I have come to see one Lazare, who has been sent here for observation," he added.

"Impossible," said Dr. Truc, with finality.

"This is an order from the court," said Frémont. "Stand aside, if you please."

"Chapter 14 of the revised laws of May, 1798, as amended by chapter 4 of the law of March, 1909, expressly states that visitors shall not be admitted to private sanitoriums except between the hours of nine a.m. and five p. m.," the doctor said. "Good evening, gentlemen, and good night. I shall be happy to receive you in the morning, or at any rate, I shall receive you," said Dr. Truc.

The soft persuasive voice of Maitre François Ronron introduced a more diplomatic note into the conversation. "My dear doctor," said the lawyer, bowing. "You have overlooked, perhaps, the amendment to the law you have just quoted, enacted in February, 1923. That provides, if my memory serves me, for visits at all hours to patients accused of major crimes or felonies, provided . . . ah, provided that the counsel for the defense agrees. I am Ronron, counsel for the defense, and I have no objection to having my client questioned. A mere formality, doctor. A bagatelle. We shall not trouble you long. I know what it is to have my hours of rest and recreation broken into, and promise you every consideration."

"Who are these other men?" the doctor asked, visibly uneasy. The names of Sergeant Schlumberger and Professor de la Poussière did nothing to allay his anxiety. He did not like the look of things at all, and especially he was chagrined at having muffed that amendment of February, 1923. That, for him, was a distinctly bad omen.

The differences between Frémont on the one hand and Truc on the other might have been smoothed over for a while had not a nurse let out a shriek and come running into the vestibule.

"Help! Sound the emergency alarm! A crowd of thieves are hiding behind the telephone booth," she cried. Coincidently guards and huskies began appearing from all directions.

"That tears it," said Hjalmar, grinning. "Well, Kvek. You work on the left-hand side and I'll take the right." And without ado he charged into a couple of guards in white jerseys, clipping one with his elbow as he dealt the other such a jab in the pantry that he doubled up and fell writhing to the floor. Tom Jackson, who had slipped his glasses into an inside pocket, set to work on the casualties while Hjalmar reached out for more. K. Parker Seldon, fitted out with his teeth but somewhat hampered by his Volga boatman's costume, started straight for Dr. Truc and was joined by the mad inventor, Passepartout, who still had his precious stick of stovewood.

Gongs clanged, signal lights flashed. The turmoil spread from ward to ward until old women were diving from their beds as if they were springboards, girls were dancing ring around a rosie, bearded fathers of families were gamboling to and fro, and the chorus of howls from the violent ward took on Wagnerian proportions, with Stravinsky's *Sacre du Printemps* thrown in.

There is no telling what might have happened had not Homer Evans appeared at the head of the main stairway, and beside him, Miriam, automatic in hand.

"Silence," Evans shouted above the din, and nearly every head was turned in his direction. The exceptions were those of Passepartout and Schlumberger. In his wild excitement, Alsatians looked all the same to the inventor and he had brought down his stick of wood on the sergeant's collar bone with such force that the latter's solid frame was hard put to stand up under the blow. It was Maitre François Ronron who saved the day.

"Why, Passepartout. How are you? I haven't seen you for years," the lawyer said, suavely, and the inventor, haunted by the echo of a familiar voice, tossed aside his weapon and his intent to commit mayhem, and said:

"You see before you a man gravely wronged. They think I'm crazy but I'm not."

Hjalmar and Kvek, while waiting for further instructions, were comparing notes. The painter had accounted for six opponents, the Russian only five, but Kvek was always a good loser. Politely he took one hundred francs from his pocket and handed it to Hjalmar, who accepted it with a deprecatory air.

"If everyone will do his best to preserve order, and Dr. Truc will send his strong-arm squads away, I have something to say that will be of interest to all concerned," Homer said. When the doctor and the guards hesitated, he nodded to Miriam, who shot away in rapid succession the four accents on the plaster motto "Liberté, Égalité, Fraternité" that had been mounted above the main doorway.

"That cost six francs eighty," said Dr. Truc, indignantly, but just then he caught sight of Dr. Hyacinthe Toudoux who was advancing, swords in hand.

"Give 'em room," said Hjalmar, whose sportsmanship was always impeccable.

"Dr. Toudoux," said Evans severely. "You had best postpone your bout until I get through talking."

"As you say. But this time he shall not get away," said the medical examiner.

"May I have an explanation of this outrage?" demanded Dr. Truc. "Chapters 7 and 8 of the law of December, 1843 . . ."

"I realize that this appears unwarranted and unusual," said Evans, coolly. "The fact is that the murderer of the Marquis de la Rose d'Antan is in this building, and the object of our coming is to arrest the perpetrator of that picturesque crime."

"Preposterous," Dr. Truc said, although visibly shaken. "The suspect Lazare has already been arrested and committed for observation."

"I shall demonstrate his innocence without delay," Evans promptly replied. "But it's awkward, meeting here on the main stairway and in the entrance hall, doctor. Could not a selected number of our company hold a confidential session in another more suitable room?"

"I have nothing to fear," said Dr. Truc. "I am always ready to lend myself to the cause of law and order . . . as set forth in the statutes and upheld by the courts . . ."

"That's different," murmured Maitre Ronron, smiling.

The guards and nurses, aching with curiosity and some of them smarting from the blows of Kvek and Jansen, were hustled away to quiet the patients, who were carrying on in a frightful manner behind tightly locked doors. Dr. Truc led the way to his main salon, in the private wing, followed by the members of the expedition from Paris, the black-haired nurse, Sofia Alexandrovna, and K. Parker Seldon, who had promised to be good. Miriam was dispatched to fetch the suspect, Lazare, but Schlumberger insisted on accompanying her, since the patient was under arrest.

The pre-arranged signal was sounded and Sergeant Bonnet entered with Xerxes, handcuffed and sullen; Mathilde Dubonnet who was pale but soon spotted Hjalmar and smiled; Madame de la Poussière; Melchisadek; Hydrangea; and last of all, Gus, who looked as if he were in a cocoon, so painstakingly was he bound. The Louis XIV salon had been built for holding fancy-dress balls, with chairs ranged around four sides and a small platform at one end for an orchestra.

"Be seated, ladies and gentlemen," Homer said, and after they had all complied he added: "Since this concerns so vitally the interests of the Marchioness de la Rose d'Antan, I think she should be present. Will you ask her to come down, please, Mademoiselle Dargomyzshkov?"

Sofia left the room, and after a silence which was broken only by nervous coughs and shuffling of feet, she returned with the Marchioness, in her absurd old-fashioned gown with high neck and puff sleeves. Nevertheless, Madame de la Rose d'Antan crossed the floor with such pathetic dignity that Hélène de la Poussière burst into tears, hurried to her old friend's side and greeted her with such emotion that it was communicated to the whole gathering.

"Eugénie, my dear. How you have suffered! How unjust has been your fate," sobbed Hélène.

"One must fulfill one's destiny," the Marchioness said, resignedly. "If I have suffered from the duplicity of others, I have one satisfaction. I have inflicted no pain on another. What I have done, I have done deliberately, and not with cruelty."

"Ladies and gentlemen," Homer began. "I have a long story to tell you, which involves certain acts performed by persons in this room. If any of these acts are described incorrectly, I invite the person in question to challenge my statement and publicly tell the truth. The truth, my friends, will stand up under any inquiry. Falsehood, however clever on the surface, is bound to have a flaw. Therefore I warn you all, although to most of you no such admonition is necessary, to think at least twice before trying to deceive this company, which includes members of the most respected professions, officers of the law whose integrity has never been questioned, brave men, sensitive women, and more than one offender against the laws of God and man. They are not always similar, those two codes of laws, as in an ideal state they should be . . . Now, I shall begin."

But another interruption was due. No one except Dr. Hyacinthe Toudoux, whose eyes had been glued on Dr. Balthazar St.-J. Truc, noticed that the latter, under cover of the confusion that attended the seating of the guests, had backed into the bedroom. The medical examiner, emitting growls of satisfaction, followed quite as stealthily. He got into the bedroom just in time to see the rear of his host as Dr. Truc was climbing out of a window, from which a balcony led to a fire escape half hidden in the luxurious growth of ivy. Toudoux, with a hand that had by no means lost its accuracy in spite of its possessor's years, plunged the point of a sword into the exposed posterior of the fleeing alienist and promised so earnestly to wet the remaining foil in the heart's blood of his victim, from below and behind, that Dr. Truc backed into the room again.

"Precede me into the salon," ordered Dr. Toudoux. "Ah. Imposter! Color blind, eh?" Each word was emphasized with a wicked jab and was followed by a squeal of pain and rage.

A gasp of astonishment was heard when the host showed up, emitting short shrieks, in the doorway of his own salon but the explanation of that phenomenon was not long in forthcoming. The assembly caught sight of Dr. Toudoux and saw what he had in his hand.

"Excuse me, Mr. Chairman," the medical examiner said to Evans, bowing, after the alienist was seated but had not ceased squirming. "One of the offenders against decency was trying to make his get-away."

"Oh, much obliged," Evans said. "He wouldn't have got very far."

"I begin to see," whispered K. Parker Seldon to Hjalmar and Kvek, "that Europe is wonderful, after all."

23

In Which Love and Duty Become Irreconcilable

As a matter of precaution, Evans asked Hjalmar to sit near the door leading into the laboratory, Kvek to guard the main entrance, and Miriam to take her place at his left, near the platform, and discourage anyone else from attempting to leave the room. The variegated company, from the racial, sartorial, moral and intellectual points of view, afforded an impressive spectacle in the sixteenth-century ballroom with glittering old-fashioned chandeliers, a polished floor of inlaid wood tastefully patterned, the gilded backs and pale upholstery of the chairs and the slightly risqué character of the Personnes and Fragonards between the wall mirrors. The ceiling had been done by Tiepolo, at a time when he was deservedly suffering from the seven days' itch, which lent the composition a vibrant effect that had been praised highly by certain critics.

There was tense silence when Homer started speaking, punctuated only by suppressed gasps and sighs and the squeaking of the antique furniture. Dr. Balthazar Truc sat stoically in his chair, glaring at the shelf of law books that could be seen through the bedroom doorway. The Marchioness de la Rose d'Antan half closed her eyes and simply waited. Lazare was beside K. Parker Seldon, as passive as the other was intense.

"Most of you," Evans began, "in common with the public generally, think of this case as having begun with the theft of *The Pansy*, and that its criminal phases ended with the murder of the Marquis de la Rose d'Antan. For a clear understanding of what I am about to tell you, it is first necessary that you shed those misconceptions.

"The roots of this crime go very deep, indeed, and I shall not attempt to bare every unimportant tendril. Let us take off from the point when the resources of the late Marquis began to dwindle to such a degree that he found it difficult to borrow large sums of money. He had squandered his patrimony and exhausted the normal credit extended by acquaintances or admirers of his family. He had placed his wife in this institution which furnishes to its patients, quarters and appointments far below the standard suggested by this room. Her income he had thus appropriated, but it was not enough.

"What does an aristocrat of that type do when pressed for cash? His first step is to borrow from—I will not say 'sharks', but lenders, who, for greater risk insist on a higher rate of interest. These men are to be found, not in banking establishments, but here and there, engaged in some form of business which brings them large sums spasmodically which have to be invested without preconceived plans. The Marquis came in contact with a member of our group who is with us tonight, a man whose name is Hagup Bogigian, according to his passport, and Xerxes, if one reads the firm name on the sign at his place of business."

All eyes were turned toward Xerxes, who showed pained surprise.

"Why shouldn't I lend money to the Marquis?" the Armenian asked. "Besides, I never got it back. He got into me for 200,000 francs at compound interest. But I didn't murder him for that. If I murdered every guy who owes me money, I'd have Landru beat to a frazzle."

"Please," interrupted Homer, holding up his hand for silence. "Let us not jump ahead of the story. We must follow it, phase after phase, and overlook no salient details. When I wish to announce who murdered the Marquis de la Rose d'Antan, I shall do so."

He paused dramatically, and Miriam could hear her heart pounding. "Steady, my girl," she whispered, then gave Homer her full attention, except for the corner of her eye glued on the bedroom door.

"I merely said that Xerxes lent the Marquis a total of 200,000 francs."

"At compound interest," Xerxes muttered.

Mathilde indignantly hissed for silence.

"The need and possession of money bridge distances between social strata, so Xerxes and the Marquis became acquaintances, if not friends. Of course there came a time when even our adventurous Monsieur 'X' could risk his coin no longer, and that was a painful moment for both. To the debtor it meant less debauchery and waste, to the creditor the horrid prospect of losing what he had already lent. Xerxes decided that he must find some way for the Marquis to make a good-sized haul.

"The director of an American museum in Woodburn,

Oregon, I believe, complained one day to Xerxes that in the whole state of Oregon there was not a single Egyptian mummy, while California possessed two. That gave Xerxes the germ of an idea . . ."

"Aw, what was the harm in that?" objected Xerxes, his dark eyes burning eloquently beneath his wrinkled forehead.

"Patience, my good man," Evans said. "I am here to state facts, not to judge human actions. Heaven forbid that I should go in for that."

"A lot of people do," said the Armenian, disconsolately.

"Now, securing a mummy is not an easy task. First Xerxes consulted an encyclopedia, probably the Britannica, to get a general idea of how mummies are made. Then it struck him that his client, the Marquis, had quite a few mummies, ready made, in the Louvre. He proposed to the Marquis that they sell one of them to Woodburn, Oregon, believing that the relic would never be missed. He was informed by the Minister of Beaux Arts that many scholars fairly doted on mummies and would raise a world scandal if an eyebrow were filched from a dead Egyptian king.

"It is not in the nature of our Monsieur 'X' to give up easily. He applied to the problem the principles of his trade. If the real thing could not be had, why not make a mummy? For that purpose, of course, a corpse was necessary. Why not buy a corpse? Unfortunately, the state refuses to let human bodies be bartered about, after life has become extinct. Before that, almost anything goes, but once a man is dead he cannot be auctioned off except to certain qualified scientists for purposes of study."

Evans shifted his position on the platform slightly, and turned suddenly to Dr. Balthazar Truc. Extending his hand toward the indignant alienist, Homer said, in a sharper tone, "That brings us to Dr. Balthazar Truc. He is a scientist . . ."

"Bah!" said Toudoux. "He is a coward and a fraud."

"Nevertheless," continued Homer, "within the meaning of the word, as used in the statutes, Dr. Truc is a scientist. He has passed an examination, has been granted a certificate."

"Chapter 53 of the law of August . . ."

"Laws should not be made in August," Evans said. "Heat puts legislators in a vicious mood. However, let me tell you all how Xerxes and Dr. Truc got together. The story is a slight digression, but pertinent nonetheless. Xerxes' partner, an Englishman, indulged a bit too freely in order to celebrate the Armistice and just after Christmas got into such a state that Xerxes had to put him away. The Briton's condition was not grave [grunts from Jackson], but he wasn't in fit shape to hang around the store in the avenue de l'Opéra where the swell trade might get a glimpse of him soused. Dr. Truc, however, by means best known to him, kept the poor chap on edge for six weeks, until, in fact, his fee would equal the asking price of a large rug he wanted for his bedroom. Lest you all feel bad for Xerxes, I want to assure you that the rug is an imitation. Now men who will exchange quack cures for fake rugs have something in them that draws Xerxes to them irresistibly. Our Armenian colleague learned that Dr. Truc had the necessary credentials for buying corpses, and tactfully the proposition was made and cautiously accepted. Truc procured a stiff from the morgue, turned it over to Bogigian, and, like Pilate, washed his hands. Of course, Pilate never had any such soap as Cosmidor or Garlin, so his hands were never washed as thoroughly as those of the doctor."

Dr. Truc rose solemnly and faced the gathering. "Ladies and gentlemen," he said, sonorously. "An innocent action of mine is being made to appear in a criminal light. The law expressly states that a registered physician, having secured a license, may purchase human bodies for dissection . . . Dr. Toudoux will bear me out."

"I'll *kick* you out," growled Toudoux.

"The law also says," continued Truc, "and Maitre Ronron will agree, that once a physician has bought a corpse, in the words of the statute 'he may dispose of said body or bodies in such manner and at such time and place as he sees fit, provided: that the remains of such body or bodies is not disposed of in such manner, and at such time or place, as to constitute a public nuisance, under the meaning of the act of July 4, 1776.' If Mr. Evans, our chairman, desires to do full justice to one and all, he should confirm my statement."

"Granted," Evans said. "Let us go on. Xerxes, with a corpse on his hands, takes the same to his warehouse in the *rue* Réaumur, unbeknown to everyone except his watchman, who has such good reasons for keeping his mouth closed that I will not, in fairness, disclose them. With the encyclopedia open to the letter 'M,' Xerxes learns that the ancient Egyptians removed the inner organs of pharaohs, before stuffing them with asphalt and natron. The watchman is dispatched for asphalt, Xerxes deciding that the natron or sodium sesquicarbonate, being expensive, can be omitted.

"Ladies and gentlemen. It is more difficult than is at first supposed to dispose of parts of human bodies secretly. Xerxes turned out a creditable mummy, but the spare innards constituted a major problem. Finally he placed them in a jar of alcohol which he concealed in a corner of his warehouse where only he would be likely to go.

"Well. The mummy, after having been certified by the Minister of Beaux Arts and Public Monuments, was sold to the Woodburn Museum, for a handsome price. Lumber was booming just then and the Oregonians were feeling that the best was none too good for them.

"A second time the operation was repeated with success, mummy No. 2 going to Austin, Texas, at a time when cattle were fetching top prices. Then came the chance the resourceful M. 'X' had been hoping for. An American multi-millionaire, Mr. T. Prosper Stables, having heard that mummies were going around, put in a bid for a genuine pharaoh, with wrapping intact, and a pedigree beyond question, for the Manhattan Museum. There, of course, a number of keen Egyptologists would inspect the treasure, and scholars are more critical of historical relics than are lumber men or ranchers."

Frémont and Schlumberger, side by side, perched on the straight-backed gilded chairs with their feet on the highly polished floor, listened doggedly, one more impatient than the other. Noticing their perturbation, Evans smiled and assured them that he would be as brief as possible.

"The Marquis, by that time, was desperate for money, and Xerxes offered him a generous sum, and the cancellation of old debts, if he would make possible the removal of an unidentified mummy from the Louvre and give the

307

name of some pharaoh so little known that the experts in New York would have no cause for suspicion. In short, the Marquis consented to have the unidentified mummy taken from the Louvre, and a false one substituted. The unknown king was to be called Neferkesokar, about whose reign nothing whatever was known except the name of the monarch and the years he occupied the throne.

"Hugo Weiss, an American philanthropist and business man who dislikes the multi-millionaire Stables, for sound and excellent reasons, got wind of the proposed sale and sent word to Professor de la Poussière, asking him to investigate."

Frémont grunted. "It's an odd way to send word, by making scratches on a tombstone, and a soft one at that," the chief of detectives grumbled.

"Professor de la Poussière, ladies and gentlemen, is the foremost Egyptologist in France," Evans continued.

"Too generous," the professor murmured.

"A year ago, the professor made a successful expedition to Egypt, where he uncovered the long-lost secrets of the reign of Neferkesokar and identified the unknown in the Louvre as Neferkesokar's twin brother, Tout-or-Nada . . ."

"Ha! Ha! Ho! Ho! Bless my soul," roared Lazare.

"The remains of Neferkesokar consist of a shin bone and a bit of skull, while Tout-or-Nada is in a perfect state of preservation. Of course, the professor did not publish his findings before his report was in shape, so Xerxes and the Marquis went on blithely with their plans. Early last week, my friends . . ."

"Thank God, we're getting up to date," said Schlumberger.

". . . Early last week," Evans went on, "the conspirators found out that the professor was about to publish the facts that would expose them and shatter their dream of wealth. The American was willing to pay a cool million, and for a million dollars men like Xerxes and the Marquis will do nearly anything."

"I didn't kill the Marquis," Xerxes cried, rising plaintively to his feet.

"One thing at a time," cautioned Evans. "Let me explain what the Marquis did. This part of the tale is extremely important. The Marquis hired a certain gang leader, who for ethical reasons I shall not name, to shift the unknown mummy from its mummycase in the Egyptian room of the Louvre and hide it for safe keeping in a near-by sarcophagus in the Assyrian corridor. Thus the casket of the unknown pharaoh was left empty for a day or two, and was to have been filled with a mummy manufactured by Xerxes, who was growing more adept as his experience in embalming ripened."

"Not noticeably," grunted Lazare.

"But *The Pansy*," Chief Frémont could not help exclaiming. "The chair promised me to find the painting. The Watteau! The 30 by 20 worth three million francs!"

"I'm coming to that," Evans said. "The gang leader knew the Marquis was broke, the Marquis knew the gang leader worked only for cash in advance. Xerxes could raise enough to cover the transfer of the mummies by night. But when it became necessary to kidnap and kill the professor . . ."

A shriek startled the already tense assembly as Hélène

de la Poussière turned white and slid from her chair to the floor in a dead faint. Hydrangea was at her side in an instant, and revived her gently as Homer continued his elucidation.

"A bargain between the Marquis and the master criminal was struck, and that was where *The Pansy* entered into the proceedings."

"I don't understand," said Frémont.

"I shall try to make it clear," Homer said. "The gang chieftain agreed to murder the professor . . ."

"Now see what you've gone and done," said Hydrangea reproachfully. "I jus' got this lady brought around and you start right off talkin' about murder again." For the professor's wife had swooned once more.

"I'm sorry," said Hélène, on reviving. "Pray continue, with no thought for me." Hjalmar left his post a moment and offered a pint bottle he had tucked in a hip pocket in case of emergency. Hélène, although unaccustomed to drinking from a bottle, swallowed a few drops of the brandy and thanked the painter courteously. "I feel easier," she said, the roses returning to her cheeks, to match her scarf. "Please go on."

"The gang leader agreed to murder the professor for one third of the million to be paid for Tout-or-Nada, passed off as Neferkesokar. As security, he insisted that one of the expensive paintings from the Louvre be delivered to him, promising to return it unharmed to the national museum when he got his $333,333.33. It was a desperate maneuver, but there was no alternative. The Marquis chose *The Pansy* of Watteau because of its small size . . ."

Frémont was on his feet, gesticulating. "Then The

Singe has *The Pansy*. I shall haul him in. Bonnet! Schlumberger . . ."

"I beg of you, be calm. I promised you the painting and you shall have it. Not later than tomorrow morning," Evans said, with pardonable severity. The officers subsided.

"It was arranged," Evans said, "that the Marquis should leave Paris and establish a perfect alibi at the time when *The Pansy* was removed. The thief, who shall remain anonymous for the time being . . ."

"Anonymous," Frémont said, indignantly. "Anonymous, indeed! Just let me lay my hands on him. I'll teach him to let loose pandemonium in the world of art . . ."

Dr. Truc looked at the irate Chief with speculative eyes. "On the verge of a breakdown," he sighed, in his best professional manner. "A few weeks of absolute quiet . . ."

"The thief," said Evans, "left the painting, well wrapped, behind the bar of the Bal des Vêtements Brulés, *rue* Cardinal Lemoine. There The Singe—I may as well call him that, since the Chief has already let slip his name—there The Singe was to garner the masterpiece and dangle it over the Marquis' head, in a figurative way. That was never accomplished. The Singe, true to his oral contract, seized Professor de la Poussière . . ."

Madame de la Poussière only smiled, and accepted another nip from Hjalmar's bottle. "Go easy, my dear. The case is not yet over," the professor counseled, *sotto voce*.

"However, The Singe was too bright to shed human blood without the security in his hand, so he delayed the execution of his prisoner, and meanwhile two things happened that were embarrassing for him, one of which the Chief prefers I should not make public. The second was the discovery of the body of the Marquis de la Rose d'Antan in Tout-or-Nada's mummy case, wrapped in Alsatian linen and rather clumsily embalmed . . ."

"No sesquicarbonate of sodium, or very little," said Lazare. "Won't last five hundred years."

"Now," said Evans. "I shall explain why, instead of a stray corpse acquired by purchase, the body of the Marquis was found in the Louvre. Also why the plans of Xerxes, The Singe, and all others involved went wrong. Xerxes, in search of a body to fill the void in Tout-or-Nada's mummy case, drove his roadster to Luneville . . ."

"The heel," said Mathilde. "I'll bet he took along a chippy."

"On the way he stopped near Mantes to buy a couple of sacks of asphalt from a barge called the 'Poor but Honest'."

The Chief, Schlumberger and Bonnet were all on their feet and each had pulled out a gleaming pair of handcuffs. But before they could advance on the sweating Armenian, Evans begged them to desist.

"Arriving at the delightful sanitorium, that is, delightful from certain points of view, Xerxes found that Dr. Truc was in Paris but upon questioning Gus, our uncommunicative member who is proving himself no Houdini, he was told that a body was handy and that Gus would turn it over at a reduced price if Xerxes would not tell the doctor about the transaction."

That was too much for Dr. Truc. Rising and glaring at Gus, he pointed his finger scornfully and said: "You crook. You ungrateful lout."

"You see. I didn't kill him," wailed Xerxes.

"I have never said you did," Homer admitted. "When you got the body as far as your warehouse and laid it out on a slab, preparatory to embalming, you got the shock of your life. You were too frightened to do your best reasoning, so you embalmed your partner in crime, rolled him in Alsatian bandages purchased from a doodlesack collector, hid him in the Louvre, to which you carried keys, and tried to look busy in your high-class store."

The trio of officers, with the handcuffs ready, started in Gus's direction, and the tied-up bruiser began to roar his innocence in French and Finnish. Again the Chief and his sergeants got the stop signal from the chairman *pro tem*. That only served to deflect them toward Dr. Balthazar Truc who tried to run and was prevented by Dr. Toudoux.

"I have broken no laws," Dr. Truc insisted. "I have kept the letter of each and every statute. I invoke my rights under common law, the constitution . . . Maitre Ronron. Explain what I mean . . ."

"I must insist that order be preserved, even by the police," Evans said. "We are now approaching the most painful moment on this session. I must tell you how the Marquis met his death."

The men and women seated with their backs to the walls gave a gasp of horror as the Marchioness rose deliberately to her feet. She looked haughtily around the room, inclined her head to the chairman as if in forgiveness, and turning toward the officers, extended her hands, palms downward, in a gesture of resignation.

"I am ready," she said, without faltering, and only

winced when Hélène de la Poussière crashed from her chair, this time out for the count.

The assembly was electrified by a flash of color as Hydrangea, dark eyes smouldering, threw herself in the path of the advancing Frémont.

"Bertram," said Hydrangea, her atavistic sense of the dramatic bringing her for the moment to the level of a Duse, "Bertram, if you lay one han' on this poor high-born lady, I takes the first bateau, and that means all is off between you and me and from henceforth until hell freezes over we'll be absent one from another."

The agony of Frémont's face was piteous to behold. "But, my dear. She's confessed," he said.

"You hol' your horses till Mistah Evans done gets through," the aroused ex-Blackbird said. "An' remember my final ultimatum."

Every one had arisen and their faces showed such approval of Hydrangea's stand that Evans found it difficult to restore quiet again. Through it all the Marchioness had not changed her position. Her wrists were still extended, without a tremor. Her eyes were steady and calm.

"I am ready," she repeated. "Why trouble yourself with further details?"

"Madame, please be seated," Evans said, stepping down to escort her back to her chair. "I hope you understand how painful this has been to me."

"I understand," said the Marchioness, softly.

"I'm sorry," said Evans, when he regained the platform. "In order to make you all understand what has happened, I must touch upon matters that I should much prefer to conceal." Miriam, just below him, was limp with grief and disappointment. In fact, there was scarcely a dry eye in the room. "Madame de la Rose d'Antan was railroaded here by her husband and held prisoner five years in defiance of all justice by Dr. Balthazar Truc. And if Dr. Truc wishes to leave this room alive . . ." Evans' voice was like cold steel and Miriam sat straight up in her chair again. "If this jackal of science does not wish to feel the force of the indignation now suppressed by the men here present, I should advise him to sit quietly where he is and not to quote statutes or precedents.

"This woman, this martyr," Evans continued, "was denied proper food, subjected to unnecessary nervous strain, kept in contact with dangerous lunatics, and even prevented from obtaining proper clothes. The Marquis purposely and cleverly did everything to break down her mind and spirit, and in this he was abetted by the proprietor of this nefarious establishment. In the course of the five years, the Marquis visited his imprisoned wife only once, and that, ladies and gentlemen, was last Saturday. He had a double purpose in making the call, first to establish an alibi and second, to borrow his wife's jewelry, the only possession he had left to her. When she saw him standing before her, the Marchioness calmly reached for a hat pin and pierced his heart. She was intending to inform the authorities and confess when Gus blundered along and she saw an unexpected opening. She knew Gus would do anything for money, so she stripped off her valuable rings and offered them to him if he would dispose of the body quietly. That is all. You know the rest."

"You haven't told us how Lazare happened to have

a jar full of the Marquis' tripes in his shop," said Schlumberger, crest-fallen but tenacious.

"Oh, those. If you'd have looked closer you would
have found two more sets of pickled human interiors."

"The devil!" the Alsatian exclaimed.

"Indeed!" said Lazare, surprised.

"Xerxes, always nervous about the relics in his ware-
house, got an inspiration one day when he was in
Monsieur Lazare's shop to buy a stuffed cat for Mme.
Dubonnet."

"Mimi!" said Mathilde. "She's mine. That fresh ghoul
will get nothing back . . ."

"Please," said Evans. "Questions of property will be
discussed later. I was saying that Xerxes noticed several
shelves on which were rows of jars and various innards
of animals in alcohol . . . interesting bits Lazare had
found in the course of his work . . . things of scientific
value. When Xerxes found himself in possession of the
parts of the Marquis, he did some heavy thinking. Then
he went to Lazare's shop and bought a chimpanzee . . ."

"But why a chimpanzee?" asked Frémont.

"The chimp, as Xerxes knew, was in a corner of the
back room where Lazare could not get at him in less than
ten minutes of effort. While Lazare extricated the
mounted ape, Xerxes reverted to the pursuits of his
younger days and took a wax impression of the padlock,
so that he could have keys made. The *place* St. André des
Arts is not frequented at night, so Xerxes was able to
enter and leave *Au Sens de Mesur* at will, and on each
visit he left a jar of incriminating evidence behind him.
Lazare, who has not had occasion to move the jars for

many years, quite naturally did not notice that new objects were finding their way into them."

"I must clean the place thoroughly some day, but I dread it," the taxidermist said, and sighed.

Evans turned kindly toward the Marchioness de la Rose d'Antan.

"It must be a comfort to you," he said, "that in ending the life of one despicable man you saved that of another who is worthy, indeed. For had not the Marquis ceased to be, The Singe would have felt bound to do away with Professor de la Poussière. As it was, the professor's life was spared and our Chief of Detectives, Frémont, found a most unusual and ingenious way to reach his side. Of course, after that he was safe and sound."

A cheer rose for Frémont, whose face turned suddenly red, then mauve. He tried to object, but Evans gave him no opportunity. The credit for the rescue was to go to Frémont. That had been agreed.

"Well, I'm waiting," said the Marchioness, and again held forth her hands for the harsh metal cuffs.

An agonized groan arose from the whole assembly. Hydrangea reassumed her defiant and protective pose. Miriam abandoned her post and, sobbing, hurried to the Marchioness' side, as also did Hélène de la Poussière and Mathilde Dubonnet. The four women, three white and one colored, forming a weeping barricade.

The face of Chief of Detectives Frémont changed from red to pale green. "I have sworn to do my duty, God help me, and I shall," he said at last.

24

The Law Is Honored in the Breach and Elsewhere

THERE is no telling what might have happened had not Maitre François Ronron, when events had reached the impasse described at the conclusion of the preceding chapter, stepped deliberately to the platform. The distinguished attorney cleared his throat, which in the tense silence sounded like a snow slide on Mount Blanc, took his glasses from their case and waved them gently to and fro.

"Mr. Chairman, Madame la Marchioness, ladies and gentlemen," the lawyer said. "Mr. Evans, in commenting on the laws of God and man, made a remark which might have been interpreted as derogatory toward the latter. I will admit that in many instances, man-made law, which has to cover many situations obviously not foreseen by the Deity when He framed the Commandments, leaves loopholes for injustices but it has its uses just the same, and in the case before us, if the chairman will permit me, I should like to point out how our statutes may be put to an excellent use."

"By all means," Evans said.

"I shall make my point at once, then elaborate, if any of those present wish to ask questions," Maitre Ronron said. "The courts of France, however wisely, have, on recommendation of two licensed physicians and a near relative, and after hearing the evidence, declared that Madame de la Rose d'Antan is of unsound mind and therefore is in no way responsible for her actions. Need I say more? Put up your handcuffs, if you please, Monsieur Frémont, and request your subordinates to do the same with theirs. The Marchioness is at perfect liberty to go back to her room whenever she wishes, and may sleep peacefully tonight in the knowledge that she is safe from prosecution."

Such a lusty cheer arose that the beaming attorney was obliged to pause, Hjalmar and Kvek raised K. Parker Seldon to their shoulders and began to parade around the room. Tom Jackson danced a buck and wing in which he was outdone by Melchisadek. Hydrangea shouted "Praise the Lord Jehovah," while Hélène de la Poussière fainted for the fourth time and was carried to a divan by the exultant Miriam and Mathilde Dubonnet. When the demonstration subsided, after Homer had earnestly requested silence, the Chief approached the platform for a whispered consultation, shooting dark looks at Dr. Balthazar Truc.

"I regret to say," continued Maitre Ronron, "that as matters now stand, there seem to be no legal grounds on which the police, without a judicial inquiry, can arrest the proprietor of this establishment. Legally, the unfortunate people between these gruesome walls have been given into his care, for such treatment as in his judgment he sees fit to mete out. If he decided, for instance, that the Marchioness de la Rose d'Antan is better off in old-fashioned clothes, he has the authority to withhold the creations of Maggy R . . ."

"Rouff," prompted Evans.

"Of Maggy Rouff, so kindly sent her by Madame de la Poussière. That is merely an example of the scope of the powers the law has put into the hands of men of science, who take an oath the very thought of which must make a man shudder who flagrantly abuses his prerogatives."

"You mean we can't pinch Truc?" asked Frémont, indignantly.

"Not tonight, at any rate," the lawyer said. "We have just seen how the laws of man, if carelessly framed, may work one moment in a benevolent manner and the next provide a refuge for a scoundrel."

"It's very simple," said Dr. Hyacinthe Toudoux, reaching for the foils again. "Let me run him through. I assure you, ladies and gentlemen, that I would perform that salutary act with the keenest pleasure, and accept whatever consequences might follow, legal or otherwise." He bowed to the Marchioness who acknowledged his salutation with a gracious nod of her head and a glance of warm approval in her eyes.

The lawyer turned to Evans. "Let us keep within bounds," he said. "There is much to be done. Tomorrow I shall, with the permission of Dr. Toudoux, and any other physician he may select, enter a petition in behalf of the Marchioness. No one here doubts that her sanity and probity can be established before any court in the land, without delay."

"Then I shall be free? I can go where I will, do what

I like?" asked the Marchioness, moved but still in remarkable control of herself.

"I can promise that, Madame," said Maitre Ronron,
and wild joy pervaded the room.

Dr. Balthazar Truc, being careful to keep his distance
from Dr. Hyacinthe Toudoux, came forward, rubbing
his hands. "I assure you, gentlemen, I shall do all in my
power . . ."

"You will sit down at your desk and write an order,
to the effect that Madame de la Rose d'Antan may be
safely left in my care, and I shall take her away from
here tonight," the lawyer said. "I will see to it that a
physician is in constant attendance until the formalities
of her release have been attended to. Then, if I were you,
I should either leave France by the first plane or commit
suicide, preferably both. None of us here intends that you
shall continue your chicanery, even though you have
dishonored the law of your country by perverting its
intent."

"Don't be too severe," Evans said, and when Miriam
looked at him in astonishment she was sure that he had
winked at her. "But let us be thorough. Suppose, Chief,
you take a look around the premises to make sure there
is no evidence on which an arrest can be made?" And
when Frémont passed near him, he added, in a whisper:
"Begin with the bedroom."

The Chief, accompanied by Bonnet and Schlumberger,
started off, side by side, and a moment later the others
heard an exultant yell. Frémont came running out of
the bedroom, handcuffs in hand, and threw himself on
Dr. Truc. After the latter's wrists had been locked together, the Chief began burbling and pointing.

Maitre Ronron, followed by Hjalmar, Tom Jackson, Kvek, Hydrangea and Miriam, burst into the bedroom and there, hanging on the wall near the canopied four-posted bed was *The Pansy*.

In a jiffy, Sergeant Schlumberger had whipped out a silk handkerchief, and carefully took down the famous Watteau. Bonnet stared at the frame through a reading glass. "Not a fingerprint. Wiped clean," he said. "We've got him dead to rights, just the same."

Dr. Balthazar Truc was so dumbfounded that he could not even attempt an explanation. If ever a man appeared guilty, that man was the proprietor of the Sens Unique. The frame in which *The Pansy* was reposing was not unlike the frames of the Boucher and Fragonards that also graced the walls of the bed-chamber. Truc could offer no alibi. He had previously admitted having been in Paris on the day of the theft and, in his demoralized condition, could not account for his movements or his time. He was hustled into the Chief's limousine and after the names of a dozen willing witnesses had been inscribed in Frémont's notebook, the Chief, his prisoner and the chastened Sergeant Schlumberger were driven along the moonlit road leading toward the capital.

The second car in the east-bound cavalcade contained the Marchioness de la Rose d'Antan and Hélène de la Poussière, who was to be her hostess until her sanity could be technically established. And to be on hand in case their joy proved too much for them, Dr. Toudoux, his foils having been chucked into the baggage rack, rode with them. Kvek, Hjalmar and Tom Jackson escorted K. Parker Seldon to the Plaza Athénée where the business man got into possession of his clothes again and they all settled down to an appropriate carouse. At the end of two unforgettable weeks, however, Seldon still carried under his arm the battered copy of *Ulysses*.

It will not be necessary to say how Lazare felt when he received from Hugo Weiss a request that he spend two years in Egypt, which the taxidermist had never seen, to act as the genial millionaire's Egyptian representative, with instructions to explore and report at will. His enthusiasm was in no way dampened by the fact that his pocket was picked on his first night in Cairo. Madame de la Poussière, accompanied by the professor, made her coveted voyage to New York, where her husband was given a touching reception by American scholars and she was welcomed in the best society. In fact, the professor began to take an interest in the modern world and she, observing how her husband was respected abroad, started reading his books and was fascinated with the lore of ancient Egypt. That brought them closer together and resulted in an ideal companionship.

The idyllic existence of K. Parker Seldon, of the American Jar and Bottle Corporation, with the second Mrs. Seldon, née Dargomyzshkov, is the awe of Des Moines and the boys there complain that when a tall handsome Russian blows into town, as he often does, their dates with Isabel, Seldon's daughter, are automatically called off.

The romance between the former Marchioness de la Rose d'Antan and Dr. Hyacinthe Toudoux, the medical examiner, was given brief mention in the Paris papers at the request of the principals, themselves. It was nonetheless touching on that account. The Marchioness, after her release, could not dismiss from her mind the recol-

lection of Toudoux, sword in hand, with Dr. Balthazar
St.-J. Truc stuck on the end of it, as he had entered the
ballroom on that historic night in Luneville. The
medical examiner, on the other hand, had been over-
whelmed by the Marchioness' poise and bravery and in
his dreams repeatedly heard her speak those fateful
words, "I am ready." Consequently his proposal took a
rather rare form, for he simply asked her: "Are you
ready?" and she said, "Why, yes, Hyacinthe, I am."

Xerxes got two years for embalming without a license
and his partner, Basil Hamborough, got the affairs of
Lewson-Phipps & Xerxes into such a hash within a
month after Xerxes went to jail that old Phipps himself,
the doodlesack collector, had to come to Paris and run
the business. The authorities, appreciating the old man's
predicament, were very lenient about giving him passes
to the Santé prison, so that he could ask the Armenian's
advice.

American visitors at the Bal Tabarin have often remarked that the little girl with curly hair, fourth from
the left, has a bit on her show-mates in the matter of
dancing and popularity. Had they scanned the front row,
they might have seen there Maitre François Ronron, who,
having met Nicole in Hjalmar's studio, took a fancy to
the girl. Having no children of his own, he became
solicitous for her welfare and formed the habit of watching her rather closely to be sure that she did not fall
into bad company, as some of the show girls unfortunately did. Nicole, however much she appreciated the
lawyer's kind attentions, never lost a violent jealousy
directed toward Mathilde Dubonnet, the painting of
whom by Jansen won first prize at the Salon d'Automne.

Whenever there was in the audience a blonde woman resembling Mathilde, Nicole could not give her best performance.

A short time after the Louvre murder case had disappeared from the press, Homer and Miriam were enjoying their long-delayed excursion to the old walled town of Langres, in the Haute Marne. They did not read the papers, and consequently missed the story of the trial of Dr. Balthazar Truc for the theft of *The Pansy*. Dr. Truc, it was said, made a poor impression on the jury. He had been so accustomed to defending himself on account of acts he had really performed that when it came to denying a theft he had not committed the alienist was completely at sea. What helped break down his morale, and caused him such despondency that in the end he confessed, was the upward progress of American Jar and Bottle stock as listed in the New York *Herald* (Paris edition). During the trial it jumped from 32 to 174, until bottle and jar news crowded crime and politics from the front pages. Also, Dr. Truc concluded bitterly, when reading of the nuptials of the Marchioness and Dr. Hyacinthe Toudoux, that Eugénie had not been fond of him, as she had implied, but merely had been using him as a means to an end while he had been trusting her. And, of course, when it was mentioned by Dr. Toudoux, before the Academy of Science, that Truc had, in his studies of the human liver, ignored the difference between herbivores and carnivores, that august body burst into hilarious laughter, for the first time since Michel Servet had announced, nearly a century before, that blood went round and round in the veins.

The day after Truc's conviction and sentence to ten

years on Devil's Island, a cryptic note, forwarded from the apartment in the *rue* Campagne Première, was received by Homer Evans, who read it, smiled and handed it to Miriam. The text was as follows:

O.K. WITH ME. HE HAD IT COMING.

The note was signed: "THE SINGE."

The next Homer Evans story, entitled MAYHEM IN B-FLAT, *gets off to a breathtaking start when a dog nearly bites a Guarnarius. Then Leffingwell Baxter of Boston, after complaining bitterly that a French chef has put nutmeg on Yorkshire pudding, breathes his last over a game of checkers with a phantom opponent.*

That The Singe, ruthless gang leader of the St. Julien Rollers, and Homer Evans have a common ancestor in the person of the Baron de Vans, pal of William the Conqueror, lends spice to the clashes between those forceful personalities. And Hjalmar Jansen, in order to entertain Anton Diluvio, harassed virtuoso, takes him for a ride on the Presque Sans Souci.

Do not worry, reader, because there is a fiddle and a recital involved. Anyone, even if he cannot tap out Bei Mir Bist du Schoen *with one finger, can understand the story, and the worse one feels about music, the better one can enjoy seeing musicians get theirs.*

To be published April 1.

THERE ARE NO DE LUXE LIMITED EDITIONS OF THIS BOOK
PRINTED ON BIRCH BARK, ARTIFICIAL SILK, TINTED CELO-
PHANE OR PAPYRUS, SIGNED BY THE AUTHOR AND NUMBERED
FROM 1 TO —, OR PERFUMED WITH FRANKINCENSE, MYRRH,
CHYPRE OR NEW-MOWN HAY. IT IS INTENDED FOR
READING, AND FOR THAT REASON IS LIGHT IN
WEIGHT, AND IS PRINTED IN LEGIBLE TYPE ON
GOOD HOUSEHOLD PAPER, BUT THE READER,
ALL STATEMENTS TO THE CONTRARY
NOTWITHSTANDING, MAY PUT, LAY
OR EVEN THROW IT DOWN
WHENEVER HE FEELS SO
INCLINED.

A CATALOG OF SELECTED DOVER
BOOKS IN ALL FIELDS OF INTEREST

THE ART NOUVEAU STYLE, edited by Roberta Waddell. 579 rare photographs of works in jewelry, metalwork, glass, ceramics, textiles, architecture and furniture by 175 artists—Mucha, Seguy, Lalique, Tiffany, many others. 288pp. 8⅜ × 11¼.
23515-7 Pa. $9.95

AMERICAN COUNTRY HOUSES OF THE GILDED AGE (Sheldon's "Artistic Country-Seats"), A. Lewis. All of Sheldon's fascinating and historically important photographs and plans. New text by Arnold Lewis. Approx. 200 illustrations. 128pp. 9⅜ × 12¼.
24301-X Pa. $7.95

THE WAY WE LIVE NOW, Anthony Trollope. Trollope's late masterpiece, marks shift to bitter satire. Character Melmotte "his greatest villain." Reproduced from original edition with 40 illustrations. 416pp. 6⅛ × 9¼.
24360-5 Pa. $7.95

BENCHLEY LOST AND FOUND, Robert Benchley. Finest humor from early 30's, about pet peeves, child psychologists, post office and others. Mostly unavailable elsewhere. 73 illustrations by Peter Arno and others. 183pp. 5⅜ × 8½.
22410-4 Pa. $3.50

ISOMETRIC PERSPECTIVE DESIGNS AND HOW TO CREATE THEM, John Locke. Isometric perspective is the picture of an object adrift in imaginary space. 75 mindboggling designs. 52pp. 8¼ × 11.
24123-8 Pa. $2.75

PERSPECTIVE FOR ARTISTS, Rex Vicat Cole. Depth, perspective of sky and sea, shadows, much more, not usually covered. 391 diagrams, 81 reproductions of drawings and paintings. 279pp. 5⅜ × 8½.
22487-2 Pa. $4.00

MOVIE-STAR PORTRAITS OF THE FORTIES, edited by John Kobal. 163 glamor, studio photos of 106 stars of the 1940s: Rita Hayworth, Ava Gardner, Marlon Brando, Clark Gable, many more. 176pp. 8⅜ × 11¼.
23546-7 Pa. $6.95

STARS OF THE BROADWAY STAGE, 1940-1967, Fred Fehl. Marlon Brando, Uta Hagen, John Kerr, John Gielgud, Jessica Tandy in great shows—*South Pacific, Galileo, West Side Story,* more. 240 black-and-white photos. 144pp. 8⅜ × 11¼.
24398-2 Pa. $8.95

ILLUSTRATED DICTIONARY OF HISTORIC ARCHITECTURE, edited by Cyril M. Harris. Extraordinary compendium of clear, concise definitions for over 5000 important architectural terms complemented by over 2000 line drawings. 592pp. 7½ × 9⅜.
24444-X Pa. $14.95

THE EARLY WORK OF FRANK LLOYD WRIGHT, F.L. Wright. 207 rare photos of Oak Park period, first great buildings: Unity Temple, Dana house, Larkin factory. Complete photos of Wasmuth edition. New Introduction. 160pp. 8⅜ × 11¼.
24381-8 Pa. $7.95

LIVING MY LIFE, Emma Goldman. Candid, no holds barred account by foremost American anarchist: her own life, anarchist movement, famous contemporaries, ideas and their impact. 944pp. 5⅜ × 8½. 22543-7, 22544-5 Pa., Two-vol. set $13.00

UNDERSTANDING THERMODYNAMICS, H.C. Van Ness. Clear, lucid treatment of first and second laws of thermodynamics. Excellent supplement to basic textbook in undergraduate science or engineering class. 103pp. 5⅜ × 8.
63277-6 Pa. $3.50

SMOCKING: TECHNIQUE, PROJECTS, AND DESIGNS, Dianne Durand. Foremost smocking designer provides complete instructions on how to smock. Over 10 projects, over 100 illustrations. 56pp. 8¼ × 11.   23788-5 Pa. $2.00

AUDUBON'S BIRDS IN COLOR FOR DECOUPAGE, edited by Eleanor H. Rawlings. 24 sheets, 37 most decorative birds, full color, on one side of paper. Instructions, including work under glass. 56pp. 8¼ × 11.   23492-4 Pa. $3.95

THE COMPLETE BOOK OF SILK SCREEN PRINTING PRODUCTION, J.I. Biegeleisen. For commercial user, teacher in advanced classes, serious hobbyist. Most modern techniques, materials, equipment for optimal results. 124 illustrations. 253pp. 5⅜ × 8½.   21100-2 Pa. $4.50

A TREASURY OF ART NOUVEAU DESIGN AND ORNAMENT, edited by Carol Belanger Grafton. 577 designs for the practicing artist. Full-page, spots, borders, bookplates by Klimt, Bradley, others. 144pp. 8⅜ × 11¼.   24001-0 Pa. $5.95

ART NOUVEAU TYPOGRAPHIC ORNAMENTS, Dan X. Solo. Over 800 Art Nouveau florals, swirls, women, animals, borders, scrolls, wreaths, spots and dingbats, copyright-free. 100pp. 8⅛ × 11.   24366-4 Pa. $4.00

HAND SHADOWS TO BE THROWN UPON THE WALL, Henry Bursill. Wonderful Victorian novelty tells how to make flying birds, dog, goose, deer, and 14 others, each explained by a full-page illustration. 32pp. 6½ × 9¼. 21779-5 Pa. $1.50

AUDUBON'S BIRDS OF AMERICA COLORING BOOK, John James Audubon. Rendered for coloring by Paul Kennedy. 46 of Audubon's noted illustrations: red-winged black-bird, cardinal, etc. Original plates reproduced in full-color on the covers. Captions. 48pp. 8¼ × 11.   23049-X Pa. $2.25

SILK SCREEN TECHNIQUES, J.I. Biegeleisen, M.A. Cohn. Clear, practical, modern, economical. Minimal equipment (self-built), materials, easy methods. For amateur, hobbyist, 1st book. 141 illustrations. 185pp. 6⅛ × 9¼.   20433-2 Pa. $3.95

101 PATCHWORK PATTERNS, Ruby S. McKim. 101 beautiful, immediately useable patterns, full-size, modern and traditional. Also general information, estimating, quilt lore. 140 illustrations. 124pp. 7⅞ × 10¾.   20773-0 Pa. $3.50

READY-TO-USE FLORAL DESIGNS, Ed Sibbett, Jr. Over 100 floral designs (most in three sizes) of popular individual blossoms as well as bouquets, sprays, garlands. 64pp. 8¼ × 11.   23976-4 Pa. $2.95

AMERICAN WILD FLOWERS COLORING BOOK, Paul Kennedy. Planned coverage of 46 most important wildflowers, from Rickett's collection; instructive as well as entertaining. Color versions on covers. Captions. 48pp. 8¼ × 11.
20095-7 Pa. $2.50

CARVING DUCK DECOYS, Harry V. Shourds and Anthony Hillman. Detailed instructions and full-size templates for constructing 16 beautiful, marvelously practical decoys according to time-honored South Jersey method. 70pp. 9¼ × 12¼.
24083-5 Pa. $4.95

TRADITIONAL PATCHWORK PATTERNS, Carol Belanger Grafton. Cardboard cut-out pieces for use as templates to make 12 quilts: Buttercup, Ribbon Border, Tree of Paradise, nine more. Full instructions. 57pp. 8¼ × 11.
23015-5 Pa. $3.50

CHILDREN'S BOOKPLATES AND LABELS, Ed Sibbett, Jr. 6 each of 12 types based on *Wizard of Oz, Alice,* nursery rhymes, fairy tales. Perforated; full color. 24pp. 8¼ × 11. 23538-6 Pa. $3.50

READY-TO-USE VICTORIAN COLOR STICKERS: 96 Pressure-Sensitive Seals, Carol Belanger Grafton. Drawn from authentic period sources. Motifs include heads of men, women, children, plus florals, animals, birds, more. Will adhere to any clean surface. 8pp. 8½ × 11. 24551-9 Pa. $2.95

CUT AND FOLD PAPER SPACESHIPS THAT FLY, Michael Grater. 16 colorful, easy-to-build spaceships that really fly. Star Shuttle, Lunar Freighter, Star Probe, 13 others. 32pp. 8¼ × 11. 23978-0 Pa. $2.50

CUT AND ASSEMBLE PAPER AIRPLANES THAT FLY, Arthur Baker. 8 aerodynamically sound, ready-to-build paper airplanes, designed with latest techniques. Fly *Pegasus, Daedalus, Songbird,* 5 other aircraft. Instructions. 32pp. 9¼ × 11¼. 24302-8 Pa. $3.95

SIDELIGHTS ON RELATIVITY, Albert Einstein. Two lectures delivered in 1920-21: *Ether and Relativity* and *Geometry and Experience.* Elegant ideas in non-mathematical form. 56pp. 5⅜ × 8½. 24511-X Pa. $2.25

FADS AND FALLACIES IN THE NAME OF SCIENCE, Martin Gardner. Fair, witty appraisal of cranks and quacks of science: Velikovsky, orgone energy, Bridey Murphy, medical fads, etc. 373pp. 5⅜ × 8½. 20394-8 Pa. $5.95

VACATION HOMES AND CABINS, U.S. Dept. of Agriculture. Complete plans for 16 cabins, vacation homes and other shelters. 105pp. 9 × 12. 23631-5 Pa. $4.95

HOW TO BUILD A WOOD-FRAME HOUSE, L.O. Anderson. Placement, foundations, framing, sheathing, roof, insulation, plaster, finishing—almost everything else. 179 illustrations. 223pp. 7⅞ × 10¾. 22954-8 Pa. $5.50

THE MYSTERY OF A HANSOM CAB, Fergus W. Hume. Bizarre murder in a hansom cab leads to engrossing investigation. Memorable characters, rich atmosphere. 19th-century bestseller, still enjoyable, exciting. 256pp. 5⅜ × 8. 21956-9 Pa. $4.00

MANUAL OF TRADITIONAL WOOD CARVING, edited by Paul N. Hasluck. Possibly the best book in English on the craft of wood carving. Practical instructions, along with 1,146 working drawings and photographic illustrations. 576pp. 6½ × 9¼. 23489-4 Pa. $8.95

WHITTLING AND WOODCARVING, E.J Tangerman. Best book on market; clear, full. If you can cut a potato, you can carve toys, puzzles, chains, etc. Over 464 illustrations. 293pp. 5⅜ × 8½. 20965-2 Pa. $4.95

AMERICAN TRADEMARK DESIGNS, Barbara Baer Capitman. 732 marks, logos and corporate-identity symbols. Categories include entertainment, heavy industry, food and beverage. All black-and-white in standard forms. 160pp. 8⅛ × 11. 23259-X Pa. $6.95

DECORATIVE FRAMES AND BORDERS, edited by Edmund V. Gillon, Jr. Largest collection of borders and frames ever compiled for use of artists and designers. Renaissance, neo-Greek, Art Nouveau, Art Deco, to mention only a few styles. 396 illustrations. 192pp. 8⅜ × 11¼. 22928-9 Pa. $6.00

THE MURDER BOOK OF J.G. REEDER, Edgar Wallace. Eight suspenseful stories by bestselling mystery writer of 20s and 30s. Features the donnish Mr. J.G. Reeder of Public Prosecutor's Office. 128pp. 5⅜ × 8½. (Available in U.S. only)
24374-5 Pa. $3.50

ANNE ORR'S CHARTED DESIGNS, Anne Orr. Best designs by premier needlework designer, all on charts: flowers, borders, birds, children, alphabets, etc. Over 100 charts, 10 in color. Total of 40pp. 8¼ × 11. 23704-4 Pa. $2.50

BASIC CONSTRUCTION TECHNIQUES FOR HOUSES AND SMALL BUILDINGS SIMPLY EXPLAINED, U.S. Bureau of Naval Personnel. Grading, masonry, woodworking, floor and wall framing, roof framing, plastering, tile setting, much more. Over 675 illustrations. 568pp. 6½ × 9¼. 20242-9 Pa. $8.95

MATISSE LINE DRAWINGS AND PRINTS, Henri Matisse. Representative collection of female nudes, faces, still lifes, experimental works, etc., from 1898 to 1948. 50 illustrations. 48pp. 8⅜ × 11¼. 23877-6 Pa. $2.50

HOW TO PLAY THE CHESS OPENINGS, Eugene Znosko-Borovsky. Clear, profound examinations of just what each opening is intended to do and how opponent can counter. Many sample games. 147pp. 5⅜ × 8½. 22795-2 Pa. $2.95

DUPLICATE BRIDGE, Alfred Sheinwold. Clear, thorough, easily followed account: rules, etiquette, scoring, strategy, bidding; Goren's point-count system, Blackwood and Gerber conventions, etc. 158pp. 5⅜ × 8½. 22741-3 Pa. $3.00

SARGENT PORTRAIT DRAWINGS, J.S. Sargent. Collection of 42 portraits reveals technical skill and intuitive eye of noted American portrait painter, John Singer Sargent. 48pp. 8¼ × 11⅛. 24524-1 Pa. $2.95

ENTERTAINING SCIENCE EXPERIMENTS WITH EVERYDAY OBJECTS, Martin Gardner. Over 100 experiments for youngsters. Will amuse, astonish, teach, and entertain. Over 100 illustrations. 127pp. 5⅜ × 8½. 24201-3 Pa. $2.50

TEDDY BEAR PAPER DOLLS IN FULL COLOR: A Family of Four Bears and Their Costumes, Crystal Collins. A family of four Teddy Bear paper dolls and nearly 60 cut-out costumes. Full color, printed one side only. 32pp. 9¼ × 12¼.
24550-0 Pa. $3.50

NEW CALLIGRAPHIC ORNAMENTS AND FLOURISHES, Arthur Baker. Unusual, multi-useable material: arrows, pointing hands, brackets and frames, ovals, swirls, birds, etc. Nearly 700 illustrations. 80pp. 8⅜ × 11¼.
24095-9 Pa. $3.75

DINOSAUR DIORAMAS TO CUT & ASSEMBLE, M. Kalmenoff. Two complete three-dimensional scenes in full color, with 31 cut-out animals and plants. Excellent educational toy for youngsters. Instructions; 2 assembly diagrams. 32pp. 9¼ × 12¼. 24541-1 Pa. $4.50

SILHOUETTES: A PICTORIAL ARCHIVE OF VARIED ILLUSTRATIONS, edited by Carol Belanger Grafton. Over 600 silhouettes from the 18th to 20th centuries. Profiles and full figures of men, women, children, birds, animals, groups and scenes, nature, ships, an alphabet. 144pp. 8⅜ × 11¼. 23781-8 Pa. $4.95

SURREAL STICKERS AND UNREAL STAMPS, William Rowe. 224 haunting, hilarious stamps on gummed, perforated stock, with images of elephants, geisha girls, George Washington, etc. 16pp. one side. 8¼ × 11. 24371-0 Pa. $3.50

GOURMET KITCHEN LABELS, Ed Sibbett, Jr. 112 full-color labels (4 copies each of 28 designs). Fruit, bread, other culinary motifs. Gummed and perforated. 16pp. 8¼ × 11. 24087-8 Pa. $2.95

PATTERNS AND INSTRUCTIONS FOR CARVING AUTHENTIC BIRDS, H.D. Green. Detailed instructions, 27 diagrams, 85 photographs for carving 15 species of birds so life-like, they'll seem ready to fly! 8¼ × 11. 24222-6 Pa. $2.75

FLATLAND, E.A. Abbott. Science-fiction classic explores life of 2-D being in 3-D world. 16 illustrations. 103pp. 5⅜ × 8. 20001-9 Pa. $2.00

DRIED FLOWERS, Sarah Whitlock and Martha Rankin. Concise, clear, practical guide to dehydration, glycerinizing, pressing plant material, and more. Covers use of silica gel. 12 drawings. 32pp. 5⅜ × 8½. 21802-3 Pa. $1.00

EASY-TO-MAKE CANDLES, Gary V. Guy. Learn how easy it is to make all kinds of decorative candles. Step-by-step instructions. 82 illustrations. 48pp. 8¼ × 11. 23881-4 Pa. $2.50

SUPER STICKERS FOR KIDS, Carolyn Bracken. 128 gummed and perforated full-color stickers: GIRL WANTED, KEEP OUT, BORED OF EDUCATION, X-RATED, COMBAT ZONE, many others. 16pp. 8¼ × 11. 24092-4 Pa. $2.50

CUT AND COLOR PAPER MASKS, Michael Grater. Clowns, animals, funny faces...simply color them in, cut them out, and put them together, and you have 9 paper masks to play with and enjoy. 32pp. 8¼ × 11. 23171-2 Pa. $2.25

A CHRISTMAS CAROL: THE ORIGINAL MANUSCRIPT, Charles Dickens. Clear facsimile of Dickens manuscript, on facing pages with final printed text. 8 illustrations by John Leech, 4 in color on covers. 144pp. 8⅜ × 11¼. 20980-6 Pa. $5.95

CARVING SHOREBIRDS, Harry V. Shourds & Anthony Hillman. 16 full-size patterns (all double-page spreads) for 19 North American shorebirds with step-by-step instructions. 72pp. 9¼ × 12¼. 24287-0 Pa. $4.95

THE GENTLE ART OF MATHEMATICS, Dan Pedoe. Mathematical games, probability, the question of infinity, topology, how the laws of algebra work, problems of irrational numbers, and more. 42 figures. 143pp. 5⅜ × 8½. (EBE) 22949-1 Pa. $3.50

READY-TO-USE DOLLHOUSE WALLPAPER, Katzenbach & Warren, Inc. Stripe, 2 floral stripes, 2 allover florals, polka dot; all in full color. 4 sheets (350 sq. in.) of each, enough for average room. 48pp. 8¼ × 11. 23495-9 Pa. $2.95

MINIATURE IRON-ON TRANSFER PATTERNS FOR DOLLHOUSES, DOLLS, AND SMALL PROJECTS, Rita Weiss and Frank Fontana. Over 100 miniature patterns: rugs, bedspreads, quilts, chair seats, etc. In standard dollhouse size. 48pp. 8¼ × 11. 23741-9 Pa. $1.95

THE DINOSAUR COLORING BOOK, Anthony Rao. 45 renderings of dinosaurs, fossil birds, turtles, other creatures of Mesozoic Era. Scientifically accurate. Captions. 48pp. 8¼ × 11. 24022-3 Pa. $2.50

THE BOOK OF WOOD CARVING, Charles Marshall Sayers. Still finest book for beginning student. Fundamentals, technique; gives 34 designs, over 34 projects for panels, bookends, mirrors, etc. 33 photos. 118pp. 7¾ × 10⅝. 23654-4 Pa. $3.95

CARVING COUNTRY CHARACTERS, Bill Higginbotham. Expert advice for beginning, advanced carvers on materials, techniques for creating 18 projects—mirthful panorama of American characters. 105 illustrations. 80pp. 8⅜ × 11. 24135-1 Pa. $2.50

300 ART NOUVEAU DESIGNS AND MOTIFS IN FULL COLOR, C.B. Grafton. 44 full-page plates display swirling lines and muted colors typical of Art Nouveau. Borders, frames, panels, cartouches, dingbats, etc. 48pp. 9⅜ × 12¼. 24354-0 Pa. $6.95

SELF-WORKING CARD TRICKS, Karl Fulves. Editor of *Pallbearer* offers 72 tricks that work automatically through nature of card deck. No sleight of hand needed. Often spectacular. 42 illustrations. 113pp. 5⅜ × 8½. 23334-0 Pa. $3.50

CUT AND ASSEMBLE A WESTERN FRONTIER TOWN, Edmund V. Gillon, Jr. Ten authentic full-color buildings on heavy cardboard stock in H-O scale. Sheriff's Office and Jail, Saloon, Wells Fargo, Opera House, others. 48pp. 9¼ × 12¼. 23736-2 Pa. $3.95

CUT AND ASSEMBLE AN EARLY NEW ENGLAND VILLAGE, Edmund V. Gillon, Jr. Printed in full color on heavy cardboard stock. 12 authentic buildings in H-O scale: Adams home in Quincy, Mass., Oliver Wight house in Sturbridge, smithy, store, church, others. 48pp. 9¼ × 12¼. 23536-X Pa. $4.95

THE TALE OF TWO BAD MICE, Beatrix Potter. Tom Thumb and Hunca Munca squeeze out of their hole and go exploring. 27 full-color Potter illustrations. 59pp. 4¼ × 5½. (Available in U.S. only) 23065-1 Pa. $1.75

CARVING FIGURE CARICATURES IN THE OZARK STYLE, Harold L. Enlow. Instructions and illustrations for ten delightful projects, plus general carving instructions. 22 drawings and 47 photographs altogether. 39pp. 8⅜ × 11. 23151-8 Pa. $2.50

A TREASURY OF FLOWER DESIGNS FOR ARTISTS, EMBROIDERERS AND CRAFTSMEN, Susan Gaber. 100 garden favorites lushly rendered by artist for artists, craftsmen, needleworkers. Many form frames, borders. 80pp. 8¼ × 11. 24096-7 Pa. $3.50

CUT & ASSEMBLE A TOY THEATER/THE NUTCRACKER BALLET, Tom Tierney. Model of a complete, full-color production of Tchaikovsky's classic. 6 backdrops, dozens of characters, familiar dance sequences. 32pp. 9⅜ × 12¼. 24194-7 Pa. $4.50

ANIMALS: 1,419 COPYRIGHT-FREE ILLUSTRATIONS OF MAMMALS, BIRDS, FISH, INSECTS, ETC., edited by Jim Harter. Clear wood engravings present, in extremely lifelike poses, over 1,000 species of animals. 284pp. 9 × 12. 23766-4 Pa. $9.95

MORE HAND SHADOWS, Henry Bursill. For those at their 'finger ends," 16 more effects—Shakespeare, a hare, a squirrel, Mr. Punch, and twelve more—each explained by a full-page illustration. Considerable period charm. 30pp. 6½ × 9¼. 21384-6 Pa. $1.95

JAPANESE DESIGN MOTIFS, Matsuya Co. Mon, or heraldic designs. Over 4000 typical, beautiful designs: birds, animals, flowers, swords, fans, geometrics; all beautifully stylized. 213pp. 11⅜ × 8¼. 22874-6 Pa. $7.95

THE TALE OF BENJAMIN BUNNY, Beatrix Potter. Peter Rabbit's cousin coaxes him back into Mr. McGregor's garden for a whole new set of adventures. All 27 full-color illustrations. 59pp. 4¼ × 5½. (Available in U.S. only) 21102-9 Pa. $1.75

THE TALE OF PETER RABBIT AND OTHER FAVORITE STORIES BOXED SET, Beatrix Potter. Seven of Beatrix Potter's best-loved tales including Peter Rabbit in a specially designed, durable boxed set. 4¼ × 5½. Total of 447pp. 158 color illustrations. (Available in U.S. only) 23903-9 Pa. $10.80

PRACTICAL MENTAL MAGIC, Theodore Annemann. Nearly 200 astonishing feats of mental magic revealed in step-by-step detail. Complete advice on staging, patter, etc. Illustrated. 320pp. 5⅜ × 8½. 24426-1 Pa. $5.95

CELEBRATED CASES OF JUDGE DEE (DEE GOONG AN), translated by Robert Van Gulik. Authentic 18th-century Chinese detective novel; Dee and associates solve three interlocked cases. Led to van Gulik's own stories with same characters. Extensive introduction. 9 illustrations. 237pp. 5⅜ × 8½. 23337-5 Pa. $4.50

CUT & FOLD EXTRATERRESTRIAL INVADERS THAT FLY, M. Grater. Stage your own lilliputian space battles.By following the step-by-step instructions and explanatory diagrams you can launch 22 full-color fliers into space. 36pp. 8¼ × 11. 24478-4 Pa. $2.95

CUT & ASSEMBLE VICTORIAN HOUSES, Edmund V. Gillon, Jr. Printed in full color on heavy cardboard stock, 4 authentic Victorian houses in H-O scale: Italian-style Villa, Octagon, Second Empire, Stick Style. 48pp. 9¼ × 12¼. 23849-0 Pa. $3.95

BEST SCIENCE FICTION STORIES OF H.G. WELLS, H.G. Wells. Full novel *The Invisible Man,* plus 17 short stories: "The Crystal Egg," "Aepyornis Island," "The Strange Orchid," etc. 303pp. 5⅜ × 8½. (Available in U.S. only) 21531-8 Pa. $4.95

TRADEMARK DESIGNS OF THE WORLD, Yusaku Kamekura. A lavish collection of nearly 700 trademarks, the work of Wright, Loewy, Klee, Binder, hundreds of others. 160pp. 8¾ × 8. (Available in U.S. only) 24191-2 Pa. $5.95

THE ARTIST'S AND CRAFTSMAN'S GUIDE TO REDUCING, ENLARGING AND TRANSFERRING DESIGNS, Rita Weiss. Discover, reduce, enlarge, transfer designs from any objects to any craft project. 12pp. plus 16 sheets special graph paper. 8¼ × 11. 24142-4 Pa. $3.50

TREASURY OF JAPANESE DESIGNS AND MOTIFS FOR ARTISTS AND CRAFTSMEN, edited by Carol Belanger Grafton. Indispensable collection of 360 traditional Japanese designs and motifs redrawn in clean, crisp black-and-white, copyright-free illustrations. 96pp. 8¼ × 11. 24435-0 Pa. $3.95

KEYBOARD WORKS FOR SOLO INSTRUMENTS, G.F. Handel. 35 neglected works from Handel's vast oeuvre, originally jotted down as improvisations. Includes Eight Great Suites, others. New sequence. 174pp. 9⅜ × 12¼.
24338-9 Pa. $7.50

AMERICAN LEAGUE BASEBALL CARD CLASSICS, Bert Randolph Sugar. 82 stars from 1900s to 60s on facsimile cards. Ruth, Cobb, Mantle, Williams, plus advertising, info, no duplications. Perforated, detachable. 16pp. 8¼ × 11.
24286-2 Pa. $2.95

A TREASURY OF CHARTED DESIGNS FOR NEEDLEWORKERS, Georgia Gorham and Jeanne Warth. 141 charted designs: owl, cat with yarn, tulips, piano, spinning wheel, covered bridge, Victorian house and many others. 48pp. 8¼ × 11.
23558-0 Pa. $1.95

DANISH FLORAL CHARTED DESIGNS, Gerda Bengtsson. Exquisite collection of over 40 different florals: anemone, Iceland poppy, wild fruit, pansies, many others. 45 illustrations. 48pp. 8¼ × 11. 23957-8 Pa. $1.75

OLD PHILADELPHIA IN EARLY PHOTOGRAPHS 1839-1914, Robert F. Looney. 215 photographs: panoramas, street scenes, landmarks, President-elect Lincoln's visit, 1876 Centennial Exposition, much more. 230pp. 8⅞ × 11¾.
23345-6 Pa. $9.95

PRELUDE TO MATHEMATICS, W.W. Sawyer. Noted mathematician's lively, stimulating account of non-Euclidean geometry, matrices, determinants, group theory, other topics. Emphasis on novel, striking aspects. 224pp. 5⅜ × 8½.
24401-6 Pa. $4.50

ADVENTURES WITH A MICROSCOPE, Richard Headstrom. 59 adventures with clothing fibers, protozoa, ferns and lichens, roots and leaves, much more. 142 illustrations. 232pp. 5⅜ × 8½. 23471-1 Pa. $3.95

IDENTIFYING ANIMAL TRACKS: MAMMALS, BIRDS, AND OTHER ANIMALS OF THE EASTERN UNITED STATES, Richard Headstrom. For hunters, naturalists, scouts, nature-lovers. Diagrams of tracks, tips on identification. 128pp. 5⅜ × 8. 24442-3 Pa. $3.50

VICTORIAN FASHIONS AND COSTUMES FROM HARPER'S BAZAR, 1867-1898, edited by Stella Blum. Day costumes, evening wear, sports clothes, shoes, hats, other accessories in over 1,000 detailed engravings. 320pp. 9⅜ × 12¼.
22990-4 Pa. $10.95

EVERYDAY FASHIONS OF THE TWENTIES AS PICTURED IN SEARS AND OTHER CATALOGS, edited by Stella Blum. Actual dress of the Roaring Twenties, with text by Stella Blum. Over 750 illustrations, captions. 156pp. 9 × 12.
24134-3 Pa. $8.50

HALL OF FAME BASEBALL CARDS, edited by Bert Randolph Sugar. Cy Young, Ted Williams, Lou Gehrig, and many other Hall of Fame greats on 92 full-color, detachable reprints of early baseball cards. No duplication of cards with *Classic Baseball Cards*. 16pp. 8¼ × 11. 23624-2 Pa. $3.50

THE ART OF HAND LETTERING, Helm Wotzkow. Course in hand lettering, Roman, Gothic, Italic, Block, Script. Tools, proportions, optical aspects, individual variation. Very quality conscious. Hundreds of specimens. 320pp. 5⅜ × 8½.
21797-3 Pa. $4.95

CATALOG OF DOVER BOOKS

THE RIME OF THE ANCIENT MARINER, Gustave Doré, S.T. Coleridge. Doré's finest work, 34 plates capture moods, subtleties of poem. Full text. 77pp. 9¼ × 12.
22305-1 Pa. $4.95

SONGS OF INNOCENCE, William Blake. The first and most popular of Blake's famous "Illuminated Books," in a facsimile edition reproducing all 31 brightly colored plates. Additional printed text of each poem. 64pp. 5¼ × 7.
22764-2 Pa. $3.50

AN INTRODUCTION TO INFORMATION THEORY, J.R. Pierce. Second (1980) edition of most impressive non-technical account available. Encoding, entropy, noisy channel, related areas, etc. 320pp. 5⅜ × 8½.
24061-4 Pa. $4.95

THE DIVINE PROPORTION: A STUDY IN MATHEMATICAL BEAUTY, H.E. Huntley. "Divine proportion" or "golden ratio" in poetry, Pascal's triangle, philosophy, psychology, music, mathematical figures, etc. Excellent bridge between science and art. 58 figures. 185pp. 5⅜ × 8½.
22254-3 Pa. $3.95

THE DOVER NEW YORK WALKING GUIDE: From the Battery to Wall Street, Mary J. Shapiro. Superb inexpensive guide to historic buildings and locales in lower Manhattan: Trinity Church, Bowling Green, more. Complete Text; maps. 36 illustrations. 48pp. 3⅞ × 9¼.
24225-0 Pa. $2.50

NEW YORK THEN AND NOW, Edward B. Watson, Edmund V. Gillon, Jr. 83 important Manhattan sites: on facing pages early photographs (1875-1925) and 1976 photos by Gillon. 172 illustrations. 171pp. 9¼ × 10.
23361-8 Pa. $7.95

HISTORIC COSTUME IN PICTURES, Braun & Schneider. Over 1450 costumed figures from dawn of civilization to end of 19th century. English captions. 125 plates. 256pp. 8⅜ × 11¼.
23150-X Pa. $7.50

VICTORIAN AND EDWARDIAN FASHION: A Photographic Survey, Alison Gernsheim. First fashion history completely illustrated by contemporary photographs. Full text plus 235 photos, 1840-1914, in which many celebrities appear. 240pp. 6½ × 9¼.
24205-6 Pa. $6.00

CHARTED CHRISTMAS DESIGNS FOR COUNTED CROSS-STITCH AND OTHER NEEDLECRAFTS, Lindberg Press. Charted designs for 45 beautiful needlecraft projects with many yuletide and wintertime motifs. 48pp. 8¼ × 11.
24356-7 Pa. $2.50

101 FOLK DESIGNS FOR COUNTED CROSS-STITCH AND OTHER NEEDLE-CRAFTS, Carter Houck. 101 authentic charted folk designs in a wide array of lovely representations with many suggestions for effective use. 48pp. 8¼ × 11.
24369-9 Pa. $2.25

FIVE ACRES AND INDEPENDENCE, Maurice G. Kains. Great back-to-the-land classic explains basics of self-sufficient farming. The one book to get. 95 illustrations. 397pp. 5⅜ × 8½.
20974-1 Pa. $4.95

A MODERN HERBAL, Margaret Grieve. Much the fullest, most exact, most useful compilation of herbal material. Gigantic alphabetical encyclopedia, from aconite to zedoary, gives botanical information, medical properties, folklore, economic uses, and much else. Indispensable to serious reader. 161 illustrations. 888pp. 6½ × 9¼. (Available in U.S. only)
22798-7, 22799-5 Pa., Two-vol. set $16.45

DECORATIVE NAPKIN FOLDING FOR BEGINNERS, Lillian Oppenheimer and Natalie Epstein. 22 different napkin folds in the shape of a heart, clown's hat, love knot, etc. 63 drawings. 48pp. 8¼ × 11. 23797-4 Pa. $1.95

DECORATIVE LABELS FOR HOME CANNING, PRESERVING, AND OTHER HOUSEHOLD AND GIFT USES, Theodore Menten. 128 gummed, perforated labels, beautifully printed in 2 colors. 12 versions. Adhere to metal, glass, wood, ceramics. 24pp. 8¼ × 11. 23219-0 Pa. $2.95

EARLY AMERICAN STENCILS ON WALLS AND FURNITURE, Janet Waring. Thorough coverage of 19th-century folk art: techniques, artifacts, surviving specimens. 166 illustrations, 7 in color. 147pp. of text. 7⅞ × 10¾. 21906-2 Pa. $9.95

AMERICAN ANTIQUE WEATHERVANES, A.B. & W.T. Westervelt. Extensively illustrated 1883 catalog exhibiting over 550 copper weathervanes and finials. Excellent primary source by one of the principal manufacturers. 104pp. 6⅛ × 9¼. 24396-6 Pa. $3.95

ART STUDENTS' ANATOMY, Edmond J. Farris. Long favorite in art schools. Basic elements, common positions, actions. Full text, 158 illustrations. 159pp. 5⅜ × 8½. 20744-7 Pa. $3.95

BRIDGMAN'S LIFE DRAWING, George B. Bridgman. More than 500 drawings and text teach you to abstract the body into its major masses. Also specific areas of anatomy. 192pp. 6½ × 9¼. (EA) 22710-3 Pa. $4.50

COMPLETE PRELUDES AND ETUDES FOR SOLO PIANO, Frederic Chopin. All 26 Preludes, all 27 Etudes by greatest composer of piano music. Authoritative Paderewski edition. 224pp. 9 × 12. (Available in U.S. only) 24052-5 Pa. $7.50

PIANO MUSIC 1888-1905, Claude Debussy. Deux Arabesques, Suite Bergamesque, Masques, 1st series of Images, etc. 9 others, in corrected editions. 175pp. 9⅜ × 12¼. (ECE) 22771-5 Pa. $5.95

TEDDY BEAR IRON-ON TRANSFER PATTERNS, Ted Menten. 80 iron-on transfer patterns of male and female Teddys in a wide variety of activities, poses, sizes. 48pp. 8¼ × 11. 24596-9 Pa. $2.25

A PICTURE HISTORY OF THE BROOKLYN BRIDGE, M.J. Shapiro. Profusely illustrated account of greatest engineering achievement of 19th century. 167 rare photos & engravings recall construction, human drama. Extensive, detailed text. 122pp. 8¼ × 11. 24403-2 Pa. $7.95

NEW YORK IN THE THIRTIES, Berenice Abbott. Noted photographer's fascinating study shows new buildings that have become famous and old sights that have disappeared forever. 97 photographs. 97pp. 11⅜ × 10. 22967-X Pa. $7.50

MATHEMATICAL TABLES AND FORMULAS, Robert D. Carmichael and Edwin R. Smith. Logarithms, sines, tangents, trig functions, powers, roots, reciprocals, exponential and hyperbolic functions, formulas and theorems. 269pp. 5⅜ × 8½. 60111-0 Pa. $4.95

HANDBOOK OF MATHEMATICAL FUNCTIONS WITH FORMULAS, GRAPHS, AND MATHEMATICAL TABLES, edited by Milton Abramowitz and Irene A. Stegun. Vast compendium: 29 sets of tables, some to as high as 20 places. 1,046pp. 8 × 10½. 61272-4 Pa. $19.95

TOLL HOUSE TRIED AND TRUE RECIPES, Ruth Graves Wakefield. Popovers, veal and ham loaf, baked beans, much more from the famous Mass. restaurant. Nearly 700 recipes. 376pp. 5⅜ × 8½. 23560-2 Pa. $4.95

FAVORITE CHRISTMAS CAROLS, selected and arranged by Charles J.F. Cofone. Title, music, first verse and refrain of 34 traditional carols in handsome calligraphy; also subsequent verses and other information in type. 79pp. 8⅜ × 11. 20445-6 Pa. $3.50

CAMERA WORK: A PICTORIAL GUIDE, Alfred Stieglitz. All 559 illustrations from most important periodical in history of art photography. Reduced in size but still clear, in strict chronological order, with complete captions. 176pp. 8⅜ × 11¼. 23591-2 Pa. $6.95

FAVORITE SONGS OF THE NINETIES, edited by Robert Fremont. 88 favorites: "Ta-Ra-Ra-Boom-De-Aye," "The Band Played On," "Bird in a Gilded Cage," etc. 401pp. 9 × 12. 21536-9 Pa. $12.95

STRING FIGURES AND HOW TO MAKE THEM, Caroline F. Jayne. Fullest, clearest instructions on string figures from around world: Eskimo, Navajo, Lapp, Europe, more. Cat's cradle, moving spear, lightning, stars. 950 illustrations. 407pp. 5⅜ × 8½. 20152-X Pa. $5.95

LIFE IN ANCIENT EGYPT, Adolf Erman. Detailed older account, with much not in more recent books: domestic life, religion, magic, medicine, commerce, and whatever else needed for complete picture. Many illustrations. 597pp. 5⅜ × 8½. 22632-8 Pa. $7.95

ANCIENT EGYPT: ITS CULTURE AND HISTORY, J.E. Manchip White. From pre-dynastics through Ptolemies: scoiety, history, political structure, religion, daily life, literature, cultural heritage. 48 plates. 217pp. 5⅜ × 8½. (EBE) 22548-8 Pa. $4.95

KEPT IN THE DARK, Anthony Trollope. Unusual short novel about Victorian morality and abnormal psychology by the great English author. Probably the first American publication. Frontispiece by Sir John Millais. 92pp. 6½ × 9¼. 23609-9 Pa. $2.95

MAN AND WIFE, Wilkie Collins. Nineteenth-century master launches an attack on out-moded Scottish marital laws and Victorian cult of athleticism. Artfully plotted. 35 illustrations. 239pp. 6⅛ × 9¼. 24451-2 Pa. $5.95

RELATIVITY AND COMMON SENSE, Herman Bondi. Radically reoriented presentation of Einstein's Special Theory and one of most valuable popular accounts available. 60 illustrations. 177pp. 5⅜ × 8. (EUK) 24021-5 Pa. $3.95

THE EGYPTIAN BOOK OF THE DEAD, E.A. Wallis Budge. Complete reproduction of Ani's papyrus, finest ever found. Full hieroglyphic text, interlinear transliteration, word-for-word translation, smooth translation. 533pp. 6½ × 9¼. (USO) 21866-X Pa. $8.95

COUNTRY AND SUBURBAN HOMES OF THE PRAIRIE SCHOOL PERIOD, H.V. von Holst. Over 400 photographs floor plans, elevations, detailed drawings (exteriors and interiors) for over 100 structures. Text. Important primary source. 128pp. 8⅜ × 11¼. 24373-7 Pa. $5.95

REASON IN ART, George Santayana. Renowned philosopher's provocative, seminal treatment of basis of art in instinct and experience. Volume Four of *The Life of Reason.* 230pp. 5⅜ × 8. 24358-3 Pa. $4.50

LANGUAGE, TRUTH AND LOGIC, Alfred J. Ayer. Famous, clear introduction to Vienna, Cambridge schools of Logical Positivism. Role of philosophy, elimination of metaphysics, nature of analysis, etc. 160pp. 5⅜ × 8½. (USCO) 20010-8 Pa. $2.75

BASIC ELECTRONICS, U.S. Bureau of Naval Personnel. Electron tubes, circuits, antennas, AM, FM, and CW transmission and receiving, etc. 560 illustrations. 567pp. 6½ × 9¼. 21076-6 Pa. $8.95

THE ART DECO STYLE, edited by Theodore Menten. Furniture, jewelry, metalwork, ceramics, fabrics, lighting fixtures, interior decors, exteriors, graphics from pure French sources. Over 400 photographs. 183pp. 8⅜ × 11¼. 22824-X Pa. $6.95

THE FOUR BOOKS OF ARCHITECTURE, Andrea Palladio. 16th-century classic covers classical architectural remains, Renaissance revivals, classical orders, etc. 1738 Ware English edition. 216 plates. 110pp. of text. 9½ × 12¾. 21308-0 Pa. $11.50

THE WIT AND HUMOR OF OSCAR WILDE, edited by Alvin Redman. More than 1000 ripostes, paradoxes, wisecracks: Work is the curse of the drinking classes, I can resist everything except temptations, etc. 258pp. 5⅜ × 8½. (USCO) 20602-5 Pa. $3.95

THE DEVIL'S DICTIONARY, Ambrose Bierce. Barbed, bitter, brilliant witticisms in the form of a dictionary. Best, most ferocious satire America has produced. 145pp. 5⅜ × 8½. 20487-1 Pa. $2.50

ERTÉ'S FASHION DESIGNS, Erté. 210 black-and-white inventions from *Harper's Bazar,* 1918-32, plus 8pp. full-color covers. Captions. 88pp. 9 × 12. 24203-X Pa. $6.50

ERTÉ GRAPHICS, Erté. Collection of striking color graphics: *Seasons, Alphabet, Numerals, Aces* and *Precious Stones.* 50 plates, including 4 on covers. 48pp. 9⅜ × 12¼. 23580-7 Pa. $6.95

PAPER FOLDING FOR BEGINNERS, William D. Murray and Francis J. Rigney. Clearest book for making origami sail boats, roosters, frogs that move legs, etc. 40 projects. More than 275 illustrations. 94pp. 5⅜ × 8½. 20713-7 Pa. $2.25

ORIGAMI FOR THE ENTHUSIAST, John Montroll. Fish, ostrich, peacock, squirrel, rhinoceros, Pegasus, 19 other intricate subjects. Instructions. Diagrams. 128pp. 9 × 12. 23799-0 Pa. $4.95

CROCHETING NOVELTY POT HOLDERS, edited by Linda Macho. 64 useful, whimsical pot holders feature kitchen themes, animals, flowers, other novelties. Surprisingly easy to crochet. Complete instructions. 48pp. 8¼ × 11. 24296-X Pa. $1.95

CROCHETING DOILIES, edited by Rita Weiss. Irish Crochet, Jewel, Star Wheel, Vanity Fair and more. Also luncheon and console sets, runners and centerpieces. 51 illustrations. 48pp. 8¼ × 11. 23424-X Pa. $2.50

YUCATAN BEFORE AND AFTER THE CONQUEST, Diego de Landa. Only significant account of Yucatan written in the early post-Conquest era. Translated by William Gates. Over 120 illustrations. 162pp. 5⅜ × 8½.　　23622-6 Pa. $3.50

ORNATE PICTORIAL CALLIGRAPHY, E.A. Lupfer. Complete instructions, over 150 examples help you create magnificent "flourishes" from which beautiful animals and objects gracefully emerge. 8⅛ × 11.　　21957-7 Pa. $2.95

DOLLY DINGLE PAPER DOLLS, Grace Drayton. Cute chubby children by same artist who did Campbell Kids. Rare plates from 1910s. 30 paper dolls and over 100 outfits reproduced in full color. 32pp. 9¼ × 12¼.　　23711-7 Pa. $3.50

CURIOUS GEORGE PAPER DOLLS IN FULL COLOR, H. A. Rey, Kathy Allert. Naughty little monkey-hero of children's books in two doll figures, plus 48 full-color costumes: pirate, Indian chief, fireman, more. 32pp. 9¼ × 12¼.

24386-9 Pa. $3.50

GERMAN: HOW TO SPEAK AND WRITE IT, Joseph Rosenberg. Like *French, How to Speak and Write It.* Very rich modern course, with a wealth of pictorial material. 330 illustrations. 384pp. 5⅜ × 8½. (USUKO)　　20271-2 Pa. $4.75

CATS AND KITTENS: 24 Ready-to-Mail Color Photo Postcards, D. Holby. Handsome collection; feline in a variety of adorable poses. Identifications. 12pp. on postcard stock. 8¼ × 11.　　24469-5 Pa. $2.95

MARILYN MONROE PAPER DOLLS, Tom Tierney. 31 full-color designs on heavy stock, from *The Asphalt Jungle, Gentlemen Prefer Blondes,* 22 others. 1 doll. 16 plates. 32pp. 9⅜ × 12¼.　　23769-9 Pa. $3.50

FUNDAMENTALS OF LAYOUT, F.H. Wills. All phases of layout design discussed and illustrated in 121 illustrations. Indispensable as student's text or handbook for professional. 124pp. 8⅛ × 11.　　21279-3 Pa. $4.50

FANTASTIC SUPER STICKERS, Ed Sibbett, Jr. 75 colorful pressure-sensitive stickers. Peel off and place for a touch of pizzazz: clowns, penguins, teddy bears, etc. Full color. 16pp. 8¼ × 11.　　24471-7 Pa. $2.95

LABELS FOR ALL OCCASIONS, Ed Sibbett, Jr. 6 labels each of 16 different designs—baroque, art nouveau, art deco, Pennsylvania Dutch, etc.—in full color. 24pp. 8¼ × 11.　　23688-9 Pa. $2.95

HOW TO CALCULATE QUICKLY: RAPID METHODS IN BASIC MATHE-MATICS, Henry Sticker. Addition, subtraction, multiplication, division, checks, etc. More than 8000 problems, solutions. 185pp. 5 × 7¼.　　20295-X Pa. $2.95

THE CAT COLORING BOOK, Karen Baldauski. Handsome, realistic renderings of 40 splendid felines, from American shorthair to exotic types. 44 plates. Captions. 48pp. 8¼ × 11.　　24011-8 Pa. $2.25

THE TALE OF PETER RABBIT, Beatrix Potter. The inimitable Peter's terrifying adventure in Mr. McGregor's garden, with all 27 wonderful, full-color Potter illustrations. 55pp. 4¼ × 5½. (Available in U.S. only)　　22827-4 Pa. $1.75

BASIC ELECTRICITY, U.S. Bureau of Naval Personnel. Batteries, circuits, conductors, AC and DC, inductance and capacitance, generators, motors, trans-formers, amplifiers, etc. 349 illustrations. 448pp. 6½ × 9¼.　　20973-3 Pa. $7.95

READY-TO-USE BORDERS, Ted Menten. Both traditional and unusual interchangeable borders in a tremendous array of sizes, shapes, and styles. 32 plates. 64pp. 8¼ × 11. 23782-6 Pa. $3.50

THE WHOLE CRAFT OF SPINNING, Carol Kroll. Preparing fiber, drop spindle, treadle wheel, other fibers, more. Highly creative, yet simple. 43 illustrations. 48pp. 8¼ × 11. 23968-3 Pa. $2.50

HIDDEN PICTURE PUZZLE COLORING BOOK, Anna Pomaska. 31 delightful pictures to color with dozens of objects, people and animals hidden away to find. Captions. Solutions. 48pp. 8¼ × 11. 23909-8 Pa. $2.25

QUILTING WITH STRIPS AND STRINGS, H.W. Rose. Quickest, easiest way to turn left-over fabric into handsome quilt. 46 patchwork quilts; 31 full-size templates. 48pp. 8¼ × 11. 24357-5 Pa. $3.25

NATURAL DYES AND HOME DYEING, Rita J. Adrosko. Over 135 specific recipes from historical sources for cotton, wool, other fabrics. Genuine premodern handicrafts. 12 illustrations. 160pp. 5⅜ × 8½. 22688-3 Pa. $2.95

CARVING REALISTIC BIRDS, H.D. Green. Full-sized patterns, step-by-step instructions for robins, jays, cardinals, finches, etc. 97 illustrations. 80pp. 8¼ × 11. 23484-3 Pa. $3.00

GEOMETRY, RELATIVITY AND THE FOURTH DIMENSION, Rudolf Rucker. Exposition of fourth dimension, concepts of relativity as Flatland characters continue adventures. Popular, easily followed yet accurate, profound. 141 illustrations. 133pp. 5⅜ × 8½. 23400-2 Pa. $3.00

READY-TO-USE SMALL FRAMES AND BORDERS, Carol B. Grafton. Graphic message? Frame it graphically with 373 new frames and borders in many styles: Art Nouveau, Art Deco, Op Art. 64pp. 8¼ × 11. 24375-3 Pa. $3.50

CELTIC ART: THE METHODS OF CONSTRUCTION, George Bain. Simple geometric techniques for making Celtic interlacements, spirals, Kellstype initials, animals, humans, etc. Over 500 illustrations. 160pp. 9 × 12. (Available in U.S. only) 22923-8 Pa. $6.00

THE TALE OF TOM KITTEN, Beatrix Potter. Exciting text and all 27 vivid, full-color illustrations to charming tale of naughty little Tom getting into mischief again. 58pp. 4¼ × 5½. (USO) 24502-0 Pa. $1.75

WOODEN PUZZLE TOYS, Ed Sibbett, Jr. Transfer patterns and instructions for 24 easy-to-do projects: fish, butterflies, cats, acrobats, Humpty Dumpty, 19 others. 48pp. 8¼ × 11. 23713-3 Pa. $2.50

MY FAMILY TREE WORKBOOK, Rosemary A. Chorzempa. Enjoyable, easy-to-use introduction to genealogy designed specially for children. Data pages plus text. Instructive, educational, valuable. 64pp. 8¼ × 11. 24229-3 Pa. $2.50

Prices subject to change without notice.

Available at your book dealer or write for free catalog to Dept. GI, Dover Publications, Inc., 31 East 2nd St. Mineola, N.Y. 11501. Dover publishes more than 175 books each year on science, elementary and advanced mathematics, biology, music, art, literary history, social sciences and other areas.